GREAT STORIES OF
HUMAN COURAGE

GREAT STORIES OF
HUMAN COURAGE

Selected and edited by
E. V. ODLE

LONDON
JOHN LANE THE BODLEY HEAD LIMITED

First published in 1933

ACKNOWLEDGMENTS

ACKNOWLEDGMENTS and thanks are made to the following proprietors of copyright: to Messrs. Blackwoods, Ltd., for permission to reprint "Love of Life" by Jack London, and "Fortitude" by Perceval Gibbon; to Messrs. Methuen, Ltd., for permission to reprint "The Stake and the Plumb Line" by the late Sir Gilbert Parker; to Messrs. Hodder and Stoughton and the author for the right to include "The Deserters" from the volume by A. E. W. Mason published by them; to the Tolstoi Society for permission to reprint the translation of "The Raid," by Leo Tolstoi; to the executors of the late C. E. Montague for permission to include "Action"; to Mrs. Phyllis Mégroz for permission to reprint her translation of "El Verdugo" by Honoré de Balzac, to Miss M. E. Kennedy for the right to print her translation of "Staff-Captain Ribnikov" by Alexandre Kuprin; to the executors of the late Katherine Mansfield for permission to reprint "Ma Parker"; to Mrs. Joseph Conrad for the right to include "Youth" by Joseph Conrad; to Mr. W. W. Jacobs for his permission to reprint "Three at Table"; to Mr. H. G. Wells for the right to include "The Argonauts of the Air"; to Mrs. Margaret Laurie for the right to include her translation of "The Runaway Gun" by Victor Hugo; to Captain Frank H. Shaw and Messrs. The Amalgamated Press, Ltd., for permission to reprint "The Chief of the Golden Hope"; and to Joseph Hergesheimer, Dale Collins, Albert Richard Wetjen, Francis Brett Young, F. Britten Austin, and Alan Sullivan, for their willingness to allow stories of which they are the authors to appear in this volume.

CONTENTS

ix

CONTENTS

LOVE OF LIFE

by Jack London

JACK LONDON worked and fought with hardy sailors twice his age before he went to school. Phenomenally strong in muscle, and full of adventuring spirit he had travelled half round the world, tramped through Canada and the United States and joined in the great Klondyke gold-rush before he was seventeen. Then, with his head full of stories, he came back to his home in San Francisco and began his education. He learned to write, but for many years he was only partly successful. "My manuscripts made amazing round-trip records between the Pacific and the Atlantic," he says. He was born in 1876, and by the time he died, in 1916, he had published forty volumes. He was a war correspondent during the Russo-Japanese War, and again in Mexico, in 1914. His stories are packed with adventure and "love of life," and express admirably the struggle of man with the primary forces of nature. "Love of Life" is a story of almost incredible human endurance, yet every detail rings true, for London knew the trail he describes, and he had himself borne many of the hardships of his hero.

LOVE OF LIFE

BY

Jack London

THEY limped painfully down the bank, and once
the foremost of the two men staggered among the
rough-strewn rocks. They were tired and weak, and
their faces had the drawn expression of patience which
comes of hardship long endured. They were heavily
burdened with blanket packs which were strapped to
their shoulders. Head-straps passing across the forehead
helped to support these packs. Each man carried a
rifle. They walked in a stooping posture, the shoulders
well forward, the head still farther forward, the eyes
bent upon the ground.

"I wish we had just about two of them cartridges
that's layin' in that cache of our'n," said the second man.

His voice was utterly and drearily expressionless. He
spoke without enthusiasm. But the first man, limping
into the milky stream that foamed over the rocks, vouchsafed no reply.

The other man followed at his heels. They did not
remove their footgear though the water was icy cold—
so cold that their ankles ached and their feet went numb.
In places the water dashed against their knees, and both
men staggered for footing.

The man who followed slipped on a smooth boulder,
nearly fell, but recovered himself with a violent effort,
at the same time uttering a sharp exclamation of pain.
He seemed faint and dizzy and put out his free hand,
while he reeled as though seeking support against the air.
When he had steadied himself, he stepped forward, but
reeled again and nearly fell. Then he stood still and
looked at the other man, who had never turned his head.

5

The man stood still for fully a minute, as though debating with himself. Then he called out:

"I say, Bill, I've sprained my ankle."

Bill staggered on through the milky water. He did not look round. The man watched him go, and though his face was expressionless as ever, his eyes were like the eyes of a wounded deer waiting the final slaughter.

The other man limped up the farther bank and continued straight on without looking back. The man in the stream watched him. His lips trembled a little, so that the rough thatch of brown hair which covered them was visibly agitated. His tongue even strayed out to moisten them.

"Bill!" he cried out.

It was the pleading cry of a strong man in distress, but Bill's head did not turn. The man watched him go, limping grotesquely and lurching forward with stammering gait up the slope toward the soft sky-line of the low-lying hill. He watched him go till he passed over the crest and disappeared. Then he turned his gaze and slowly took in the circle of the world that remained to him, now that Bill was gone.

Near the horizon the sun was smouldering dimly, almost obscured by formless mists and vapours which gave an impression of mass and density without outline or tangibility. The man pulled out his watch, the while resting his weight on one leg. It was four o'clock, and as the season was near the last of July or first of August —he did not know the precise date within a week or two—he knew that the sun roughly marked the north-west. He looked to the south and knew that somewhere beyond those bleak hills lay the Great Bear Lake; also, he knew that in that direction the Arctic Circle cut its forbidding way across the Canadian Barrens. This stream in which he stood was a feeder to the Coppermine River, which, in turn, flowed north and emptied into Coronation Gulf and the Arctic Ocean. He had never been there, but he had seen it once on a Hudson Bay Company chart.

6

Again his gaze completed the circle of the world about him. It was not a heartening spectacle. Everywhere was soft skyline. The hills were all low-lying. There were no trees, no shrubs, no grasses—naught but a tremendous and terrible desolation that sent fear swiftly dawning into his eyes.

"Bill!" he whispered, once, and twice—"Bill!"

He cowered in the midst of the milky water as though the vastness were pressing in upon him with overwhelming force, brutally crushing him with its complacent awfulness. He began to shake, as with an ague-fit, till the gun fell from his hand with a splash. This served to rouse him. He fought with his fear and pulled himself together, groping in the water and recovering the weapon. He hitched his pack farther over on his left shoulder, so as to take a portion of its weight from off the injured ankle. Then he proceeded, slowly and carefully, wincing with pain, to the bank.

He did not stop. With a desperation that was madness, unmindful of the pain, he hurried up the slope to the crest of the hill over which his comrade had disappeared—more grotesque and comical by far than that limping, jerking comrade. But at the crest he saw a shallow valley, empty of life. He fought with his fear again, overcame it, hitched the pack still farther over on his left shoulder, and lurched on down the slope.

The bottom of the valley was soggy with water, which the thick moss held, sponge-like, close to the surface. This water squirted out from under his feet at every step, and each time he lifted a foot the action culminated in a sucking sound as the wet moss reluctantly released its grip. He picked his way from muskeg to muskeg, and followed the other man's footsteps along and across the rocky ledges which thrust like islets through the sea of moss.

Though alone, he was not lost. Farther on he knew he would come to where dead spruce and fir, very small

7

and shrivelled, bordered the shore of a little lake, the
tit-chinniehilie in the tongue of the country, the "land of
little sticks." And into that lake flowed a small stream,
the water of which was not milky. There was rush-
grass on that stream—this he remembered well—but no
timber, and he would follow till its first trickle ceased at
a divide. He would cross this divide to the first trickle
of another stream flowing to the west, which he would
follow until it emptied into the river Dease; and here
he would find a cache, under an upturned canoe and
piled over with many rocks. And in this cache would
be ammunition for his empty gun, fish-hooks and lines,
a small net—all the utilities for the killing and snaring
of food. Also, he would find flour—not much—a piece
of bacon, and some beans.

Bill would be waiting for him there, and they would
paddle away south, down the Dease to the Great Bear
Lake. And south across the lake they would go, ever
south, till they gained the Mackenzie. And south, still
south they would go—while the winter raced vainly
after them, and the ice formed in the eddies, and the
days grew chill and crisp—south to some warm Hudson
Bay Company post, where timber grew tall and generous
and there was grub without end.

These were the thoughts of the man as he strove
forward. But hard as he strove with his body, he strove
equally hard with his mind, trying to think that Bill
had not deserted him, that Bill would surely wait for
him at the cache. He was compelled to think this
thought, or else there would not be any use to strive,
and he would have lain down and died. And as the
dim ball of the sun sank slowly into the north-north-
west, he covered every inch, and many times, of his and
Bill's flight south before the down-coming winter. And
he conned the grub of the cache and the grub of the
Hudson Bay Company post over and over again, this
man, for he was very hungry. He had not eaten for
two days; for a far longer time he had not had all he

wanted to eat. Often he stooped and picked pale muskeg berries, put them into his mouth, and chewed and swallowed them. A muskeg berry is a bit of seed enclosed in a bit of water. In the mouth the water melts away and the seed chews sharp and bitter. The man knew there was no nourishment in the berries, but he chewed them patiently, with a hope greater than knowledge and defying experience.

At nine o'clock he stubbed his toe on a rocky ledge, and from sheer weariness and weakness staggered and fell. He lay for some time, without movement, on his side. Then he slipped out of the pack-straps and clumsily dragged himself into a sitting posture. It was not yet dark, and in the lingering twilight he groped about among the rocks for shreds of dry moss. When he had gathered a heap he built a fire—a smouldering, smudgy fire—and put a tin pot of water on to boil.

He unwrapped his pack, and the first thing he did was to count his matches. There were sixty-seven. He counted them three times to make sure. He divided them into several portions, wrapping them in oil-paper, disposing of one bunch in his empty tobacco-pouch, of another bunch in the inside band of his battered hat, of a third bunch under his shirt on the chest. This accomplished, a panic came upon him, and he un-wrapped them all and counted them again. There were still sixty-seven.

He dried his wet footgear by the fire. The mocassins were in sodden shreds. The blanket socks were worn through in places, and his feet were raw and bleeding. His ankle was throbbing, and he gave it an examination. It had swollen to the size of his knee. He tore a long strip from one of his two blankets and bound the ankle tightly. He tore other strips and bound them about his feet to serve for both mocassins and socks. Then he drank the pot of water, steaming hot, wound his watch, and crawled between his blankets.

He slept like a dead man. The brief darkness around

9

midnight came and went. The sun arose in the north-
north-east—at least, the day dawned in that quarter,
for the sun was hidden by grey clouds.

At six o'clock he awoke, quietly, lying on his back.
He gazed straight up into the grey sky and knew that
he was hungry. As he rolled over on his elbow he was
startled by a loud snort, and saw a bull caribou regarding
him with alert curiosity. The animal was not more than
fifty feet away, and instantly into the man's mind leaped
the vision and the savour of a caribou steak sizzling and
frying over a fire. Mechanically he reached for the
empty gun, drew a bead, and pulled the trigger. The
bull snorted and leaped away, his hoofs rattling and
clattering as he fled across the ledges.

The man cursed and flung the empty gun from him.
He groaned aloud as he started to drag himself to his
feet. It was a slow and arduous task. His joints were
like rusty hinges. They worked harshly in their sockets
with much friction, and each bending or unbending was
accomplished only through a sheer exertion of will.
When he finally gained his feet, another minute or so
was consumed in straightening up so that he could stand
erect as a man should stand.

He crawled up a small knoll and surveyed the prospect. There were no trees, no bushes, nothing but a grey
sea of moss scarcely diversified by grey rocks, grey-
coloured lakelets, and grey streamlets. The sky was
grey. There was no sun or hint of sun. He had no idea
of north, and he had forgotten the way he had come to
this spot the night before. But he was not lost. He knew
that. Soon he would come to the land of the little sticks.
He felt that it lay off to the left, somewhere, not far,
possibly just over the next low hill.

He went back to put his pack into shape for travelling.
He assured himself of his three separate parcels of
matches, though he did not stop to count them. But
he did linger, debating over a squat moose-hide sack.

It was not large. He could hide it under his two hands. He knew that it weighed fifteen pounds—as much as all the rest of the pack—and it worried him. He finally set it to one side and proceeded to roll the pack. He paused to gaze at the squat moose-hide sack. He picked it up hastily, with a defiant glance about him, as though the desolation were trying to rob him of it; and when he arose to his feet to stagger on into the day it was included in the pack on his back.

He bore away to the left, stopping now and again to eat muskeg berries. His ankle had stiffened, his limp was more pronounced; but the pain of it was as nothing compared with the pain of his stomach. The hunger pangs were sharp. They gnawed and gnawed until he could not keep his mind steady on the course he must pursue to gain the land of little sticks. The muskeg berries did not allay this gnawing, while they made his tongue and the roof of his mouth sore with their irritating bite.

He came upon a valley where rock ptarmigan rose on whirring wings from the ledges and muskegs. "Ker-ker-ker," was the cry they made. He threw stones at them, but could not hit them. He placed his pack on the ground and stalked them as a cat stalks a sparrow. The sharp rocks cut through the legs of his trousers till his knees left a tail of blood. But the hurt was lost in the hurt of his hunger. He squirmed over the wet moss, saturating his clothes and chilling his body, but he was not aware of it, so great was his fever for food. And always the ptarmigan rose whirring before him, till their "ker-ker-ker" became a mock to him, and he cursed them and cried aloud at them with their own cry.

Once he crawled upon one that must have been asleep. He did not see it till it shot up in his face from its rocky nook. He made a clutch as startled as was the rise of the ptarmigan, and there remained in his hand three tail-feathers. As he watched its flight he hated it

11

as though it had done him some terrible wrong. Then
he returned and shouldered his pack.

As the day wore along he came into valleys or swales
where game was more plentiful. A band of caribou
passed by, twenty and odd animals, tantalizingly within
rifle range. He felt a wild desire to run after them, a
certitude that he could run them down. A black fox
came toward him carrying a ptarmigan in his mouth.
The man shouted. It was a fearful cry; but the fox,
leaping away in fright, did not drop the ptarmigan.

Late in the afternoon he followed a stream, milky
with lime, which ran through sparse patches of rush-
grass. Grasping these rushes firmly near the root, he
pulled up what resembled a young onion-sprout no
larger than a shingle-nail. It was tender and his teeth
sank into it with a crunch that promised deliciously
of food. But its fibres were tough. It was composed
of stringy filaments, saturated with water like the
berries, and devoid of nourishment. But he threw off
his pack and went into the rush-grass on hands
and knees, crunching and munching like some bovine
creature.

He was very weary, and often wished to rest—to lie
down and sleep; but he was continually driven on, not
so much by his desire to gain the land of little sticks as
by his hunger. He searched small ponds for frogs, and
dug up the earth with his nails for worms, though he
knew that neither frogs nor worms existed so far north.
He looked into every pool of water vainly, until, as the
long twilight came on, he discovered a solitary fish, the
size of a minnow, in such a pool. He plunged his arm
in up to the shoulder, but it eluded him. He reached for
it with both hands, and stirred up the milky mud at the
bottom. In his excitement he fell in, wetting himself to
the waist. Then the water was too muddy to admit of
his seeing the fish, and he was compelled to wait until
the sediment had settled.

12

The pursuit was renewed till the water was again muddied. But he could not wait. He unstrapped the tin bucket and began to bale the pool. He baled wildly at first, splashing himself and flinging the water so short a distance that it ran back into the pool. He worked more carefully, striving to be cool, though his heart was pounding against his chest and his hands were trembling. At the end of half an hour the pool was nearly dry, not a cupful of water remained, and there was no fish. He found a hidden crevice among the stones through which it had escaped to the adjoining and larger pool—a pool which he could not empty in a night and a day. Had he known of the crevice he could have closed it with a rock at the beginning, and the fish would have been his.

Thus he thought, and crumpled up and sank down upon the wet earth. At first he cried softly to himself, then he cried loudly, to the pitiless desolation that ringed him around; and for a long time after he was shaken by great, dry sobs.

He built a fire and warmed himself by drinking quarts of hot water and made camp on a rocky ledge in the same fashion he had the night before. The last thing he did was to see that his matches were dry and to wind his watch. The blankets were wet and clammy. His ankle pulsed with pain. But he knew only that he was hungry, and through his restless sleep he dreamed of feasts and banquets and of food served and spread in all imaginable ways.

He awoke, chilled and sick. There was no sun. The grey of earth and sky had become deeper, more profound. A raw wind was blowing, and the first flurries of snow were whitening the hill-tops. The air about him thickened and grew white while he made a fire and boiled more water. It was wet snow, half rain, and the flakes were large. At first they melted as soon as they came in contact with the earth, but more fell, covering the ground, putting out the fire, spoiling his supply of moss-fuel.

13

This was the signal for him to strap on his pack and stumble onward, he knew not where. He was not concerned with the land of little sticks, nor with Bill and the cache under the upturned canoe by the river Dease. He was mastered by the verb "to eat." He was hunger-mad. He took no heed of the course he pursued, so long as that course led him through the swale bottoms. He felt his way through the wet snow to the watery muskeg berries, and went by feel as he pulled up the rush-grass by the roots. But it was tasteless stuff and did not satisfy. He found a weed that tasted sour, and he ate all he could find of it, which was not much, for it was a creeping growth, easily hidden under the several inches of snow.

He had no fire that night, nor hot water, and crawled under his blanket to sleep the broken hunger-sleep. The snow turned into a cold rain. He awakened many times to feel it falling on his upturned face. Day came—a grey day and no sun. It had ceased raining. The keenness of his hunger had departed. Sensibility, so far as concerned the yearning for food, had been exhausted. There was a dull, heavy ache in his stomach, but it did not bother him so much. He was more rational, and once more he was chiefly interested in the land of little sticks and the cache by the river Dease.

He ripped the remnant of one of his blankets into strips and bound his bleeding feet. Also, he re-cinched the injured ankle and prepared himself for a day of travel. When he came to his pack he paused long over the squat moose-hide sack, but in the end it went with him.

The snow had melted under the rain, and only the hill-tops showed white. The sun came out, and he succeeded in locating the points of the compass, though he knew now that he was lost. Perhaps, in his previous day's wanderings, he had edged away too far to the left. He now bore off to the right to counteract the possible deviation from his true course.

14

Though the hunger pangs were no longer so exquisite, he realized that he was weak. He was compelled to pause for frequent rests when he attacked the muskeg berries and rush-grass patches. His tongue felt dry and large, as though covered with a fine hairy growth, and it tasted bitter in his mouth. His heart gave him a great deal of trouble. When he had travelled a few minutes it would begin a remorseless thump, thump, thump, and then leap up and away in a painful flutter of beats that choked him and made him go faint and dizzy.

In the middle of the day he found two minnows in a large pond. It was impossible to bale it, but he was calmer now and managed to catch them in his tin bucket. They were no longer than his little finger, but he was not particularly hungry. The dull ache in his stomach had been growing duller and fainter. It seemed almost that his stomach was dozing. He ate the fish raw, masticating with painstaking care, for the eating was a pure act of reason. While he had no desire to eat, he knew that he must eat to live.

In the evening he caught three more minnows, eating two and saving the third for breakfast. The sun had dried stray shreds of moss, and he was able to warm himself with hot water. He had not covered more than ten miles that day, and the next day, travelling whenever his heart permitted him, he covered no more than five miles. But his stomach did not give him the slightest uneasiness. It had gone to sleep. He was in a strange country, too, and the caribou were growing more plentiful, also the wolves. Often their yelps drifted across the desolation, and once he saw three of them slinking away before his path.

Another night, and in the morning, being more rational, he untied the leather string that fastened the squat moose-hide sack. From its open mouth poured a yellow stream of coarse gold-dust and nuggets. He roughly divided the gold in halves, caching one half on

15

a prominent ledge, wrapped in a piece of blanket, and returning the other half to the sack. He also began to use strips of the one remaining blanket for his feet. He still clung to his gun, for there were cartridges in that cache by the river Dease.

This was a day of fog, and this day hunger awoke in him again. He was very weak, and was afflicted with a giddiness which at times blinded him. It was no uncommon thing now to stumble and fall; and stumbling once, he fell squarely into a ptarmigan nest. There were four newly-hatched chicks, a day old, little specks of pulsating life, no more than a mouthful, and he ate them, ravenously, thrusting them alive into his mouth and crunching them like eggshells between his teeth. The mother ptarmigan beat about him with great outcry. He used his gun as a club with which to knock her over, but she dodged out of reach. He threw stones at her, and with one chance shot broke a wing. Then she fluttered away, running, trailing the broken wing, with him in pursuit.

The little chicks had no more than whetted his appetite. He hopped and bobbed clumsily along on his injured ankle, throwing stones and screaming hoarsely at times; at other times hopping and bobbing silently along, picking himself up grimly and patiently when he fell, or rubbing his eyes with his hand when the giddiness threatened to overpower him.

The chase led him across swampy ground in the bottom of the valley, and he came upon footprints in the moss. They were not his own—he could see that. They must be Bill's. But he could not stop, for the mother ptarmigan was running on. He would catch her first, then he would return and investigate.

He exhausted the mother ptarmigan; but he exhausted himself. She lay panting on her side. He lay panting on his side, a dozen feet away, unable to crawl to her. And as he recovered, she recovered, fluttering out of

16

reach as his hungry hand went out to her. The chase was resumed. Night settled down, and she escaped. He stumbled from weakness and pitched head foremost on his face, cutting his cheek, his pack upon his back. He did not move for a long while; then he rolled over on his side, wound his watch, and lay there until morning.

Another day of fog. Half of his last blanket had gone into foot-wrappings. He failed to pick up Bill's trail. It did not matter. His hunger was driving him too compellingly . . . only . . . only he wondered if Bill, too, were lost. By midday the irk of his pack became too oppressive. Again he divided the gold, this time merely spilling half of it on the ground. In the afternoon he threw the rest of it away, there remaining to him only the half-blanket, the tin bucket, and the rifle.

A hallucination began to trouble him. He felt confident that one cartridge remained to him. It was in the chamber of the rifle, and he had overlooked it. On the other hand, he knew all the time that the chamber was empty. But the hallucination persisted. He fought it off for hours, then threw his rifle open and was confronted with emptiness. The disappointment was as bitter as though he had really expected to find the cartridge.

He plodded on for half an hour, when the hallucination again arose. Again he fought it, and still it persisted, till for very relief he opened his rifle to unconvince himself. At times his mind wandered farther afield, and he plodded on, a mere automaton, strange conceits and whimsicalities gnawing at his brain like worms. But these excursions out of the real were of brief duration, for ever the pangs of the hunger-bite called him back. He was jerked back abruptly once, from such an excursion, by a sight that caused him nearly to faint. He reeled and swayed, doddering like a drunken man to keep from falling. Before him stood a horse. A horse! He could not believe his eyes. A thick mist was in

17

them, intershot with sparkling points of light. He rubbed his eyes savagely to clear his vision, and beheld, not a horse, but a great brown bear. The animal was studying him with bellicose curiosity.

The man had brought his gun half-way to his shoulder before he realized. He lowered it, and drew his hunting-knife from its beaded sheath at his hip. He ran his thumb along the edge of his knife. It was sharp; the point was sharp. He would fling himself upon the bear and kill it. But his heart began its warning thump, thump, thump. Then followed the wild upward leap and tattoo of flutters, the pressing as of an iron band about his forehead, the creeping of the dizziness into his brain.

His desperate courage was evicted by a great surge of fear. In his weakness, what if the animal attacked him! He drew himself up to his most imposing stature, gripping the knife, and staring hard at the bear. The bear advanced clumsily a couple of steps, reared up, and gave vent to a tentative growl. If the man ran, he would run after him. But the man did not run. He was animated now with the courage of fear, the courage of the cornered rat. He, too, growled—savagely, terribly, voicing the fear that is to life germane, and that lies twisted about life's deepest roots.

The bear edged away to one side, growling menacingly, himself appalled by this mysterious creature that appeared upright and unafraid. But the man did not move. He stood like a statue till the danger was past, when he yielded to a fit of trembling and sank down into the wet moss.

He pulled himself together and went, afraid now in a new way. It was not the fear that he should die passively from lack of food, but that he should be destroyed violently before starvation had exhausted the last particle of the endeavour in him that made toward surviving. There were the wolves. Back and forth across the desolation drifted their howls, weaving the very air into a fabric of menace that was so tangible that he found himself, arms in the air, pressing it back from him as it might be the walls of a wind-blown tent.

Now and again the wolves, in packs of two and three, crossed his path. But they sheered clear of him. They were not in sufficient numbers; and, besides, they were hunting the caribou, which did not battle, while this strange creature that walked erect might scratch and bite.

In the late afternoon he came upon scattered bones where the wolves had made a kill. The *debris* had been a caribou calf an hour before, squawking and running and very much alive. He contemplated the bones, clean-picked and polished, pink with the cell-life in them which had not yet died. Could it possibly be that he might be that ere the day was done? Such was life, eh? A vain and fleeting thing. It was only life that pained. There was no hurt in death. To die was to sleep. It meant cessation, rest. Then why was he not content to die?

But he did not moralize long. He was squatting in the moss, a bone in his mouth, sucking at the shreds of life that still dyed it faintly pink. The sweet meaty taste, thin and elusive almost as a memory, maddened him. He closed his jaws on the bones and crunched. Sometimes it was the bone that broke, sometimes his teeth. Then he crushed the bones between rocks, pounded them to a pulp, and swallowed them. He pounded his fingers, too, in his haste, and yet found a moment in which to feel surprise at the fact that his fingers did not hurt much when caught under the descending rock.

Came two frightful days of snow and rain. He did not know when he made camp, when he broke camp. He travelled in the night as much as in the day. He rested wherever he fell, crawled on whenever the dying life in him flickered up and burned less dimly. He, as a man, no longer strove. It was the life in him, unwilling

to die, that drove him on. He did not suffer. His
nerves had become blunted, numb, while his mind was
filled with weird visions and delicious dreams.

But ever he sucked and chewed on the crushed bones
of the caribou calf, the least remnants of which he had
gathered up and carried with him. He crossed no more
hills or divides, but automatically followed a large stream
which flowed through a wide and shallow valley. He
did not see this stream, or this valley. He saw nothing
save visions. Soul and body walked or crawled side
by side, yet apart, so slender was the thread that bound
them.

He awoke, in his right mind, lying on his back on a
rocky ledge. The sun was shining bright and warm.
Afar off he heard the squawking of caribou calves. He
was aware of vague memories of rain, and wind, and
snow, but whether he had been beaten by the storm for
two days or two weeks he did not know.

For some time he lay without movement, the genial
sunshine pouring upon him, and saturating his miserable body with its warmth. A fine day, he thought.
Perhaps he could manage to locate himself. By a
painful effort he rolled over on his side. Below him
flowed a wide and sluggish river. Its unfamiliarity
puzzled him. Slowly he followed it with his eyes,
winding in wide sweeps among the bleak, bare hills,
bleaker and barer, and lower-lying than any hills he
had yet encountered. Slowly, deliberately, without
excitement or more than the most casual interest, he
followed the course of the strange stream toward the
skyline, and saw it emptying into a bright and shining
sea. He was still unexcited. Most unusual, he thought,
a vision or a mirage—more likely a vision, a trick of his
disordered mind. He was confirmed in this by sight
of a ship lying at anchor in the midst of the shining sea.
He closed his eyes for a while, then opened them.
Strange how the vision persisted. Yet not strange. He
knew there were no seas or ships in the heart of the

Barren-lands, just as he had known there was no cartridge in the empty rifle.

He heard a snuffle behind him, a half-choking gasp or cough. Very slowly, because of his exceeding weakness and stiffness, he rolled over on his other side. He could see nothing near at hand, but he waited patiently. Again came the snuffle and cough, and, outlined between two jagged rocks, not a score of feet away, he made out the grey head of a wolf. The sharp ears were not pricked so sharply as he had seen them on other wolves, the eyes were bleared and bloodshot, the head seemed to droop limply and forlornly. The animal blinked continually in the sunshine. It seemed sick. As he looked, it snuffled and coughed again.

This, at least, was real, he thought, and turned on the other side so that he might see the reality of the world which had been veiled from him before by the vision. But the sea still shone in the distance, and the ship's spars were plainly discernible. Was it reality after all? He closed his eyes for a long while, and thought, and then it came to him. He had been making north by east, away from the Dease Divide, and into the Coppermine Valley. This wide and sluggish river was the Coppermine. That shining sea was the Arctic Ocean. That ship was a whaler, strayed east, far east, from the mouth of the Mackenzie, and it was lying at anchor in Coronation Gulf. He remembered the Hudson Bay Company chart he had seen long ago, and it was all clear and reasonable to him.

He sat up and turned his attention to immediate affairs. He had worn through the blanket-wrappings, and his feet were like shapeless lumps of raw meat. His last blanket was gone. Rifle and knife were both missing. He had lost his hat somewhere, with the bunch of matches in the band, but the matches against his chest were safe and dry.

He was calm and collected. Though extremely weak,

he had no sensation of pain. He was not hungry. The thought of food was not even pleasant to him, and whatever he did was done by his reason alone. He ripped off the legs of his trousers to the knees, and bound them about his feet. Somehow he had succeeded in retaining the tin bucket. He would have some hot water before he began what he foresaw was to be a terrible journey to the ship.

His movements were slow. He shook as with a palsy. When he started to collect dry moss he found he could not rise to his feet. He tried again and again, then contented himself with crawling about on hands and knees. Once he crawled near to the sick wolf. The animal dragged itself reluctantly out of his way, licking its chops with a tongue which seemed hardly to have the strength to curl. The man noticed that the tongue was not the customary healthful red. It was a yellowish brown, and seemed coated with a rough and half-dry mucus.

After he had drunk a quart of hot water, the man found he was able to stand, and even to walk as well as a dying man might be supposed to walk. Every minute or so he was compelled to rest. His steps were feeble and uncertain, just as the wolf's that trailed him were feeble and uncertain; and that night, when the shining sea was blotted out by blackness, he knew he was nearer to it by no more than four miles.

Throughout the night he heard the cough of the sick wolf, and now and then the squawking of caribou calves. There was life all around him; but it was strong life, very much alive and well, and he knew the sick wolf clung to the sick man's trail in the hope that the man would die first. In the morning on first opening his eyes, he beheld it regarding him with a wistful and hungry stare. It stood crouched, with tail between its legs, like a miserable and woe-begone dog.

The sun rose brightly, and all morning the man tottered and fell toward the ship on the shining sea.

The weather was perfect. It was the brief Indian summer of the high latitudes. It might last a week. To-morrow or next day it might be gone.

In the afternoon the man came upon a trail. It was of another man who did not walk, but who dragged himself on all fours. The man thought it might be Bill, but he thought in a dull, uninterested way. He had no curiosity. In fact, sensation and emotion had left him. He was no longer susceptible to pain. Stomach and nerves had gone to sleep. Yet the life that was in him drove him on. He was very weary, but it refused to die. It was because it refused to die that he still ate muskeg berries and minnows, drank his hot water, and kept a wary eye on the sick wolf.

He followed the trail of the other man who dragged himself along, and soon came to the end of it—a few fresh-picked bones where the moss was marked by the footpads of many wolves. He saw a squat, moose-hide sack, mate to his own, which had been torn by sharp teeth. He picked it up, though its weight was almost too much for his feeble fingers. Bill had carried it to the last. Ha! ha! he would have the laugh on Bill. He would himself survive and carry it to the ship in the shining sea. His mirth was hoarse and ghastly, like a raven's croak, and the sick wolf joined him, howling lugubriously. The man ceased suddenly. How could he have the laugh on Bill if that were Bill —if those bones, so pinky-white and clean, were Bill!

He turned away. Well, Bill had deserted him; but he would not take the gold.

He came to a pool of water. Stooping over in quest of minnows, he jerked his head back as though he had been stung. He had caught sight of his reflected face. So horrible was it that sensibility awoke long enough to be shocked. There were three minnows in the pool, which was too large to drain, and after several ineffectual attempts to catch them in the tin bucket he forbore.

23   c

He was afraid, because of his great weakness, that he might fall in and drown.

That day he decreased the distance between him and the ship by three miles, the next day by two—for he was crawling now, as Bill had crawled—and the end of the fifth day found the ship still seven miles away, and him unable to make even a mile a day. Still the Indian summer held on, and he continued to crawl and faint turn and turn about, and ever the sick wolf coughed and wheezed at his heels. His knees had become raw meat like his feet, and though he padded them with the shirt from his back, it was a red track he left behind him on the moss and stones. Once, glancing back, he saw the wolf licking hungrily his bleeding trail, and he saw sharply what his own end might be . . . unless . . . unless he could get the wolf. Then began as grim a tragedy of existence as was ever played—a sick man that crawled, a sick wolf that limped, two creatures dragging their dying carcasses across the desolation and hunting each other's lives.

His mind had begun to wander again and to be perplexed by hallucinations, while his lucid intervals grew rarer and shorter.

He was awakened once, from a faint, by a wheeze close in his ear. The wolf leaped lamely back, losing its footing and falling in its weakness. It was ludicrous, but he was not amused. He was too far gone for that. But his mind was for the moment clear, and he lay and considered. The ship was no more than four miles away. He could see it quite distinctly when he rubbed the mists out of his eyes, and he could see the white sail of a small boat cutting the water of the shining sea. But he could never crawl those four miles. He knew that, and was very calm in the knowledge. He knew that he could not crawl half a mile. And yet he wanted to live. It was unreasonable that he should die after all he had undergone. Fate asked too much of him.

And, dying, he declined to die. It was stark madness, perhaps, but in the very grip of death he defied death and refused to die.

He closed his eyes and composed himself with infinite precaution. He steeled himself to keep above the suffocating languor that lapped like a rising tide through all the wells of his being. It was very like a sea, this deadly languor, that rose and rose and drowned his consciousness bit by bit. Sometimes he was all but submerged, swimming through oblivion with a faltering stroke; and again, by some strange alchemy of soul, he would find another shred of will and strike out more strongly again.

Without a movement he lay on his back, and he could hear, slowly drawing nearer and nearer, the wheezing intake and output of the sick wolf's breath. It drew closer, ever closer, through an infinitude of time, and he did not move. It was at his ear. The harsh, dry tongue grated like sandpaper against his cheek. His hands shot out—or at least he willed them to shoot out. The fingers were curved like talons, but they closed on empty air. Swiftness and certitude require strength, and the man had not this strength.

The patience of the wolf was terrible. The man's patience was no less terrible. For half a day he lay motionless, fighting off unconsciousness. Sometimes the languid sea rose over him and he dreamed long dreams, but ever through it all, waking and dreaming, he waited for the wheezing breath and the harsh caress of the tongue.

He did not hear the breath, and he slipped slowly from some dream to the feel of the tongue along his hand. He waited. The fangs pressed softly, the pressure increased, the wolf was exerting its last strength in an effort to sink teeth in the food for which it had waited so long. But the man had waited long, and the lacerated hand closed on the jaw. Slowly, while the wolf struggled feebly and the hand clutched feebly, the

25

other hand crept across to a grip. Five minutes later the whole weight of the man's body was on top of the wolf. The hands had not sufficient strength to choke the animal, but the face of the man was pressed close to the throat of the wolf, and the mouth was full of hair. At the end of half an hour the man was aware of a warm trickle in his throat. It was not pleasant. It was like molten lead being forced into his stomach, but it was forced by his will alone. Later, the man rolled over on his back and slept.

There were some members of a scientific expedition on the whaleship *Bedford*. From the deck they remarked a strange object on the shore. It was moving down the beach towards the water. They were unable to classify it, and, being scientific men, they climbed into the whaleboat alongside and went ashore to see. And they saw something that was alive but that could hardly be called a man. It was blind, unconscious. It squirmed along the ground like some monstrous worm. Most of its efforts were ineffectual, but it was persistent, and it writhed and twisted and went ahead perhaps a score of feet an hour.

Three weeks afterwards the man lay in a bunk on the whaleship *Bedford* and, with tears streaming down his wasted cheeks, told who he was and what he had undergone. He also babbled incoherently of his mother, of sunny Southern California, and a home among the orange-groves and flowers.

The days were not many after that when he sat at table with the scientific men and ship's officers. He gloated over the spectacle of so much food, watching it anxiously as it went into the mouths of others. With the disappearance of each mouthful an expression of deep regret came into his eyes. He was quite sane, yet he hated those men at meal-time because they ate so much food. He was haunted by a fear that it would not last. He enquired of the cook, the cabin-boy, the captain, concerning the food stores. They reassured him countless times, but he could not believe them, and pried cunningly about the lazarette to see with his own eyes.

It was noticed that the man was getting fat. He grew stouter each day. The scientific men shook their heads and theorized. They limited the man at his meals, but still his girth increased, and his body swelled prodigiously under his shirt.

The sailors grinned. They knew. And when the scientific men set a watch on the man, they knew too. They saw him slouch for'ard after breakfast, and, like a mendicant with outstretched palm, accost a sailor. The sailor grinned and passed him a fragment of sea biscuit. He clutched it avariciously, looked at it as a miser looks at gold, and thrust it into his shirt-bosom. Similar were the donations from other grinning sailors.

The scientific men were discreet. They left him alone. But they privily examined his bunk. It was lined with hard tack; every nook and cranny was filled to overflowing with hardtack. Yet he was sane. He was taking precautions against another possible famine, that was all. He would recover from it, the scientific men said; and he did, ere the *Bedford*'s anchor rumbled down in San Francisco Bay.

27

UNCONQUERED
by Ben Ames Williams

BEN AMES WILLIAMS was born in Macon, Mississippi, in 1889, and graduated at Dartmouth College. In common with many of the younger American authors Williams sought experience of active life before settling down to a literary career. He has written dramatic stories of war and the sea, and he has also written quiet stories of the trout brooks and woodcock covers of a village called "Fraternity," the origin of which is his native home. In 1926 he was awarded the O. Henry Memorial Prize for one of the best stories of that year. "Unconquered," written in 1918, is a remarkable piece of work, fully bearing out its author's creed that "In every great story there is a moment which would have been supremely effective on the stage; in every dramatic situation there is a short story."

BEN AMES WILLIAMS was born in Macon, Mississippi, in 1889, and graduated at Dartmouth College. In common with many of the younger American authors Williams sought experience of active life before settling down to a literary career. He has written dramatic stories of war and the sea; and he has also written quiet stories of the trout brooks and woodcock covers of a village called "Fraternity," the origin of which is his native home. In 1926 he was awarded the O. Henry Memorial Prize for one of the best stories of that year. "Unconquered," written in 1918, is a remarkable piece of work, fully bearing out its author's creed that "In every great story there is a moment which would have been supremely effective on the stage; in every dramatic situation there is a short story."

UNCONQUERED

BY

BEN AMES WILLIAMS

THIS was in the first months after the War. The old Frenchman was still in uniform. His round-topped, gold-braided cap lay on the table at his elbow, beside the open box of cigarettes and the half-empty glass. The breast and the sleeve of his tunic bore testimony to his honourable service.

He was a short man, a heavy man, with a large stomach, and solid shoulders; and his head hunched forward in a leonine fashion. His eyes were blue; and his hair was thick, and coarse, and white as snow. He was in New York on some business of reconstruction. . . . And while the other men had been exchanging reminiscences, he had stared with thoughtful eyes at a large framed print upon the wall before him.

This print was a reproduction of a painting thoroughly familiar. It portrayed an old man, a man of middle age, a boy, a fife, a drum and a flag. . . . And one who looked at it could feel the brush of the wind through the banner's waving folds, and hear the scream of shrill fifes piping in the air.

Hinchcliffe, who knew the Frenchman better than the others, observed this scrutiny, and asked a question softly. The Frenchman smiled.

"I was thinking, sir," he told Hinchcliffe, "that I have witnessed a scene like that, in my time."

His words came in a little pause in the conversation of the others, so that they all heard, and waited for him to continue. And Hinchcliffe ventured to urge quietly: "Tell us."

The Frenchman lifted his hand in a deprecating

33

fashion; they insisted. He sipped at his glass, and in the end he nodded. Barton lighted a fresh cigar. Hinchcliffe shifted to a more comfortable position in his chair. Hughes beckoned the nearest attendant with a silent forefinger. The Frenchman began to speak.

His tone was level and unemotional; his articulation was precise. Only an odd construction of sentences now and then betrayed his unfamiliarity with the tongue. His eyes were on the framed print upon the wall; and they seemed to look through it, and beyond. . . .

It was, in the beginning (said the old Frenchman), one of those valorous and devoted regiments to which fall the hardest and most honourable tasks.

The men came, for the most part, from the Argonne; they were rugged stock, men of the farms and of the hills. Simple and direct . . . good soldiers. . . . And Frenchmen.

It chanced that when the War came, this regiment fought in its own homeland. The men knew every foot of the hills they defended, the ravines which they turned into death-traps, the forests through which they marched, the meadows where they skirmished. They knew this land, and by the same token, they loved it. It was as though they had their roots in the soil. They could not be torn from it. They waited for the Germans at ten kilometres from the frontier—you remember, my friends, how we waited for them here so that they might not say we had provoked the conflict—and when the Germans came, this regiment stopped its immediate foe and held the Germans in their tracks.

At this time, the French invasion toward Muelhausen was prospering; but at the same time, the Germans were crushing Belgium, and pouring through, so that they turned our flank and we were forced to go back. That was very unpleasant, and for a little time, at the very first, it was dangerous. But in a few days we were safely disengaged, and the enemy was exhausting himself to come up with us, and our counter-stroke was preparing.

34

But to give us time for this retreat and preparation, certain organizations had to be sacrificed. This regiment was one. It was ordered to stand firm, to hold. . . . It held. The enemy attacked on the front and was repulsed; but on either side, our lines gave way, and the second day saw the regiment attacked on the right flank, and the left.

It was well posted, upon a hill that dominated two good roads, and it held. . . .

But the Germans poured past them on either side; and in the press of more important matters to the southward, the work of overwhelming this regiment was delayed. A containing force was left to hold them, starve them. . . . And the main battle swept away and left them stranded there.

The men had fought tirelessly; they were prepared to fight on, and to die. But when it became apparent that the Germans did not propose to push matters, and when it became clear that another day would see hunger among them, the commander determined to strike. He had, at this time, some three hundred fit men of the regiment remaining. They were no longer of use where they stood. And the regiment was not accustomed to be idle.

Therefore, that night, a little after midnight, when it was very dark and only the occasional flashes from the German positions illumined the blackness, the regiment attacked. They went down in three lines, a hundred men to a line, with their commander and their officers ahead. And they flung themselves upon the Germans.

The Germans were surprised. They had expected another day or two of waiting, and then an easy surrender. Instead, they found themselves beset by swarming enemies—stout men with long bayonets who sweated and swore and struck. The first charge of the French cut through the encircling lines; the remnant of the regiment might have escaped even then. But there had been no orders to escape, so they turned to right

35

and left, along the German positions, and flung the huddled enemy back and back and back.

The word was passed that their commander had fallen; and this man—he was my very good friend and comrade, gentlemen—had been beloved by them. Therefore they continued to fight with bitterness in their hearts until the resistance melted before them. There may have been a thousand Germans left to hold this battered remnant of a regiment; but those who lived, out of that thousand, fled before the three hundred.

They fled, and were lost in the night; and the flame from a fired straw-stack nearby illumined the field, so that the Frenchmen could look into each other's eyes and consider what was to be done.

Their commissioned officers were dead, gentlemen; but there was an under-officer in that regiment named Jacques Fontaine. He was a big man, a farmer; and he was a very serious and practical and thrifty man. Also, he knew that country, and many of the men of the regiment were his neighbours, and all of them knew him for what he was.

Therefore it seemed natural that he should take the command that night. He called to a man named Lupec, and spoke with him. This Lupec was a little, wry-necked man, as shrewd as a fox. And Lupec advised Jacques Fontaine, and the big farmer shouted aloud to the panting men of the regiment, where they stood about him in the red trousers and the blue coats that had made our army so vulnerable in that first rush of war. He looked about him, and he shouted to them. . . .

He bade them strip cartridges and rifles from the dead; and he told them to take what provisions they could find. And when this was done, they were to scatter, and rendezvous the next night but one in a certain ravine which all that country knew.

This ravine was in the heart of the forest. It was well hidden; it might be defended. There was water
36

in it; and there were farms upon the borders of the forest where food might be had.

When, a little before dawn, a German force came back and descended upon them, the men melted before it like the morning mists before the sun; and the Germans did not know what to do, so they made camp, and cooked, and ate, and slept. And the men of the regiment made their way, singly, and by twos and threes, through the forest toward the ravine that was the rendezvous.

This spot was called in your tongue, gentlemen, the Ravine of the Cold Tooth.

Now modern warfare, gentlemen, is a curious and inconsistent thing. It is vast, and yet it is minute.

This battered regiment, added to the French armies at that moment, would have been of small account. A burst of shrapnel, a mine, an unimportant counter-thrust might have accounted for them all. Their weight in an attack would have been inconsiderable.

But this regiment which did not know how to surrender, and which was at large behind the German lines, was another matter, my friends. It was worth well nigh a division to France. For an army is as vulnerable as it is vast, gentlemen; and it can do only one thing at a time.

The Emperor discovered this truth, long ago, in Spain. When he scattered his army to overcome the guerillas, he exposed himself to the blows of the Iron Duke; and when he effected a concentration to attack Wellington, the Spanish peasants sliced off every straggler. He was incessantly harassed, and he lost that campaign; and that was his first defeat.

The warfare of to-day—or, let us say, the warfare of yesterday, which we hope will never be the warfare of to-morrow—the warfare of yesterday was like that. The army's front is like the front of a dam, vast and impregnable; but behind that front is bolstered and strengthened

37

and buttressed by many little lines of communication and supply, just as a dam may be buttressed on the lower side. A division may shatter itself in vain against the army's front; a hundred men may cut one of those little lines behind.

This was the fact which aided Jacques Fontaine and his men, the regiment.

You must understand, also, gentlemen, that in the heat of open battle, a fighting-line is an unstable thing. It sways, and bends, and yields, and rebounds; and fragments are broken off from it. They return to their places, or they do not return. At times, the line itself is shattered, its component parts are thrown to every side. In open country, these component parts—men, gentlemen—may be run down and sabred by the cavalry, or they may surrender.

In wooded land, however, it is hard to exterminate men who will yield to nothing less than extermination. Cavalry can work through the forest only in small patrols, and along defined paths and roads. And for infantry, the carrying of a wood is slow and painful work.

Therefore, when an army makes a considerable advance, it leaves in its rear many small and scattered parties of the enemy. It was so when the Germans thrust down into France, gentlemen. There were many Frenchmen left behind to wander and hide in the forest, to starve, or yield, or die. . . . Or, perhaps, to survive.

This will explain to you, my friends, the growth of the regiment under Jacques Fontaine's command. When they scattered, after dispersing the German force which had been set to hold them, there were scarce a hundred of them without wounds. When they gathered at the Ravine of the Cold Tooth, straggling parties had swelled that number, so that Jacques Fontaine, counting, with his big forefinger pointing in turn toward each man and his lips mumbling as he counted, found that he had a force of two hundred and seven hardy and energetic men.

And he was pleased.

The first thing this man did, gentlemen, was to reconstitute the regiment. A regiment, you understand, is an immortal thing. It cannot die. When every man of it is dead, the regiment still lives; because a regiment is an idea, and ideas are eternal. Jacques Fontaine was a slow man, my friends; and you would have considered him a dull man. Nevertheless, this conception of the immortality of the regiment was a part of his heart and his soul. If you had told him the regiment was destroyed, he would have been very sorry for you.

They had saved their regimental colours, you understand; the banner with its honourable decorations. They had saved this, and Jacques Fontaine's first act was to assign six men to guard this banner. He explained to them, carefully, that they were to seclude themselves. They were to engage in no enterprise involving hazard; and they were to keep the standard immaculate and unstained. They were to fight only to defend it; and they were to save it by evasion and flight when they could, and fight only when they must.

Jacques Fontaine understood, gentlemen, that the banner is the regiment.

When he had made this arrangement, he called Lupec, and they found a man skilled in writing, and they prepared a regimental roll. Those stragglers from other regiments who had joined them were mustered in after a formula which Jacques Fontaine devised. In the end, two hundred and seven men were one body and one soul, and Jacques Fontaine was satisfied with the arrangement.

Having counted his men, he began, thriftily, to consider their equipment.

He found that these two hundred and seven men had two hundred and fifty-four rifles. A hundred or so of these rifles were German; and for these weapons there was a plentiful supply of German ammunition. But there were very few cartridges for the French rifles; there were only the long, needle-like bayonets.

39

Jacques Fontaine was vexed with this discovery. He was one of those penurious peasants whom De Maupassant knew how to paint, my friends. He could not bear poverty, or waste. He derived a solid satisfaction from the mere possession of wealth; and his conception of wealth was strictly in accord with academic economic principles. Any useful article was wealth to him.

He perceived that while his command was wealthy in rifles and bayonets, it was very badly off indeed for cartridges.

He sat down on a big rock at the head of the ravine, while the men with little fires cooked supper in the deeps below him; and he took off his hat and scratched his head and considered what to do. Another man might have chosen his course more swiftly; it required some hours for Jacques Fontaine to make up his mind.

But when he rose from the rock, this man had laid out before his feet the path they were to follow through the four interminable and glorious years which were to come.

Any other man would have been wise enough to know that the plan he had chosen was impossible. Jacques Fontaine was valorously stupid. He did not know he could not do that which he planned to do, gentlemen. Therefore, he did the impossible.

The German armies, at this time, were throwing themselves against our barricade of steel and fire along the Marne; and by every possible avenue, they were hurrying forward munitions and guns and all supplies. They gave little thought to the stragglers in the forests behind them. They knew that stragglers are not dangerous to an organized force. It is only when the stragglers organize that they become a peril.

Jacques Fontaine had organized these stragglers. At dawn, on the third day after that first rendezvous, he flung his men upon a wagon train that threaded one of the forest roads.

This train was escorted by a troop of some five score

Uhlans; it was upon a road which was guarded by
patrols of three and four men stationed at every farm.
Yet in a dip between two hills, the single Uhlan in
advance found his way blocked by felled trees in the
road, and at the same time other trees, cut almost
through and held erect by ropes until the appointed
time, crashed down upon his comrades behind.

With the crashing of these trees was mingled the
crashing discharge of two hundred rifles. And after
the first discharge out of a hundred troopers scarce fifty
remained upon their horses; and after the second volley,
not thirty men were still unharmed. And after the
third, there were only fugitive Uhlans galloping headlong back to give the alarm.

Before these fugitives were out of sight, Jacques
Fontaine and his men flung themselves upon the loaded
wagons. The two foremost wagons bore cartridges.
They laid open the boxes with axe and bayonet; and
they plunged in their hands.

It was hopeless to attempt to make away with the
wagons themselves. Thick forest lay on every hand.
Therefore, by Jacques' order, each man took all the
cartridges he could bear, and raced back into the wood,
and hid the precious things between rocks, and beneath
logs, and in every cranny he could find; and when he
had disposed of his burden he returned and took as
many more as he could carry. The men filled their
pockets, their belts, their pouches, their hats. . . .
Some of them dropped the cartridges inside the legs of
their trousers, so that the things hung heavy about their
knees. And when this was done, of the two wagon
loads, no cartridges remained.

The men took also the rifles and revolvers of the fallen
Germans; and they stripped their own dead of weapons.
And then they slipped into the forest, and scattered,
and fled away.

The hunt began within the hour; and for a week, the
men were chivvied through the woods like hares. Dogs

bayed upon their trails; they hid in caves, in trees, in the thick-growing underbrush; they lay for hours in the pools with only mouth and nose and eyes exposed above the water. And some of them were shot, and some were taken alive. . . . And some took Germans with them when they died.

Lupec was one of those who were captured. On the fourth day, weary and utterly exhausted, he fell asleep in a crevice beneath two boulders; and a German stumbled on him. His captor took him, at gun point, back through the forest toward a cross-road where the Germans were encamped.

When they came in sight of this place, his captor halted to stare, and Lupec also looked. The Germans were busy; they were engaged in hanging three Frenchmen by the necks to a beech tree beside the farm-house there.

Lupec had no desire to thrust his wry neck into a noose. Therefore, he turned and plunged into the man who had captured him, and knocked the man down. Even then he found time to snatch up the German's rifle and turn and fire; and he saw the German officer who was watching the hangings pitch drunkenly forward on his saddle. So that Lupec was grinning as he plunged into the forest again.

He made good his escape; and thus he was able to bring to Jacques Fontaine, when the pursuit relaxed, the word of the hangings.

The big farmer was displeased with this news; because, you understand, my friends, he had reconstituted the regiment, so that he considered that he and his comrades were soldiers of France, and as such entitled to better treatment than a noose. He frowned blackly at Lupec's report; and he sent out men to discover if there had been other hangings.

He found that eleven Frenchmen had been murdered in this fashion, gentlemen; and Jacques Fontaine nodded at this, and made a calculation upon his fingers. He was slow at figures, you understand; but he knew what he wished to do. He made his calculations; and he sent out his men to the farms and the cross-roads, and he gave them careful orders. . . .

They obeyed him so well, my friends, that on the second day he was able to hang twenty-two Germans, two for each Frenchman, upon the same tree where the men of his regiment had been hung.

When the Germans discovered these pendant figures, looking like sacks of old clothes in their dirty, baggy uniforms, they were violently wrathful; and for two weeks more the forests were scoured in an effort to exterminate the remnants of the regiment.

But there were no more Frenchmen hanged.

To understand the history of the four years which followed, gentlemen, it is necessary to understand the man Jacques Fontaine; it is necessary to understand the spirit of Frenchmen. It is necessary, in short, to comprehend France.

I believe I may be forgiven for holding that valour is a trait of most Frenchmen. And by valour I do not mean the bravery which can be taught, which is merely a form of habit. You may take the most craven material and teach it the habit of obedience, and you have what passes for a brave soldier; but the Frenchman is valorous before he is a soldier, and he is valorous when he is no longer a soldier. The whining beggar has valour; so has the peasant, and the comfortable bourgeois, and the man of birth and breeding. You will find it universally, my friends.

This is perhaps because the French are the great phrase-makers of the world. The turn of a phrase comes easily to them; and the turn of a phrase captivates and conquers them, so that they will die for it. Danton made a phrase that saved France. Verdun made another. Combine the two, my friends, and you have the spirit of France. Dare—and yield not. The valour

43

of France is the valour that will die rather than violate those mighty phrases. . . .

Thus I say Jacques Fontaine was valorous. Bravery is a tangible thing; valour defends the intangible. Bravery is steadfast, and it is sensible. Valour may be foolhardy. Valour is a form of pride. And Jacques Fontaine was proud. Thus, when the Germans hanged men of the regiment, he hanged Germans. He would have done the same knowing that he himself must be hanged forthwith thereafter. For valour does not consider consequences.

But Jacques Fontaine was not only valorous; he was thrifty. And it was the combination of these two characteristics that enabled him to survive. It is this same combination which has enabled France to survive, my friends. She is valorous, but she is thrifty. She is audacious; but she is pre-eminently logical. Thus Jacques Fontaine; valorous and thrifty, audacious and logical.

Thrift was bred in him. It was thrift which enabled him to survive and keep his regiment alive. He saved supplies, munitions, guns, men. . . . He had no other belongings save the things of war; therefore he hoarded these things, and when his stores ran short, he secured fresh supplies.

When his stores ran short, he foraged through the land, and he raided the German trains. When munitions threatened to fail, he watched his opportunity to replenish them. When guns wore out, he got new ones. And when the wastage of these operations, the unceasing perils of this life reduced the numbers in his command, he attacked and liberated a convoy of prisoners and recruited his regiment once more.

Through it all, he kept careful records of his regimental life. These records show that at one time, this man and his tattered remnant of a regiment possessed three German machine-guns, four hundred rifles, and almost fifty thousand cartridges. Besides clothing,

44

and stores of food, all hidden in caches in the forest depths.

It was inevitable that he should be hunted. There were at least four determined attempts by the Germans to exterminate the regiment. One of these occupied six weeks; it cut the roll from a hundred and eighty men down to less than sixty; it reduced weapons and supplies to a minimum; and for the full six weeks, the men saw each other only now and then, in groups of two or three. For this was the secret of their survival; they scattered before the hunt, they became units, as difficult to find as the beasts of the forest in which they dwelt.

Yet always they survived. That is to say, a nucleus of men always survived; and the regiment could never die. The regimental colours were never captured; the regimental records were never found. And Jacques Fontaine, and Lupec, and a handful of others of the original regiment, preserved themselves and held the rest together.

Picture it to yourselves, my friends, if you can; this handful of men, cohering, enduring; and all around them by the hundred thousand, the enemy. Behind every tree, a possible rifle; in every wood, a potential ambush; in every comrade, the danger of a spy. . . .

There were three spies in the regiment during those four years. The first was suspected and killed before he had reached the rendezvous. The second was detected on the third day when he stiffened at a barked command in German. The third, alone, was clever; he deceived them, he lived among them, he learned their plans, and when the chance came, he brought down a German force upon the rendezvous when almost the full command was there.

But Jacques Fontaine had never grown careless; he had made it a rule from the beginning to post twenty guards in a wide circle about the Ravine of the Cold Tooth when the regiment was assembled. And one of

45

these guards escaped the attempt to overcome him, and gave warning just in time. The regiment flung out of the ravine, broke boldly through the jaws of the German's trap, left half its strength in German hands.

But the remnant escaped, and lived.

In the winter of 1915, this regiment was reduced to twenty-seven men. The next winter, at the time of the great hunt, when the men were tracked through the snow, they were cut down to fifty-four. The fall of 1917 was the time of the spy; and some seventy men went through that winter like the beasts, some of them nursing wounds for months on end. They stirred from their hiding-places only once, and that was when they cut off a German patrol in which the spy rode, and took him from his comrades and hanged him to the beams of a barn.

They had been forced to leave the Ravine of the Cold Tooth, since the Germans knew that spot; they hid now under the shoulder of one of the little mountains. And there, that winter, and the next spring, their numbers grew again. . . .

They had ninety men in March; and the friendly peasants brought to them by devious ways soldiers of England and of France who were cut off in the great offensive of that year, so that in May they numbered a hundred and fifty men; and in June, close to two hundred. . . . And the Germans were too much concerned with other matters to divert so much as a regiment to run them down. . . .

When in due time the hour came for them to fulfil their destiny, my friends, this regiment which Jacques Fontaine had kept alive numbered three hundred and ninety men, with rifles for all, and two machine-guns, and cartridges to feed those clamouring things. . . . And Jacques prepared to strike his blow for France.

It is certain, my friends, that I have failed to give you any comprehensive picture of the life of this poor

regiment during the years of its isolation. It is impossible
for you, who have always been well fed and comfortable,
to imagine the hunger, the cold, the loneliness, the
misery. Some of you have faced peril, perhaps for hours
on end. There was never a moment when their lives
were secure. They were like the animals in the forest
about them; they slept fitfully; they squatted on their
haunches while they ate, and were alert to spring to their
feet at the least alarm. They subsisted on berries, on
nuts, on uncooked grain pilfered from the fields which
the Germans forced the peasants to cultivate; they
snared rabbits, they were able, now and then, to kill
larger game. And when desperation drove them, they
attacked the Germans and wrested food from them at
the price of blood.

This existence was at best an ordeal; and when the
Germans found time to try to hunt them down, it became
torment. Regiments encircled them, beating through the
woods, searching every brake and gully and ravine.
Dogs tracked them, baying on their trails; their footprints in the snow, bloody and stumbling, led their
pursuers through the forest. At one time, one of the
little German princelings gave great sport to his friends
by organizing a hunt for these men as he would have
organized a hunt for the wild boars. When the beaters
overcame a Frenchman, they took his weapons and let
him go, and then the princeling and his friends charged
the unarmed man with levelled lance, and ran him
through.

The Frenchmen spoiled this sport by a stubborn refusal
to run before the horses. Robbed of their weapons, they
stood erect and faced their foe and took the steel in
their breasts, so that the princeling was furious, and those
with him were shamed, and the sport was broken off. . . .

Of such things as this was existence for these men. . . .

But I have been unjust in failing, before this, to speak
of the peasants who helped them. Word of this regiment
had gone abroad through the forest and the mountains.

And wherever they went, they were welcomed, and given food, and shelter, and clothed. . . . And the peasants brought recruits to them, and brought them warnings and information. They made endurance possible. . . .

It was the peasants, in the end, who brought the word to Jacques Fontaine that told him his hour had come to strike. They came and they said the great battle to the southward was rolling nearer every day. This was at the time, you understand, when we had begun to push the Germans back; it was at the time when they were giving way each time a little more easily than the time before. We advanced one mile to-day two miles to-morrow, three the day after. . . .

And the word of this was abroad among the peasants in that part of France and of Belgium which the Germans still held. They were fermenting, as though these rumours of approaching liberation had been yeast cast among them.

They came, and they told Jacques Fontaine. And Jacques Fontaine, and wry-necked Lupec, cast about them to find a task for their hands.

The Germans were making up their mind, at this time, to draw back to a new defensive line, where they counted on being able to hold us at last. And they were withdrawing slowly, a little here, and a little there, and a little yonder, day by day. Behind them they left a ruined country, every house destroyed, every fruit tree cut off at the roots. . . . But they were going back and back. . . .

There was one line of railway along which the trains were pounding, day by day; and this line ran north and south past the fringe of the forest and the mountains where Jacques Fontaine and his regiment were hiding. The regiment was scattered, groups of four men and five and six dwelt here and there among the ravines. But when Jacques Fontaine and Lupec had considered, and secretly scouted back and forth, and had decided upon what they wished to do, they sent runners to gather the regiment together.

There was a spot where the railway line which the Germans were burdening so heavily crossed a little stream. On the north bank of this stream, and overlooking the bridge which spanned it, there rose a rocky hillock; and this hillock was topped by one of those ancient, ruined châteaux which were the chief beauty of France before the War. On three sides, sheer precipices fell away from the walls of this old châtcau; on the other side, the way of ascent was steep and hard.

A dozen men could hold this spot against an army, so long as cannon were not concerned in the affair. And Jacques Fontaine believed the Germans had other uses for their cannon at this time.

So he gathered his regiment, and drew them near the spot he had chosen, and waited his time to strike.

There was, you understand, a guard set about this bridge. But the guard was not strong, for a strong guard was not considered necessary. There were soldiers passing constantly, working slowly northward in the great retreat; and the long trains of stores and supplies crossed one after another, through every day.

It was like a river of men and of supplies, one of the rivers of war. And on a certain night, Jacques Fontaine dammed that river. His men swept down, they overwhelmed the guard upon the bridge . . . And they fired the petard which the Germans had themselves laid, to destroy that bridgc when their forces should be across. They fired the petard, and the bridge disappeared in a great flame of orange fire; and Jacques Fontaine and his men fell back swiftly into the night. When dawn came, they were all within the walls of the old château, high above the bridge, commanding it. And when the German pioneers swarmed out to repair the bridge, Jacques and his men began to fire.

They swept the pioneers away, for they were marksmen all. They had been trained for four years never

to waste a cartridge; that was the thrift of Jacques
Fontaine. And they wasted none now. They did not
use the two machine-guns. Those were reserved to repel
the attack that was sure to come. They used their
rifles, and they strove to make every bullet take its toll.

A troop train came north in the morning, and the
Germans flung the men against the old château, up the
steep path. The Frenchmen slaughtered them; they
built a barricade of German bodies before the very
muzzles of their guns. And more trains came, and were
held up, by the destroyed bridge. The dammed river
began to rise, and grumble, and fret and fume. . . .
The pioneers, down by the ruined bridge, strove fruit-
lessly under the hail of lead.

The second day, the Germans brought guns to bear.
At first, there was only shrapnel, and it spattered harm-
lessly. But after that came high explosive; and each great
shell, detonating amid the ruined walls of the château,
turned every stone and pebble into a missile that swept
to right and left and all about in a storm of death.

When three hundred men are huddled in a narrow
area, a single shell will kill half of them. This happened,
on that day. An hour after the bombardment began, not
a hundred men remained alive upon the top of that little
peak; an hour after that, scarce fifty remained. . . .

But while it was easy to kill the first hundred, and
while it was not difficult to kill the second hundred, it
was very hard indeed to complete the extermination of
the force. A dozen men may live where a hundred
would perish; and at noon the riflemen in the ruins of
the old château still kept the ruined bridge cleared of
men, and none could toil there.

By that time, the congestion on the southern bank of
the river had become so great that that tide overflowed.
And Jacques Fontaine, with a scarf bound around his
chest to crush back the blood that was leaking from his
great body, could see and hear the roar of the French
guns, ten miles away, harassing the fleeing enemy. . . .

By mid-afternoon, French shells began to fall amid the huddle on the southern bank of the river; and at nightfall the Germans broke there. . . .

They broke . . . they poured across the stream, wading, swimming, drowning. They broke in flight to escape the merciless guns. And the French 'planes overhead, till dark was fully fallen, marked their going, and signalled the guns that harassed the fleeing men.

Before that, the Frenchmen had been silenced; the Frenchmen of Jacques Fontaine, in the old château. There were some few of them still unwounded; there were others who breathed and groaned as they slowly died. There were not enough of them to keep the bridge clear; but that duty no longer was required of them. They had held up a division, till the French armies could come up and rout it. And the Germans, flinging one last charge against the old château, drew off to the north and left Jacques Fontaine and his men masters of the field.

I was with the army that came up to that bridge at dawn, my friends. And I was one of those who saw, floating in the first light above the ruined walls of the old château, a flicker of glorious colour. . . . A banner, floating there. . . .

Our skirmishers were flung across, pressing northward. Our engineers swarmed upon the ruined bridge, rebuilding. . . .

And one patrol of men turned aside, by the road that led toward the château. They went to solve this riddle, gentlemen. They went to discover who it was that had set there, the banner of France.

They went carefully, one man ahead, others behind. They feared a trap; they did not understand. . . .

I was with them. We came, thus, to a turn in the road; and we rounded it, and we saw our advance man at the halt, upon his horse, in the road ahead.

Toward this man were marching, down the road from the château, four men.

51

One of these men was tall, and strong, and bulky. And there was a scarf about his chest; and the scarf was red.

Of the others, two marched proudly; two who had come unscathed through the hell where that château had stood. And the fourth, though there was a smeared bandage about his face and eyes, so that he held to the arm of Jacques Fontaine; this fourth man, my friends, held his head as high as any; and his shoulders were erect, and his steps were firm.

It was this fourth man who bore, resting it against his hip and steadying it with his other hand, the flag.

They came on, these four, heads high. And though they were haggard, and stained, and worn, the banner above them was unsullied, and unsoiled. . . .

As they came toward us, we could hear them singing, in cracked and hoarse voices. Singing those immortal words of Rouget de l'Isle. . . .

When they came near our vedette, where he sat his horse so quietly, they halted. And I saw then that these men still wore the red trousers and blue coats of their ancient uniforms, which they had preserved for this occasion through the years. And we were all very still as we listened so that we heard the vedette challenge, in a ringing voice:

"*Qui vive?*"

There was, for me, something splendidly symbolic in the scene. For to that challenge those battered but unconquerable men gave answer with one voice, one word.

"*Qui vive?*" the vedette challenged.

And the four answered hoarsely:

"France!"

FORTITUDE

by Perceval Gibbon

PERCEVAL GIBBON was born at Trelech, Carmarthenshire, in 1879, and received most of his education at the famous Moravian school, Germany. His first love was for the sea, but although, like Joseph Conrad, he passed many years in the British Merchant Service there is little trace in his fiction of seafaring experiences. Most of the adventures described in his stories are derived from his observations and activities as a war correspondent in Africa, America and Central Europe. He was essentially an imaginative reporter of life either directly witnessed or overheard in the course of his journalistic travels. "Fortitude," originally published under the title of "Vrouw Grobelaar's Own Story," is the best of a collection of South African tales, and purporting to be the reminiscences of an aged Dutch woman. Gibbon also wrote an excellent volume of war stories under the title of "Those Who Smiled." He died in 1926.

PERCEVAL GIBBON was born at Trelech, Carmarthenshire, in 1879, and received most of his education at the famous Moravian school, Germany. His first love was for the sea, but although, like Joseph Conrad, he passed many years in the British Merchant Service there is little trace in his fiction of seafaring experiences. Most of the adventures described in his stories are derived from his observations and activities as a war correspondent in Africa, America and Central Europe. He was essentially an imaginative reporter of life either directly witnessed or overheard in the course of his journalistic travels. "Fortitude," originally published under the title of "Vrouw Grobelaar's Own Story," is the best of a collection of South African tales, and purporting to be the reminiscences of an aged Dutch woman. Gibbon also wrote an excellent volume of war stories under the title of "Those Who Smiled." He died in 1926.

E

FORTITUDE

BY

Perceval Gibbon

"BUT what are you going to live on?" asked the Vrouw Grobelaar. "You haven't got a farm."

"We're going to live in a town," answered Katje proudly.

I interrupted here, and tried to make the old lady understand that even schoolmasters received some money for their work, and that there would be enough for two, without frills.

She had no answer for the moment, but sat and looked at us both very thoughtfully. Still, there was no hostility in her aspect; she had not her war-like manner, and seemed engrossed rather with an estimate of the situation than of its consequences. I had looked for opposition and disparagement at least, volubly voiced and backed with a bloody example of a failure in marriage, and I know that Katje shared my misgivings. But here was something different.

"You—you are not angry?" asked Katje after a while.

The old lady stared. "Angry! No, of course not. It is not altogether my affair, Katje. As time goes on, I grow nervous of stirring any broth but my own. If it were a matter of mere wisdom, and knowledge of life, and the cool head of an elder, I should not be afraid to handle you to suit my ideas; but this is a graver piece of business. Wisdom has nothing to do with it: those who are wise in their love are often foolish in their life. You've got your man, and if you want him you'll marry him in despite of the tongues of men and of angels. I know; I did it myself."

"You?" cried Katje.

"Yes, me," retorted the Vrouw Grobelaar. "Why not? Do you think that a person of sense has no feelings? When I was a girl I was nearly as big a fool as some others I could name, and got more out of it, in happiness and experience, than ever they will."

"Tell us about it," suggested Katje.

"I am telling you," snapped the old lady. "Don't interrupt. Sit down. Don't fidget, nor giggle. There!"

"When I was a girl," she began at last, "my father's farm was at Windhoek, and beyond the nek to the south, an easy two miles from our beacons, there lived one Kornel du Plessis. I came to know him, somehow. I saw him here and there, till I had no wish to see any but him, and we understood one another very well. Ah, Katje, girls are light things; but I truly think that in those days few Boer maids had much mind for trivial matters in their loves when once the man was found right and sound. Even at this length of time I have a thrill in remembering Kornel: a big man, and heavy, with thick shoulders, but very quick on his feet, and eyes that were grey, with pleasant little puckers at the corners. He sat far back in his saddle and lolled to the gait of the horse easily; such men make horse masters, and masters of women. That is to say, they are masters of all.

"There was no kissing behind the kraal and whispering at windows. Neither of us had a mind for such meannesses. He came to my father's house and took food with us, and told my father the tale of his sheep and cattle, and the weight of the mortgage on his farm. Though he was not rich, he was young and keen, and my father knew well that the richest are not those who begin life with riches. There would have been no hindrance to a marriage forthwith, but for some law business in the town, of which I never understood the truth. But it concerned the land and house of Kornel, and my father would not say the last word till that should be settled.

"It dragged on for a long while, that law matter, and the conversations between Kornel and my father ran mainly in guesses about it, with much talk that was very forlorn of interest. But what did it matter to me? I had the man, and knew I could keep him: had I foreseen the future, even then I would not have cared. But for all that, I was very uneasy one hot day when Kornel rode over with a grave face and eyes that looked as though he had not slept the night before.

"My father gave him a sharp look, and pulled strongly at his pipe, like a man who prepares for ticklish business.

"'You have news?' he asked.

"Kornel nodded and looked at me. It was a look as though he would ask me to spare and forgive. I smiled at him, and came and stood at his side.

"'From what you have told me,' began my father, looking very wise, 'the water right may cut you off from the pastures. Is that so?'

"'No,' said Kornel, 'all that is wrong.'

"'H'm. Indeed! Then you will have to carry your north beacon farther to the east and lose the dam.'

"'Wrong again,' answered Kornel patiently.

"'Then you have won your case,' said my father, very eager to name the truth and prove his wisdom.

"'Dear me!' said Kornel; 'you have no idea at all of the matter. You are quite out in your guesses. I have not won my case: I have lost it, and the land and the house and the stock along with it. I came over on a horse that is no more mine than this chair is. For all I know, my very trousers may belong to the other man. There you have it. What do you say to that?'

"'Then you have nothing at all?' asked my father.

"'I have a piece of waste on the dorp road, near the spruit,' answered Kornel. 'There is a kind of hut on it. That is all. It is only two morgen' (four acres).

59

"My father sat shaking his head in silence for a long time, while Kornel clenched and unclenched his hands and stared at the floor and frowned. I put my hand on his shoulder, and he trembled.

"'It is an affliction,' said my father at last, 'and no doubt you know very well what you have done to deserve it. But it might be worse. You might have had a wife, and then what would you have done?'

"One is wise to honour one's parents always, but one cannot be blind. I think my father might sometimes have spoken less and done better for it.

"'We have talked about Christina yonder,' continued my father, pointing at me with the stem of his pipe. 'It is a good thing it went no further than talk.'

"'But it did,' I said quickly. 'It went much further. It went to my promise and Kornel's; and if I am ready to keep mine now, I shall not look to see him fail in his.'

"Ah! He never needed any but the smallest spur. Your true man kindles quickly. At my word he sprang up and his arm folded me. I gasped in the grip of it.

"My father had a way of behaving like a landdrost (magistrate) at times, and now he wrinkled his forehead and smiled very wisely.

"'When one's bed is on the veld,' he said, 'it is not the time to remember a promise to a girl. It is easier to find a bed-fellow than a blanket sometimes. And then, I am to be considered, and I cannot suffer this kind of thing.'

"'I think you will have to manage it,' answered Kornel.

"'Do you?' said my father. 'Well, I have nothing to give you. Christina, come here to me!'

"Kornel loosed his arm and set me free, but I stayed where I was.

"'Father,' I cried, 'I have promised Kornel.'

"'Come here!' he said again. Then, when I did not move, disobeying him for the first time in my life, his face darkened. 'Are you not coming?' he said.

60

"'No!' I answered, and my man's arm took me again, tight—tight, Katje.

"'Well,' said my father, 'you had better be off, the two of you. Do not come here again.'

"'We can do that much to please you,' answered Kornel, with his head very high. 'Come, Christina!'

"And I followed him from my father's house. I had not even a hat for my head.

"We were married forthwith, of course—no later than the next day—and the day after that I rode with my man to the plot beside the dorp spruit to see our home that had to be. That was a great day for me; and to be going in gentle companionship with Kornel across the staring veld and along the empty road was a most wonderful thing, and its flavour is still a relish to my memory. I knew that he feared what we were to see —the littleness and mean poverty of it, after the spaciousness of the farm; but most of all it galled him that I should see it on this our first triumphant day. He was very gentle and most loving, but shadows grew on his face, and there was a track of worry between his brows that spurred me. I knew what I had to do, now that our fortunes were knitted, and I did it.

"The plot was a slope from the edge of the dorp to the little spruit, not fenced nor sundered in any way from the squalid brick which houses the lower end of Dopfontein. Full in face of it was the location of the Kafirs; around it and close at hand were the gross and dirty huts of the off-colours (half-castes). The house, which was in the middle of the plot, was a bulging hovel of green brick, no more stately or respectable than any of the huts round about. As our horses picked their way through the muck underfoot, and we rode down to it, the off-colours swarmed out of their burrows and grinned and pointed their fingers at us.

"Kornel helped me from my saddle, and we went together to see the inside of the house. It was very foul and broken, with the plain traces of Kafirs in each of its two rooms, and a horrid litter everywhere. As I looked round I saw Kornel straighten himself quickly, and my eyes went to his.

"'This is our home,' he said bluntly, with a twitching of the cheek.

"I nodded.

"'Perhaps,' he said in the same hard voice, as if he were awaiting an onslaught of reproach—'perhaps I was wrong to bring you to this, but it is too late to tell me so now. It is not much——'

"I broke in and laughed. 'You will not know it when I have set it to rights,' I answered. 'It shall be a home indeed by the time I am through with it.'

"His cheek twitched yet, as though some string under the flesh were quivering with the strain.

"'It's you and me against all the evil luck in the world,' he cried, but his face was softening.

"I cowered within the arm he held out to me, and told him I was all impatience to begin the fight. And he cried on my shoulder, and I held him to me and soothed him from a spring of motherhood that broke loose in my heart.

"Within a week we were living in the place, and, Katje! I hope you will feel yet for some roof what I felt for that, with all its poorness. It was the first home of my wifehood: I loved it. I worked over it as later I worked over the children God bestowed on me, purging it, remaking it, spending myself on it, and gilding it with the joy of the work. From the beams of the roof to the step of the door I cleansed it with my hands, marking it by its spotlessness for the habitation of white folk among the yellow people all round. Kornel did little to aid me in that—for the most part he was seeking work in the town; and even when he was at home I drove him sharply from the labour that was mine, and mine alone. The yellow people were very curious about it all, and would stand and watch me through the door till Kornel sjamboked them away; and even then some of their fat talkative women would come round with offers of help and friendship. But though we were fallen to poverty, we had not come so low as that; and few came to me a second time, and none a third.

"Still, though Kornel humbled himself and asked very little money, there was no work to be had in the dorp. No storekeeper had a use for him, and the transport agents had too many riders already. Day after day went by, and each day he came back more grim, with a duller light in those kind eyes of his and a slower twinkle.

"'You must trust in yourself,' I told him, as he sat by the table and would have it that he was not hungry.

"'I trust in you,' he answered, with a pitiable attempt at his old sparkle. 'You have proved yourself; I have not—yet, and I could do the work of three Kafirs, too.'

"The next day he came home at noon, with a swing in his gait and his fingers working.

"'I've got work,' he said, 'at last.'

"I stopped sewing and looked at him. 'Is it a white man's work?' I asked him.

"'It is work,' he retorted.

"'Very well,' I said; 'but, remember, we sink or soar together, and in neither case will I blame you. If you get white man's work, you shall have a white man's wife; but if you are going to do the work of Kafirs——'

"'Yes,' he said; 'and what then?'

"'In that case,' I answered, 'I shall do washing to eke it out and be a level mate for you.'

"'By God, you won't!' he cried, and his hand came down hard on the table. There was no mistaking his face; the command and the earnestness of it lighted up his eyes. I stared at him in a good deal of surprise, for though I had known it was there, this was the first I had seen of the steel strain in my man.

"'Call it Kafir work, or what you please,' he went

63   F

on, with a briskness of speech that made answer impossible. 'You will keep this house and concern yourself with that only. The gaining of money is my affair. Leave it to me therefore.'

"I cast down my eyes, knowing I must obey, but a little while after I asked him again what the work was to be.

"'Making bricks,' he answered. 'Here we have the spruit at our door and mud for the picking up. It needs only a box-mould or two, and it will be funny if I can't turn out as many good bricks in a day as three lazy Kafirs. Old Pagan, the contractor, has said he will buy them, so now it only remains to get to work.'

"As he said this, I noticed the uneasiness that kept him from meeting my eye, for in truth it was a sorry employ to put his strength to—a dirty toil, all the dirtier for the fact that only Kafirs handled it in Dopfontein, and the pay was poor. From our door one could always see the brick-making going on along the spruit, with the mud-streaked niggers standing knee-deep in the water, packing the wet dirt into the boxes, and spilling them out to be baked in the sun or fired, as the case might be. There was too much grime and discomfort to it to be a respectable trade.

"But Kornel went to work at once, carrying down box-moulds from the contractor's yard, and stacking them in the stiff grey mud at the edge of the spruit. I went with him to see him start. He waded down over his boots, into the slow water, and plunged his arms elbow-deep into the mud.

"'Here's to an honest living,' he said, and lifted a great lump of slime into the first box and kneaded it close. Then, as he set it aside and reached for the next, he looked up to me with a smile that was all awry. My heart bled for him.

"'But there's no time to be polite,' he said, as the mud squelched into the next box. 'Here's the time to prove how a white man can work when he goes about it.

64

So run back to the house, my kleintje, and leave me to make my fortune.'

"And forthwith he braced himself and went at that sorry work with all his fine strength. I had not the heart to stay by him: I knew that my eyes upon him were like offering him an insult, and yet I never looked at him save in love. But once or twice I glanced from the doorway and saw him bowed still over that ruthless task, slaving doggedly, as good men do with good work.

"When the evening meal was due he came in, drenched from head to foot, and patched and lathered with the pale sticky mud; but though he was so tired that he drooped like a sick man where he stood, his face was bright again and his eyes were once more a-twinkle with hope and confidence.

"As he changed his clothes and washed himself, he talked cheerily to me through the wall, with a spirit like a boy's.

"'I've begun, at any rate,' he called out, 'and that's a great thing. If I go as far forward as I've gone back, I shall be satisfied. Where did you say the comb was?'

"And all through supper he chatted in the same vein, rejoicing in the muscles that ached with work and in his capacity to do more and bear more than the Kafirs who were his rivals. For me, I was pleased enough and thankful to hear the heart of him thus vocal, and to mark the man I knew of old and chose to be my mate come to light in this labourer, new from his toil.

"We did not sit late that night, for, with all his elation and reawakened spirits, Kornel was weary to the honest bone of him, and swayed with sleep as he stood on his feet. He rolled into my clean, cool sheets with a grunt of utter satisfaction. 'This is comfort indeed,' he said drowsily, as I leaned over him, and he was asleep before I had answered.

"At daylight he rose and went forth to the spruit again, and there all day he laboured earnestly. Each time that I looked towards him I saw his back bent and his arms plunging in the mud, while the rows of wet bricks grew longer and multiplied. I heard him whistling at it—some English melody he had gathered long before at a wapenschauw—with a light heart, the while he was up to his knees in the dirty water, with the mud plastered all over him.

"By and by I went down to the bank and asked him how he did. He straightened himself, grimacing humorously at the stiffness of his back, and answered me cheerily.

"'To-morrow old Pagan will come down and pay for what I have done,' he said. 'I think he will be surprised at the amount. His Kafirs have no such appetite for it as I.' And he laughed.

"It was a dreadful business he had taken in hand, and work hard beyond believing. The boxes stood in a pile above the stream, and each had to be reached down as one was filled, and as soon as two were full, Kornel must climb the bank to set them aside. When all were full, they had to be turned out on the level ground, and all this, as you can see, meant that he must scramble up and down in the heavy mud, taxing every spring in his poor body. Yet he toiled ceaselessly, attacking the job with a kind of light-hearted desperation that made nothing of its hardships, bringing to it a tough and unconquerable joy in the mere effort, which drove him ever like a spur.

"As I watched him delving, I thought that here a woman could render some measure of help, and as he turned from talking to me I began to empty out the boxes that were ready and to stack them again on the pile. I had not yet turned out ten bricks when he saw me, and paused in his melancholy work.

"'Stop that!' he cried, and scrambled out of the spruit to where I stood. 'I suppose,' he went on, 'you would like your father to know that I had suffered you to work for me like a Kafir.'

"'Kornel!' I cried in horror.

66

"But he was white on the cheekbones and breathing hard, and I could not soften him.

"'Rich man's daughter or poor man's wife,' he said, 'you are white, and must keep your station. It is my business to sell myself, not yours. Get you back to the house I have given you, and stay there.'

"And with that he picked up the soft bricks I had turned for him, and threw them one by one into the spruit.

"'Poverty and meanness and all,' he added, 'it shall not be said at your father's house that you worked for me. Nor that you lacked aught it became you to have, neither,' he added, with a quick heat of temper. 'Get to your house.'

"I slunk off, crying like a child, while he went back to the mud—and the labour.

"Next day came Pagan to pay for the work that was done. He drove up in his smart cart, and tiptoed his way daintily to the edge of the spruit where the bricks lay. He was an old man, very cleanly dressed; with hard white hair on his head and face, and a quick manner of looking from side to side, like a little bird. In all his aspect there was nothing but spoke of easy wealth and the serenity of a well-ordered life; there was even that unkindly sharpness of tone and manner that is a dead weight on the well-to-do. My husband was at work when he drove up, but he straightened his back, squared his broad shoulders, and came up from the mud, walking at the full of his height and smiling down at the rich man with half-closed eyes.

"'Daag, Heer Pagan,' he said to him, in the tone of one who needs and desires nothing, and held out his hand—mud from the elbow—with something lordly in the gesture. The rich man cocked his head quickly, in the way he had, and hung in the breeching for a moment, ere he rendered his hand to Kornel, with a reddening of the cheek above his white whisker that betrayed him, I thought, for a paltry soul.

67

"'I've come to see your bricks,' he said curtly, 'and to pay for 'em, if they're all right.'

"'Ah, the bricks,' said Kornel airily. 'Yes, to be sure. There they are. Go and count them, if you like, and then you can come to me at my house where the Vrouw du Plessis (which was me) will give us some coffee.'

"I was watching, you may be sure, and again I saw the wintry red swell above the white whisker, and I clenched my hands in wrath and contempt at the creature's littleness. I was sure he would have liked to sweep my man's courtesy aside, and certainly the politeness had a prick in it. He was rich, and old, and fat, with a consequence in his mien and an air that hinted he was used to deference, and Kornel was but a muddy brick-moulder. Yet there stood my man, so easy in his quiet speech, so sure of himself, so dangerous a target for contempt, that the rich man only stammered. Kornel nodded as though he understood the invitation to be accepted, and walked up to the house, leaving old Pagan to count the bricks and follow.

"I kissed him as he came in. 'You've trampled his dirty soul under your heel,' I said, 'and I love you for it. I love to see you upright and a man of purpose: whatever comes of it, I shall honour you always.'

"He kissed me and laughed. 'Nothing will happen, if we are lucky,' he said. 'There is more in John Pagan than the big stomach and the money. But we mustn't crawl to him; I'll wager he never crawled himself when he was poor.'

"I set the coffee ready, spreading the table with a fine cloth I had brought from Kornel's farm, one of the few things we had taken with us, and presently in came old Pagan. Directly I saw him I felt a doubt of him: there was a kind of surreptitious viciousness showing in his sour smile that warned me. He was like a man who is brewing an unpleasant joke.

68

"'Ah, Mrs. du Plessis,' he said, 'your man will have been working very hard.'

"'You know what brick-moulding is, then?' I said. "He grinned. 'A little,' he said; 'yes, a little. There's few jobs I haven't put a hand to in my time. Work's a fine thing, when a man knows how to work.'

"'You are very right,' agreed Kornel.

"'This is good coffee,' said John Pagan, as he stirred his cup. 'In fact, it's better than the bricks.'

"'A better hand was at work on it,' said Kornel.

"'So I should judge,' answered Pagan sleekly. 'I should like another cup of this coffee, if I may trouble you, Mrs. du Plessis.'

"He laid his cup on the table and bit his nails while I filled it, glancing round at my poor room the while and smiling to himself.

"'Yes,' he said, 'I like the coffee, but I don't like the bricks. They're no good at all.'

"We both stared at him, silent and aghast, and the white-haired old man chuckled in our stricken faces.

"'What is wrong with them?' demanded Kornel at last. His face was white, but he spoke quite naturally.

"'Aha!' old Pagan laughed. 'Ye see, there's no trade that ye can take up without a bit o' learning, not even makin' mud-bricks. The very same thing happened to me. Lord, it's past forty years ago! I turned out six hundred dozen, and had 'em thrown on my hands. It nearly broke my heart.'

"'I can understand that,' said Kornel. 'But what is wrong with my bricks?'

"Old Pagan set his cup back on the table and sat up in his chair. As he began to speak he hitched back the sleeves of his coat and moved his neck in his white collar.

"'See here!' he said. 'It's a little thing, like turning up the toe of a horseshoe, but just as essential. When ye set your full moulds out to dry, did ye set 'em on edge, to drain away the water? Ye did not? Well, that's what's wrong. They're just mud-pies—lumps o' damp dirt, that'll crumble as soon as they're dry. There's ninety dozen of 'em, by my count, and there'll not be three dozen that ye could use in any way consistent wi' conscience. Do ye take my meanin'?'

"Kornel nodded very thoughtfully.

"'Well, you'll just need to get to work again,' said the old man. 'Maybe I'm not exactly keen on invitations and greetings and the like, but you'll not be able to teach me anything on bricks. So if you're thinking anything about the splendour o' your work, wait till ye're master of it before you waste more thought. I'm your better as a craftsman,' he said, with a glance towards me.

"I was red all over, what with shame and sorrow, but I marked that the paltriness seemed to have gone from John Pagan as soon as he began to talk of work. He turned then to Kornel with a briskness that was not unkindly.

"'I was relying on you for bricks,' he said, 'for you can work, and that's a fact. Perhaps you'll let me have a hundred dozen by Thursday, eh? I'm waitin' on them. And if you'll make sure of it, I'll do wi' ye what's my common custom, and that's pay half the price in advance. How'll that suit?'

"Kornel rose from his chair and stammered thanks, and John Pagan paid the money onto the table.

"'I'll be down on Thursday to see the bricks,' he said, 'and don't forget the dodge I told ye. And maybe Mrs. du Plessis'll be willing to give me coffee again when I come. So good day to ye, and mind—drain 'em!'

"When he was gone Kornel and I looked at each other and laughed emptily. Then he went out to the mud again to make ready for Thursday.

"So it was we lived for a time that was shorter than it seemed, building on the mud of our shaky fortunes a pride that our poverty could not overturn. Kornel had a saying that seemed irreligious but very true. 'There are ministers and farmers and lawyers who are rich,'

70

he would observe, 'but there's no money in work.' I have since been won to believe that there is a flaw in the argument, but for us it was true, and bitterly true. We were never on the right side of ten shillings; we were never out of sight of the thin brink of want. That we were preserved and kept clear of disaster was due only to the toil of Kornel and my own anxious care for the spending of the money. I found out that a wife who is strong has a great trade to drive in upholding her house, and I, at any rate, was proficient in maintaining cleanliness, in buying and making food, and preserving in my home the atmosphere of happiness and welcome that anchors a man to his own place. Take it all in all, we were happy, and yet I would not pretend that there were not grim hours when we wondered if the mere living were worth all that it cost. Kornel, hard as iron always, grew lean and stooped, and there appeared in his face a kind of wild care that frightened me. From the chill upcoming of the dawn to the rising of the wind at evening he taxed himself remorselessly at the sorry work in the mud, while I scrubbed and scraped and plotted and prayed to make the meagre pay cover wants that were pared meagre enough. Yes, there were certainly times when we thought the cost too great, but God be praised! we never thought it at the same moment, and the stronger always upheld the weaker.

"And there was never any shame in the matter. Even as we feared nothing, we were never ashamed. Never!

"One morning, about an hour before high sun, when the dust lay thick on the road that passed our land, and the neighbourhood around was feverish with the fuss of the Kafirs and yellow folk, I stood for a moment at my door, looking down to where Kornel was fervently at work in the spruit. There was always traffic on the road at that hour, and something drew me to look towards it. At once I saw my father. He was riding

71

in, dressed in his best clothes, very solemn and respectable, with his beard flowing over his chest. At the same moment he saw me, and seemed to start in his saddle and glance quickly at all about—at my poor little house, the litter that lay around, the squalor of the town-end we lived in, and the laborious bent back of my man as he squattered about in the mud. He checked his horse an instant, as though by an impulse—for my father, though I honoured him, was a weak man, in whom no purpose was steadfast. I saw the wavering in his face and the uncertainty of his big pale eyes; and then, half-nodding to me as though in an embarrassment, he pushed on and entered the town. I went down and told Kornel.

"'H'm!' He stood as though in thought, looking up to me from the water. 'Your father, eh? Would you like him to come and see you?'

"I nodded.

"He laughed and climbed up the bank to me. 'So would I!' he said. 'I have a stiffness in my back that makes me inclined for anything rather than this work —even your father.'

"We walked up to the house together, and Kornel's brow was creased with thought, while his lips smiled.

"'You see,' he said, 'we want nothing from him— nothing at all, so we can't afford to be humble. Have we any money at all?'

"'We have three shillings,' I answered, 'and I owe one shilling for food.'

"'That's not enough,' he said, shaking his head. 'You say he saw me working? We must have thirty shillings at least; we must treat him well; I can't let him off, now that he has seen so much. We'll stuff him till he bulges like a rotten cask, and wishes he could make bricks as I can. I wonder if Pagan would pay me in advance for a thousand dozen. I'll go and ask him.'

"He started for the door at once, but turned and came back to me.

72

"'He said once he had nothing to give me,' he whispered to me. 'Do you grudge me this, kleintje?'

"'Not I,' I answered. 'I only wish we could do more.'

"He kissed me, and was off in a moment. Pagan made no difficulty about the money. He looked at Kornel shrewdly when my man made the request, and paid at once.

"'It suits me ye should be a wee thing in my debt,' he said. 'But you're so damned proud, there's times I'm scared of ye. Sign yer name here.'

"'Now,' said Kornel, when he had put the money in my hand, 'get what you need for a dinner that will tickle the ou pa's stomach, and a bottle of whisky. There never was a deacon that did not suffer from some complaint that whisky would ease; and I'll get into what clean clothes I have and go to look for him.'

"So I bought the dinner. I was willing enough to suffer the emptiness to come, if only I could wipe from my father's memory his impression of my man's poverty; but all the same, in case he should refuse to visit us, I bought things that would last long enough to serve ourselves until the thirty shillings should have been earned. They made a good show: for I have never been a fool in the matter of food, and I knew my father's tastes. I promised myself that his dinner should be his chief memory of that day, at all events. He was, I fear, the kind of man who remembers his good dinners better than anything else.

"It was a long time before they came, and I had given up all hope of the visit when I heard their voices. Or rather, it was Kornel's voice that I heard, in a tone of careless civility, like one who performs a casual duty of politeness. He was talking nonsense in a slow drawl, and as they picked their way from the road to the house my father looked up to him in a kind of wonder.

"'The evenings are pleasant here,' Kornel was saying, 'we have a little time to ourselves then, for people have learned at last not to trouble us much. One sees the sun go down yonder across the hills, and it is very pretty. Now, on the farm, nobody ever knew how handsome the sunset is. We were like Kafirs on the farm; but life in the town is quite different.'

"He chattered on in the same strain, and my father was plainly dazed by it; so that his judgment was all fogged, and he took the words at their face value. I noticed that my father seemed a little abashed and doubtful: it was easy to see that this was the opposite of what he had expected.

"He greeted me with a touch of hesitation in his manner; but I kissed him on the forehead and tried to appear a fortunate daughter—smiling assuredly, you know, glad to exercise hospitality and to receive my father in my own house. It was not all seeming, either; for I had no shame in my condition and my husband's fortune—only a resentment for those who affected to expect it.

"'You are looking well,' said my father, staring at me. 'How do you like the life you are living?'

"Kornel smiled boldly across to me, and I laughed.

"'I was never so happy in my life,' I answered—and that, at any rate, was true.

"My father grunted, and sat listening to the gentle flow of talk with which Kornel gagged him the while I busied myself with the last turn of the cooking and set the table to rights. But he glanced at me from time to time with something of surprise and disapproval: perhaps a white woman with no Kafir servant had never met his eyes before. Kornel did not miss the expression of his face.

"'We will show you something new in the dinner line,' he remarked knowingly. 'There are things you can't teach to a Kafir, you know.'

"'What things?' demanded my father.

"'Ah, you shall see in a moment,' answered Kornel, nodding mysteriously. 'Christina will show you. Have you ever heard of a ragout?'

74

"My father shook his head. Neither had I; but I held my tongue.

"'Well,' said Kornel, 'a ragout is a fowl cooked as Christina has cooked it. It is a very favourite dish among the rich men in Johannesburg. If you will draw up your chair to the table you shall see.'

"It is true that I had a good hand with a fowl, stewed in a fashion of my own, which was mainly the outcome of ignorance and emergency; but it was very fortunate that on that day of all days the contrivance should have turned out so well. It was tender, and the flesh was seasoned to just the right flavour by the stuff I stewed with it—certain herbs, Katje, and a hint of a whiff of garlic. Garlic is a thing you must not play with: like sin, you can never undo it, whatever forgiveness you win. But a leaf or two bruised between two clean pebbles, and the pebbles coiled with the stew, spices the whole thing as a touch of devil spices a man.

"You may be sure I was anxious about it, and watched Kornel and my pa as they started to eat. Kornel swallowed his first mouthful with an appearance of keen judgment; then he winked swiftly to me, and nodded slightly. It was his praise of the dish. Oh, if you had known my man, you would not need telling that that was enough for me. My father commenced to eat as though curious of the food before him. He gave no sign of liking or otherwise; but presently he squared his shoulders, drew his chair closer to the table, and gave his mind to the matter.

"'That's right, walk into it,' said Kornel.

"'It is very good indeed,' said my father, eating thoughtfully, and presently I helped him to some more. Kornel gave him soda-water with whisky in it, and thereafter there were other things to eat—nearly thirty shillings' worth. After that they sat and smoked, and drank the strong coffee I made for them, and passed the whisky bottle to and fro between them. All the while Kornel babbled amiably of foolish things—sunsets, and

Shakespeare and the ways of women—till I caught myself wondering whether indeed he relished the change from the wide clean veld of the farm to this squalid habitation of toil.

"'I suppose,' said my father at last, when Kornel had finished talking about sunsets—'I suppose a ragoo, as you call it, is very expensive to make?'

"'I really couldn't say,' answered Kornel, 'but I should think not.'

"'H'm; and you think a Kafir could not be taught to make them?'

"Kornel laughed. 'I should be sorry to try,' he said.

"My father pondered on that for a while, smoking strongly and glancing from time to time at me.

"'I'm growing an old man,' he said at last, 'and old men are lonely at the best.'

"'Some seem to wish it,' said Kornel.

"'I say they are lonely,' repeated my father sharply. 'I have no wife, and I cannot be bothered with getting another at my time of life.' He shook his grey head sadly. 'Not that I should have to look far for one,' he added, however.

"Kornel laughed, and my father looked at him angrily.

"'If it had not been for you,' he said, 'I should still have had my daughter Christina to live with me. I am tired of being alone, and I cannot nurse the wrong done me by my own flesh and blood. You and Christina had better come out to the farm and live with me.'

"'And leave my business?' asked Kornel.

"'Oh, there is mud and water on the farm, if your business pleases you,' retorted my father. 'But out there we do not take the bread out of the mouths of Kafirs.'

"'I see,' answered Kornel briefly; and I, who watched him, knew from his voice that there was to be no truce after that—that we should still earn our livelihood by the mud bricks.

"'You will come?' asked my father.

76

"'Good Lord, no!' replied Kornel. 'You would weary me to death in a week. I don't mind being civil when we meet, but live with you! It would be to make oneself a vegetable.'

"My father heard him out with a grave face, and then rose to his feet. There was a stateliness in his manner that grieved me, for when a man meets a rebuff with silence and dignity he is ageing.

"'You are right perhaps,' he said. 'I don't know, but you may be. Anyhow, I have enjoyed an excellent meal, and I thank you. Good-bye, Christina!'

"When he was gone, Kornel turned to me.

"'It is evident you cannot have both a husband and a father,' he said; 'but I am sorry for the rudeness, kleintje. He is a greater man than I.'

"'I think you might have made it otherwise,' I answered, for my heart ached for my father.

"He shrugged his shoulders. 'You must manage to forgive me,' he said. 'I have a thousand dozen bricks to make, and that will be punishment enough.'

"'But you will not start again to-night!' I cried, for it was already the thin end of evening, and he was taking off his clean clothes.

"'A thousand dozen is a big handful,' he answered, smiling. 'There's nothing like getting a grip on the work ahead.'

"So in a few minutes he was down in the water again, and the mud flew as he worked at the heart-breaking task he had taken upon him. After all, the 'ragout' was expensive to make. It came dearer than we expected.

"Late into the night he held on, though thrice I went out to the bank of the stream to beg him to quit it and come to bed. There was a great pale moon that night, which threw up the colours of things strongly, and I have yet in my mind—and my heart—that picture—the stained water, and the bank of grey mud over it, and between the two my Kornel bent over the endless

77

boxes, vehemently working with no consideration for the limits of his strength. His arms gleamed with the wet, and were ceaseless; he might have been a dumb machine, without capacity for weariness. If he had toiled before, now he toiled doubly: there was a trouble in his mind to be sweated out and a debt of money to be repaid. And also, like a peril always near at hand, there was the thin margin that stood between us and starvation.

"When he came to bed at length, he lay down without the greeting he was wont to give me—lapsed into his place beside me with the limpness of a man spent to the utmost ounce. He slept without turning on his side, his worn hands, half-closed, lying loosely on the quilt. Yet within an hour after daylight he rose with narrow, sleep-burdened eyes, fumbled into his clothes, and staggered out to the spruit again, to resume his merciless work with the very fever of energy. The Kafirs that worked leisurely on the next plot stopped to look at him and to wonder at the speed with which the rows of drying bricks lengthened and multiplied. I saw them pointing as I stood at the door, heavy-hearted and anxious, and envied the ease of their manner of life, and the simplicity that could be content with such work at such a wage. Yes, I have envied Kafirs, Katje: there are times for all women when we envy the dead.

"But it was the day after that that the trouble came upon us, great and violent and unawaited. Kornel had been up at daybreak again, working as strongly as ever, though his mouth was loose with the strain and his face very yellow and white. The drying and the dry bricks were lying on the ground in long rows, and some which were hard were already stacked to make room for others. It was a tremendous output for one man in the time it had taken; and when the Kafirs turned out, gabbling and laughing as usual, they stopped to look in surprise at our plot and the great quantity of bricks. They gathered in a group, and talked among

78

themselves and pointed, and presently I was aware
there was something toward. One of them in particular
—a great brown brute, with bulky shoulders and huge
arms—seemed to be concerned in the affair: he stared
continually towards Kornel, and talked loudly, his
voice running up into the squeak of a Kafir when he is
excited, or angry, or afraid; and presently he stepped
over our border line and walked down to the bricks.
He was jabbering to himself all the time as he stooped
and picked up bricks and examined them closely, and
glanced down to the spruit where Kornel was still
working.

"I watched him, but I said nothing, hoping he would
go away before Kornel saw him; but he kept on, and
presently my man looked up.

"He saw the Kafir at once, and climbed up the bank
pretty quickly. There was something like a smile on
his face, a look as though he had found the relief he
needed. He walked swiftly over to the Kafir.

"'What are you doing here?' he demanded, keeping his eyes unwinkingly on the staring eyes of the
Kafir.

"The latter held a dried brick in his great paw, and
now he thrust it forward and broke into a torrent of
speech. He accused Kornel of having trespassed in the
night and stolen the bricks of the Kafirs. No man, he
said, could have made so many by himself; and then
he began to call names. I shuddered and put my hands
before my face, and took them down again in time to
see Kornel's fist fly up and out, and the great Kafir reel
back from a vicious blow in the face.

"But he gave way for a moment only. Next instant
he recovered and his huge arm rose, and I screamed
and ran forward as the brick, dry and hard as a stone,
struck Kornel on the head, and tumbled him, loosely,
like a dead man, among the rows of bricks about him.
I did not see the Kafir run away—I saw only the thin
white face of my man turned up to the sun, and the

blood that ran from his brown hair. I lifted his head and called to him; but his head lolled on his shoulders, and I let him lie while I ran out crying to find help.

"It was some of the yellow folk who carried him in for me, and brought the German doctor. Kornel was on the bed when he came, and he caused the cut to be bandaged, and then spoke abstrusely of the effect of the blow, so that I understood nothing at all. I learned, however, how I was to tend him, how feed him, and how he would lie unconscious for long intervals when there would be nothing at all to do for him. But he told me I had nothing to fear in the end. Indeed, he had a kind of cheeriness which seems to belong to doctors, which did much to comfort me and steady me for what was to come. Kornel would not die, he said; and it was that assurance I chiefly needed.

"The day went slowly for me, I can tell you. There was yet food enough in the house to last us a little while, and I made a mess for Kornel, and ate what I wanted myself. He recovered his sense of things once or twice, but when night came he dropped off again into a stupor from which he was not to be roused, and it was then I left him. I felt as though I were a traitor to him in his weakness; but my mind had buzzed hopelessly all day about the problem of our mere living, and I saw nothing else for it, so down I went to the spruit to earn what I might for my sick husband.

"The moon gave me light, and I had watched Kornel often enough to know how to go about the work. But the water, as it flowed about my legs, bit me with a chill that made me gasp, and the effort of the work, the constant bending and lifting, tried every muscle in my body. I had seen the cruelty of the work in its traces on Kornel, and knew how little it gave and how much it took; but with this first trial of it came the realization, never lost since, of how gallant a man I had chosen to stand between me and the world, and how much I owed him. I had not time to think a great deal, for the torture of brick-making is partly in the fact that while it wrenches the body, it joins the mind to its infinite triviality. If you think, you do not pack the mud as it must be packed, and the sun crumbles your bricks to dust. It is no task for a real man at all; even for a woman, it debases, it unmakes, it breaks.

"I worked hard at it, husbanding my strength, and within an hour I was weak and foolish with the effort. Twice I had left it to go in and see if all was well with Kornel, and this rested me; but I was now resolved that I must rest no more, if ever our debt was to be paid and bread earned for the grim days to come. So I stayed in the bitter water and worked on, till even the sense of pain was dulled and it seemed that I was past the capacity of feeling.

"I was toiling thus (never mind my old troubles, Katje dear; this is years ago) when a sound came to my ears that caused me to look up. It had been going on for some time, persisting till it gained my notice, and suddenly I became aware that there were men on our ground among the bricks. I climbed half-way up the bank to look at them, where they could not see me; and I saw several dark figures bent to some business or moving here and there. I caught the sound of hushed voices, too, though no words, and then the hot wrath set my blood racing as I realized what was going on. The Kafirs, who knew my man was wounded and helpless—the very beast who had felled him—were stealing the bricks he had laboured so stoutly to make. My head swam with a delirium of vivid anger at the meanness of the crime, and without calculation, with no thought of fear, I scrambled up and ran at them, shouting.

"I suppose they were surprised at my coming out of the spruit, and some of them ran as soon as they heard me. Others stood and waited ominously—you know what a Kafir is with a woman—and doubtless I should have met my last earthly troubles then and there, but

81

that from the road beyond us there were other shouts, and men came running.

"I saw the forms of the rescuers as they raced up, and marked one tall young man who ran past me with his arm lifted before him. There was a flash and a bang, and I sat down heavily as the white men shot at the Kafirs, who were now all running to cover. It took but an instant, and I remember it as one remembers a thing seen at night by a lightning flash, sharp, and feverish.

"'Ye've no need to be feard,' someone said to me, 'they're only my clerks, but they're a handy lot.'

"A short stout man was standing over me, and as I looked up I saw it was old Pagan. Away in the darkness there were yet cries and the sound of blows, where the white men pursued the Kafirs.

"'Ye see,' continued the old man, 'I heard o' what had happened, an' I counted on this. I'm a man o' experience, Mrs. du Plessis, an' the very same thing happened to me once. So I got a few o' my lads along, and we've been waitin' for what ye might call the eventuality. I'm no' exactly a negrophilist, ye ken. An' after seein' you squatterin' about in the mud yonder, while yer husband was sick a-bed, there was no holdin' the lads. No' that I endeavoured to restrain them, in any precise sense.'

"Away in the darkness a Kafir shrieked agonizedly. "'There ye are,' said the old man. 'Yon's chivalry. If ye had been a man, they'd never ha' put their hearts into it like that.'

He helped me to my feet and gave me an arm towards the house.

"'There's just one thing,' he said, 'and it's this. I'm no' quite the slave-driver ye might take me for—workin' in the night to drag a pittance out o' me! For instance, I've a job in the store that yer man can have, if it'll suit him, and if you're willing yerself. It's no' a big thing, but it's white. And for the present while,

I dare say I can advance ye enough to be going on with. And me and the lads 'll say no word about seein' you at yer work.'

"What is the use of carrying this tale on? It was there we ceased to have the troubles that go to making tales, and entered upon the ordered life of good industry and clean living. But, Katje, of all that came afterwards, money and success, and even children, there was nothing to knit us as did the sorry months by the spruit, when my Kornel proved himself the man I knew him to be. Be happy, Katje; be happy at any rate."

I think she has been happy.

THE OPEN BOAT
by Stephen Crane

STEPHEN CRANE, author of *The Red Badge of Courage*—one of the greatest novels of military experience ever written—was a mere youth and, like F. Britten Austin, entirely innocent of active warfare when he wrote that marvellous account of a volunteer's shattering ordeal under gun-fire. Later, he acted as war correspondent in the Balkans and in Cuba. To have written *The Red Badge of Courage* at twenty-five was in itself a pledge of immortality, but Crane unfortunately did not live to achieve the further brilliant promise of his youth. He was born in 1871 and died in 1900. His short stories are remarkable for their depth of feeling and lucidity of expression. *The Open Boat* is a masterpiece of graphic, restrained writing, and its note of courage is all the more evident because it is never over-stressed.

THE OPEN BOAT

BY

STEPHEN CRANE

NONE of them knew the colour of the sky. Their eyes glanced level, and were fastened upon the waves that swept towards them. These waves were of the hue of slate, save for the tops, which were of foaming white, and all of the men knew the colours of the sea. The horizon narrowed and widened, and dipped and rose, and at all times its edge was jagged with waves that seemed thrust up in points like rocks. Many a man ought to have a bath-tub larger than the boat which here rode upon the sea. These waves were most wrongfully and barbarously abrupt and tall, and each froth-top was a problem in small-boat navigation.

The cook squatted in the bottom and looked with both eyes at the six inches of gunwale which separated him from the ocean. His sleeves were rolled over his fat forearms, and the two flaps of his unbuttoned vest dangled as he bent to bail out the boat. Often he said: "Gawd! That was a narrow clip." As he remarked it he invariably gazed eastward over the broken sea.

The oiler, steering with one of the two oars in the boat, sometimes raised himself suddenly to keep clear of water that swirled in over the stern. It was a thin little oar, and it seemed often ready to snap.

The correspondent, pulling at the other oar, watched the waves and wondered why he was there.

The injured captain, lying in the bow, was at this time buried in that profound dejection and indifference which comes, temporarily at least, to even the bravest and most enduring when, willy nilly, the firm fails, the army loses, the ship goes down. The mind of the master of a vessel is rooted deep in the timbers of her, though he commanded for a day or a decade, and this captain had on him the stern impression of a scene in the grey of dawn of seven turned faces, and later a stump of a topmast with a white ball on it, that slashed to and fro at the waves, went low and lower, and down. Thereafter there was something strange in his voice. Although steady, it was deep with mourning, and of a quality beyond oration or tears.

"Keep 'er a little more south, Billie," said he.

"'A little more south,' sir," said the oiler in the stern.

A seat in this boat was not unlike a seat upon a bucking broncho, and by the same token a broncho is not much smaller. The craft pranced and reared, and plunged like an animal. As each wave came, and she rose for it, she seemed like a horse making at a fence outrageously high. The manner of her scramble over these walls of water is a mystic thing, and, moreover, at the top of them were ordinarily these problems in white water, the foam racing down from the summit of each wave, requiring a new leap, and a leap from the air. Then, after scornfully bumping a crest, she would slide and race and splash down a long incline, and arrive bobbing in front of the next menace.

A singular disadvantage of the sea lies in the fact that after successfully surmounting one wave you discover that there is another behind it just as important and just as nervously anxious to do something effective in the way of swamping boats. In a ten-foot dinghy one can get an idea of the resources of the sea in the line of waves that is not probable to the average experience which is never at sea in a dinghy. As each slaty wall of water approached, it shut all else from the view of the men in the boat, and it was not difficult to imagine that this particular wave was the final outburst of the ocean, the last effort of the grim water. There was a terrible grace in the move of the waves, and they came in silence, save for the snarling of the crests.

In the wan light, the faces of the men must have been grey. Their eyes must have glinted in strange ways as they gazed steadily astern. Viewed from a balcony, the whole thing would doubtless have been weirdly picturesque. But the men in the boat had no time to see it, and if they had had leisure there were other things to occupy their minds. The sun swung steadily up the sky, and they knew it was broad day because the colour of the sea changed from slate to emerald-green, streaked with amber lights, and the foam was like tumbling snow. The process of the breaking day was unknown to them. They were aware only of this effect upon the colour of the waves that rolled towards them.

In disjointed sentences the cook and the correspondent argued as to the difference between a life-saving station and a house of refuge. The cook had said: "There's a house of refuge just north of the Mosquito Inlet Light, and as soon as they see us they'll come off in their boat and pick us up."

"As soon as who see us?" said the correspondent.

"The crew," said the cook.

"Houses of refuge don't have crews," said the correspondent. "As I understand them, they are only places where clothes and grub are stored for the benefit of shipwrecked people. They don't carry crews."

"Oh, yes, they do," said the cook.

"No, they don't," said the correspondent.

"Well, we're not there yet, anyhow," said the oiler, in the stern.

"Well," said the cook, "perhaps it's not a house of refuge that I'm thinking of as being near Mosquito Light. Perhaps it's a life-saving station."

"We're not there yet," said the oiler, in the stern.

As the boat bounced from the top of each wave, the wind tore through the hair of the hatless men, and as the craft plopped her stern down again the spray splashed past them. The crest of each of these waves was a hill, from the top of which the men surveyed, for a moment, a broad, tumultuous expanse, shining and wind-riven. It was probably splendid. It was probably glorious, this play of the free sea, wild with lights of emerald and white and amber.

"Bully good thing it's an on-shore wind," said the cook. "If not, where would we be? Wouldn't have a show."

"That's right," said the correspondent.

The busy oiler nodded his assent.

Then the captain, in the bow, chuckled in a way that expressed humour, contempt, tragedy, all in one. "Do you think we've got much of a show now, boys?" said he.

Whereupon the three were silent, save for a trifle of hemming and hawing. To express any particular optimism at this time they felt to be childish and stupid, but they all doubtless possessed this sense of the situation in their minds. A young man thinks doggedly at such times. On the other hand, the ethics of their condition were decidedly against any open suggestion of hopelessness. So they were silent.

"Oh, well," said the captain, soothing his children. "We'll get ashore all right."

But there was that in his tone which made them think, so the oiler quoth: "Yes, if this wind holds!"

The cook was bailing. "Yes, if we don't catch hell in the surf."

Canton-flannel gulls flew near and far. Sometimes they sat down on the sea, near patches of brown seaweed that rolled on the waves with a movement like carpets on a line in a gale. The birds sat comfortably in groups, and they were envied by some in the dinghy, for the wrath of the sea was no more to them than it was to a covey of prairie chickens a thousand miles inland. Often they came very close and stared at the men with black, bead-like eyes. At these times they were uncanny and sinister in their unblinking scrutiny, and the men hooted angrily at them, telling them to be gone. One came, and evidently decided to alight on the top of the captain's head. The bird flew parallel to the boat and did not circle, but made short sidelong jumps in the air in chicken-fashion. His black eyes were wistfully fixed upon the captain's head.

"Ugly brute!" said the oiler to the bird. "You look as if you were made with a jack-knife." The cook and the correspondent swore darkly at the creature. The captain naturally wished to knock it away with the end of the heavy painter; but he did not dare to do it, because anything resembling an emphatic gesture would have capsized this freighted boat, and so, with his open hand, the captain gently and carefully waved the gull away. After it had been discouraged from the pursuit, the captain breathed easier on account of his hair, and others breathed easier because the bird struck their minds at this time as being somehow gruesome and ominous.

In the meantime, the oiler and the correspondent rowed. And also they rowed. They sat together in the same seat, and each rowed an oar. Then the oiler took both oars; then the correspondent took both oars; then the oiler; then the correspondent. They rowed and they rowed. The very ticklish part of the business was when the time came for the reclining one in the stern to take his turn at the oars. By the very last star of truth, it is easier to steal eggs from under a hen than it was to change seats in the dinghy. First, the man in the stern slid his hand along the thwart and moved with care, as if he were of Sèvres. Then the man in the rowing-seat slid his hand along the other thwart. It was all done with the most extraordinary care. As the two sidled past each other the whole party kept watchful eyes on the coming wave, and the captain cried:

"Look out, now!"

The brown mats of seaweed that appeared from time to time were like islands, bits of earth. They were travelling, apparently, neither one way nor the other.

93

They were, to all intents, stationary. They informed the men in the boat that it was making progress slowly towards the land.

The captain, rearing cautiously in the bow, after the dinghy soared on a great swell, said that he had seen the lighthouse at Mosquito Inlet. Presently the cook remarked that he had seen it. The correspondent was at the oars then, and for some reason he wished to look at the lighthouse, but his back was towards the far shore and the waves were important, and for some time he could not seize an opportunity to turn his head. But at last there came a wave more gentle than the others, and when at the crest of it he swiftly scoured the western horizon.

"See it?" said the captain.

"No," said the correspondent slowly. "I didn't see anything."

"Look again," said the captain. He pointed. "It's exactly in that direction."

At the top of another wave the correspondent did as he was bid, and this time his eyes chanced on a small still thing on the edge of the swaying horizon. It was precisely like the point of a pin. It took an anxious eye to find a lighthouse so tiny.

"Think we'll make it, Captain?"

"If this wind holds and the boat don't swamp, we can't do much else," said the captain.

The little boat, lifted by each towering sea, and splashed viciously by the crests, made progress that in the absence of seaweed was not apparent to those in her. She seemed just a wee thing wallowing, miraculously top-up, at the mercy of five oceans. Occasionally a great spread of water, like white flames, swarmed into her.

"Bail her, cook," said the captain serenely.

"All right, Captain," said the cheerful cook.

It would be difficult to describe the subtle brotherhood of men that was here established on the seas. No one

94

said that it was so. No one mentioned it. But it dwelt in the boat, and each man felt it warmed him. They were a captain, an oiler, a cook, and a correspondent, and they were friends, friends in a more curiously iron-bound degree than may be common. The hurt captain, lying against the water-jar in the bow, spoke always in a low voice and calmly, but he could never command a more ready and swiftly obedient crew than the motley three of the dinghy. It was more than a mere recognition of what was best for the common safety. There was surely in it a quality that was personal and heartfelt. And after this devotion to the commander of the boat, there was this comradeship that the correspondent, for instance, who had been taught to be cynical of men, knew even at the time was the best experience of his life. But no one said that it was so. No one mentioned it.

"I wish we had a sail," remarked the captain. "We might try my overcoat on the end of an oar, and give you two boys a chance to rest." So the cook and the correspondent held the mast and spread wide the overcoat. The oiler steered, and the little boat made good way with her new rig. Sometimes the oiler had to scull sharply to keep a sea from breaking into the boat, but otherwise sailing was a success.

Meanwhile, the lighthouse had been growing slowly larger. It had now almost assumed colour, and appeared like a little grey shadow on the sky. The man at the oars could not be prevented from turning his head rather often to try for a glimpse of this little grey shadow.

At last, from the top of each wave, the men in the tossing boat could see land. Even as the lighthouse was an upright shadow on the sea. It certainly was thinner than paper. "We must be about opposite New Smyrna," said the cook, who had coasted this shore often in schooners. "Captain, by the way, I believe they abandoned that life-saving station there about a year ago."

"Did they?" said the captain.

The wind slowly died away. The cook and the

correspondent were not now obliged to slave in order to hold high the oar. But the waves continued their old impetuous swooping at the dinghy, and the little craft, no longer under way, struggled woundily over them. The oiler or the correspondent took the oars again.

Shipwrecks are *apropos* of nothing. If men could only train for them and have them occur when the men had reached pink condition, there would be less drowning at sea. Of the four in the dinghy none had slept any time worth mentioning for two days and two nights previous to embarking in the dinghy, and in the excitement of clambering about the deck of a foundering ship they had also forgotten to eat heartily.

For these reasons, and for others, neither the oiler nor the correspondent was fond of rowing at this time. The correspondent wondered ingenuously how in the name of all that was sane could there be people who thought it was amusing to row a boat. It was not an amusement; it was a diabolical punishment, and even a genius of mental aberrations could never conclude that it was anything but a horror to the muscles and a crime against the back. He mentioned to the boat in general how the amusement of rowing struck him, and the weary-faced oiler smiled in full sympathy. Previously to the foundering, by the way, the oiler had worked double-watch in the engine-room of the ship.

"Take her easy now, boys," said the captain. "Don't spend yourselves. If we have to run a surf you'll need all your strength, because we'll sure have to swim for it. Take your time."

Slowly the land rose from the sea. From a black line it became a line of black, and a line of white—trees and sand. Finally the captain said that he could make out a house on the shore.

"That's the house of refuge, sure," said the cook. "They'll see us before long, and come out after us."

The distant lighthouse reared high.

"The keeper ought to be able to make us out now, if he's looking through a glass," said the captain. "He'll notify the life-saving people."

"None of those other boats could have got ashore to give word of the wreck," said the oiler in a low voice, "else the lifeboat would be out hunting us."

Slowly and beautifully the land loomed out of the sea. The wind came again. It had veered from the north-east to the south-east. Finally a new sound struck the ears of the men in the boat. It was the low thunder of the surf on the shore. "We'll never be able to make the lighthouse now," said the captain. "Swing her head a little more north, Billie," said he.

" 'A little more north,' sir," said the oiler.

Whereupon the little boat turned her nose once more down the wind, and all but the oarsman watched the shore grow. Under the influence of this expansion, doubt and direful apprehension were leaving the minds of the men. The management of the boat was still most absorbing, but it could not prevent a quiet cheerfulness. In an hour, perhaps, they would be ashore.

Their backbones had become thoroughly used to balancing in the boat, and they now rode this wild colt of a dinghy like circus men. The correspondent thought that he had been drenched to the skin, but happening to feel in the top pocket of his coat, he found therein eight cigars. Four of them were soaked with sea water; four were perfectly scathless. After a search, somebody produced three dry matches, and thereupon the four waifs rode impudently in their little boat, and with an assurance of an impending rescue shining in their eyes, puffed at the big cigars and judged well. Each took a drink of water.

"Cook," remarked the captain, "there don't seem to be any signs of life about your house of refuge."

"No," replied the cook. "Funny they don't see us."

A broad stretch of lowly coast lay before the eyes of

the men. It was of dunes topped with dark vegetation. The roar of the surf was plain, and sometimes they could see the white lip of a wave as it spun up the beach. A tiny house was blocked out black upon the sky. Southward, the slim lighthouse lifted its little grey length.

Tide, wind, and waves were swinging the dinghy northward. "Funny they don't see us," said the men.

The surf's roar was here dulled, but its tone was, nevertheless, thunderous and mighty. As the boat swam over the great rollers, the men sat listening to this roar. "We'll swamp sure," said everybody.

It is fair to say here that there was not a life-saving station within twenty miles in either direction, but the men did not know this fact, and in consequence they made dark and opprobrious remarks concerning the eyesight of the nation's life-savers. Four scowling men sat in the dinghy and surpassed records in the invention of epithets.

"Funny they don't see us."

The lightheartedness of a former time had completely faded. To their sharpened minds it was easy to conjure pictures of all kinds of incompetency and blindness, and, indeed, cowardice. There was the shore of the populous land, and it was bitter to them that from it came no sign.

"Well," said the captain ultimately, "I suppose we'll have to make a try for ourselves. If we stay out here too long we'll none of us have strength left to swim after the boat swamps."

And so the oiler, who was at the oars, turned the boat straight for the shore. There was a sudden tightening of muscles. There was some thinking.

"If we don't all get ashore," said the captain—"if we don't all get ashore, I suppose you fellows know where to send news of my finish?"

They then briefly exchanged some addresses and admonitions. As for the reflections of the men, there was a great deal of rage in them. Perchance they might

98

be formulated thus: "If I am going to be drowned—if I am going to be drowned—if I am going to be drowned, why, in the name of the seven mad gods who rule the sea, was I allowed to come thus far and contemplate sand and trees? Was I brought here merely to have my nose dragged away as if I was about to nibble the sacred cheese of life? It is preposterous. If this old ninny-woman, Fate, cannot do better than this, she should be deprived of the management of men's fortunes. She is an old hen who knows not her intention. If she has decided to drown me, why did she not do it in the beginning, and save me all this trouble? The whole affair is absurd. . . . But no, she cannot drown me. Not after all this work." Afterwards the man might have had an impulse to shake his fist at the clouds: "Just you drown me, now, and then hear what I call you!"

The billows that came at this time were more formidable. They seemed always just about to break and roll over the little boat in a turmoil of foam. There was a preparatory and long growl in the speech of them. No mind unused to the sea would have concluded that the dinghy could ascend those sheer heights in time. The shore was still afar. The oiler was a wily surfman. "Boys," he said swiftly, "she won't live three minutes more, and we're too far out to swim. Shall I take her to sea again, Captain?"

"Yes, go ahead!" said the captain.

This oiler, by a series of quick miracles, and fast and steady oarsmanship, turned the boat in the middle of the surf and took her safely to sea again.

There was a considerable silence as the boat bumped over the furrowed sea to deeper water. Then somebody in gloom spoke.

"Well, anyhow, they must have seen us from the shore by now."

The gulls went in slanting flight up the wind towards the grey desolate east. A squall, marked by

99

dingy clouds, and clouds of brick-red, like smoke from a burning building, appeared from the southeast.

"What do you think of those life-saving people? Ain't they peaches?"

"Funny they haven't seen us."

"Maybe they think we're out here for sport! Maybe they think we're fishin'. Maybe they think we're damned fools."

It was a long afternoon. A changed tide tried to force them southward, but the wind and wave said northward. Far ahead, where coastline, sea and sky formed their mighty angle, there were little dots which seemed to indicate a city on the shore.

"St. Augustine?"

The captain shook his head. "Too near Mosquito Inlet."

And the oiler rowed, and then the correspondent rowed. Then the oiler rowed. It was a weary business. The human back can become the seat of more aches and pains than are registered in books for the composite anatomy of a regiment. It is a limited area, but it can become the theatre of innumerable muscular conflicts, tangles, wrenches, knots, and other discomforts.

"Did you ever like to row, Billie," asked the correspondent.

"No," said the oiler. "Hang it!"

When one exchanged the rowing-seat for a place in the bottom of the boat, he suffered a bodily depression that caused him to be careless of everything save an obligation to wiggle one finger.

There was cold sea swashing to and fro in the boat, and he lay in it. His head, pillowed on a thwart, was within an inch of the swirl of a wave crest, and sometimes a particularly obstreperous sea came inboard and drenched him once more. But these matters did not annoy him. It is almost certain that if the boat had capsized he would have tumbled comfortably out upon the ocean as if he felt sure that it was a great soft mattress.

"Look! There's a man on the shore!"

"Where?"

"There! See'm? See'm?"

"He's stopped. Look! He's facing us!"

"He's waving at us!"

"So he is! By thunder!"

"Ah, now we're all right! Now we're all right! There'll be a boat here for us in half an hour."

"He's going on. He's running. He's going up to that house there."

The remote beach seemed lower than the sea, and it required a searching glance to discern the little black figure. The captain saw a floating stick, and they rowed to it. A bath towel was by some weird chance in the boat, and tying this on the stick, the captain waved it. The oarsman did not dare turn his head, so he was obliged to ask questions.

"What's he doing now?"

"He's standing still again. He's looking, I think. . . . There he goes again. Towards the house. . . . Now he's stopped again."

"Is he waving at us?"

"No, not now. He was, though."

"Look! There comes another man!"

"Look at him go, would you."

"Why, he's on a bicycle. Now he's met the other man. They're both waving at us. Look!"

"There comes something up the beach."

"What the devil is that thing?"

"Why, it looks like a boat."

"Why, certainly it's a boat."

"No, it's on wheels."

"Yes, so it is. Well, that must be the lifeboat. They drag them along shore on a wagon."

"That's the lifeboat, sure."

"No, by heaven, it's—it's an omnibus."

"I tell you it's a lifeboat."

"It's not! It's an omnibus. I can see it plain. One of these big hotel omnibuses."

"By thunder, you're right. It's an omnibus, sure as Fate. What do you suppose they are doing with an omnibus. Maybe they are goin' around collectin' the life-crew, hey?"

"That's it, likely. Look! There's a fellow waving a little black flag. He's standing on the steps of the omnibus. There come those other two fellows. Now they're all talking together. Look at the fellow with the flag. Maybe he ain't waving it!"

"So it is. It's his coat. He's taken it off, and is waving it around his head. But wouldn't you look at him swing it!"

"Oh, say, there isn't any life-saving station there. That's just a winter resort hotel omnibus that has brought some of the boarders to see us drown."

"What's that idiot with the coat mean? What's he signalling, anyhow?"

"It looks as if he were trying to tell us to go north. There must be a life-saving station up there."

"No. He thinks we're fishing. Just giving us a merry hand. See? Ah, there, Willie!"

"Well, I wish I could make something of those signals. What do you suppose he means?"

"He don't mean anything. He's just playing."

"Well, if he'd just signal us to try the surf again, or to go to sea and wait, or go north, or go south, or go to hell—there would be some reason in it. But look at him. He just stands there and keeps his coat revolving like a wheel. The ass!"

"There come more people."

"Now, there's quite a mob. Look! Isn't that a boat?"

"Where? Oh, I see where you mean. No, that's no boat."

"That fellow is still waving his coat."

"He must think we like to see him do that. Why don't he quit it? It don't mean anything."

"I don't know. I think he is trying to make us go north. It must be that there's a life-saving station there somewhere."

"Say, he ain't tired yet. Look at 'im wave."

"Wonder how long he can keep that up. He's been revolving his coat ever since he caught sight of us. He's an idiot. Why aren't they getting men to bring a boat out? A fishing-boat—one of those big yawls—could come out here all right. Why don't he do something?"

"Oh, it's all right now."

"They'll have a boat out here for us in less than no time, now that they've seen us."

A faint yellow tone came into the sky over the low land. The shadows on the sea slowly deepened. The wind bore coldness with it, and the men began to shiver.

"Holy smoke!" said one, allowing his voice to express his impious mood. "If we keep on monkeying out here! If we've got to flounder out here all night!"

"Oh, we'll never have to stay here all night! Don't you worry. They've seen us now, and it won't be long before they'll come chasing out after us."

The shore grew dusky. The man waving a coat blended gradually into this gloom, and it swallowed in the same manner the omnibus and the group of people. The spray, when dashed uproariously over the side, made the voyagers shrink and swear like men who were being branded.

"I'd like to catch the chump who waved the coat. I feel like socking him one, just for luck."

"Why? What did he do?"

"Oh, nothing, but then he seemed so damned cheerful."

In the meantime the oiler rowed, and then the correspondent rowed, and then the oiler rowed. Grey-faced and bowed forward, they mechanically, turn by turn, plied the leaden oars. The form of the lighthouse had vanished from the southern horizon, but finally a pale star appeared, just lighting from the sea. The streaked saffron in the west passed before the all-merging darkness, and the sea to the east was black. The land had vanished, and was expressed only by the low and dreary thunder of the surf.

"If I am going to be drowned—if I am going to be drowned—if I am going to be drowned, why, in the name of the seven mad gods who rule the sea, was I allowed to come thus far and contemplate sand and trees? Was I brought here merely to have my nose dragged away as I was about to nibble the sacred cheese of life?"

The patient captain, drooped over the water-jar, was sometimes obliged to speak to the oarsman.

"Keep her head up! Keep her head up!"

" 'Keep her head up,' sir." The voices were weary and low.

This was surely a quiet evening. All save the oarsman lay heavily and listlessly in the boat's bottom. As for him, his eyes were just capable of noting the tall black waves that swept forward in a most sinister silence, save for an occasional subdued growl of a crest.

The cook's head was on a thwart, and he looked without interest at the water under his nose. He was deep in other scenes. Finally he spoke. "Billie," he murmured, dreamfully, "what kind of pie do you like best?"

"Pie?" said the oiler and the correspondent agitatedly. "Don't talk about those things, blast you!"

"Well," said the cook, "I was just thinking about ham sandwiches, and——"

A night on the sea in an open boat is a long night. As darkness settled finally, the shine of the light, lifting from the sea in the south, changed to full gold. On the northern horizon a new light appeared, a small bluish gleam on the edge of the waters. These two lights were the furniture of the world. Otherwise there was nothing but waves.

Two men huddled in the stern, and distances were so magnificent in the dinghy that the rower was enabled to keep his feet partly warmed by thrusting them under his companions. Their legs, indeed, extended far under the rowing seat, until they touched the feet of the captain forward. Sometimes, despite the efforts of the tired oarsman, a wave came piling into the boat, an icy wave of the night; and the chilling water soaked them anew. They would twist their bodies for a moment and groan, and sleep the dead sleep once more, while the water in the boat gurgled about them as the craft rocked.

The plan of the oiler and the correspondent was for one to row until he lost the ability, and then arouse the other from his sea-water couch in the bottom of the boat.

The oiler plied the oars until his head drooped forward, and the overpowering sleep blinded him. And he rowed yet afterwards. Then he touched a man in the bottom of the boat and called his name. "Will you spell me for a little while?" he said meekly.

"Sure, Billie!" said the correspondent, awakening and dragging himself to a sitting position. They exchanged places carefully, and the oiler, cuddling down the sea-water at the cook's side, seemed to go to sleep instantly.

The correspondent, as he rowed, looked down at the two men sleeping underfoot. The cook's arm was around the oiler's shoulders, and, with their fragmentary clothing and haggard faces, they were the babes of the sea, a grotesque rendering of the old babes in the wood.

Later he must have grown stupid at his work, for suddenly there was a growling of water, and a crest came with a roar and a swash into the boat, and it was a wonder that it did not set the cook afloat in his life-belt. The cook continued to sleep, but the oiler sat up, blinking his eyes and shaking with the new cold.

"Oh, I'm awfully sorry, Billie," said the correspondent contritely.

"That's all right, old boy," said the oiler, and lay down again and was asleep.

Presently it seemed that even the captain dozed, and the correspondent thought that he was the one man afloat on all the oceans. The wind had a voice as it came over the waves, and it was sadder than the end.

There was a long, loud swishing astern of the boat, and a gleaming trail of phosphorescence, like blue flame, was furrowed on the black water. It might have been made by a monstrous knife.

Then there came a stillness, while the correspondent breathed with open mouth and looked at the sea.

Suddenly there came another swish and another long flash of bluish light, and this time it was alongside the boat, and might almost have been reached with an oar. The correspondent saw an enormous fin speed like a shadow through the water, hurling the crystalline spray and leaving the long glowing trail.

The correspondent looked over his shoulder at the captain. His face was hidden and he seemed to be asleep. He looked at the babes of the sea. They certainly were asleep. So, being bereft of sympathy, he leaned a little way to one side and swore softly into the sea.

But the thing did not then leave the vicinity of the boat. Ahead or astern, on one side or the other, at intervals long or short, fled the long sparkling streak, and there was to be heard the whirroo of the dark fin. The speed and power of the thing was greatly to be admired. It cut the water like a gigantic and keen projectile.

The presence of this biding thing did not affect the man with the same horror that it would if he had been picnicker. He simply looked at the sea dully, and swore in an undertone.

Nevertheless, it is true that he did not wish to be

alone. He wished one of his companions to awaken by chance and keep him company with it. But the captain hung motionless over the water-jar, and the oiler and the cook in the bottom of the boat were plunged in slumber.

"If I am going to be drowned—if I am going to be drowned—if I am going to be drowned, why, in the name of the seven mad gods who rule the sea, was I allowed to come thus far and contemplate sand and trees?"

During this dismal night, it may be remarked that a man would conclude that it was really the intention of the seven mad gods to drown him, despite the abominable injustice of it. For it was certainly an abominable injustice to drown a man who had worked so hard, so hard. The man felt it would be a crime most unnatural. Other people had drowned at sea since galleys swarmed with painted sails, but still——

When it occurs to a man that Nature does not regard him as important, and that she feels that she would not maim the universe by disposing of him, he at first wishes to throw bricks at the temple, and he hates deeply the fact that there are no bricks and no temples. Any visible expression of Nature would surely be pelleted with his jeers.

Then, if there be no tangible thing to hoot, he feels, perhaps, the desire to confront a personification and indulge in pleas, bowed to one knee, and with hands supplicant, saying: "Yes, but I love myself."

A high cold star on a winter's night is the word he feels that she says to him. Thereafter he knows the pathos of his situation.

The men in the dinghy had not discussed these matters, but each had, no doubt, reflected upon them in silence and according to his mind. There was seldom any expression upon their faces save the general one of complete weariness. Speech was devoted to the business of the boat.

To chime the notes of his emotion, a verse mysteriously entered the correspondent's head. He had even forgotten this verse, but it suddenly was in his mind.

"A soldier of the Legion lay dying in Algiers,
   There was a lack of woman's nursing, there was dearth
      of woman's tears;
But a comrade stood beside him, and he took that
      comrade's hand,
And he said: 'I never more shall see my own, my
      native land.' "

In his childhood the correspondent had been made acquainted with the fact that a soldier of the Legion lay dying in Algiers, but he had never regarded the fact as important. Myriads of his schoolfellows had informed him of the soldier's plight, but the dinning had naturally ended by making him perfectly indifferent. He had never considered it his affair that a soldier of the Legion lay dying in Algiers, nor had it appeared to him as a matter for sorrow. It was less to him than the breaking of a pencil's point.

Now, however, it quaintly came to him as a human, living thing. It was no longer merely a picture of a few throes in the breast of a poet, meanwhile drinking tea and warming his feet at the grate; it was an actuality —stern, mournful and fine.

The correspondent plainly saw the soldier. He lay on the sand with his feet straight and still. While his pale left hand was upon his chest in an attempt to thwart the going of his life, the blood came between his fingers. In the far Algerian distance, a city of low square forms was set against a sky that was faint with the last sunset hues. The correspondent, plying the oars and dreaming of the slow and slower movements of the lips of the soldier, was moved by a profound and perfectly impersonal comprehension. He was sorry for the soldier of the Legion who lay dying in Algiers.

The thing which had followed the boat and waited, had evidently grown bored at the delay. There was no longer to be heard the slash of the cut-water, and there was no longer the flame of the long trail. The light in the north still glimmered, but it was apparently no nearer to the boat. Sometimes the boom of the surf rang in the correspondent's ears, and he turned the craft seaward then, and rowed harder. Southward, someone had evidently built a watchfire on the beach. It was too low and too far to be seen, but it made a shimmering roseate reflection upon the bluff back of it, and this could be discerned from the boat. The wind came stronger, and sometimes a wave suddenly ranged out like a mountain cat, and there was to be seen the sheen and sparkle of a broken crest.

The captain, in the bow, moved on his water-jar, and sat erect. "Pretty long night," he observed to the correspondent. He looked at the shore. "Those life-saving people take their time."

"Did you see that shark playing around?"

"Yes, I saw him. He was a big fellow, all right."

"Wish I had known you were awake."

Later the correspondent spoke into the bottom of the boat.

"Billie!" There was a slow and gradual disentanglement. "Billie, will you spell me?"

"Sure!" said the oiler.

As soon as the correspondent touched the cold comfortable sea-water in the bottom of the boat, and had huddled close to the cook's life-belt, he was deep in sleep, despite the fact that his teeth played all the popular airs. This sleep was so good to him that it was but a moment before he heard a voice call his name in a tone that demonstrated the last stages of exhaustion.

"Will you spell me?"

"Sure, Billie!"

The light in the north had mysteriously vanished, but

the correspondent took his course from the wide-awake captain.

Later in the night they took the boat farther out to sea, and the captain directed the cook to take one oar at the stern and keep the boat facing the seas. He was to call out if he should hear the thunder of the surf. This plan enabled the oiler and the correspondent to get respite together.

"We'll give those boys a chance to get into shape again," said the captain. They curled down again and, after a few preliminary chatterings and trembles, slept once more the dead sleep. Neither knew they had bequeathed to the cook the company of another shark, or perhaps the same shark.

As the boat caroused on the waves, spray occasionally bumped over the side and gave them a fresh soaking, but this had no power to break their repose. The ominous slash of the wind and the water affected them as it would have affected mummies.

"Boys," said the cook, with the notes of every reluctance in his voice, "she's drifted in pretty close. I guess one of you had better take her to sea again." The correspondent, aroused, heard the crash of the toppled crests.

As he was rowing, the captain gave him some whisky and water, and this steadied the chills out of him. "If I ever get ashore and anybody shows me even a photograph of an oar . . ."

At last there was a short conversation.

"Billie . . . Billie, will you spell me?"

"Sure!" said the oiler.

When the correspondent again opened his eyes, the sea and the sky were each of the grey hue of the dawning. Later, carmine and gold were painted upon the waters. The morning appeared finally in splendour, with a sky of pure blue, and the sunlight flamed on the tips of the waves.

On the distant dunes were set many little black cottages, and a tall white windmill reared above them. No man, nor dog, nor bicycle appeared on the beach. The cottages might have formed a deserted village.

The voyagers scanned the shore. A conference was held in the boat. "Well," said the captain, "if no help is coming we might better try a run through the surf right away. If we stay out here much longer we will be too weak to do anything for ourselves at all." The others silently acquiesced in this reasoning. The boat was headed for the beach. The correspondent wondered if none ever ascended the tall wind-tower, and if then they never looked seaward. This tower was a giant, standing with its back to the plight of the ants. It represented in a degree, to the correspondent, the serenity of Nature amid the struggles of the individual —Nature in wind, and Nature in the vision of men. She did not seem cruel to him then, nor beneficent, nor treacherous, nor wise. But she was indifferent, flatly indifferent. It is, perhaps, plausible that a man in this situation, impressed with the unconcern of the universe, should see the innumerable flaws of them, and have them taste wickedly in his mind and wish for another chance. A distinction between right and wrong seems absurdly clear to him, then, in this new ignorance of the grave-edge, and he understands that if he were given another opportunity he would mend his conduct and his words, and be better and brighter during an introduction or at a tea.

"Now, boys," said the captain, "she is going to swamp, sure. All we can do is to work her in as far as possible, and then when she swamps pile out and scramble for the beach. Keep cool now, and don't jump until she swamps."

The oiler took the oars. Over his shoulders he scanned the surf. "Captain," he said, "I think I'd better bring her about, and keep her head-on to the seas, and back her in."

"All right, Billie," said the captain. "Back her in." The oiler swung the boat then, and, seated in the stern, the cook and the correspondent were obliged to look over their shoulders to contemplate the lonely and indifferent shore.

The monstrous in-shore rollers heaved the boat high until the men were again enabled to see the white sheets of water scudding up the slanted beach. "We won't get in very close," said the captain. Each time a man could wrest his attention from the rollers he turned his glance towards the shore, and in the expression of his eyes during this contemplation there was a singular quality. The correspondent, observing the others, knew that they were not afraid, but the full meaning of their glances was shrouded.

As for himself, he was too tired to grapple fundamentally with the fact. He tried to coerce his mind into thinking of it, but the mind was dominated at this time by the muscles, and the muscles said they did not care. It merely occurred to him that if he should drown it would be a shame.

There were no hurried words, no pallor, no plain agitation. The men simply looked at the shore. "Now, remember to get well clear of the boat when you jump," said the captain.

Seaward the crest of a roller suddenly fell with a thunderous crash, and the long white comber came roaring down upon the boat.

"Steady now!" said the captain. The men were silent. They turned their eyes from the shore to the comber and waited. The boat slid up the incline, leaped at the furious top, bounced over it, and swung down the long back of the wave. Some water had been shipped, and the cook bailed it out.

But the next crest crashed also. The tumbling boiling flood of white water caught the boat and whirled it almost perpendicular. Water swarmed in from all sides. The correspondent had his hands on the gunwale at this time, and when the water entered at that place he swiftly withdrew his fingers, as if he objected to wetting them.

The little boat, drunken with this weight of water, reeled and snuggled deeper into the sea.

"Bail her out, cook! Bail her out."

"All right, Captain," said the cook.

"Now, boys, the next one will do for us, sure," said the oiler. "Jump clear of the boat."

The third wave moved forward, huge, furious, implacable. It fairly swallowed the dinghy, and almost simultaneously the men tumbled into the sea. A piece of life-belt had lain in the bottom of the boat, and as the correspondent went overboard he held this to his chest with his left hand.

The January water was icy, and he reflected immediately that it was colder than he had expected to find it on the coast of Florida. This appeared to his dazed mind as a fact important enough to be noted at the time. The coldness of the water was sad; it was tragic. The fact was somehow so mixed with his opinion of his own situation that it seemed almost a proper reason for tears. The water was cold.

When he came to the surface he was conscious of little but the noisy water. Afterwards he saw his companions in the sea. The oiler was ahead in the race. He was swimming strongly and rapidly. Off to the correspondent's left, the cook's great white and corked back bulged out of the water, and in the rear the captain was hanging with his one good hand to the keel of the overturned dinghy.

There is a certain immovable quality to a shore, and the correspondent wondered at it amid the confusion of the sea.

It seemed also very attractive, but the correspondent knew that it was a long journey, and he paddled leisurely. The piece of life-preserver lay under him, and sometimes he whirled down the incline of a wave as if he were on a hand-sled.

But finally he arrived at a place in the sea where travel was beset with difficulty. He did not pause swimming to inquire what manner of current had caught him, but there his progress ceased. The shore was set before him like a bit of scenery on a stage, and he looked at it and understood each detail of it.

As the cook passed, much farther to the left, the captain was calling to him, "Turn over on your back, Cook! Turn over on your back and use the oar."

"All right, sir." The cook turned on his back, and, paddling with an oar, went ahead as if he were a canoe.

Presently the boat also passed to the left of the correspondent with the captain clinging with one hand to the keel. He would have appeared like a man raising himself to look over a board fence, if it were not for the extraordinary gymnastics of the boat. The correspondent marvelled that the captain could still hold to it.

They passed on, nearer to shore—the oiler, the cook, the captain—and following them went the water-jar, bouncing gaily over the seas.

The correspondent remained in the grip of this strange new enemy—a current. The shore, with its white slope of sand and its green bluff, topped with little silent cottages, was spread like a picture before him. It was very near to him then, but he was impressed as one who in a gallery looks at a scene from Brittany or Holland.

He thought: "I am going to drown! Can it be possible? Can it be possible?" Perhaps an individual must consider his own death to be the final phenomenon of nature.

But later a wave perhaps whirled him out of this small, deadly current, for he found suddenly that he could again make progress towards the shore. Later still, he was aware that the captain, clinging with one hand to the keel of the dinghy, had his face turned away from the shore and towards him, and was calling his name. "Come to the boat! Come to the boat!"

In his struggle to reach the captain and the boat, he

reflected that when one gets properly wearied, drowning must really be a comfortable arrangement, a cessation of hostilities accompanied by a large degree of relief, and he was glad of it, for the main thing in his mind for some months had been horror of the temporary agony. He did not wish to be hurt.

Presently he saw a man running along the shore. He was undressing with most remarkable speed. Coat, trousers, shirt, everything flew magically off him.

"Come to the boat," called the captain.

"All right, Captain." As the correspondent paddled, he saw the captain let himself down to bottom and leave the boat. Then the correspondent performed his one little marvel of the voyage. A large wave caught him and flung him with ease and supreme speed completely over the boat and far beyond it. It struck him even then as an event in gymnastics, and a true miracle of the sea. An overturned boat in the surf is not a plaything to a swimming man.

The correspondent arrived in water that reached only to his waist, but his condition did not enable him to stand for more than a moment. Each wave knocked him into a heap, and the undertow pulled at him.

Then he saw the man who had been running and undressing, and undressing and running, come bounding into the water. He dragged ashore the cook, and then waded towards the captain, but the captain waved him away, and sent him to the correspondent.

He was naked, naked as a tree in winter, but a halo was about his head, and he shone like a saint. He gave a strong pull, and a long drag, and a bully heave at the correspondent's hand. The correspondent, schooled in the minor formulæ, said, "Thanks, old man." But suddenly the man cried: "What's that?" He pointed a swift finger. The correspondent said: "Go."

In the shadows, face downwards, lay the oiler. His forehead touched sand that was periodically, between each wave, clear of the sea.

The correspondent did not know all that transpired afterwards. When he achieved safe ground he fell, striking the sand with each particular part of his body. It was as if he had dropped from a roof, but the thud was grateful.

It seems that instantly the beach was populated with men with blankets, clothes and flasks, and women with coffee-pots and all the remedies sacred to their minds. The welcome of the land to the men from the sea was warm and generous, but a still and dripping shape was carried slowly up the beach, and the land's welcome for it could only be the different and sinister hospitality of the grave.

When it came night, the white waves paced to and fro in the moonlight, and the wind brought the sound of the great sea's voice to the men on shore, and they felt they could then be interpreters.

CIRCUMSTANCE

by Harriet Prescott Spofford

HARRIET ELIZABETH SPOFFORD (1835-1921) was one of a group of women authors who helped to lay the foundations of American fiction in the early nineteenth century. Writing of the stories that he read as an editor in those days, the eminent critic, William Deans Howells said: "There were people of my own age, say of twenty or twenty-one, and my partners, both sexes, in the awful joy of Miss Prescott's (not yet Mrs. Spofford's) tremendous story of 'Circumstance,' still unsurpassed of its kind. We thrilled over it severally and collectively (the whole 20,000 of us) and we are still ready to swear it unsurpassed, though we are now over seventy or eighty years old and 200,000 in number."

CIRCUMSTANCE

BY

HARRIET PRESCOTT SPOFFORD

SHE had remained, during all that day, with a sick
neighbour,—those eastern wilds of Maine in that
epoch frequently making neighbours and miles synonymous,—and so busy had she been with care and cook-
ery, that she did not at first observe the approaching
night. But finally the level rays, reddening the snow,
threw their gleam upon the wall; and, by the sombre
desk and nook her broad hornward casement flung
forth her return. Home lay some three miles distant
across a copse, a meadow, and a piece of wood,—the
woods being a fringe on the skirts of the great forests
that stretch far away into the north. That home was
one of a dozen log-houses lying a few furlongs apart
from each other, with their half-cleared demesnes
separating them at the rear from a wilderness unbroken
save by stealthy native or deadly panther tribes.

She was in a no wise exalted frame of spirit,—on the
contrary, rather depressed by the pain she had witnessed and the fatigue she had endured; but in certain
temperaments such a condition throws open the mental
pores, so to speak, and renders one receptive of every
influence. Through the little copse she walked slowly,
with her cloak folded about her, lingering to imbibe the
sense of shelter, the sunset filtered in purple through the
mist of woven spray and twig, the companionship of
growth not sufficiently dense to band against her, the
sweet home-feeling of a young and tender wintry wood.
It was, therefore, just on the edge of the evening that she
emerged from the place and began to cross the meadowland. At one hand lay the forest to which her path

132

CIRCUMSTANCE

BY

HARRIET PRESCOTT SPOFFORD

SHE had remained, during all that day, with a sick neighbour—those eastern wilds of Maine in that epoch frequently making neighbours and miles synonymous—and so busy had she been with care and sympathy that she did not at first observe the approaching night. But finally the level rays, reddening the snow, threw their gleam upon the wall, and, hastily donning cloak and hood, she bade her friend farewell and sallied forth on her return. Home lay some three miles distant, across a copse, a meadow, and a piece of woods—the woods being a fringe on the skirts of the great forests that stretch far away into the north. That home was one of a dozen log-houses lying a few furlongs apart from each other, with their half-cleared demesnes separating them at the rear from a wilderness untrodden save by stealthy native or deadly panther tribes.

She was in a no wise exalted frame of spirit—on the contrary, rather depressed by the pain she had witnessed and the fatigue she had endured; but in certain temperaments such a condition throws open the mental pores, so to speak, and renders one receptive of every influence. Through the little copse she walked slowly, with her cloak folded about her, lingering to imbibe the sense of shelter, the sunset filtered in purple through the mist of woven spray and twig, the companionship of growth not sufficiently dense to band against her, the sweet home-feeling of a young and tender wintry wood. It was, therefore, just on the edge of the evening that she emerged from the place and began to cross the meadowland. At one hand lay the forest to which her path wound; at the other the evening star hung over a tide of failing orange that slowly slipped down the earth's broad side to sadden other hemispheres with sweet regret. Walking rapidly now, and with her eyes wide open, she distinctly saw in the air before her what was not there a moment ago, a something—cold, white, and ghastly, waved by the likeness of four wan hands—that rose with a long inflation and fell in rigid folds, while a voice, shaping itself from the hollowness above, spectral and melancholy, sighed, "The Lord have mercy on the people! The Lord have mercy on the people!" Three times the sheet with its corpse-covering outline waved beneath the pale hands, and the voice, awful in its solemn and mysterious depth, sighed, "The Lord have mercy on the people!" Then all was gone, the grey sky was obstructed by no deathly blot; she looked about her, shook her shoulders decidedly, and, pulling on her hood, went forward once more.

She might have been a little frightened by such an apparition if she had led a life of less reality than frontier settlers are apt to lead; but dealing with hard fact does not engender a flimsy habit of mind, and this woman was too sincere and earnest in her character, and too happy in her situation to be thrown by antagonism merely upon superstitious fancies and chimeras of second-sight. She did not even believe herself subject to an hallucination, but smiled simply, a little vexed that her thought could have framed such a glamour from the day's occurrences, and not sorry to lift the bough of the warder of the woods and enter and disappear in their sombre path. If she had been imaginative, she would have hesitated at her first step into a region whose dangers were not visionary; but I suppose that the thought of a little child at home would conquer that propensity in the most habituated. So, biting a bit of spicy birch, she went along. Now and then she came to a gap where the trees had been partially felled, and here she found that the lingering twilight was explained by that peculiar and perhaps electric film which sometimes sheathes the sky in diffused light for very many hours before a brilliant aurora.

Suddenly, a swift shadow, like the fabulous flying-dragon, writhed through the air before her, and she felt herself instantly seized and borne aloft. It was that wild beast—the most savage and serpentine and subtle and fearless of our latitudes—known by hunters as the Indian Devil, and he held her in his clutches on the broad floor of a swinging fir-bough. His long sharp claws were caught in her clothing, he worried them sagaciously a little, then, finding that ineffectual to free them, he commenced licking her bare white arm with his rasping tongue and pouring over her the wide streams of his hot breath.

So quick had this flashing action been that the woman had had no time for alarm, moreover, she was not of the screaming kind; but now, as she felt him endeavouring to disentangle his claws, and the horrid sense of her fate smote her, and she saw instinctively the fierce plunge of those weapons, the long strips of flesh torn from her bones, the agony, the quivering disgust—itself a worse agony—while by her side and holding her in his great lithe embrace the monster crouched, his white tusks whetting and gnashing, his eyes glaring through all the darkness like balls of fire—a shriek that rang in every forest hollow, that startled every winter-housed thing, that stirred and woke the last needle of the tasselled pines, tore through her lips. A moment afterwards, the beast left the arm, once white, now crimson, and looked up alertly.

She did not think at this instant to call upon God. She called upon her husband. It seemed to her that she had but one friend in the world—that was he; and again the cry, loud, clear, prolonged, echoed through the woods. It was not the shriek that disturbed the creature at his relish; he was not born in the woods to be scared of an owl, you know—what then? It must have been the echo, most musical, most resonant, repeated and yet repeated, dying with long sighs of sweet sound, vibrated from rock to river and back again from depth to depth of cave and cliff. Her thought flew after it; she knew that, even if her husband heard it, he yet could not reach her in time; she saw that while the beast listened he would not gnaw—and this she *felt* directly, when the rough, sharp, and multiplied stings of his tongue retouched her arm. Again her lips opened by instinct, but the sound that issued thence came by reason. She had heard that music charmed wild beasts —just this point between life and death intensified every faculty—and when she opened her lips the third time it was not for shrieking, but for singing.

A little thread of melody stole out, a rill of tremulous motion: it was the cradle-song with which she rocked her baby—how could she sing that? And then she remembered the baby sleeping rosily on the long settee before the fire; the father, cleaning his gun, with one foot on the green wooden rundle; the merry light from the chimney dancing out and through the room, on the rafters of the ceiling with their tassels of onions and herbs, on the log walls painted with lichens and festooned with apples, on the king's arm slung across the shelf with the old pirate's cutlass, on the snow-pile of the bed, and on the great brass clock—dancing, too, and lingering on the baby, with his fringed gentian eyes, his chubby fists clenched on the pillow, and his fine breezy hair fanning with the motion of his father's foot. All this struck her in one, and made a sob of her breath, and she ceased.

Immediately the long red tongue was thrust forth again. Before it touched, a song sprang to her lips, a wild sea song, such as some sailor might be singing far out on trackless blue water that night, the shrouds whistling with frost and the sheets glued in ice—a song with the wind in its burden and the spray in its chorus. The monster raised his head and flared the fiery eyeballs upon her, then fretted the imprisoned claws a moment and was quiet; only the breath like the vapour from some hell-pit still swathed her.

Her voice, at first faint and fearful, gradually lost its quiver, grew under her control and subject to her modulation; it rose on long swells, it fell in subtle cadences, now and then its tones pealed out like bells from distant belfries on fresh sonorous mornings. She sung the song through, and wondering lest his name of Indian Devil were not his true name, and if he would not detect her, she repeated it. Once or twice now, indeed, the beast stirred uneasily, turned, and made the bough sway at his movement. As she ended, he snapped his jaws together, and tore away the fettered member, curling it under him with a snarl—when she burst into the gayest reel that ever answered a fiddle-bow.

How many a time she had heard her husband play it on the homely fiddle made by himself from birch and cherrywood; how many a time she had seen it danced on the floor of their one room, to the patter of wooden clogs and the rustle of homespun petticoat; how many a time she had danced it herself—and did she not remember once, as they joined clasps for right-hands-round, how it had lent its gay, bright measure to her life? And here she was, singing it alone, in the forest, at midnight, to a wild beast! As she sent her voice trilling up and down its quick oscillations between joy and pain, the creature who grasped her uncurled his paw and scratched the bark from the bough; she must vary the spell, and her voice spun leaping along the projecting points of tune of a hornpipe. Still singing, she felt herself twisted about with a low growl and a lifting of the red lip from the glittering teeth; she broke the hornpipe's thread, and commenced unravelling a lighter, livelier thing, an Irish jig.

Up and down and round about her voice flew, the beast threw back his head so that the diabolical face fronted hers, and the torrent of his breath prepared her for his feast as the anaconda slimes his prey. Frantically she darted from tune to tune; his restless movements followed her. She tired herself with dancing and vivid national airs, growing feverish and singing spasmodically as she felt her horrid tomb yawning wider. Touching in this manner all the slogan and keen clan cries, the beast moved again, but only to lay the disengaged paw across her with heavy satisfaction. She did not dare to pause; through the clear cold air, the frosty starlight, she sang. If there were yet any tremor in the tone, it was not fear—she had learned the secret of sound at last; nor could it be chill—far too high a fervour throbbed her pulses; it was nothing but the thought of the log-house and of what might be passing within it. She fancied the baby stirring in his sleep and moving his pretty lips—her husband rising and opening the door, looking out after her, and wondering at her absence. She fancied the light pouring through the chink and then shut in again with all the safety and comfort and joy, her husband taking down the fiddle and playing lightly with his head inclined, playing while she sang, while she sang for her life to an Indian Devil. Then she knew he was fumbling for and finding some shining fragment and scoring it down the yellowing hair, and unconsciously her voice forsook the wild war tunes and drifted into the half-gay, half-melancholy *Rosinthe Bow.*

Suddenly she woke pierced with a pang, and the daggered tooth penetrated her flesh—dreaming of safety she had ceased singing and lost it. The beast had regained the use of all his limbs, and now, standing and raising his back, bristling and growling, with sounds that would have been like hisses but for their deep and fearful sonority, he withdrew step by step towards the trunk of the tree, still with his flaming eyes upon her. She was all at once free, on one end of the bough, twenty feet from the ground. She did not measure the distance, but rose to drop herself down, careless of any death, so that it were not this. Instantly, as if he scanned her thoughts, the creature bounded forward with a yell and caught her again in his dreadful hold. It might be that he was not greatly famished; for, as she suddenly flung up her voice again, he settled himself composedly on the bough, still clasping her with invincible pressure to his rough, ravenous breast, and listening in a fascination to the sad, strange U-la-lu that now moaned forth in loud, hollow tones above him. He half closed his eyes, and sleepily reopened and shut them again.

What rending pains were close at hand! Death! And what a death! Water, be it cold or warm, that which buoys up blue icefields, or which bathes tropical coasts with currents of balmy bliss, is yet a gentle conqueror, kisses as it kills, and draws you down gently through darkening fathoms to its heart. Death at the sword is the festival of trumpet and bugle and banner, with glory ringing out around you and distant hearts thrilling through yours. No gnawing disease can bring such hideous end as this; for that is a fiend bred of your own flesh, and this—is it a fiend, this living lump of appetites? What dread comes with the thought of perishing in flames! But fire, let it leap and hiss never so hotly, is something too remote, too alien, to inspire us with such loathly horror as a wild beast, if it have a life, that life is too utterly beyond our comprehension.

All this she felt as she charmed him, and what force it lent to her song God knows. If her voice should fail! If the damp and cold should give her any fatal hoarseness! If all the silent powers of the forest did not conspire to help her! The dark, hollow night rose indifferently over her; the wide, cold air breathed rudely past her, lifted her wet hair and blew it down again; the great boughs swung with a ponderous strength,

127   K

now and then clashed their iron lengths together and shook off a sparkle of icy spears or some long-lain weight of snow from their heavy shadows. The green depths were utterly cold and silent and stern. These beautiful haunts that all the summer were hers and rejoiced to share with her their bounty, these heavens that had yielded their largesse, these stems that had thrust their blossoms into her hands, all these friends of three moons ago forgot her now and knew her no longer.

Feeling her desolation, wild, melancholy, forsaken songs rose thereon from that frightful aerie—weeping, wailing tunes, that sob among the people from age to age, and overflow with otherwise unexpressed sadness —all rude, mournful ballads—old tearful strains, that Shakespeare heard the vagrants sing, and that rise and fall like the wind and tide—sailor-songs, to be heard only in lone mid-watches beneath the moon and stars —ghastly rhyming romances, such as that famous one of the *Lady Margaret*, when

> "She slipped on her gown of green
> A piece below the knee—
> And 'twas all a long, cold winter's night
> A dead corpse followed she."

Still the beast lay with closed eyes, yet never relaxing his grasp. Once a half-whine of enjoyment escaped him—he fawned his fearful head upon her; once he scored her cheek with his tongue; savage caresses that hurt like wounds. How weary she was! And yet how terribly awake! How fuller and fuller of dismay grew the knowledge that she was prolonging her anguish and playing with death! How appalling the thought that with her voice ceased her existence! Yet she could not sing for ever; her throat was dry and hard, her very breath was a pain, her mouth was hotter than any desert-worn pilgrim's—if she could but drop upon her burning tongue one atom of the ice that glittered about her!—but both of her arms were pinioned in the giant's vice. She remembered the apparition, and for the first time in her life shivered with spiritual fear. Was it hers? She asked herself, as she sang, what sins she had committed, what life she had led, to find her punishment so soon, and in these pangs, and then she sought eagerly for some reason why her husband was not up and abroad to find her.

He failed her—her one sole hope of life—and without being aware of it, her voice forsook the songs of suffering and sorrow for old Covenanting hymns—hymns with which her mother had lulled her, which the class-leader pitched in the chimney-corners—grand and sweet Methodist hymns, brimming with melody and with all fantastic involutions of tune to suit that ecstatic worship, hymns full of the beauty of holiness, steadfast, relying, sanctified by the salvation they had lent to those in worse extremity than hers, for they had found themselves in the grasp of hell, while she was but in the jaws of death. Out of this strange music, peculiar to one character of faith, and than which there is none more beautiful in its degree nor owning a more potent sway of sound, her voice soared into the glorified chants of churches. What to her was death by cold or famine or wild beasts? "Though He slay me, yet will I trust in Him," she sang. High and clear through the frore fair night, the level moonbeams splintering in the wood, the scarce glints of stars in the shadowy roof of branches, these sacred anthems rose—rose as a hope from despair, as some snowy spray of flower-bells from blackest mould. Was she not in God's hands? Did not the world swing at His will? If this were in His great plan of Providence, was it not best, and should she not accept it?

"He is the Lord our God; His judgments are in all the earth."

Never ceasing in the rhythm of her thoughts, articulated in music as they thronged, the memory of her first communion flashed over her. Again she was in that distant place on that sweet spring morning. Again the congregation rustled out, and the few remained, and she trembled to find herself among them. How well she remembered the devout, quiet faces, too accustomed to the sacred feast to glow with their inner joy, how well the snowy linen at the altar, the silver vessels slowly and silently shifting, and as the cup approached and passed, how the sense of delicious perfume stole in and heightened the transport of her prayer!

Perhaps another would not have felt so much ecstasy as satisfaction on that occasion; but it is true, of a later disciple, who had said, "The Lord bestoweth His blessings there, where He findeth the vessels empty." "And does it need the walls of a church to renew my communion?" she asked. "Does not every moment stand a temple four-square to God? And in that morning, with its buoyant sunlight, was I any dearer to the Heart of the World than now?" "My beloved is mine, and I am His," she sang over and over again, with all varied inflection and profuse tune. How gently all the winter-wrapt things bent towards her then! Into what relation with her had they grown! How this common dependence was the spell of their intimacy! How at one with Nature had she become! How all the night and the silence and the forest seemed to hold its breath, and to send its soul up to God in her singing! It was no longer despondency, that singing. It was neither prayer nor petition. She had left imploring: "How long wilt Thou forget me, O Lord?" "Lighten mine eyes, lest I sleep the sleep of death." "For in death there is no remembrance of Thee," with countless other such fragments of supplication. She cried rather, "Yea, though I walk through the valley of the shadow of death, I will fear no evil, for Thou art with me; Thy rod and Thy staff, they comfort me."

Then she thought of the Great Deliverance, when He drew her up out of many waters, and the flashing old psalm pealed forth triumphantly:

"The Lord descended from above, and bow'd the
    heavens high;
And underneath his feet he cast the darkness of the sky.
On cherubs and on cherubims full royally he rode;
And on the wings of all the winds came flying all
    abroad."

She remembered, "In Thy presence is fulness of joy;
at Thy right hand there are pleasured for evermore";
and "God will redeem my soul from the power of the
grave; for He shall receive me"; "He will swallow up
death in victory"; not once now did she say, "Lord,
how long wilt Thou look on?   Rescue my soul from
their destructions, my darling from the lions," for she
knew that "the young lions roar after their prey and
seek their meat from God."   "O Lord, Thou preservest
man and beast," she said.

She had no comfort or consolation in this season, such
as sustained the Christian martyrs in the amphitheatre.
She was not dying for her faith, there were no palms in
heaven for her to wave,—but how many a time had she
declared, "I had rather be a door-keeper in the house
of my God, than to dwell in the tents of wickedness!"
And as the broad rays here and there broke through
the dense covert of shade and lay in rivers of lustre on
crystal sheathing and frozen fretting of trunk and limb
and on the great spaces of refraction, they builded up
visibly that house, the shining city on the hill, and
singing, "Beautiful for situation, the joy of the whole
earth, is Mount Zion, on the sides of the north, the city
of the Great King," her vision climbed to that higher
picture where the angel shows the dazzling thing, the
holy Jerusalem descending out of heaven from God,
with its splendid battlements and gates of pearls, and its
foundations—the eleventh a jacinth, the twelfth an
amethyst—with its great white throne, and the rainbow
round about it, in sight like unto an emerald—"And
there shall be no night there, for the Lord God giveth
them light," she sang.

131

What whisper of dawn now rustled through the wilderness? How the night was passing! And still the beast crouched upon the bough, changing only the posture of his head that again he might command her with those charmed eyes. Half their fire was gone—she could almost have released herself from his custody— yet, had she stirred, no one knows what malevolent instinct might have dominated anew. But of that she did not dream; long ago stripped of any expectation, she was experiencing in her divine rapture how mystically true it is that "he that dwelleth in the secret place of the Most High shall abide under the shadow of the Almighty."

Slow clarion cries now wound from the distance as the cocks caught the intelligence of day and re-echoed it faintly from farm to farm—sleepy sentinels of night, sounding the foe's invasion, and translating that dim intuition to ringing notes of warning. Still she chanted on. A remote crash of brushwood told of some other beast on his depredations, or some night-belated traveller groping his way through the narrow path. Still she chanted on. The far, faint echoes of the chanticleers died into distance, the crashing of the branches grew nearer. No wild beast that, but a man's step, a man's form in the moonlight, stalwart and strong, on one arm slept a little child, in the other hand he held his gun. Still she chanted on.

Perhaps, when her husband last looked forth, he was half ashamed to find what a fear he felt for her. He knew she would never leave the child so long but for some direst need—and yet he may have laughed at himself, as he lifted and wrapped it with awkward care, and loading his gun and strapping on his horn, opened the door again and closed it behind him, going out and plunging into the darkness and dangers of the forest. He was more singularly alarmed than he would have been willing to acknowledge.

As he drew nearer the heart of the forest, that intimation of melody seemed to grow more actual, to take body and breath, to come and go on long swells and ebbs of the night breeze, to increase with tune and words, till a strange, shrill singing grew ever clearer, and, as he stepped into an open space of moonbeams, far up in the branches, rocked by the wind, and singing, "How beautiful upon the mountains are the feet of him that bringeth good tidings, that publisheth peace," he saw his wife—but, great God in heaven! how?   Some mad exclamation escaped him, but without diverting her.   The child knew the singing voice, though never heard before in that unearthly key, and turned towards it through the veiling dreams.   With a celerity almost instantaneous, it lay, in the twinkling of an eye, on the ground at the father's feet, while his gun was raised to his shoulder and levelled at the monster covering his wife with shaggy form and flaming gaze—his wife so ghastly white, so rigid, so stained with blood, her eyes so fixedly bent above, and her lips, that had indurated into the chiselled pallor of marble, parted only with that flood of solemn song.

I do not know if it were the mother instinct that for a moment lowered her eyes—those eyes, so lately riveted on heaven, now suddenly seeing all lifelong bliss possible. A thrill of joy pierced and shivered through her like a weapon, her voice trembled in its course, her glance lost its steady strength, fever flushes chased each other over her face, yet she never once ceased chanting.   She was quite aware that if her husband shot now the bullet must pierce her body before reaching any vital part of the beast—and yet better that death, by his hand, than the other.   But this her husband also knew, and he remained motionless, just covering the creature with the sight. He dared not fire lest some wound not mortal should break the spell exercised by her voice.

Now and then he examined his gun to see if the damp were injuring its charge, now and then he wiped the great drops from his forehead.   Again the cocks crowed with the passing hour—the last time they were heard on that night. Cheerful home sound then, how full of safety and all comfort and rest it seemed! What sweet morning incidents of sparkling fire and sunshine, of gay household bustle, shining dresser, and cooing baby, of steaming cattle in the yard, and brimming milk-pails at the door!

Now as she sung on in the slow, endless, infinite moments, the fervent vision of God's peace was gone. Just as the grave had lost its sting, she was snatched back again into the arms of earthly hope. In vain she tried to sing, "There remaineth a rest for the people of God"—her eyes trembled on her husband's, and she could think only of him, and of the child, and of happiness that yet might be, but with what a dreadful gulf of doubt between! She shuddered now in the suspense; all calm forsook her; she was tortured with dissolving heats or frozen with icy blasts; her face contracted, growing small and pinched; her voice was hoarse and sharp—every tone cut like a knife—the notes became heavy to lift—withheld by some hostile pressure— impossible. One gasp, a convulsive effort, and there was silence—she had lost her voice.

The beast made a sluggish movement—stretched and fawned like one awakening—then, as if he would have yet more of the enchantment, stirred her slightly with his muzzle. As he did so a sidelong hint of the man standing below with the raised gun smote him; he sprung round furiously, and, seizing his prey, was about to leap into some unknown airy den of the topmost branches now waving to the slow dawn. The late moon had rounded through the sky so that her gleam at last fell full upon the bough with fairy frosting; the wintry morning light did not yet penetrate the gloom. The woman, suspended in mid-air an instant, cast only one agonized glance beneath, but across and through it, ere the lids could fall, a withering sheet of flame—a rifle-

134

crack, half heard, was lost in the terrible yell of desperation that bounded after it and filled her ears with savage echoes, and in the wide arc of some eternal descent she was falling—but the beast fell under her.

I think that the moment following must have been too sacred for us, and perhaps the three have no special interest again till they issue upon the shadows of the wilderness upon the white hills that skirt their home. The father carries the child hushed again into slumber, the mother follows with no such feeble step as might be anticipated; and as they slowly climb the steep under the clear grey sky and the paling morning star, she stops to gather a spray of the red rose berries or a feathery tuft of dead grasses for the chimney-piece of the log-house, or a handful of brown ones for the child's play —and of these quiet happy folk you would scarcely dream how lately they had stolen from under the banner and encampment of the great King Death. The husband proceeds a step or two in advance; the wife lingers over a singular footprint in the snow, stoops and examines it, then looks up with a hurried word. Her husband stands alone on the hill, his arms folded across the babe, his gun fallen—stands defined against the pallid sky like a bronze.

What is there in their home, lying below and yellowing in the light, to fix him with such a stare? She springs to his side. There is no home there. The log-house, the barns, the neighbouring farms, the fences, are all blotted out and mingled in one smoking ruin. Desolation and death were indeed there, and beneficence and life in the forest. Tomahawk and scalping knife, descending during that night, had left behind them only this work of their accomplished hatred and one subtle footprint in the snow.

For the rest—the world was all before them, where to choose.

135

ACTION
by C. E. Montague

CHARLES EDWARD MONTAGUE was born in 1867 and educated at Oxford. He adopted journalism as a profession, and his brilliantly sardonic novel, *A Hind Let Loose*, reveals an intimate if somewhat disillusioning knowledge of life in a newspaper office. For many years he was the chief leader writer for the *Manchester Guardian*, thus anonymously guiding public opinion on important issues of the day. During the European war, although almost over military age, he joined up and served with distinction, afterwards describing his experiences in a volume of trenchant stories entitled *Disenchantment*. In a further novel, *Right off the Map*, Montague exposes the foibles and fallacies of patriotism, but he was a great lover of his country, and his novels and tales show the English character at its best. *Action* is a story of this kind, showing how an Englishman who had lived to the utmost was prepared to go out on a top note. Montague died in 1928.

ACTION

BY

C. E. MONTAGUE

WHEN Christopher Bell awoke, just fifty-two, he woke
in one September morning to feel a slight numbi-
ness all down his right side. Some of the numbness was
in his right arm; a good deal of it in his right thigh,
along its outside; rather less in his right foot; and just
a little in his head—all over the hinterland of his right
ear.

It seemed a big percentage of him gone, "to sleep,"
at one time. He lay still for a minute, to let it pass off.
But it didn't, so he began to speculate. When he got
up would he be able to stand?; and no well-marked but
would his head go on working all right, until that bit
of it stiff? Just how hard a pinch would it mean but
to be, that some god or devil had given him in the
night?

He tried. Yes, he could stand (walk too) and sit up.
No portion of him was absolutely non-extant. But the
numbness went on. And somehow he couldn't feel sure
that some part of the right flank of his body or brain
would not give way, without notice, and give him a
cropper. You never know how deliciously sure you have
been of yourself, of every scrap of yourself, till all the
days of your health, till some small gadget inside you is
put out of action. Bell made this deep reflection while
going downstairs to his solitary breakfast. He kept one
hand on the banisters.

Christopher Bell was the reigning sovereign of a
respectable dynasty of "merchant princes" in Manchester. For several generations his clan had embraced
the higher civilization so far as English public schools

ACTION

BY

C. E. Montague

WHEN Christopher Bell was just fifty-two, he woke
up one September morning to feel a slight numbness all down his right side. Some of the numbness was
in his right arm; a good deal of it in his right thigh,
along its outside; rather less in his right foot; and just
a little in his head—all over the hinterland of his right
ear.

It seemed a big percentage of a man to "go to sleep"
at one time. He lay still for a minute, to let it pass off.
But it didn't. So he began to speculate. When he got
up would he be able to stand? And to walk straight?
Would his head go on working all right, with that bit
of it stiff? Just how hard a punch would it turn out
to be, that some god or devil had given him in the
night?

He tried. Yes, he could stand, walk, dress and shave.
No portion of him was absolutely on strike. But the
numbness went on. And somehow he couldn't feel sure
that some part of the right flank of his body or brain
would not give way, without notice and give him a
cropper. You never know how deliciously sure you have
been of yourself, of every scrap of yourself, till all the
days of your health, till some small gadget inside you is
put out of action. Bell made this deep reflection while
going downstairs to his solitary breakfast. He kept one
hand on the banisters.

Christopher Bell was the reigning sovereign of a
respectable dynasty of "merchant princes" in Manchester. For several generations his clan had embraced
the higher civilization so far as English public schools

and universities lead to such embraces. He had read
with understanding and relish, and he had travelled
with open eyes. He could value the great things in the
arts and in science—indeed, in the whole ampler life of
the race. And always, till now, his blood had pretty
well bubbled with health. He had rowed, run, swum
and ridden well. To his body, at forty years old, the
War had brought a second boyhood of happy absorption
in efforts merely physical.

Half-way through the War, the wife he had loved in
every tissue of body and soul had died of something
brought on by too passionate overwork for the cause.
The news came to Bell in a hospital where he had just
begun to grow a new skin on a face and hands well
flayed and charred by chemical warfare. He could
not see at the time, so a nurse read the telegram out.
His face was buried deep in a canary-coloured mask of
wadding stained with picric acid; so the nurse could not
tell how he took it—only knew that he thanked her very
civilly through the little blow-hole left for his mouth. I
fancy Bell was hanging on hard to the thought that he
still had two children, a boy and a girl, both in their
'teens. Soldiers, even educated ones, are apt to grow
sentimental, especially when wounded. Bell, the War
widower, lay, week by week, behind his fancy-dress
mask, staying his mind on an ingenuous vision of an
improved world to come after the War. He saw it as a
young man and a young woman standing in summer
twilight, under the stars, with their eyes all a-shine at
the loveliness of the life which it had taken so much
pain and shame to make possible for them.

Many soldiers hugged these quaint fancies, in their
bad times. They helped, for the moment. It was
afterwards that they had to be paid for. In the foul
enervatory air that filled England and Europe just after
the War, Bell's boy and girl drifted feebly into failure.
Both were married lovelessly now, each to another small
waste product of that waste-producing time. Some-

where out of Bell's sight these forfeited objects of his pride and joy were shuffling punily through life. He gathered that they were rather ashamed of him as an old slowcoach provincial.

Bell was not given to wallowing in self-pity. Still, as you see, he had had his losses, like another.

Your British merchant prince, in these days, is prone to lose heart, get himself up as an owner of land and beeves, and melt weakly into the common herd of squires who know not, poor fellows, what it is to go on 'Change. Bell was different. He had pride. He stuck, as his father had done, to his post among the garrison of the smutty city that had done well by them. He lived where he could hear the Town Hall clock strike twelve when the traffic was quiet at night, and a north wind blowing. He liked the sound, he was so oddly civic a person.

To this old-fashioned hobby Bell added some cheap habits less rare in rich men. He stood on guard against his wealth, lest it should cut him off from the sight and sound of ordinary and unprincely men, for whom his regard had been redoubled by four years of living with them in the War. Because of this fad he nearly always went into the city by tram. This morning he walked the three hundred yards from his house to the tram's stopping-place with deliberate caution. He could not be sure of that sleepy right leg. He was still distrusting it temperately when he had taken his seat and was tendering his fare to town.

The conductor rejected the tender, at sight. "We doan't taake boottons," he said with civil composure.

Bell examined the bright disc that he had offered as a sixpence. Behold, a silvery trouser-button. Last night it had come off and he had slipped it into a pocket. He put his finger-tips ruefully up to his eyes. "I'm sorry," he said to the man as he gave the right coin.

"It's all reet, sir," the conductor said quietly. Once

143

he saw that no pulling of legs had been intended, his tact and sympathy were perfect.

He passed on to collect other fares. But a new care remained in Bell's mind. Sight, too? Was that going? Sight, touch, the whole sensory apparatus losing precision, entering on the long slope to decay—the silver cord going loose and the golden bowl crackling? When a man who has known how to read feels the first clap of the hand of Time on his shoulder, he has plenty of ready prompters to ruefulness; so many excellent poets have found handsome words for the mists and mellow poignancy of man's autumn, the lapse from the old vigour and vision into mere drug-taker's dreams while we are led down the avenue lined with over-blown roses, to lie in the dust at its end.

Bell kept his head. But his memory was beginning to bulge with lovely quotations not conducive to high spirits—"Bare ruined choirs where late the sweet birds sang," and all that lot.

The morning's office work did him good, while it lasted. He had more than most men of the gift of forgetting himself in the excitement of getting a job to come right—any old job, the dictating of letters, anything. And just now the affairs of his firm were of quite stirring interest. Like many others it had been making large losses for several years. Bell's game was to keep these losses as low as he could without stopping the work and wages of a moorland villageful of people who spun and wove cotton for Bell to sell for less than it cost to make it.

This unacquisitive practice brought Bell into great infamy. Most of his fellow-employers wanted to close all the factories down, or half-close them down, and leave the work-people to live on their fat. So Bell was an arrant traitor to them. Still, he was an employer; and so, to ardent Socialist eyes, he was a sucker of blood, *ex officio*. This lively cross-fire of censures braced Bell.

144

If it had to be woe unto you when all men spoke well of you, it might be safer when everyone slated you hard. Anyhow, it livened you up, like a good stinging wind that has blown across snow. While he schemed to find some not quite ruinous sale for the stuff that piled itself up at the mills, Bell could forget the thing that had clawed him in its clutch during the night.

But the clouds return after the rain: luncheon-time set his mind free to worry, the way your sore tongue returns to the amusement of hurting itself on the sharp point of a tooth lately broken. He lunched at the club; and, twice in the one hour it took him, his mind accused younger members of paying him the pestilential kind of unarguing deference which is really the civil refusal of youth to keep its communications open with age. Could they have noticed the way he walked down the stairs—a canny way, like a horse's when it is afraid on a slippery slope? One younger man opened the door of the billiard-room for him. Damn these good manners that ain't good at all!

Going home at twilight in the tram, Bell thought over all this so absorbedly that he kept his legs crossed the whole way. So, when he stood up, to get off, his right leg had gone clean asleep. It was only asleep in the common and blameless way. Still, he couldn't know that at first. For all he could tell, a second stroke might have fallen, and this time a real knock-out. Of course he kept his fears dark; still, he stepped off the car with such unconcealable care that the conductor slipped a friendly hand under his arm and led him slowly to the safety of the footpath, like a blind man or a drunk.

When Bell had walked a few yards by himself the extra numbness was gone. But the other numbness remained. And so did the feel of that patiently guarding hand under his arm. Of course, he had not needed it. Still, perhaps he would presently. "*Mene, mene,*" etc.—every wall seemed to be covered with sinister

145

shreds of writing. An object for everybody's protection, a call on everyone's forbearance—that was the kind of pest that he might become. Soon too, perhaps. This kind of plague crept on and on. It never turned back. Five years might bring an invalid chair and a male nurse to put him to bed and to see that he was carted securely about from place to place, to sprawl in the sun— Mentone, the Canaries, Egypt, all the places to which the decayed butterflies of our commonwealth were brought to lie out and doze in the warmth when too much eating and idling had brought them back all the way to the status of larvæ. Disgusting!

Bell gazed steadily into this smiling future while eating his dinner alone. From the table he went straight, like a man who knew what he needed, to that shelf in his study on which there were all his pet Alpine books. No other sport had ever so wholly ravished his soul as mountaineering. On the high snows it seemed as if magical fires were lit in your blood; the flame of life burned amazingly there; something was added unto a man as divine as whatever it is that makes its way into the vapid juice of a fruit and turns it to wine. Nowhere else in the world was the taste of success so wholly and indefeasibly sweet as it was on the tip of some spire of granite and ice that had all but turned you back in despair by the Daphnean rigour of its resistance. There, uplifted on the swell of the round earth, you could see how men had come to dream Gardens of Eden and Ages of Gold.

He took from the shelf a great climber's narratives of his greatest adventures. Two of these, in especial, could always entrance Bell as soon as he had read a few lines: their vividness gave him an almost physical sense of what they described. Each was a case of cutting steps up a long and extremely steep slope of ice. And in each case the slope had, at one point, ceased even to slope. For just a few feet of its height it had become as vertical as the wall of a house: each man of the party had had to hold himself into the perpendicular wall by sheer strength and good hand-hold against gravitation.

In each case the party had come safely through. But with how big a margin of safety, as engineers say? Bell wondered. A pretty big one, he fancied. Few good climbers slipped in really difficult places; all their faculties were bent up too intently for that, with danger about; they were above their own every-day form. But what if such a party were to try paring and paring away at that pretty wide margin? Something like an experiment, that! To what untold heights of achievement might not the party attain before all the margin was gone! And, of course, the party might be a party of one.

Bell had once had a holiday dream of climbing a crag that grew steeper and steeper till it was vertical first, and then overhung, more and more, but still he climbed on and on because the crag beetled out over a warm summer sea, so that, when he lost hold in the end, he would only fall from one pleasure into another, out of a mountaineer's paradise into a swimmer's. Cut out the old fear of death in that way, or some other, and —why, you could do anything.

As he sat back with the open book on his knees, a light wind stirred the trees in the garden. It may have been this that called up another old notion of his. This one had visited him in a wood close to Arras in 1916. During some dark windless weeks of that autumn the unfallen leaves had been fading inertly from green to a dull rusty red, and so down to a dead russet brown; the whole burning heart of the year was collapsing into shabby ashes. Then a night of frost came and then a gale on a day of broken sunshine thrown wildly about between clouds. As the gale stripped the trees it had seemed almost to blow them aflame; sparks of brave yellow flew in the air; the dun beech-leaves took light

147

and fell lustrously. Somehow the sight had filled Bell, at the time, with a wish that, when he had to go, he might do it like that—all astir and aglow, by one of the "violent" deaths, as most of the easy ones seemed to be called. Anything but to lie on a bed in a hushed room, with the lights low and life's jolly noises shut out, and people whispering among the shadows. One wrench for the undecayed body, and then unbreakable sleep—what end could equal it?

Now, almost suddenly, these several notions ran into one, as raindrops do on a newly wet window. Here was the moment to put into practice that old and sound choice of his between the long decrepitude of the flesh and the one clear-cut and summary pang that saves you it all. Suicide? Oh, no. But just to carry on, right to the end, the piquant experiment of paring and paring away that limiting and restraining margin of safety which mountaineers, even the boldest, keep in reserve. Had not all things conspired to free him from too much love of remaining alive—bereavement and baulked hope and now this first lick of fire from heaven, soon to blast the whole of him by degrees? Why, Fate had brought him the fulfilment of his old dream. No precipice in the world would now have an abhorred death waiting at its foot—merely a warm quiet sea of painless forgetfulness.

Only—he must be quick, before the accursed thing that was setting to work on him could pith so much of the vigour out of his body that he could not make his own way to a place—already he had a good place in his mind—where he might try the thing out.

At the end of September a savoursome blend of jollity and melancholy pervades the little Val d'Anniviers. The summer hotels of Zinal, at the head of the valley, are closing. Down the bridle path, through forests of fir, the hotel staffs stream along joyously, laden with the year's vintage of tips, to their snug winter homes in the Rhone Valley below. Reconverted, after four months of restraint and disguise, into young, natural Swiss men and women, they caper like Alpine cows let out in the spring. Shouting, chaffing and singing, they seem to flout with their merriment Nature's yearly menace to marmots and men. And Nature answers them back. Almost hour by hour the new snow creeps down the forested slopes of the valley and grizzles more of its firs; the morning dew lies late, and even at noon the weakening sun hangs lazily low above the main chain of the Alps. You feel, all about you, a big closing-in, the rustle of a heavy curtain falling upon a good time that is played out at last.

As Bell walked the six miles up from Vissoye to Zinal, he breasted that jovial current of waiters and chamber-maids thawed and rehumanized. Jove! they were good to see and to hear, with their jokes and catches and bold, friendly, unobsequious looks at every man and brother they met. But everything was good in this place. Even the smell of Vissoye and its pigs, as he passed, had been the smell of the best holiday of his boyhood. How he had liked life—every bit of it, coloured or plain, the high lights and the low! Even the jars had been part of the makings of the incomparable adventure. He wondered whether the mere feel of things—common things, all sorts of things—could ever have given anyone else such raptures of secret contentment as they had given to him.

He had made sure of a room at Zinal. He dined by the light of one lamp in a corner of the hotel's dining-room, now empty and shadowy. An elderly woman waited upon him; everyone else in the house had gone down the valley; she had been left for a week or two more, to cook, wait, make a bed and draw out a bill for anyone mad enough to turn up so belatedly. Bell had known her for thirty years—ever since her marriage to an old guide of his, recently killed on the Meije. She told him how their son Pierre was now a guide, too, rather to her alarm. She seemed amazingly glad to see Bell, as if he were a bit of some good old world that had been slipping away. And he——? she asked. Was he making a *grande course*, as always? Surely not, at this time of year?

He fenced with her apt, friendly questions. He felt like a liar. Indeed, he was one, pretty well, for he fully meant to deceive. He would go for a walk by himself, he said, after breakfast to-morrow—perhaps to the Arpitetta Alp only, perhaps rather further.

She looked at him sadly, with pleasant directness. "All alone, now!" she said simply. "And once it was you and Madame——and Gaspard and me. Ah! the good times." She had all humanity's fate in her face, like an old woman drawn by Rembrandt—hopes and happy love and then the dust of the day, dimming the roses, and then great loneliness and inconsolable tears. Would Monsieur have coffee, she asked.

Bell could face her no longer. It was too treacherous. No, he said, he would want nothing more. Let her go to bed early, like all the good marmots. So would he too, when he had smoked a little end of tobacco.

When she was gone, he sat by a fire of logs she had lit for him in the small smoking-room. To his surprise he found he had nothing to do. There could be no saying good-bye, no specious last letter to write, no will to be made, no manifesto of any sort to be left. People do not do such things just before unforeseen accidents —for the wood must look raw at the break. A real good tip for the widow of Gaspard would have to be left in an obvious place: that was all.

It went beyond having nothing to do. There was nothing to think. He had no fears of post-mortem torture to busy his brain, for the God of his faith was no fiend. He was equally void of covetous hopes of a sensational "good time" when the breath should be out of his body. So far he might have expected his mind to be free. The strange thing was to find how much of one's usual matter for thought is taken away if, in twenty hours or so, one will have nothing whatever to fix up or to see to, no house or business to run, no special beat to patrol, no arts or letters to care for, nor "public duties" to mind. It was a release. But it was a queer one—a kind of vacuous and disquieting freedom, such as a man might attain who has suddenly let off the pressure of gravitation, so that he needn't keep his feet down to the earth any more—in fact, couldn't press on it hard if he tried, and so couldn't get any purchase for putting forth his strength upon anything at all. Bell's released mind did its best to think firmly of what he was going to do the next day. But no firmness came; the levers of thought could not find any fulcrum; they worked at a loss, feebly and fumblingly.

He brought over the lamp to review the inn's tiny library—two shelves freakishly peopled with the printed leavings of guests lettered, half-lettered, unlettered, conventional, independent and odd. There was the common aphrodisiac novel of commerce; there was *The Vicar of Wakefield*, all golden sunshine and wit; there were Nat Gould and the wise, humane book of the great William James on the incessant endeavours of men to find or to imagine some larger life on which to rest the frail and soon-tired figure of their own. Yes, that was it: something to lean against: something sure not to give when you put your whole weight on it, in any state of yourself: that was where peace and strength were to be had; nowhere else. So he fancied, at least; he could not be sure; he was still in that vacuum where his thoughts had no pivot to work on: the wheels did not bite on the road: the cogs would not engage: he thought and he felt, but gropingly, not with the sure and eager drive of a mind and heart that have found themselves by forgetting themselves.

The place that Bell had picked for his purpose was on the west side of the Schallijoch. The Schallijoch, as you may know, is a dip in the ridge that joins the Weisshorn to the Schallihorn. Even the lowest point of the dip is more than twelve thousand feet high. The last part of the rise to the ridge from the west is up one of the steepest slopes of ice that are climbed. That is if you mount it where it is least steep. At some other points it is steeper than any slope that is climbed, or thought to be climbable. The surface of this wall of ice undulates like a sheet of hammered copper—here a concave patch and there a convex one. Though the wall at its steepest leans back from the straight, as a whole, it has parts—the upper halves of these hollows, and lower halves of these bulges—at which it is vertical for some feet at a time; and at two or three parts it even overhangs slightly. These last, avoided by climbers happily wedded to life, were what Bell had in mind. He would start up the wall at the steepest part he could find; as he went on he would make, at each stage, for the point where there seemed to be most of an over-hang. He would do the thing honestly—try all that was in him to bring the climb off, reach the ridge and prove that, in this small matter, man could do more than he knew. With careful timing he would be up, if up at all, about dusk. In that unlikely event he would carry the test a step further and try to come down his ice ladder by feel, in the dark, instead of descending the gentle snow slopes on the eastern side of the pass.

He worked out a time-table. Three hours' walk up to the Arpitetta Alp from Zinal. Three more up from the Alp to the foot of the final ice-wall. Half an hour for eating; another half-hour for sundries, and four for the ultimate work on the wall. Eleven hours in all. To-morrow's evening dusk would be over by seven. He would push off at eight in the morning.

Probably you would have thought him rather a pleasant sight as he quitted Zinal—the outward figure of a hale, fit mountaineer; just a little stricken with years, but vigorous; brindled, but not at all bald;

leanly and brownly good-looking; turning out by himself, with his axe under his arm and a little luncheon in his pocket, for a walk among the feet of old sporting friends like the Weisshorn and the Rothhorn. How can you tell by the looks of a man that he would not feel the point of a pin if you ran it into his thigh, or that this exemption from pain is causing any disturbance of his spirits?

Nobody was to be seen at the emerald Alp of Arpitetta. Like the almost deserted Zinal, like yesterday's valley path streaming with walkers carrying bundles, the empty hovels on the Alp recalled the sight of a whole countryside in flight before the army of an invader. The ashes left from the cheesemaker's fire were wet with drippings from the roof; the rough wooden crane used for swinging the cauldron over the flames flapped in a draught from the door. Outside, the intoxicant beauty of gentian and orchis was over for the year; the rich grass had spread back over the trodden mud of the milking-place; but snow was lying a few hundred feet higher up. The invader was near.

Bell's legs were liking the work. The numb one was numb, but it did not give out; it would not let him down. By one o'clock he had reached the tail end—some would call it the snout—of the big Weisshorn Glacier, eaten his rations and set a first foot on the rough convex of honeycombed ice, with water flushing out its millions of cells; for the sun was on it. He pawed the stuff tenderly with his axe. Perdition catch his soul but he did love it—strong as iron, carvable as cheese: what genius could have conceived so delicious a union of opposites if, by some disaster, no glaciers had been made?

By three o'clock he was through the freak shapes of the icefall, across the snowfield above it, and close to the wall that he sought. Yes, its great width and height had the wavy surface that he remembered. It showed like a vast relief map of some low rolling downland, modelled in ice and then set up to stand on its edge. Off to his right, as he looked up, the general angle was easiest. That was the regular way—very steep but quite practicable. That was of no use for his purpose. Far away to his left the slope looked ferocious enough. But down it an almost continuous fall of stones of all sizes, broke away from the sun-warmed rocks of the Weisshorn, came sliding and hissing, or bounding and smashing explosively. That was no use either. That way would be suicide, not experiment.

He soon saw what he wanted—almost directly above him. There, nearly all the way up to the ridge, the ice was steep and bare and blue, and the face of it waved more at this place than anywhere else. Several broad bosses of rocks must have underlain the smooth surface. Over these the close-fitting ice swelled like a stocking upon a bent knee. Up to the centre of each of these bosses the ice bulged out overhangingly; just above each centre it would recede at a more merciful angle; but nowhere in the whole thousand feet of ascent would a man have a foothold to stand on, unless he made it.

Bell conscientiously tightened each boot-lace and puttee-string. Then he set off for the point where he had descried the best overhang. It was half-way, as he judged, to the top of the wall. If he should conquer that one, then he would look for another, more bulgy.

He cut his steps with almost fanatical care. He had a disagreeable sense of doing something furtive: he couldn't help asking himself, against his own will, "What if somebody saw?" damn somebody, another part of him said. Still, he cut every step as if he defied the whole solar system to say that it was not the work of a good craftsman bent upon keeping alive. So he rose slowly. It took a good two hours' work to mount a third of the way to the ridge. But then he was close to what mattered more—the great bulge that he was making for.

The bulge stood out like a gigantic blister upon the

face of the ice. It must have been forty feet in diameter and it jutted so much that a stone dropped from its outermost point would only have touched the stone again some fifty feet lower. So the climax had come. To reach that outermost point he would have to climb up for twenty feet as you climb up the underside of a ladder that leans against a wall. And he would have to make the ladder, rung by rung, as he climbed it, fashion each rung out of the ice with his axe, held in one hand, while with the other hand and both feet he clung to three of the rungs made already, and held up the body against the drag of its weight. Every rung would have to be made like a letter-box in a door, big enough for the toe of a boot to go in, but so shaped that, when a hand entered, the fingers could bend down inside and grip as you grip the top of a fence. The grand, the crucial question was how long one hand and one arm could hold the body in to the projecting ice-wall. For what part of the two hours or so that the other labouring hand might require to cut that fantastical staircase? Of course, if his axe should slip out of his hand, or if one step should break, that would end the affair. But away with the thought of any such bungling.

The moment the overhang started, Bell discovered the theory of gravitation to be exceedingly true. The work was amazingly hard. When he had carved five letter-boxes, and used them, an hour had gone. He carved five more and observed that daylight was failing. Behind his back an unsensational sunset was going on at its ease. His left hand was chilled almost dead with all the ice it had gripped; his right wrist was swollen and sore with the intensity of the axe-work; his right knee had begun to shake as uncontrollably as chattering teeth; he heard his breath as if it were somebody else's; it made a dry rustling noise, like a bird struggling silently in the hand.

The centre of the boss was now, he reckoned, some eight feet above his head. Beyond it he could see nothing, as yet, but a tranquil sky with a rose-coloured flush dying out of it. Five letter-boxes more, he thought, might take him up to the nipple of this frozen breast and bring the receding slope of its upper half into his sight.

It was just at this very point that it struck him as clear, sober matter of fact, that he could not get up those eight feet. His strength was running out fast; one more good letter-box was all that he could conceive himself able to make. He made it, hacking away with slow, painful strokes, his axe-handle slippery with his sweat. He reached up his left hand to grab the new hold and dragged a foot up to its new place below. Then, just to go down fighting, he went through the movement of starting to chip out yet another step. Second by second the effort held out; his strokes were the taps of a child; his wrist felt like breaking; yet somehow he finished the hole and forced his left hand to rise up to it; then he even hauled up in its turn a right foot of infinite weight: the poor quivering knee had to straighten out next, and did it, after a long, doubtful struggle. But that was the end, he felt, of all possible effort.

By this time all his senses had the morbid exaltation that will sometimes come of fierce physical effort. His mind was at leisure, after a fashion. He was fully aware of the sunset; he did not miss the charm of its sabbatical charm: the majesty and mystery of mountains were still there, all right. A verse he had liked as a boy came into his head, as beautiful things that have built themselves into your mind are apt to do at a crisis—as people who once went to church will cry out, "Oh, God!" when a smash comes.

> "And here indeed might death be fair
> If death be dying into air,
> And souls evanished mix with the
> Illumined sky, eternal sea."

But no pretty dying for him, if death could be still headed off. He started desperately to try again, sweating and straining. No good: the feeble strokes of his axe scarcely scratched the bare ice: his left hand was frost-bitten now, past feeling anything. Only five feet to relative safety, but five more than any spur worn by his will could drive the spent body. "I'm done," he said, and ceased to struggle upwards.

Some innate impulse to take the thing well, and not to let human dignity down at a pinch, kept him resolved to hold on, foot and hand, to the last moment possible. While he clung so, the sun left him. A high Alpine sunset is sudden, like tropical ones. A cold, sharp-edged shadow raced up from the valley, chasing the sunlight before it. Pursuer and fugitive scudded up over the tops of the firs and across the bright green of the Alp that Bell had passed, and then up the ice-fall and on up the wall till the shadow came down like a great frigid hand on the sweaty back of his neck. Next moment the last warmth and light fleeted up out of sight, over the bulge. As his gaze followed, his cheeks felt the sting of a few falling granules of ice; little chips of it, rather; even a few rather big ones. A trickle of icy scraps seemed to be sliding down the upper half of the bulge, to dive into space on reaching its centre —most of them clear of his back.

Queer! Was an ice avalanche coming? No need to suppose it, though. Glaciers, crushed and huddled things, always heaving and cracking, played curious tricks and ground out all sorts of freaked rubbish. Oh! let the ice do what it liked; all his business with it was done; all that he could now attend to was a kind of dream noise, big, muted, and almost asleep, that the torrent was making, enormously far off, down in the blackening trench of the valley—that and a kind of emotional dream of himself, the dying man was doing his best to leave as was meet—a figure at which he

could look, as it were, from outside, and dreamily feel
it to be rather touching.

Into this semi-dream there managed to enter, also, a
sound more abrupt—a little noise like the low, startled
cry that some women give when they see a horse fall
or a big window smashed. The cry worked itself into
his dream, but also it roused him. "Getting light-
headed," he thought. But he wasn't. Almost as quick
as that thought, a new sound, a light hissing rub, rushed
down to his ears and an ice-axe slid over the bulge
overhead and out into the air; it whizzed past the back
of his head.

To anyone versed in high mountains an ice-axe loose
and falling in any such place is a portent of horror, like
a child's pony galloping riderless home, or a boat adrift,
bottom uppermost, in a Thames lasher. It means that
somebody may have just lost the power to move, without
help, at a place where a man unable to move will soon
be unable to live. Suddenly Bell's mind took eyes to
itself: it saw a party of some sort above him, trying to
cut its way down the ice-wall, straight towards the
deadly bulge that now beetled over himself. At this
hour! And by such a route! They must be mad:
so he thought—forgetting himself. And now one of them
was disabled—perhaps had disabled the whole of his
party—had tethered it to the ice-wall. The idea was
frightful to Bell.

Another sound came. From somewhere not far overhead there broke, like an explosion, the singular cry that
Swiss peasants and some mountaineers employ as a
long-distance hail. No other noise of purely human
production will carry so far. Harsh, wild and long, it
starts, as the noise of a rocket does, at its maximum
loudness, and then wails itself out in a dying fall that
has an effect of collapse into despair. Though com-
monly uttered on quite cheerful occasions, it might be
the passionate scream of some wretched animal terrified
by the solitude of a desolate place and trying to empty

into one impetuous lamentation all its burden of loneliness and desire.

Bell held his breath as the sinking shriek thinned away
into silence. Then he counted off the seconds half-
aloud, by guesswork, as bomb-throwers learnt to do in
the War. The count ran to seven—eight—nine, and just
as Bell was muttering "ten," the great yell smashed into
the silence again. Yes, he had expected that. Someone
above was in the last extremity of danger—was trying
the last shift of all, the most all-but-hopeless of all—was
sending out the Alpine signal of distress into this stone
and snow desert where autumn and night had joined to
make it utterly certain that no answer would come. It
was like praying to God, for dear life, that a well of
fresh water might open itself in the dry middle of the
Sahara.

Up to that point of time, as you have seen, Bell had
been the kind of dual creature that most of us are for
nearly the whole of our days. Part of him had toiled,
sweated and ached, and another part of him had been
sorry for that one. But, from the moment the second
yell came, this two-fold arrangement was somehow
abolished. All craving or any need for any part of
himself to be troubled about any other was over: now
there was nothing at all to work out any more, no next
move to be consciously planned, nor hesitant will to be
coaxed or hustled, nor any plaguey choice to be made.
All of the man was one unit at last, and it lived intently
and intensely, moved by some force which it had no
more desire to question than flames have to ask, "Why
burn upwards?"

The next mystery was that out of the mind so suddenly
lightened there seemed, as it were, to overflow lightness
into Bell's body of lead. Strangely empowered, his left
foot was rising already to thrust itself into the next
letter-box; almost gaily his right arm, freed from its
preoccupation with pain, was beginning to hack a new
hand-hold above. How long it took him to make it he

could not have told, then or after. For time, too, was abolished; long trains of executive, practical thought could run on to their end instantaneously; courses, whole courses, of study of relevant things—the state of the ice, minute changes of gradient, the swift regelation following sundown—were carried out without any sense of duration. One of the revelatory trances had come, in which even a plain man sees for once that an eternity need not be long and that in a single moment he may have everlasting life.

A minor, but still a piquant discovery was that he had never really known till now what it was to cut a good sizable strip off that old margin of safety which he had imagined himself to have all but used up. His new letter-boxes now are marvels of sketchy adequacy; they were high art in the skimpiness of the means that they took to their end; triumphs of confident "cheek" to Nature; they bluffed that august power quite wittily. Almost before the vocalist overhead had completed the long S.O.S. of the mountains—it takes three minutes in all—Bell had his chest up to the dead centre of the bulge and saw what he had come for.

Some thirty feet higher up, a woman in mountain kit, with no axe and no hold for hand or foot, was dangling at a long rope's end. Her body revolved a little as it hung against the steep ice, but she was making no voluntary movement. The rope constricting her chest was held with one straining hand by a man perched eighty feet higher up. He was clearly unable to move, hand or foot, without being dragged off his stance by the weight of the woman. He stood on one foot—his right: it seemed to be firmly placed on a tiny step; and a little above his head, he had the pick of his axe driven well into the ice. To the steep bracket thus formed by the axe-head the man was holding on stoutly with his right hand.

The sorry sight explained itself. The woman must have been cutting steps down the slope; she must have slipped from a step, and dropped her axe with the shock. The man had checked her fall well, but both were hung up as immovably as a couple of stoats nailed to a gamekeeper's door. And now the rope must be slowly killing the woman. Just as Bell's head topped the bulge she called out in a strangled voice to the man, "Can you cut the rope, Teddy? I'm done, anyhow. Think of the kiddies. You *must*." The man held on.

Bell gave tongue as loudly as the dry brown fur lining his mouth would allow. "Well held, sir!" he roared. "It's all right. I'm coming."

Not once in a long and respectable Alpine career had Bell thought he would ever entrust his person to ledges quite so narrow as those on which he made the rest of his way up to that pendent woman. And yet he had never, in any hard place, felt such absolute freedom from any uneasiness. As he romped up, he sang out, at intervals, "There in three minutes," "Just two minutes more," "Only one minute now," "Half a shake—I'm just there." Then he arrived. He cut a big step close to where the woman's feet hung, planted his own firmly on it, and then stooping and straightening up again, took the weight of her, sitting, on his right shoulder. Lest she be fainting he put up his right hand behind her, to hold her in place.

She was none of your fainters, though she was white, yellow, greenish, all the bad colours that beauty itself may have to put on in bad times. "She's a good 'un," Bell thought, as she sat quiet, panting.

"*You're* a great sportsman," she gasped, when she had breath enough.

Feeling all the weight off the rope of a sudden, the man above shouted down thickly, "Sure you have got her, sir?"

"Right as rain," she called up from her perch.

Bell added, "Leave the rope slack and dig in. We'll come up when you're comfy."

The man gave a tuneless yodel of joy and was plying

his axe the same instant; chips and wedges of ice came pelting down from the great step that he must be cutting, from which to make the whole caravan fast. In five minutes he ceased hacking, braced himself, drew in the slack of the rope and announced that now he could hold up a cow for a day.

Bell let the woman cannily down till her feet found a trim ledge that he had managed to scratch out while holding her up. But some four or five feet of smooth ledgeless ice intervened between this and the lowest step the woman had cut, coming down, before she slipped off. Some new ones had to be made. "Care to cut 'em?" Bell asked. "Or shall I?"

She ruefully opened the hands in which no axe was now held. "I dropped it," she said, "like a mug. I feel sick with shame."

"Have mine," he said, holding it out.

Her open boy face shone with joyous relief, as if at a gift of free absolution from sin. Even now their lives hung on this axe that he was entrusting to her, the convicted axe-dropper. She took it. "You're a very generous person," she said. "Now I'll unrope and go up by myself, and you shall tie on."

He shook his head firmly. "You mustn't unrope."

Her eyes broke out in a quick sparkle of anger. "You've *got* to rope up," she said, flushing. "I know that I've done a dud thing and can't preach. But what about you? Climbing alone! Coming up out of no-where, almost at night! Up a worse slope than this beast! Think it bears looking into? Eh? Well, do you mean to rope up, or shall both of us climb in this way that you seem to think right?"

Bell fairly funked the scrutiny of the young woman's fiery simplicity. When once simplicity sets out to inquire, what else is so penetrating "Well, you tie on in the middle," he said, "and I at the end."

"That's fair," she agreed. A few feet of spare rope were let down by her husband. In two or three minutes, at most, the man who would have shuffled off the mortal coil was securely girt with the most delectable of its loops, the cheerfullest symbol of human determination not to withdraw from the banquet of life—only to salt a dish now and then with a few little hazards.

The last daylight was gone when the three stood safe on the level roof of the ridge, scrunching its gritty, granular snow somewhat shyly, though partly kept in countenance by the dark, which is itself a shy, friendly thing.

Bell, now a mere dual creature again, had been wondering, all the way up the last flight of ice-stairs, how he could give these married lovers a chance to re-assert their lately threatened right to possession of each other's lips. Best, he thought, just to turn his back on them when he got up, and try to look busy, coiling the rope.

But they also seemed to have some sort of plan. The man was waiting above the last step, to shake Bell by the hand—really to shake him—and mumbling something which Bell did not desire to make out more clearly. The cup of his consternation was filled when the lady raised his disengaged hand to her lips, a gesture for which he had not been prepared by her vivacity lower down.

Then, with one silent consent, they all stampeded away from the key of emotion.

"You travel light, sir," said Bell, just to say something trivial. The other two seemed to carry not so much as a prune or a biscuit between them.

"Well—" said the man, and then Bell imagined the two must be having a quiet laugh in the dark.

"Oh! I know I can't talk," Bell admitted. "The fact is, I didn't expect to be coming right over the pass."

"Same here," said the man. "We just walked up from Randa—meant to go only as far as the hut for the

Weisshorn, eat our sandwiches there and go back to dinner. Then—it *was* rather mad, but the snow was so toppingly good—we thought we might just rush the Scallijoch before dark, sleep at Zinal and come back to-morrow."

"Gosh! it was rash!" exclaimed Bell, off his guard. He felt sure, the next instant, the man was quite seeing the humour of such a rebuke from such a sinner. Hastily trying to cover the slip, Bell made another. He asked, "How on earth did you miss the way down?"

The man didn't exactly say, "How did *you* miss the way up?" but he did say, "Yes, it was stupid, but—well, you know how it isn't so easy to see a way down from above as it is from below?"

"Hadn't we better push off?" said Bell, rather hurriedly. "We'll be getting friz up here." But it was not the cold that he minded. It was the heat. It felt as if he couldn't move his tongue without burning his fingers.

The three truants had luck. Just such a full moon as they needed, not having a lantern, was on the point of rising from behind the snowy mass of the Mischabel, beyond the forest glen of the Visp. The mounting light could no longer contain itself. Its bright animation was pulsing up the dark violet of the sky in tremulous waves. It would be easy, by such a light as was coming, to follow the downward track left by the couple, on their way up, almost to the door of the old Weisshorn hut, a refuge squat, squalid, flea-haunted and cramped, but divinely rich in raw materials for manufacturing heat, against a long night of hard frost.

At any time it is rather exciting to walk in the dark, and in silence, with anyone whom you like but don't yet know very well. What is he thinking about? You? And, if so, in what way? Barring you? Liking you? Wanting to throw down the conventional fence and talk frankly? An hour or two of this blindfold contact between mind and mind may so work on them both that when their eyes meet under a lamp at the end of the walk it may feel as if they had had a long and intimate conversation, leaving each of them just slightly anxious to know that the other has taken nothing amiss. Even thus, with friendly and deprecating looks, did they regard each other by candle-light two hours later among the strong shadows and smells of the hut.

In ten minutes more the man's wife, who had walked like a true Joan of Arc, was exercising the blessed privilege of healthy tired young people of thirty or so. While she slept like a prosperous babe, her man and Bell smoked as they lay in the hay at the big sleeping-shelf's other end. Smoking helps to keep talk good. A man can puff at his pipe between each thing he really wants to say and the next. No gap-filling rubble is required.

Bell ascertained that the man's name was Gollen and that he was a doctor—the Harley Street species of doctor. Bell gave in return his own name and description. Then they enjoyed one of those unembarrassing pauses. Then Bell said, somewhat brusquely, "There's one thing we have to get straight."

"Go it," said Gollen.

"You seem to imagine you're under some sort of obligation to me."

"Well, you see, we're alive. And, before you appeared, our number was up."

"So was mine."

"Oh, every one's is, in a sense! 'All condemned to death,' doesn't somebody say, 'with an indefinite reprieve'? But ours wasn't indefinite. We were booked to go west in five minutes."

"I was to do it in one. In less. I should have dropped off my holds in ten seconds if you people hadn't blown in."

"Hullo?"

"Sure thing. I was done. I had never known until then how far doneness could go. That's how it felt, anyhow. Then your wife's axe came along. That by itself held me on for a jiffy or two. And then you hollered—gad! you *can* holler—and everything changed. There was something new in me, or around me, at work on me, somehow. Every bit of soreness and worry and funk was taken right off me—nothing was left in the world but one energy—just an enveloping, mastering sort of a push. It went up like a flame and it took me along—it made everything easy and light. And it wasn't only a thing in the mind. Old brother body himself was roped into the movement; some of the waft of this impulse seemed to get itself into my muscles. D'you follow these ravings?"

"Rather. Physicians aren't the fools that they were. We don't go on missing out what the mind—or the soul, if you like—has to say to all the dynamic affairs of the body."

Bell puffed his pipe for a while. Then he said: "See? That's how you two preserved me. So, if thanking is what we're about, thank y' kindly."

Gollen, too, smoked in silence for the next minute or two, before asking: "The ice overhung where you were when I first caterwauled?"

"Can't tell you the angle. Hadn't got a clinometer thing. Of course, it wasn't a motoring road."

Gollen laughed. Bell liked Gollen's face when he laughed, so far as it could be seen among the tangle of wry shadows thrown about the hut by a small flame that still leapt in the stove. Gollen's face made Bell think of a trade term—"good ordinary." He had blunt, goodish features, strong and good-tempered. A straight, friendly man, you would say, and easily amused; a good man to be in a hole with. Bell enjoyed such men. They made the world go round. As he was thinking so, Gollen suddenly asked: "I say—why did you do it?"

As Bell did not answer at once, Gollen added: "Of course, it's cheek—asking. Tell me to go to hell, if you like, and I'll warmly approve. Only—well, I'm a doctor."

Bell cut the thing short. He answered at once what Gollen might go on to ask in another few minutes: "Yes —the spring's running dry. The salt losing its savour, you know—the wine going flat. And worse coming."

Again Gollen did the bold thing. "Any particular evil?" he said.

Bell liked the man. And when two men would both have been dead a few hours ago if either had failed at a pinch, they may soon get on terms. Bell avowed the whole business—his symptoms, his surmises and disgusts, and his specious experiment.

Gollen listened as wise doctors do. "Did that numbness cramp you to-day?" he asked at the end.

"No. But it was there all the day—except just the time—ten minutes or so, I suppose—when—" Bell hesitated for a moment.

"When you were in action?" said Gollen.

"Action?"

"Oh, I don't mean just doing violent things out of doors—pressing triggers or lassoing cows! I mean getting every Jack fibre there is in your nature alive and utterly turned on to something outside you—absorbed in it, lost in it—every bit of your consciousness taken up into some ecstasy of endeavour that's passion and peace."

Bell nodded, and Gollen went on. "I guess the great artists—all sorts of 'em—know how to bring the fit on, or it comes when they're at the top of their form—they seem to get further and further above 'emselves—hold the note out in a way that we can't—bring every tissue they have in their being to bear on the effort to get a wee touch to come right. Saints, too, I suppose—the pukka ones, like Francis, the man at Assisi: they have the knack, too; they can get more alive; they've found how to exist at a sort of top pressure. I fancy all of us get just a glimpse of the thing now and then—of what

167

living *might* be, you know—at a great turn in a game, or when we're in love, or if some beautiful thing in a book bowls us over. Only, we can't hold the note, or we can't do it yet; the pitch is too high for our reach; so we flop back into flatness. But we shall get there, I do believe that. What we've done since we started as jelly-fish is to get more and more of ourselves into action, and we shall go on till we are as much more in action—real, true action—than now as we are now than when we were jelly-fish. Why, in a few thousand years we may all be able to live half our time as you lived to-day for ten minutes."

"Something in that," Bell assented.

Gollen apologized meekly. "Sorry to verge upon 'uplift.' Still, one can't always bother about the convention that talk has got to be pessimist piffle."

Bell nodded. Reigning conventions had few less dutiful followers than he.

They smoked again for a while. Presently Gollen said, "How goes the weather?" He rose and opened the door of the hut very quietly. Bell followed him out to the hut's tiny terrace.

Nothing at all was wrong with the night. Beyond the queenly white shape of Mont Rose the moon rode gloriously high, burnished and flashing with frost, above sleeping Lombardy. Crowned in new snow and bejewelled with sparkles of light, the Weisshorn, the greatest great lady in nature, looked as lovely to Bell as when the first sight of her pale supreme grace had taken his breath away in his youth. At the height where they stood the frost had silenced every trickle of water, leaving all space to be filled with subtler challenges to the ear. The air almost crackled with crispness; it was alive with the massed animation of millions of infinitesimal crystallizations. The Schalliberg Glacier, a little away to their right, had its own living whisper, the sum of the innumerable tiny creaks and fractures of its jostling molecules of ice. Up here, where the quiet of night was suffused with this audible stir of the forces fashioning the earth, it felt as if some murmurous joint voice of all existence were abroad and life itself were trying to make its high urgency felt.

"Pretty good," Gollen said presently.

"Yes, it's all right," answered Bell.

Gollen waited a minute or two. Then he asked, "Is it all right—enough?"

"Oh, yes," said Bell, "I'm sticking on."

YOUTH

by Joseph Conrad

YOUTH
by Joseph Conrad

JOSEPH CONRAD sprang from a race of Polish exiles and patriots, and was born in the Ukraine, in 1857. He was educated at Cracow, but perhaps the most significant circumstance about his early training was the fact that his father read the best English books to him. Conrad, however, did not actually learn the English language until after he went to sea. This career was his own choice, and he succeeded in it so well that he became a master in the British Merchant Service. His own experiences and those of the characters who came under his observation are recorded, in unsurpassed style, in novels and tales of the sea which became "classics" almost as soon as they were published. *Youth* contains the very essence of sea adventure, and the unquenchable bravery of young manhood is its inspiration. To the end of his life Conrad remained a foreigner in speech, but his prose has been the envy of many British-born authors, and wherever the sea is mentioned the name of Conrad will always be echoed.

YOUTH

BY

JOSEPH CONRAD

THIS could have occurred nowhere but in England, where men and sea interpenetrate, so to speak—the sea entering into the life of most men, and the men knowing something or everything about the sea, in the way of amusement, of travel, or of bread-winning.

We were sitting round a mahogany table that reflected the bottle, the claret glasses, and our faces as we leaned on our elbows. There was a director of companies, an accountant, a lawyer, Marlow and myself. The director had been a *Conway* boy, the accountant had served four years at sea, the lawyer—a fine crusted Tory, High Churchman, the best of old fellows, the soul of honour—had been chief officer in the P. & O. service in the good old days when mail-boats were square-rigged at least on two masts, and used to come down the China Sea before a fair monsoon with stun'-sails set alow and aloft. We all began life in the merchant service. Between the five of us there was the strong bond of the sea, and also the fellowship of the craft, which no amount of enthusiasm for yachting, cruising, and so on can give, since one is only the amusement of life and the other is life itself.

Marlow (at least I think that is how he spelt his name) told the story, or rather the chronicle, of a voyage:

"Yes, I have seen a little of the Eastern seas; but what I remember best is my first voyage there. You fellows know there are those voyages that seem ordered for the illustration of life, that might stand for a symbol of existence. You fight, work, sweat, nearly kill yourself, sometimes do kill yourself, trying to accomplish some-

175

thing—and you can't. Not from any fault of yours. You simply can do nothing, neither great nor little—not a thing in the world—not even marry an old maid, nor get a wretched 600-ton cargo of coal to its port of destination.

"It was altogether a memorable affair. It was my first voyage to the East, and my first voyage as second mate; it was also my skipper's first command. You'll admit it was time. He was sixty if a day; a little man, with a broad, not very straight back, with bowed shoulders and one leg more bandy than the other, he had that queer, twisted-about appearance you see so often in men who work in the fields. He had a nut-cracker face—chin and nose trying to come together over a sunken mouth—and it was framed in iron-grey fluffy hair, that looked like a chin-strap of cotton-wool sprinkled with coal-dust. And he had blue eyes in that old face of his, which were amazingly like a boy's, with that candid expression some quite common men preserve to the end of their days by a rare internal gift of simplicity of heart and rectitude of soul.

"What induced him to accept me was a wonder. I had come out of a crack Australian clipper, where I had been third officer, and he seemed to have a prejudice against crack clippers as aristocratic and high-toned. He said to me, 'You know, in this ship you'll have to work.' I said I had to work in every ship I had ever been in. 'Ah, but this is different, and you gentlemen out of them big ships . . . but there! I daresay you will do. Join to-morrow.'

"I joined to-morrow. It was twenty-two years ago; and I was just twenty. How time passes! It was one of the happiest days of my life. Fancy! Second mate for the first time—a really responsible officer! I wouldn't have thrown up my new billet for a fortune. The mate looked me over carefully. He was also an old chap, but of another stamp. He had a Roman nose, a snow-white, long beard, and his name was Mahon, but he insisted that it should be pronounced Mann. He was well connected; yet there was something wrong with his luck, and he had never got on.

"As to the captain, he had been for years in coasters, then in the Mediterranean, and last in the West Indian trade. He had never been round the Capes. He could just write a kind of sketchy hand, and didn't care for writing at all. Both were thorough good seamen, of course, and between those two old chaps I felt like a small boy between two grandfathers.

"The ship also was old. Her name was the *Judea*. Queer name, isn't it? She belonged to a man, Wilmer, Wilcox—some name like that; but he has been bankrupt and dead these twenty years or more, and his name don't matter. She'd been laid up in Shadwell Basin for ever so long. You may imagine her state. She was all rust, dust, grime—soot aloft, dirt on deck. To me, it was like coming out of a palace into a ruined cottage. She was about 400 tons, had a primitive windlass, wooden latches to the doors, not a bit of brass about her, and a big square stern. There was on it, below her name in big letters, a lot of scrollwork, with the gilt off, and some sort of a coat of arms, with the motto, 'Do or Die' underneath. I remember it took my fancy immensely. There was a touch of romance in it, something that made me love the old thing—something that appealed to my youth!

"We left London in ballast—sand ballast—to load a cargo of coal in a northern port for Bankok. Bankok! I thrilled. I had been six years at sea, but had only seen Melbourne and Sidney, very good places, charming places in their way—but Bankok!

"We worked out of the Thames under canvas with a North Sea pilot on board. His name was Jermyn, and he dodged all day long about the galley drying his handkerchief before the stove. Apparently he never slept. He was a dismal man, with a perpetual tear sparkling at the end of his nose, who either had been in

177

trouble, or was in trouble, or expected to be in trouble —couldn't be happy unless something went wrong. He mistrusted my youth, my common sense, and my seamanship, and made a point of showing it in a hundred little ways. I dare say he was right. It seems to me I knew very little then, and I know not much more now; but I cherish a hate for that Jermyn to this day.

"We were a week working up as far as Yarmouth Roads, and then we got into a gale—the famous October gale of twenty-two years ago. It was wind, lightning, sleet, snow, and a terrific sea. We were flying light, and you may imagine how bad it was when I tell you we had smashed bulwarks and a flooded deck. On the second night she shifted her ballast into the lee bow, and by that time we had been blown off somewhere on the Dogger Bank. There was nothing for it but go below with shovels and try to right her, and there we were in that vast hold, gloomy like a cavern, the tallow dips stuck and flickering on the beams, the gale howling above, the ship tossing about like mad on her side; there we all were, Jermyn, the captain, everyone, hardly able to keep our feet, engaged on that grave-digger's work, and trying to toss shovelfuls of wet sand up to windward. At every tumble of the ship you could see vaguely in the dim light men falling down with a great flourish of shovels. One of the ship's boys (we had two), impressed by the weirdness of the scene, wept as if his heart would break. We could hear him blubbering somewhere in the shadows.

"On the third day the gale died out, and by and by a north-country tug picked us up. We took sixteen days in all to get from London to the Tyne! When we got into dock we had lost our turn for loading, and they hauled us off to a pier where we remained for a month. Mrs. Beard (the captain's name was Beard) came from Colchester to see the old man. She lived on board. The crew of runners had left, and there remained only the officers, one boy, and the steward, a mulatto who answered to the name of Abraham. Mrs. Beard was an old woman, with a face all wrinkled and ruddy like a winter apple, and the figure of a young girl. She caught sight of me once, sewing on a button, and insisted on having my shirts to repair. This was something different from the captains' wives I had known on board crack clippers. When I brought her the shirts she said: 'And the socks? They want mending, I am sure, and John's —Captain Beard's—things are all in order now. I would be glad of something to do.' Bless the old woman. She overhauled my outfit for me, and meantime I read for the first time *Sartor Resartus* and Burnaby's *Ride to Khiva*. I didn't understand much of the first then; but I remember I preferred the soldier to the philosopher at the time. One was a man, and the other was either more—or less. However, they are both dead, and Mrs. Beard is dead, and youth, strength, genius, thoughts, achievements, simple hearts—all die. . . . No matter.

"They loaded us at last. We shipped a crew. Eight able seamen and two boys. We hauled off one evening to the buoys at the dock gates, ready to go out, and with a fair prospect of beginning the voyage next day. Mrs. Beard was to start for home by a late train. When the ship was fast we went to tea. We sat rather silent through the meal, Mahon, the old couple, and I. I finished first, and slipped away for a smoke, my cabin being in a deck-house just against the poop. It was high water, blowing fresh with a drizzle; the double dock gates were opened, and the steam-colliers were going in and out in the darkness with their lights burning bright, a great plashing of propellers, rattling of winches, and a lot of hailing on the pier-heads. I watched the procession of head-lights gliding high and of green lights gliding low in the night, when suddenly a red gleam flashed at me, vanished, came into view again, and remained. The fore-end of a steamer loomed up close. I shouted down the cabin, 'Come up, quick!' and then heard a startled voice say afar in the dark, 'Stop her,

sir.' A bell jingled. Another voice cried warningly,
'We are going right into that barque, sir.' The answer
to this was a gruff 'All right,' and the next thing was a
heavy crash as the steamer struck a glancing blow with
the bluff of her bow about our fore-rigging. There was
a moment of confusion, yelling, and running about.
Steam roared. Then somebody was heard saying, 'All
clear, sir.' . . . 'Are you all right?' asked the gruff
voice. I had jumped forward to see the damage, and
hailed back, 'I think so.' 'Easy astern,' said the gruff
voice. A bell jingled. 'What steamer is that?' screamed
Mahon. By that time she was no more to us than a
bulky shadow manœuvring a little way off. They
shouted at us some name—a woman's name, *Miranda*
or *Melissa*—or some such thing. 'This means another
month in this beastly hole,' said Mahon to me, as we
peered with lamps about the splintered bulwarks and
broken braces. 'But where's the captain?'

"We had not seen or heard anything of him all that
time. We went aft to look. A doleful voice arose hailing
somewhere in the middle of the dock, '*Judea* ahoy!' . . .
How the devil did he get there? . . . 'Hallo!' we shouted.
'I am adrift in our boat without oars,' he cried.

"A belated waterman offered his services, and Mahon
struck a bargain with him for half a crown to tow our
skipper alongside; but it was Mrs. Beard that came up
the ladder first. They had been floating about the dock
in that mizzly cold rain for nearly an hour. I was never
so surprised in my life.

"It appears that when he heard my shout, 'Come up,'
he understood at once what was the matter, caught up
his wife, ran on deck and across, and down into our
boat, which was fast to the ladder. Not bad for a sixty
year-old. Just imagine that old fellow saving heroically
in his arms that old woman—the woman of his life. He
set her down on a thwart, and was ready to climb back
on board when the painter came adrift somehow, and
away they went together.

180

"Of course in the confusion we did not hear him shouting. He looked abashed. She said cheerfully, 'I suppose it does not matter my losing the train now?' 'No, Jenny—you go below and get warm,' he growled. Then to us: 'A sailor has no business with a wife—I say. There I was, out of the ship. Well, no harm done this time. Let's go and look at what that fool of a steamer smashed.'

"It wasn't much, but it delayed us three weeks. At the end of that time, the captain being engaged with his agents, I carried Mrs. Beard's bag to the railway station and put her all comfy into a third-class carriage. She lowered the window to say, 'You are a good young man. If you see John—Captain Beard—without his muffler at night, just remind him from me to keep his throat well wrapped up.' 'Certainly, Mrs. Beard,' I said. 'You are a good young man; I noticed how attentive you are to John—to Captain—' The train pulled out suddenly; I took my cap off to the old woman; I never saw her again. . . . Pass the bottle.

"We went to sea next day. When we made that start for Bankok we had been already three months out of London. We had expected to be a fortnight or so—at the outside.

"It was January, and the weather was beautiful—the beautiful sunny winter that has more charm than the summer time, because it is unexpected, and crisp, and you know it won't, it can't, last long. It's like a windfall, like a godsend, like an unexpected piece of luck.

"It lasted all down the North Sea, all down Channel; and it lasted till we were three hundred miles or so to the westward of the Lizards; then the wind went round to the sou'-west and began to pipe up. In two days it blew a gale. The *Judea*, hove to, wallowed in the Atlantic like an old candle-box. It blew day after day: it blew with spite, without interval, without mercy, without rest. The world was nothing but an immensity

of great foaming waves rushing at us, under a sky low
enough to touch with the hand and dirty like a smoked
ceiling. In the stormy space surrounding us there was
as much flying spray as air. Day after day and night
after night there was nothing round the ship but the
howl of the wind, the tumult of the sea, the noise of
water pouring over her deck. There was no rest for her
and no rest for us. She tossed, she pitched, she stood
on her head, she sat on her tail, she rolled, she groaned,
and we had to hold on while on deck and cling to our
bunks when below, in a constant effort of body and
worry of mind.

"One night Mahon spoke through the small window
of my berth. It opened right into my very bed, and I
was lying there sleepless, in my boots, feeling as though
I had not slept for years, and could not if I tried. He
said excitedly:

" 'You got the sounding-rod in there, Marlow? I
can't get the pumps to suck. By God! it's no child's
play.'

"I gave him the sounding-rod and lay down again,
trying to think of various things—but I thought only of
the pumps. When I came on deck they were still at it,
and my watch relieved at the pumps. By the light of
the lantern brought on deck to examine the sounding-rod
I caught a glimpse of their weary, serious faces. We
pumped all the four hours. We pumped all night, all
day, all the week—watch and watch. She was working
herself loose, and leaked badly—not enough to drown
us at once, but enough to kill us with the work at the
pumps. And while we pumped the ship was going from
us piecemeal: the bulwarks went, the stanchions were
torn out, the ventilators smashed, the cabin-door burst
in. There was not a dry spot in the ship. She was
being gutted bit by bit. The long-boat changed, as if
by magic, into matchwood where she stood in her
gripes. I had lashed her myself, and was rather proud
of my handiwork, which had withstood so long the

182

malice of the sea. And we pumped. And there was no break in the weather. The sea was white like a sheet of foam, like a cauldron of boiling milk; there was not a break in the clouds, no—not the size of a man's hand —no, not for as much as ten seconds. There was for us no sky, there were for us no stars, no sun, no universe —nothing but angry clouds and an infuriated sea. We pumped watch and watch for dear life; and it seemed to last for months, for years, for all eternity, as though we had been dead and gone to a hell for sailors. We forgot the day of the week, the name of the month, what year it was, and whether we had ever been ashore. The sails blew away, she lay broadside on under a weather-cloth, the ocean poured over her, and we did not care. We turned those handles, and had the eyes of idiots. As soon as we had crawled on deck I used to take a turn round with a rope about the men, the pumps, and the mainmast, and we turned, we turned incessantly, with the water to our waists, to our necks, over our heads. It was all one. We had forgotten how it felt to be dry.

"And there was somewhere in me the thought: By Jove! this is the deuce of an adventure—something you read about; and it is my first voyage as second mate— and I am only twenty—and here I am lasting it out as well as any of these men, and keeping my chaps up to the mark. I was pleased. I would not have given up the experience for worlds. I had moments of exulta-tion. Whenever the old dismantled craft pitched heavily with her counter high in the air, she seemed to me to throw up, like an appeal, like a defiance, like a cry to the clouds without mercy, the words written on her stern: '*Judea*, London. Do or Die.'

"O! Youth! The strength of it, the faith of it, the imagination of it! To me she was not an old rattle-trap carting about the world a lot of coal for a freight— to me she was the endeavour, the test, the trial of life. I think of her with pleasure, with affection, with regret—as you would think of someone dead you have loved. I shall never forget her. . . . Pass the bottle.

"One night when tied to the mast, as I explained, we were pumping on, deafened with the wind, and without spirit enough in us to wish ourselves dead, a heavy sea crashed aboard and swept clean over us. As soon as I I got my breath I shouted, as in duty bound, 'Keep on, boys!' when suddenly I felt something hard floating on deck strike the calf of my leg. I made a grab at it and missed. It was so dark we could not see each other's faces within a foot—you understand.

"After that thump the ship kept quiet for a while, and the thing, whatever it was, struck my leg again. This time I caught it—and it was a saucepan. At first, being stupid with fatigue and thinking of nothing but the pumps, I did not understand what I had in my hand. Suddenly it dawned upon me, and I shouted, 'Boys, the house on deck is gone. Leave this, and let's look for the cook.'

"There was a deck-house forward, which contained the galley, the cook's berth, and the quarters of the crew. As we had expected for days to see it swept away, the hands had been ordered to sleep in the cabin—the only safe place in the ship. The steward, Abraham, however, persisted in clinging to his berth, stupidly, like a mule—from sheer fright, I believe, like an animal that won't leave a stable falling in an earthquake. So we went to look for him. It was chancing death, since once out of our lashings we were as exposed as if on a raft. But we went. The house was shattered as if a shell had exploded inside. Most of it had gone overboard—stove, men's quarters, and their property, all was gone; but two posts, holding a portion of the bulkhead to which Abraham's bunk was attached, remained as if by a miracle. We groped in the ruins and came upon this, and there he was, out of his mind; completely and for ever mad, with this sudden shock coming upon the fag-end of his endurance. We snatched him up, lugged him aft, and pitched him head first down the cabin companion. You understand there was no time to carry him down with infinite precautions and wait to see how he got on. Those below would pick him up at the bottom of the stairs all right. We were in a hurry to go back to the pumps. That business could not wait. A bad leak is an inhuman thing.

"One would think that the sole purpose of that fiendish gale had been to make a lunatic of that poor devil of a mulatto. It eased before morning, and next day the sky cleared, and as the sea went down the leak took up. When it came to bending a fresh set of sails the crew demanded to put back—and really there was nothing to do. Boats gone, decks swept clean, cabin gutted, men without a stitch but what they stood in, stores spoiled, ship strained. We put her head for home, and—would you believe it?—the wind came east right in our teeth. It blew fresh, it blew continuously. We had to beat up every inch of the way, but she did not leak so badly, the water keeping comparatively smooth. Two hours pumping in every four is no joke —but it kept her afloat as far as Falmouth.

"The good people there live on casualties of the sea, and no doubt were glad to see us. A hungry crowd of shipwrights sharpened their chisels at the sight of that carcass of a ship. And, by Jove! they had pretty pickings off us before they were done. I fancy the owner was already in a tight place. There were delays. Then it was decided to take part of the cargo out and caulk her top-sides. This was done, the repairs finished, cargo re-shipped; a new crew came on board, and we went out—for Bankok. At the end of a week we were back again. The crew said they weren't going to Bankok—a hundred and fifty days' passage—in a some-thing hooker that wanted pumping eight hours out of the twenty-four: and the nautical papers inserted again the little paragraph: '*Judea*. Barque. Tyne to Bankok, coals; put back to Falmouth leaky and with crew refusing duty.'

"There were more delays—more tinkering. The owner came down for a day, and said she was as right as a little fiddle. Poor old Captain Beard looked the ghost of a Geordie skipper—through the worry and humiliation of it. Remember he was sixty, and it was his first command. Mahon said it was a foolish business, and would end badly. I loved the ship more than ever, and wanted awfully to get to Bankok. To Bankok! Magic name, blessed name. Mesopotamia wasn't a patch on it. Remember I was twenty, and it was my first second mate's billet, and the East was waiting for me.

"We went out and anchored in the outer roads with a fresh crew—the third. She leaked worse than ever. It was as if those confounded shipwrights had actually made a hole in her. This time we did not even go outside. The crew simply refused to man the windlass.

"They towed us back to the inner harbour, and we became a fixture, an institution of the place. People pointed us out to visitors as, 'That 'ere barque that's going to Bankok—has been here six months—put back three times.' On holidays the small boys pulling about in boats would hail, '*Judea*, ahoy!' and if a head showed above the rail shouted, 'Where you bound to?—Bankok?' and jeered. We were only three on board. The poor old skipper mooned in the cabin. Mahon undertook the cooking and unexpectedly developed all a Frenchman's genius for preparing nice little messes. I looked languidly after the rigging. We became citizens of Falmouth. Every shopkeeper knew us. At the barber's or tobacconist's they asked familiarly, 'Do you think you will ever get to Bankok?' Meantime the owner, the underwriters, and the charters squabbled amongst themselves in London, and our pay went on. . . . Pass the bottle.

186

"It was horrid. Morally it was worse than pumping for life. It seemed as though we had been forgotten by the world, belonged to nobody, would get nowhere; it seemed that, as if bewitched, we would have to live for ever and ever in that inner harbour, a derision and a byword to generations of long-shore loafers and dishonest boatmen. I obtained three months' pay and a five days' leave, and made a rush for London. It took me a day to get there and pretty well another to come back —but three months' pay went all the same. I don't know what I did with it. I went to a music-hall, I believe, lunched, dined and supped in a swell place in Regent Street, and was back to time, with nothing but a complete set of Byron's works and a new railway rug to show for three months' work. The boatman who pulled me off to the ship said: 'Hallo! I thought you had left the old thing. *She* will never get to Bankok.' 'That's all *you* know about it,' said I, scornfully—but I didn't like that prophecy at all.

"Suddenly a man, some kind of agent to somebody, appeared with full powers. He had grog-blossoms all over his face, an indomitable energy, and was a jolly soul. We leaped into life again. A hulk came alongside, took our cargo, and then we went into dry dock to get our copper stripped. No wonder she leaked. The poor thing, strained beyond endurance by the gale, had, as if in disgust, spat out all the oakum of her lower seams. She was recaulked, new-coppered, and made as tight as a bottle. We went back to the hulk and re-shipped our cargo.

"Then, on a fine moonlight night, all the rats left the ship.

"We had been infested with them. They had destroyed our sails, consumed more stores than the crew, affably shared our beds and our dangers, and now, when the ship was made seaworthy, concluded to clear out. I called Mahon to enjoy the spectacle. Rat after rat appeared on our rail, took a last look over his shoulder, and leaped with a hollow thud into the empty hulk. We tried to count them, but soon lost the tale. Mahon said: 'Well, well! don't talk to me about the intelligence of rats. They ought to have left before, when we had that narrow squeak from foundering. There you have the proof how silly is the superstition about them. They leave a good ship for an old rotten hulk, where there is nothing to eat, too, the fools! . . . I don't believe they know what is safe or what is good for them, any more than you or I.'

"And after some more talk we agreed that the wisdom of rats had been grossly overrated, being in fact no greater than that of men.

"The story of the ship was known, by this, all up the Channel from Land's End to the Forelands, and we could get no crew on the south coast. They sent us one all complete from Liverpool, and we left once more—for Bankok.

"We had fair breezes, smooth water right into the tropics, and the old *Judea* lumbered along in the sunshine. When she went eight knots everything crackled aloft, and we tied our caps to our heads; but mostly she strolled on at the rate of three miles an hour. What could you expect? She was tired—that old ship. Her youth was where mine is—where yours is—you fellows who listen to this yarn; and what friend would throw your years and your weariness in your face? We didn't grumble at her. To us, aft, at least, it seemed as though we had been born in her, reared in her, had lived in her for ages, had never known any other ship. I would just as soon have abused the old village church at home for not being a cathedral.

"And for me there was also my youth to make me patient. There was all the East before me, and all life, and the thought that I had been tried in that ship and had come out pretty well. And I thought of men of old who, centuries ago, went that road in ships that sailed no better, to the land of palms and spices, and yellow sands, and of brown nations ruled by kings more cruel than Nero the Roman, and more splendid than Solomon the Jew. The old barque lumbered on, heavy with her age and the burden of her cargo, while I lived the life of youth in ignorance and hope. She lumbered on through an interminable procession of days; and the fresh gilding flashed back at the setting sun, seemed to cry out over the darkening sea the words painted on her stern, '*Judea*, London. Do or Die.'

"Then we entered the Indian Ocean and steered northerly for Java Head. The winds were light. Weeks slipped by. She crawled on, do or die, and people at home began to think of posting us as overdue.

"One Saturday evening, I being off duty, the men asked me to give them an extra bucket of water or so— for washing clothes. As I did not wish to screw on the fresh-water pump so late, I went forward whistling and with a key in my hand to unlock the forepeak scuttle, intending to serve the water out of a spare tank we kept there.

"The smell down below was as unexpected as it was frightful. One would have thought hundreds of paraffin lamps had been flaring and smoking in that hole for days. I was glad to get out. The man with me coughed and said, 'Funny smell, sir.' I answered negligently, 'It's good for the health they say,' and walked aft.

"The first thing I did was to put my head down the square of the midship ventilator. As I lifted the lid a visible breath, something like a thin fog, a puff of faint haze, rose from the opening. The ascending air was hot, and had a heavy, sooty, paraffiny smell.

"I gave one sniff, and put down the lid gently. It was no use choking myself. The cargo was on fire.

"Next day she began to smoke in earnest. You see it was to be expected, for though the coal was of a safe kind, that cargo had been so handled, so broken up with handling, that it looked more like smithy coal than anything else. Then it had been wetted—more than once. It rained all the time we were taking it back

189

from the hulk, and now with this long passage it got heated, and there was another case of spontaneous combustion.

"The captain called us into the cabin. He had a chart spread on the table, and looked unhappy. He said, 'The coast of West Australia is near, but I mean to proceed to our destination. It is the hurricane month, too; but we will just keep her head for Bankok, and fight the fire. No more putting back anywhere, if we all get roasted. We will try first to stifle this 'ere damned combustion by want of air.'

"We tried. We battened down everything, and still she smoked. The smoke kept coming out through imperceptible crevices; it forced itself through bulkheads and covers; it oozed here and there and everywhere in slender threads, in an invisible film, in an incomprehensible manner. It made its way into the cabin, into the forecastle; it poisoned the sheltered places on the deck, it could be sniffed as high as the mainyard. It was clear that if the smoke came out the air came in. This was disheartening. This combustion refused to be stifled.

"We resolved to try water, and took the hatches off. Enormous volumes of smoke, whitish, yellowish, thick, greasy, misty, choking, ascended as high as the trucks. All hands cleared out aft.

"Then the poisonous cloud blew away, and we went back to work in a smoke that was no thicker now than that of an ordinary factory chimney.

"We rigged the force-pump, got the hose along, and by and by it burst. Well, it was as old as the ship—a prehistoric hose, and past repair. Then we pumped with the feeble head-pump, drew water with buckets, and in this way managed in time to pour lots of Indian Ocean into the main hatch. The bright stream flashed in sunshine, fell into a layer of white crawling smoke, and vanished on the black surface of coal. Steam ascended mingling with the smoke. We poured salt water as into a barrel without a bottom.

"It was our fate to pump in that ship, to pump out of her, to pump into her; and after keeping water out of her to save ourselves from being drowned, we frantically poured water into her to save ourselves from being burnt.

"And she crawled on, do or die, in the serene weather. The sky was a miracle of purity, a miracle of azure. The sea was polished, was blue, was pellucid, was sparkling like a precious stone, extending on all sides, all round to the horizon—as if the whole terrestrial globe had been one jewel, one colossal sapphire, a single gem fashioned into a planet. And on the lustre of the great calm waters the *Judea* glided imperceptibly, enveloped in languid and unclean vapours, in a lazy cloud that drifted to leeward, light and slow; a pestiferous cloud defiling the splendour of sea and sky.

"All this time, of course, we saw no fire. The cargo smouldered at the bottom somewhere. Once Mahon, as we were working side by side, said to me with a queer smile: 'Now, if she would only spring a tidy leak—like that time when we first left the Channel—it would put a stopper on this fire, wouldn't it?' I remarked irrelevantly, 'Do you remember the rats?'

"We fought the fire and sailed the ship, too, as carefully as though nothing had been the matter. The steward cooked and attended on us. Of the other twelve men, eight worked while four rested. Every one took his turn, captain included. There was equality, and if not exactly fraternity, then a deal of good feeling. Sometimes a man, as he dashed a bucketful of water down the hatchway, would yell out 'Hurrah for Bankok!' and the rest laughed. But generally we were taciturn and serious—and thirsty. Oh! how thirsty! And we had to be careful with the water. Strict allowance. The ship smoked, and the sun blazed. . . . Pass the bottle.

"We tried everything. We even made an attempt to dig down to the fire. No good, of course. No man could

191   O

remain more than a minute below. Mahon, who went first, fainted there, and the man who went to fetch him out did likewise. We lugged them out on deck. Then I leaped down to show how easily it could be done. They had learned wisdom by that time, and contented themselves by fishing for me with a chain-hook tied to a broom-handle, I believe. I did not offer to go and fetch up my shovel, which was left down below.

"Things began to look bad. We put the longboat into the water. The second boat was ready to swing out. We had also another, a fourteen-foot thing, on davits aft where it was quite safe.

"Then, behold, the smoke suddenly decreased. We redoubled our efforts to flood the bottom of the ship. In two days there was no smoke at all. Everybody was on the broad grin. This was on a Friday. On Saturday no work, but sailing the ship, of course, was done. The men washed their clothes and their faces for the first time in a fortnight, and had a special dinner given them. They spoke of spontaneous combustion with contempt, and implied *they* were the boys to put out combustion. Somehow we all felt as though we each had inherited a large fortune. But a beastly smell of burning hung about the ship. Captain Beard had hollow eyes and sunken cheeks. I had never noticed so much before how twisted and bowed he was. He and Mahon prowled soberly about hatches and ventilators, sniffing. It struck me suddenly poor Mahon was a very, very old chap. As to me, I was as pleased and proud as though I had helped to win a great naval battle. O! Youth!

"The night was fine. In the morning a homeward bound ship passed us hull down—the first we had seen for months; but we were nearing the land at last, Java Head being about 190 miles off, and nearly due north."

"Next day it was my watch on deck from eight to twelve. At breakfast the captain observed, 'It's wonderful how that smell hangs about the cabin.' About ten, the mate being on the poop, I stepped down on the main deck for a moment. The carpenter's bench stood abaft the mainmast; I leaned against it sucking at my pipe, and the carpenter, a young chap, came to talk to me. He remarked, 'I think we have done very well, haven't we?' and then I perceived with annoyance the fool was trying to tilt the bench. I said curtly, 'Don't, Chips,' and immediately became aware of a queer sensation, of an absurd delusion—I seemed somehow to be in the air. I heard all round me like a pent-up breath released—as if a thousand giants simultaneously had said 'Phoo!'—and felt a dull concussion which made my ribs ache suddenly. No doubt about it—I was in the air, and my body was describing a short parabola. But short as it was, I had time to think several thoughts in, as far as I can remember, the following order: This can't be the carpenter—What is it? —Some accident—Submarine?—Volcano?—Coals, gas! —By Jove! we are being blown up—Everybody's dead—I am falling into the after-hatch—I see fire in it.

"The coal-dust suspended in the air of the hold had glowed dull-red at the moment of the explosion. In the twinkling of an eye, in an infinitesimal fraction of a second since the first tilt of the bench, I was sprawling full length on the cargo. I picked myself up and scrambled out. It was quick like a rebound. The deck was a wilderness of smashed timber, lying crosswise like trees in a wood after a hurricane; an immense curtain of soiled rags waved gently before me—it was the mainsail blown to strips. I thought, the masts will be toppling over directly; and to get out of the way bolted on all fours towards the poop-ladder. The first person I saw was Mahon, with eyes like saucers, his mouth open, and the long white hair standing straight up on end round his head like a silver halo. He was just about to go down when the sight of the main deck stirring, heaving up, and changing into splinters before his eyes, petrified him on the top step. I did not know that I had no hair, no eyebrows, no eyelashes, that my young moustache was burnt off, that my face was black, one cheek laid open, my nose cut and my chin bleeding. I had lost my cap, one of my slippers, and my shirt was torn to rags. Of all this I was not aware. I was amazed to see the ship still afloat, the poop deck whole—and, most of all, to see anybody alive. Also the peace of the sky and the serenity of the sea were distinctly surprising. I suppose I expected to see them convulsed with horror. . . . Pass the bottle.

"There was a voice hailing the ship from somewhere —in the air, in the sky—I couldn't tell. Presently I saw the captain—and he was mad. He asked me eagerly, 'Where's the cabin-table?' and to hear such a question was a frightful shock. I had just been blown up, you understand, and vibrated with that experience; I wasn't quite sure whether I was alive. Mahon began to stamp with both feet and yelled at him, 'Good God! don't you see the deck's blown out of her?' I found my voice, and stammered out as if conscious of some gross neglect of duty, 'I don't know where the cabin-table is.' It was like an absurd dream.

"Do you know what he wanted next? Well, he wanted to trim the yards. Very placidly, and as if lost in thought, he insisted on having the foreyard squared. 'I don't know if there's anybody alive,' said Mahon, almost tearfully. 'Surely,' he said gently, 'there will be enough left to square the foreyard.'

"The old chap, it seems, was in his own berth, winding up the chronometers, when the shock sent him spinning. Immediately it occurred to him—as he said afterwards —that the ship had struck something, and he ran out into the cabin. There, he saw, the cabin-table had vanished somewhere. The deck being blown up, it had fallen into the lazarette, of course. Where we had our breakfast that morning he saw only a great hole in the floor. This appeared to him so awfully mysterious, and

impressed him so immensely, that what he saw and
heard after he got on deck were mere trifles in comparison. And, mark, he noticed directly the wheel
deserted and his barque off her course—and his only
thought was to get that miserable, stripped, undecked,
smouldering shell of a ship back again with her head
pointing at her port of destination. Bankok! That's
what he was after. I tell you this quiet, bowed, bandy-
legged, almost deformed little man was immense in the
singleness of his idea and in his placid ignorance of our
agitation. He motioned us forward with a commanding
gesture, and went to take the wheel himself.

"Yes; that was the first thing we did—trim the yards
of that wreck! No one was killed, or even disabled,
but everyone was more or less hurt. You should have
seen them! Some were in rags, with black faces, like
coal-heavers, like sweeps, and had bullet heads that
seemed closely cropped, but were in fact singed to the
skin. Others, of the watch below, awakened by being
shot out from their collapsing bunks, shivered incessantly,
and kept on groaning even as we went about our work.
But they all worked. That crew of Liverpool hard cases
had in them the right stuff. It's my experience they
always have. It is the sea that gives it—the vastness,
the loneliness surrounding their dark stolid souls. Ah!
Well! We stumbled, we crept, we fell, we barked our
skins on the wreckage, we hauled. The masts stood, but
we did not know how much they might be charred down
below. It was nearly calm, but a long swell ran from
the west and made her roll. They might go at any
moment. We looked at them with apprehension. One
could not foresee which way they would fall.

"Then we retreated aft and looked about us. The
deck was a tangle of planks on edge, of planks on end,
of splinters, of ruined woodwork. The masts rose from
that chaos like big trees above a matted undergrowth.
The interstices of that mass of wreckage were full of
something whitish, sluggish, stirring—of something that

was like a greasy fog. The smoke of the invisible fire was coming up again, was trailing, like a poisonous thick mist in some valley choked with dead wood. Already lazy wisps were beginning to curl upwards amongst the mass of splinters. Here and there a piece of timber, stuck upright, resembled a post. Half of a fife-rail had been shot through the foresail, and the sky made a patch of glorious blue in the ignobly soiled canvas. A portion of several boards holding together had fallen across the rail, and one end protruded overboard, like a gangway leading upon nothing, like a gangway leading over the deep sea, leading to death—as if inviting us to walk the plank at once and be done with our ridiculous troubles. And still the air, the sky—a ghost, something invisible was hailing the ship.

"Someone had the sense to look over, and there was the helmsman, who had impulsively jumped overboard, anxious to come back. He yelled and swam lustily like a merman, keeping up with the ship. We threw him a rope, and presently he stood amongst us, streaming with water and very crestfallen. The captain had surrendered the wheel, and apart, elbow on rail and chin in hand, gazed at the sea wistfully. We asked ourselves, What next? I thought, Now, this is something like. This is great. I wonder what will happen. O! Youth!

"Suddenly Mahon sighted a steamer far astern. Captain Beard said, 'We may do something with her yet.' We hoisted two flags, which said in the international language of the sea, 'On fire. Want immediate assistance.' The steamer grew bigger rapidly, and by and by spoke with two flags on her foremast, 'I am coming to your assistance.'

"In half an hour she was abreast, to windward, within hail, and rolling slightly, with her engines stopped. We lost our composure, and yelled all together with excitement, 'We've been blown up.' A man in a white helmet, on the bridge, cried, 'Yes! All right! All right!' and he nodded his head, and smiled, and made soothing motions with his hand as though at a lot of frightened children. One of the boats dropped in the water, and walked towards us upon the sea with her long oars. Four Calashes pulled a swinging stroke. This was my first sight of Malay seamen. I've known them since, but what struck me then was their unconcern: they came alongside, and even the bowman standing up and holding to our main-chains with the boathook did not deign to lift his head for a glance. I thought people who had been blown up deserved more attention.

"A little man, dry like a chip and agile like a monkey, clambered up. It was the mate of the steamer. He gave one look, and cried, 'O! boys—you had better quit!'

"We were silent. He talked apart with the captain for a time—seemed to argue with him. Then they went away together to the steamer.

"When our skipper came back we learned that the steamer was the *Sommerville*, Captain Nash, from West Australia to Singapore *via* Batavia with mails, and that the agreement was she should tow us to Anjer or Batavia, if possible, where we could extinguish the fire by scuttling, and then proceed on our voyage—to Bankok! The old man seemed excited. 'We will do it yet,' he said to Mahon, fiercely. He shook his fist at the sky. Nobody else said a word.

"At noon the steamer began to tow. She went ahead slim and high, and what was left of the *Judea* followed at the end of seventy fathoms of tow-rope—followed her swiftly like a cloud of smoke with mast-heads protruding above. We went aloft to furl the sails. We coughed on the yards, and were careful about the bunts. Do you see the lot of us there, putting a neat furl on the sails of that ship doomed to arrive nowhere? There was not a man who didn't think that at any moment the masts would topple over. From aloft we could not see the ship for smoke, and we worked carefully, passing the gaskets with even turns. 'Harbour furl—aloft there!' cried Mahon from below.

"You understand this? I don't think one of those chaps expected to get down in the usual way. When we did I heard them saying to each other, 'Well, I thought we would come down overboard, in a lump—sticks and all—blame me if I didn't.' 'That's what I was thinking to myself,' would answer wearily another battered and bandaged scarecrow. And, mind, these were men without the drilled-in habit of obedience. To an onlooker they would be a lot of profane scallywags without a redeeming point. What made them do it—what made them obey me when I, thinking consciously how fine it was, made them drop the bunt of the foresail twice to try and do it better? What? They had no professional reputation—no examples, no praise. It wasn't a sense of duty; they all knew well enough how to shirk, and laze, and dodge—when they had a mind to it—and mostly they had. Was it the two pounds ten a month that sent them there? They didn't think their pay half good enough. No; it was something in them, something inborn and subtle and everlasting. I don't say positively that the crew of a French or German merchantman wouldn't have done it, but I doubt whether it would have been done in the same way. There was a completeness in it, something solid like a principle, and masterful like an instinct—a disclosure of something secret—of that hidden something, that gift of good or evil that makes racial difference, that shapes the fate of nations.

"It was that night at ten that, for the first time since we had been fighting it, we saw the fire. The speed of the towing had fanned the smouldering destruction. A blue gleam appeared forward, shining below the wreck of the deck. It wavered in patches, it seemed to stir and creep like the light of a glow-worm. I saw it first, and told Mahon. 'Then the game's up,' he said. 'We had better stop this towing, or she will burst out suddenly

fore and aft before we can clear out.' We set up a yell;
rang bells to attract their attention; they towed on. At
last Mahon and I had to crawl forward and cut the
rope with an axe. There was no time to cast off the
lashings. Red tongues could be seen licking the wilderness of splinters under our feet as we made our way back
to the poop.

"Of course they very soon found out in the steamer
that the rope was gone. She gave a loud blast of her
whistle, her lights were seen sweeping in a wide circle,
she came up ranging close alongside, and stopped. We
were all in a tight group on the poop looking at her.
Every man had saved a little bundle or a bag. Suddenly
a conical flame with a twisted top, shot up forward and
threw upon the black sea a circle of light, with the two
vessels side by side and heaving gently in its centre.
Captain Beard had been sitting on the gratings still and
mute for hours, but now he rose slowly and advanced
in front of us, to the mizzen-shrouds. Captain Nash
hailed: 'Come along! Look sharp. I have mail-bags
on board. I will take you and your boats to Singapore.'

" 'Thank you! No!' said our skipper. 'We must see
the last of the ship.'

" 'I can't stand by any longer,' shouted the other.
'Mails—you know.'

" 'Aye! aye! We are all right.'

" 'Very well! I'll report you in Singapore. . . .
Good-bye!'

"He waved his hand. Our men dropped their
bundles quietly. The steamer moved ahead, and passing out of the circle of light, vanished at once from our
sight, dazzled by the fire which burned fiercely. And
then I knew that I would see the East first as commander
of a small boat. I thought it fine; and the fidelity to
the old ship was fine. We should see the last of her.
Oh, the glamour of youth! Oh, the fire of it, more
dazzling than the flames of the burning ship, throwing
a magic light on the wide earth, leaping audaciously to

the sky, presently to be quenched by time, more cruel, more pitiless, more bitter than the sea—and like the flames of the burning ship surrounded by an impenetrable night.

"The old man warned us in his gentle and inflexible way that it was part of our duty to save for the underwriters as much as we could of the ship's gear. Accordingly we went to work aft, while she blazed forward to give us plenty of light. We lugged out a lot of rubbish. What didn't we save? An old barometer fixed with an absurd quantity of screws nearly cost me my life; a sudden rush of smoke came upon me, and I just got away in time. There were various stores, bolts of canvas, coils of rope; the poop looked like a marine bazaar, and the boats were lumbered to the gunwales. One would have thought the old man wanted to take as much as he could of his first command with him. He was very, very quiet, but off his balance evidently. He wanted to take a length of old stream-cable and a kedge-anchor with him in the longboat. We said, 'Aye, aye, sir,' deferentially, and on the quiet let the things slip overboard. The heavy medicine chest went that way, two bags of green coffee, tins of paint—fancy, paint!—a whole lot of things. Then I was ordered with two hands into the boats to make a stowage and get them ready against the time it would be proper for us to leave the ship.

"We put everything straight, stepped the longboat's mast for our skipper, who was to take charge of her, and I was not sorry to sit down for a moment. My face felt raw, every limb ached as if broken, I was aware of all my ribs, and would have sworn to a twist in the backbone. The boats, fast astern, lay in a deep shadow, and all around I could see the circle of the sea lighted by the fire. A gigantic flame rose forward straight and clear. It flared fierce, with noises like the whirr of wings, with rumbles as of thunder. There were cracks,

detonations, and from the cone of flame the sparks
flew upwards, as man is born to trouble, to leaky ships,
and to ships that burn.

"What bothered me was that the ship, lying broadside
to the swell and to such wind as there was—a mere
breath—the boats would not keep astern where they
were safe, but persisted, in a pig-headed way boats have,
in getting under the counter and then swinging alongside. They were knocking about dangerously and
coming near the flames, while the ship rolled on them,
and, of course, there was always the danger of the masts
going over the side at any moment. I and my two
boat-keepers kept them off as best we could, with oars
and boat-hooks; but to be constantly at it became exas-
perating, since there was no reason why we should not
leave at once. We could not see those on board, nor
could we imagine what caused the delay. The boat-
keepers were swearing feebly, and I had not only my
share of the work but also had to keep at it two men
who showed a constant inclination to lay themselves
down and let things slide.

"At last I hailed, 'On deck there,' and someone
looked over. 'We're ready here,' I said. The head
disappeared, and very soon popped up again. 'The
captain says, 'All right, sir,' and to keep the boats well
clear of the ship.'

"Half an hour passed. Suddenly there was a frightful
racket, rattle, clanking of chain, hiss of water, and
millions of sparks flew up into the shivering column of
smoke that stood leaning slightly above the ship. The
cat-heads had burned away, and the two red-hot
anchors had gone to the bottom, tearing out after them
two hundred fathom of red-hot chain. The ship
trembled, the mass of flame swayed as if ready to
collapse, and the fore topgallant-mast fell. It darted
down like an arrow of fire, shot under, and instantly
leaping up within an oar's length of the boats, floated
quietly, very black on the luminous sea. I hailed the

deck again. After some time a man in an unexpectedly
cheerful but also muffled tone, as if he had been trying
to speak with his mouth shut, informed me, 'Coming
directly, sir,' and vanished. For a long time I heard
nothing but the whirr and roar of the fire. There were
also whistling sounds. The boats jumped, tugged at the
painters, ran at each other playfully, knocked their sides
together, or, do what we would, swung in a bunch
against the ship's side. I couldn't stand it any longer,
and swarming up a rope, clambered aboard over the
stern.

"It was as bright as day. Coming up like this, the
sheet of fire facing me, was a terrifying sight, and the
heat seemed hardly bearable at first. On a settee
cushion dragged out of the cabin, Captain Beard, his
legs drawn up and one arm under his head, slept with
the light playing on him. Do you know what the rest
were busy about? They were sitting on deck right aft,
eating bread and cheese and drinking bottled stout.

"On the background of flames twisting in fierce
tongues above their heads they seemed at home like
salamanders, and looked like a band of desperate pirates.
The fire sparkled in the whites of their eyes, gleamed on
patches of white skin seen through the torn shirts. Each
had the marks as of a battle about him—bandaged
heads, tied-up arms, a strip of dirty rag round a knee
—and each man had a bottle between his legs and a
chunk of cheese in his hand. Mahon got up. With his
handsome and disreputable head, his hooked profile, his
long white beard, and with an uncorked bottle in his
hand, he resembled one of those reckless sea-robbers of
old making merry amidst violence and disaster. 'The
last meal on board,' he explained solemnly. 'We had
nothing to eat all day, and it was no use leaving all
this.' He flourished the bottle and indicated the
sleeping skipper. 'He said he couldn't swallow anything, so I got him to lie down,' he went on; and as I
stared, 'I don't know whether you are aware, young

fellow, the man had no sleep to speak of for days—and there will be dam' little sleep in the boats.' 'There will be no boats by and by if you fool about much longer,' I said indignantly. I walked up to the skipper and shook him by the shoulder. At last he opened his eyes, but did not move. 'Time to leave her, sir,' I said quietly.

"He got up painfully, looked at the flames, at the sea sparkling round the ship, and black, black as ink farther away; he looked at the stars shining dim through a thin veil of smoke in a sky black, black as Erebus.

" 'Youngest first,' he said.

"And the ordinary seaman, wiping his mouth with the back of his hand, got up, clambered over the taffrail, and vanished. Others followed. One, on the point of going over, stopped short to drain his bottle, and with a great swing of his arm flung it at the fire. 'Take this!' he cried.

"The skipper lingered disconsolately, and we left him to commune alone for a while with his first command. Then I went up again and brought him away at last. It was time. The ironwork on the poop was hot to the touch.

"Then the painter of the longboat was cut, and the three boats, tied together, drifted clear of the ship. It was just sixteen hours after the explosion when we abandoned her. Mahon had charge of the second boat, and I had the smallest—the fourteen-foot thing. The longboat would have taken the lot of us; but the skipper said we must save as much property as we could—for the underwriters—and so I got my first command. I had two men with me, a bag of biscuits, a few tins of meat, and a breaker of water. I was ordered to keep close to the longboat, that in case of bad weather we might be taken into her.

"And do you know what I thought? I thought I would part company as soon as I could. I wanted to have my first command all to myself. I wasn't going to sail in a squadron if there was a chance for independent cruising. I would make land by myself. I would beat the other boats. Youth! All youth! The silly, charming, beautiful youth.

"But we did not make a start at once. We must see the last of the ship. And so the boats drifted about that night, heaving and setting on the swell. The men dozed, waked, sighed, groaned. I looked at the burning ship.

"Between the darkness of earth and heaven she was burning fiercely upon a disc of purple sea shot by the blood-red play of gleams; upon a disc of water glittering and sinister. A high, clear flame, an immense and lonely flame, ascended from the ocean, and from its summit the black smoke poured continuously at the sky. She burned furiously, mournful and imposing, like a funeral pile kindled in the night, surrounded by the sea, watched over by the stars. A magnificent death had come like a grace, like a gift, like a reward to that old ship at the end of her laborious days. The surrender of her weary ghost to the keeping of stars and sea was stirring like the sight of a glorious triumph. The masts fell just before daybreak, and for a moment there was a burst and turmoil of sparks that seemed to fill with flying fire the night patient and watchful, the vast night lying silent upon the sea. At daylight she was only a charred shell, floating still under a cloud of smoke and bearing a glowing mass of coal within.

"Then the oars were got out, and the boats forming in a line moved round her remains as if in procession —the longboat leading. As we pulled across her stern a slim dart of fire shot out viciously at us, and suddenly she went down, head first, in a great hiss of steam. The unconsumed stern was the last to sink; but the paint had gone, had cracked, had peeled off, and there were no letters, there was no word, no stubborn device that was like her soul, to flash at the rising sun her creed and her name.

"We made our way north. A breeze sprang up, and

about noon all the boats came together for the last time. I had no mast or sail in mine, but I made a mast out of a spare oar and hoisted a boat awning for a sail, with a boat-hook for a yard. She was certainly over-masted, but I had the satisfaction of knowing that with the wind aft I could beat the other two. I had to wait for them. Then we all had a look at the captain's chart, and after a sociable meal of hard bread and water, got our last instructions. These were simple : steer north, and keep together as much as possible. 'Be careful with that jury-rig, Marlow,' said the captain; and Mahon, as I sailed proudly past his boat, wrinkled his curved nose and hailed, 'You will sail that ship of yours under water, if you don't look out, young fellow. He was a malicious old man—and may the deep sea where he sleeps now rock him gently, rock him tenderly to the end of time.

"Before sunset a thick rain-squall passed over the two boats, which were far astern, and that was the last I saw of them for a time. Next day I sat steering my cockle-shell—my first command—with nothing but water and sky around me. I did sight in the afternoon the upper sails of a ship far away, but said nothing, and my men did not notice her. You see I was afraid she might be homeward bound, and I had no mind to turn back from the portals of the East. I was steering for Java— another blessed name—like Bankok, you know. I steered many days.

"I need not tell you what it is to be knocking about in an open boat. I remember nights and days of calm when we pulled, and the boat seemed to stand still, as if bewitched within the circle of the sea horizon. I remember the heat, the deluge of rain-squalls that kept us baling for dear life (but filled our water-cask), and I remember sixteen hours on end with a mouth as dry as a cinder and a steering-oar over the stern to keep my first command head on to a breaking sea. I did not know how good a man I was till then. I remember the

205

drawn faces, the dejected figures of my two men, and I remember my youth and the feeling that will never come back any more—the feeling that I could last for ever, outlast the sea, the earth, and all men; the deceitful feeling that lures us on to joys, to perils, to love, to vain effort—to death; the triumphant conviction of strength; the heat of life in the handful of dust, the glow in the heart that with every year grows dim, grows cold, grows small, and expires—and expires, too soon, too soon—before life itself.

"And this is how I see the East. I have seen its secret places and have looked into its very soul; but now I see it always from a small boat, a high outline of mountains, blue and afar in the morning; like faint mist at noon; a jagged wall of purple at sunset. I have the feel of the oar in my hand, the vision of a scorching blue sea in my eyes. And I see a bay, a wide bay, smooth as glass and polished like ice, shimmering in the dark. A red light burns far off upon the gloom of the land, and the night is soft and warm. We drag at the oars with aching arms, and suddenly a puff of wind, a puff faint and tepid and laden with strange odours of blossoms, of aromatic wood, comes out of the still night —the first sigh of the East on my face. That I can never forget. It was impalpable and enslaving, like a charm, like a whispered promise of mysterious delight.

"We had been pulling this finishing spell for eleven hours. Two pulled, and he whose turn it was to rest sat at the tiller. We had made out the red light in that bay and steered for it, guessing it must mark some small coasting port. We passed two vessels, outlandish and high-sterned, sleeping at anchor, and, approaching the light, now very dim, ran the boat's nose against the end of a jutting wharf. We were blind with fatigue. My men dropped the oars and fell off the thwarts as if dead. I made fast to a pile. A current rippled softly. The scented obscurity of the shore was grouped into vast masses, a density of colossal clumps of vegetation, probably,—mute and fantastic shapes. And at their foot the semi-circle of a beach gleamed faintly, like an illusion. There was not a light, not a stir, not a sound. The mysterious East faced me, perfumed like a flower, silent like death, dark like a grave.

"And I sat weary beyond expression, exulting like a conqueror, sleepless and entranced as if before a profound, a fateful enigma.

"A splashing of oars, a measured dip reverberating on the level of water, intensified by the silence of the shore into loud claps, made me jump up. A boat, a European boat, was coming in. I invoked the name of the dead; I hailed: '*Judea* ahoy!' A thin shout answered.

"It was the captain. I had beaten the flagship by three hours, and I was glad to hear the old man's voice again, tremulous and tired. 'Is it you, Marlow?' 'Mind the end of that jetty, sir,' I cried.

"He approached cautiously, and brought up with the deep-sea lead-line which we had saved—for the underwriters. I eased my painter and fell alongside. He sat, a broken figure at the stern, wet with dew, his hands clasped in his lap. His men were asleep already. 'I had a terrible time of it,' he murmured. 'Mahon is behind—not very far.' We conversed in whispers, in low whispers, as if afraid to wake up the land. Guns, thunder, earthquakes, would not have awakened the men just then.

"Looking round as we talked, I saw away at sea a bright light travelling in the night. 'There's a steamer passing the bay,' I said. She was not passing, she was entering, and she even came close and anchored. 'I wish,' said the old man, 'you would find out whether she is English. Perhaps they could give us a passage somewhere.' He seemed nervously anxious. So by dint of punching and kicking I started one of my men into a state of somnambulism, and, giving him an oar, took another and pulled towards the lights of the steamer.

"There was a murmur of voices in her, metallic

hollow clangs of the engine-room, footsteps on the deck. Her ports shone, round like dilated eyes. Shapes moved about, and there was a shadowy man high up on the bridge. He heard my oars.

"And then, before I could open my lips, the East spoke to me, but it was in a Western voice. A torrent of words was poured into the enigmatical, the fateful silence; outlandish angry words, mixed with words and even whole sentences of good English, less strange but even more surprising. The voice swore and cursed violently; it riddled the solemn peace of the bay by a volley of abuse. It began by calling me Pig, and from that went crescendo into unmentionable adjectives—in English. The man up there raged aloud in two languages, and with a sincerity in his fury that almost convinced me I had, in some way, sinned against the harmony of the universe. I could hardly see him, but began to think he would work himself into a fit.

"Suddenly he ceased, and I could hear him snorting and blowing like a porpoise. I said—

" 'What steamer is this, pray?'

" 'Eh? What's this? And who are you?'

" 'Castaway crew of an English barque burnt at sea. We came here to-night. I am the second mate. The captain is in the longboat, and wishes to know if you would give us a passage somewhere.'

" 'Oh, my goodness! I say. . . . This is the *Celestial*, from Singapore on her return trip. I'll arrange with your captain in the morning . . . and . . . I say . . . did you hear me just now?'

" 'I should think the whole bay heard you.'

" 'I thought you were a shore-boat. Now, look here —the infernal lazy scoundrel of a caretaker has gone to sleep again—curse him. The light is out, and I nearly ran foul of the end of this damned jetty. This is the third time he plays me this trick. Now, I ask you, can anybody stand this kind of thing? It's enough to drive a man out of his mind. I'll report him. . . . I'll get

the Assistant Resident to give him the sack, by . . . !
See—there's no light. It's out, isn't it? I take you to
witness the light's out. There should be a light, you
know. A red light on the ——'

" 'There was a light,' I said, mildly.

" 'But it's out, man! What's the use of talking like
this? You can see for yourself it's out—don't you? If
you had to take a valuable steamer along this God-
forsaken coast you would want a light too. I'll kick
him from end to end of his miserable wharf. You'll see
if I don't. I will——'

" 'So I may tell my captain you'll take us?' I broke
in.

" 'Yes, I'll take you. Good night,' he said, brusquely.

"I pulled back, made fast again to the jetty, and then
went to sleep at last. I had faced the silence of the East.
I had heard some of its language. But when I opened
my eyes again the silence was as complete as though it
had never been broken. I was lying in a flood of light,
and the sky had never looked so far, so high, before. I
opened my eyes and lay without moving.

"And then I saw the men of the East—they were
looking at me. The whole length of the jetty was full
of people. I saw brown, bronze, yellow faces, the black
eyes, the glitter, the colour of an Eastern crowd. And
all these beings stared without a murmur, without a
sigh, without a movement. They stared down at the
boats, at the sleeping men who at night had come to
them from the sea. Nothing moved. The fronds of
palms stood still against the sky. Not a branch stirred
along the shore, and the brown roofs of hidden houses
peeped through the green foliage, through the big leaves
that hung shining and still like leaves forged of heavy
metal. This was the East of the ancient navigators, so
old, so mysterious, resplendent and sombre, living and
unchanged, full of danger and promise. And these were
the men. I sat up suddenly. A wave of movement
passed through the crowd from end to end, passed along

209

the heads, swayed the bodies, ran along the jetty like a ripple on the water, like a breath of wind on a field— and all was still again. I see it now—the wide sweep of the bay, the glittering sands, the wealth of green infinite and varied, the sea blue like the sea of a dream, the crowd of attentive faces, the blaze of vivid colour—the water reflecting it all, the curve of the shore, the jetty, the high-sterned outlandish craft floating still, and the three boats with the tired men from the West sleeping, unconscious of the land and the people and of the violence of sunshine. They slept thrown across the thwarts, curled on bottom-boards, in the careless attitudes of death. The head of the old skipper, leaning back in the stern of the longboat, had fallen on his breast, and he looked as though he would never wake. Further out old Mahon's face was upturned to the sky, with the long white beard spread out on his breast, as though he had been shot where he sat at the tiller; and a man, all in a heap in the bows of the boat, slept with both arms embracing the stem-head and with his cheek laid on the gunwale. The East looked at them without a sound.

"I have known its fascination since; I have seen the mysterious shores, the still water, the lands of brown nations, where a stealthy Nemesis lies in wait, pursues, overtakes so many of the conquering race, who are proud of their wisdom, of their knowledge, of their strength. But for me all the East is contained in that vision of my youth. It is all in that moment when I opened my young eyes on it. I came upon it from a tussle with the sea—and I was young—and I saw it looking at me. And this is all that is left of it! Only a moment; a moment of strength, of romance, of glamour —of youth! . . . A flick of sunshine upon a strange shore, the time to remember, the time for a sigh, and --good-bye!—Night—Good-bye . . .!"

He drank.

"Ah! The good old time—the good old time. Youth

and the sea. Glamour and the sea! The good, strong sea, the salt, bitter sea, that could whisper to you and roar at you and knock your breath out of you."

He drank again.

"By all that's wonderful, it is the sea, I believe, the sea itself—or is it youth alone? Who can tell? But you here—you all had something out of life: money, love—whatever one gets on shore—and, tell me, wasn't that the best time, that time when we were young at sea; young and had nothing, on the sea that gives nothing, except hard knocks—and sometimes a chance to feel your strength—that only—what you all regret?"

And we all nodded at him: the man of finance, the man of accounts, the man of law, we all nodded at him over the polished table that like a still sheet of brown water reflected our faces, lined, wrinkled; our faces marked by toil, by deceptions, by success, by love; our weary eyes looking still, looking always, looking anxiously for something out of life, that while it is expected is already gone—has passed unseen, in a sigh, in a flash—together with the youth, with the strength, with the romance of illusions.

LIFE OF MA PARKER
by Katherine Mansfield

KATHERINE MANSFIELD was born in New Zealand, in 1889, but spent her girlhood in England and was educated at Queen's College, London. She began, when only nineteen years of age, writing short stories of a very distinctive character; and many of these early efforts, at one time thought immature, have since been recognized as masterpieces. Her first volume of stories was published in 1911, but it was not until her marriage to John Middleton Murray, then Editor of *The Nation and Athæneum*, that her contributions to that review in the form of brilliant criticisms of contemporary authors won her recognition. The influence of her style and artistry on the modern short story is incalculable: she dispensed with plot, yet her stories amply make up in point and sensitiveness of observation for this omission, as *Ma Parker*, a story of the courage that it sometimes takes to live, shows.

LIFE OF MA PARKER

BY

KATHERINE MANSFIELD

WHEN the literary gentleman, whose flat old Ma Parker cleaned every Tuesday, opened the door to her that morning, he asked after her grandson. Ma Parker stood on the doormat inside the dark little hall, and she stretched out her hand to help the gentleman shut the door before she replied. "We buried 'im yesterday, sir," she said quietly.

"Oh, dear me! I'm sorry to hear that," said the literary gentleman in a shocked tone. He was in the middle of his breakfast. He wore a very shabby dressing-gown and carried a crumpled newspaper in one hand. But he felt awkward. He could hardly go back to the warm sitting-room without saying something—something more. Then because these people set such store by funerals he said kindly, "I hope the funeral went off all right."

"Beg parding, sir?" said old Ma Parker huskily.

Poor old bird! She did look dashed.

"I hope the funeral was a—a—success," said he. Ma Parker gave no answer. She bent her head and hobbled off to the kitchen, clasping the old fish bag that held her cleaning things and an apron and a pair of felt shoes. The literary gentleman raised his eyebrows and went back to his breakfast.

"Overcome, I suppose," he said aloud, helping himself to the marmalade.

Ma Parker drew the two jetty spears out of her toque and hung it behind the door. She unhooked her worn jacket and hung that up too. Then she tied her apron and sat down to take off her boots. To take off her boots or to put them on was an agony to her, but it had been an agony for years. In fact, she was so accustomed to the pain that her face was drawn and screwed up ready for the twinge before she'd so much as untied the laces. That over, she sat back with a sigh and softly rubbed her knees.

"Gran! Gran!" Her little grandson stood on her lap in his button boots. He'd just come in from playing in the street.

"Look what a state you've made your gran's skirt into—you wicked boy!"

But he put his arms round her neck and rubbed his cheek against hers.

"Gran, gi' us a penny!" he coaxed.

"Be off with you; Gran ain't got no pennies."

"Yes, you 'ave."

"No, I ain't."

"Yes, you 'ave. Gi' us one!"

Already she was feeling for the old, squashed, black leather purse.

"Well, what'll you give your gran?"

He gave a shy little laugh and pressed closer. She felt his eyelid quivering against her cheek. "I ain't got nothing," he murmured.

The old woman sprang up, seized the iron kettle off the gas stove and took it over to the sink. The noise of the water drumming in the kettle deadened her pain, it seemed. She filled the pail, too, and the washing-up bowl.

It would take a whole book to describe the state of that kitchen. During the week the gentleman "did" for himself. That is to say, he emptied the tea leaves now and again into a jam jar set aside for that purpose, and if he ran out of clean forks he wiped over one or two on the roller towel. Otherwise, as he explained to his friends, his "system" was quite simple, and he couldn't understand why people made all this fuss about housekeeping.

"You simply dirty everthing you've got, get a hag in once a week to clean up, and the thing's done."

The result looked like a gigantic dustbin. Even the floor was littered with toast-crusts, envelopes, cigarette-ends. But Ma Parker bore him no grudge. She pitied the poor young gentleman for having no one to look after him. Out of the smudgy little window you could see an immense expanse of sad-looking sky, and whenever there were clouds, they looked very worn, old clouds, frayed at the edges, with holes in them, or dark stains like tea.

While the water was heating, Ma Parker began sweeping the floor. "Yes," she thought, as the broom knocked, "what with one thing and another I've had my share. I've had a hard life."

Even the neighbours said that of her. Many a time, hobbling home with her fish bag, she heard them, waiting at the corner, or leaning over the area railings, say among themselves, "She's had a hard life, has Ma Parker." And it was so true she wasn't in the least proud of it. It was just as if you were to say she lived in the basement-back at No. 27. A hard life . . . !

At sixteen she'd left Stratford and come up to London as kitchin-maid. Yes, she was born in Stratford-on-Avon. Shakespeare, sir? No, people were always arsking her about him. But she'd never heard his name until she saw it in the theatres.

Nothing remained of Stratford except that "sitting in the fire-place of a evening you could see the stars through the chimley," and "Mother always 'ad 'er side of bacon 'anging from the ceiling." And there was something —a bush, there was—at the front door, that smelt ever so nice. But the bush was very vague. She'd only remembered it once or twice in the hospital, when she'd been taken bad.

That was a dreadful place—her first place. She was never allowed out. She never went upstairs except for prayers morning and evening. It was a fair cellar. And the cook was a cruel woman. She used to snatch away her letters from home before she'd read them and

throw them in the range because they made her dreamy.
. . . And the beedles! Would you believe it?—until
she came to London she'd never seen a black beedle.
Here Ma always gave a little laugh, as though—not to
have seen a black beedle! Well! It was as if to say
you'd never seen your own feet.

When that family was sold up she went as "help" to
a doctor's house, and after two years there, on the run
from morning till night, she married her husband. He
was a baker.

"A baker, Mrs. Parker!" the literary gentleman would
say. For occasionally he laid aside his tomes and lent
an ear, at least, to this product called Life. "It must
be rather nice to be married to a baker!"

Mrs. Parker didn't look so sure.

"Such a clean trade!" said the gentleman.

Mrs. Parker didn't look convinced.

"And didn't you like handing the new loaves to the
customers?"

"Well, sir," said Mrs. Parker, "I wasn't in the shop
above a great deal. We had thirteen little ones and
buried seven of them. If it wasn't the 'ospital it was the
infirmary, you might say!"

"You might *indeed*, Mrs. Parker!" said the gentleman,
shuddering and taking up his pen again.

Yes, seven had gone, and while the six were still small,
her husband was taken ill with consumption. It was
flour on the lungs, the doctor told her at the time. . . .
Her husband sat up in bed with his shirt pulled over his
head, and the doctor's finger drew a circle on his back.

"Now, if we were to cut him open *here*, Mrs. Parker,"
said the doctor, "you'd find his lungs chock-a-block
with white powder. Breathe, my good fellow!" And
Mrs. Parker never knew for certain whether she saw or
whether she fancied she saw a great fan of white dust
come out of her poor dear husband's lips. . . .

But the struggle she'd had to bring up those six little
children and keep herself to herself. Terrible it had

been! Then, just when they were old enough to go to school, her husband's sister came to stop with them to help things along, and she hadn't been there more than two months when she fell down a flight of steps and hurt her spine. And for five years Ma Parker had another baby—and such a one for crying—to look after. Then young Maudine went wrong and took her sister Alice with her; the two boys emigrated, and young Jim went to India with the army, and Ethel, the youngest, married a good-for-nothing little waiter who died of ulcers the year little Lennie was born. And now little Lennie—my grandson. . . .

The piles of dirty cups, dirty dishes, were washed and dried. The ink-black knives were cleaned with a piece of potato and finished off with a piece of cork. The table was scrubbed, and the dresser and the sink that had sardine tails swimming in it. . . .

He'd never been a strong child—never from the first. He'd been one of those fair babies that everybody took for a girl. Silvery fair curls he had, blue eyes, and a little freckle like a diamond on one side of his nose. The trouble she and Ethel had had to rear that child! The things out of the newspapers they had tried him with! Every Sunday morning Ethel would read aloud while Ma Parker did her washing.

"Dear Sir,

"Just a line to let you know my little Myrtil was laid out for dead. . . . After four bottils . . . gained eight pounds in nine weeks, and *is still putting it on*."

And then the egg-cup of ink would come off the dresser and the letter would be written, and Ma would buy a postal order on her way to work next morning. But it was no use. Nothing made little Lennie put it on. Taking him to the cemetery, even, never gave him a colour; a nice shake-up in the 'bus never improved his appetite.

But he was Gran's boy from the first. . . .

"Whose boy are you?" said old Ma Parker, straightening up from the stove and going over to the smudgy window. And a little voice, so warm, so close, it half stifled her—it seemed to be in her breast under her heart —laughed out, and said, "I'm Gran's boy!"

At that moment there was a sound of steps, and the literary gentleman appeared, dressed for walking.

"Oh, Mrs. Parker, I'm going out."

"Very good, sir."

"And you'll find your half-crown in the tray of the inkstand."

"Thank you, sir."

"Oh, by the way, Mrs. Parker, said the literary gentleman quickly, "you didn't throw away any cocoa last time you were here—did you?"

"No, sir."

"*Very* strange. I could have sworn I left a teaspoonful of cocoa in the tin." He broke off. He said softly and firmly, "You'll always tell me when you throw things away—won't you, Mrs. Parker?" And he walked off, very well pleased with himself, convinced, in fact, he'd shown Mrs. Parker that under his apparent carelessness he was as vigilant as a woman.

The door banged. She took her brushes and cloths into the bedroom. But when she began to make the bed, smoothing, tucking, patting, the thought of little Lennie was unbearable. Why did he have to suffer so? That's what she couldn't understand. Why should a little angel child have to arsk for his breath and fight for it? There was no sense in making a child suffer like that. . . . From Lennie's little box of a chest there came a sound as though something was boiling. There was a great lump of something bubbling in his chest that he couldn't get rid of. When he coughed the sweat sprang out on his head; his eyes bulged, his hands waved, and the great lump bubbled as a potato knocks in a saucepan. But what was more awful than all was

222

when he didn't cough he sat against the pillow and never spoke or answered, or even made as if he heard. Only he looked offended.

"It's not your poor old Gran's doing it, my lovey," said old Ma Parker, patting back the damp hair from his little scarlet ears. But Lennie moved his head and edged away. Dreadfully offended with her he looked —and solemn. He bent his head and looked at her sideways as though he couldn't have believed it of his Gran.

But at the last . . . Ma Parker threw the counterpane over the bed. No, she simply couldn't think about it. It was too much—she'd had too much in her life to bear. She'd borne it up till now, she'd kept herself to herself, and never once had she been seen to cry. Never, by a living soul. Not even her own children had seen Ma break down. She'd kept a proud face always. But now! Lennie gone—what had she? She had nothing. He was all she'd got from life, and now he was took too. Why must it all have happened to me? she wondered. "What have I done?" said old Ma Parker. "What have I done?"

As she said those words she suddenly let fall her brush. She found herself in the kitchen. Her misery was so terrible that she pinned on her hat, put on her jacket and walked out of the flat like a person in a dream. She did not know what she was doing. She was like a person so dazed by the horror of what has happened that he walks away—anywhere, as though by walking away he could escape.

It was cold in the street. There was a wind like ice. People went flitting by, very fast; the men walked like scissors, the women trod like cats. And nobody knew —nobody cared. Even if she broke down, if at last, after all these years, she were to cry, she'd find herself in the lock-up as like as not.

But at the thought of crying it was as though little

Lennie leapt in his Gran's arms. Ah, that's what she wants to do, my dove. Gran wants to cry. If she could only cry now, cry for a long time, over everything, beginning with her first place and the cruel cook, going on to the doctor's, and then the seven little ones, death of her husband, the children's leaving her, and all the years of misery that led up to Lennie. But to have a proper cry over all these things would take a long time. All the same, the time for it had come. She must do it. She couldn't put it off any longer; she couldn't wait any more. . . . Where could she go?

"She's had a hard life, has Ma Parker." Yes, a hard life, indeed! Her chin began to tremble; there was no time to lose. But where? Where?

She couldn't go home; Ethel was there. She couldn't sit on a bench anywhere; people would come arsking her questions. She couldn't possibly go back to the gentleman's flat; she had no right to cry in strangers' houses. If she sat on some steps a policeman would speak to her.

Oh, wasn't there anywhere where she could hide and keep herself to herself and stay as long as she liked, not disturbing anybody, and nobody worrying her? Wasn't there anywhere in the world where she could have her cry out—at last?

Ma Parker stood, looking up and down. The icy wind blew out her apron into a balloon. And now it began to rain. There was nowhere.

THE DESERTERS
by A. E. W. Mason

A. E. W. MASON entered politics as a young man and was a member of Parliament for Coventry between the years 1906-10. Born in 1865, he was educated at Dulwich College and Trinity College, Cambridge. He took his political career very seriously and advanced considerably beyond the stage of the "maiden speech." Eventually, however, he realized that effective oratory is not the only qualification for success in the House of Commons and decided to devote himself to literature. Following the outbreak of the European War in 1914, he became Captain in a Manchester regiment and was subsequently appointed Major R.M.L.I. on the General Staff. He has written variously some of his novels, such as *The Four Feathers* and *At the Villa Rose*, being of an avowedly popular character. *Ensign Knightley*, a collection of brilliant short stories of military life in former days was published in 1901.

THE DESERTERS

BY

A. E. W. MASON

LIEUTENANT FEVRIER of the 69th regiment, which belonged to the first brigade of the first division of the army of the Rhine, was summoned to the Belletonge Farm just as it was getting dusk. The lieutenant hurried thither, for the Belletonge Farm opposite the woods of Colombey was the headquarters of the general of his division.

"I have been instructed," said General Montaudon, "to select an officer for a special duty. I have selected you."

Now for days, Lieutenant Fevrier's duties had consisted solely of keeping the soldiers of his company from eating unripe fruit; and here unexpectedly he was chosen from all the officers of his division for a particular exploit. The lieutenant trembled with emotion.

"My general!"

The general himself was moved.

"What your task will be," he continued, "I do not know. You will go at once to the marshal's headquarters, where the chief of the staff, General Jarras, will inform you."

Lieutenant Fevrier went immediately up to Metz. His division was entrenched on the right bank of the Mosel and beyond the forts, so that it was dark before he passed through the gates. He had never once been in Metz before; he had grown used to the monotony of camps; he had expected shuttered windows and deserted roads, and so the aspect of the town amazed him beyond measure. Instead of a town besieged, it seemed a town during a fairing. There were railway carriages, it is

229

true, in the Place Royale doing duty as hospitals; the provision shops, too, were bare, and there were no horses visible.

But on the other hand, everywhere was a blaze of light and a bustle of people coming and going upon the footpaths. The cafés glittered and rang with noise. Here one little fat burgher was shouting that the town-guard was worth all the red-legs in the trenches; another as loudly was criticizing the tactics of Bazaine, and comparing him for his invisibility to a pasha in his seraglio; while a third sprang upon a table and announced fresh victories. An army was already on the road from Paris to relieve Metz. Only yesterday Mac-Mahon had defeated the Prussians; any moment he might be expected from the Ardennes. Nor were they only civilians who shouted and complained. Lieutenant Fevrier saw captains, majors, and even generals, who had left their entrenchments to fight the siege their own way with dominoes upon the marble tables of the cabarets.

"My poor France," he said to himself; and a passer-by overhearing him answered:

"True, monsieur. Ah, but if we had a man at Metz!"

Lieutenant Fevrier turned his back upon the speaker and walked on. He, at all events, would not join in the criticisms. It was just, he reflected, because he had avoided the cafés of Metz that he was singled out for special distinction, and he fell to wondering what work it was he had to do that night. Was it to surprise a field-watch? Or to spike a battery? Or to capture a convoy? Lieutenant Fevrier raised his head. For any exploit in the world he was ready.

General Jarras was writing at a table when Fevrier was admitted to his office. The chief of the staff inclined his lamp-shade so that the light fell full upon Fevrier's face, and the action caused the lieutenant to rejoice. So much care in the choice of the officer meant so much more important a duty.

"The General Montaudon tells me," said Jarras, "that you are an obedient soldier."

"Obedience, my General, is the soldier's first lesson."

"That explains to me why it is first forgotten," answered Jarras dryly. Then his voice became sharp and curt. "You will choose fifty men. You will pick them carefully."

"They shall be the best soldiers in the regiment," said Fevrier.

"No, the worst."

Lieutenant Fevrier was puzzled. When dangers were to be encountered, when audacity was needed, one required the best soldiers. That was obvious, unless the mission meant annihilation. That thought came to Fevrier, and remembering the cafés and the officers dishonouring their uniforms, he drew himself up proudly and saluted. Already he saw his dead body recovered from the enemy, and borne to the grave beneath a tricolour. He heard the lamentations of his friends, and the firing of the platoon. He saw General Montaudon in tears. He was shaken with emotion. But Jarrass's next words fell upon him like cold water.

"You will parade your fifty men unarmed. You will march out of the lines, and to-morrow morning as soon as it is light enough for the Prussians to see that you come unarmed you will desert to them. There are too many mouths to feed in Metz."[1]

The lieutenant had it on his lips to shout, "Then why not lead us out to die?" But he kept silence. He could have flung his kepi in the general's face; but he saluted. He went out again into the streets and among the lighted cafés and reeled like a drunken man, thinking confusedly of many things; that he had a mother in Paris who might hear of his desertion before she heard of its explanation; that it was right to claim obedience but *lâche* to exact dishonour—but chiefly and above all that if he had been wise, and had made light of his duty,

[1] See the *Daily News* War Correspondence, 1870.

and had come up to Metz to rearrange the campaign with dominoes on the marble tables, he would not have been specially selected for ignominy. It was true, it needed an obedient officer to desert! And so, laughing aloud he reeled blindly down to the gates of Metz. And it happened that just by the gates a civilian looked after him, and shrugging his shoulders, remarked, "Ah! But if we had a *Man* at Metz?"

From Metz Lieutenant Fevrier ran. The night air struck cool upon him. And he ran and stumbled and fell and picked himself up, and ran again till he reached the Belletonge Farm.

"The general," he cried; and so to the general a mud-plastered figure with a white, tormented face, was admitted.

"What is it?" asked Montaudon. "What will this say?"

Lieutenant Fevrier stood with the palms of his hands extended, speechless, like an animal in pain. Then he suddenly burst into tears and wept, and told of the fine plan to diminish the demands upon the commissariat.

"Courage, my old one!" said the general. "I had a fear of this. You are not alone—other officers in other divisions have the same hard duty," and there was no inflection in the voice to tell Fevrier what his general thought of the duty. But a hand was laid soothingly upon his shoulder, and that told him. He took heart to whisper that he had a mother in Paris.

"I will write to her," said Montaudon. "She will be proud when she receives the letter."

Then Lieutenant Fevrier, being French, took the general's hand and kissed it, and the general, being French, felt his throat fill with tears.

Fevrier left the headquarters, paraded his men, laid his sword and revolver on the ground, and ordered his fifty to pile their arms. Then he made them a speech —a very short speech, but it cost him much to make it in an even voice.

"My brave," said he, "my fellow soldiers, it is easy to fight for one's country, it is not difficult to die for it. But the supreme test of patriotism is willingly to suffer shame for it. That test your country now claims of you. Attention! March!"

For the last time he exchanged a password with a French sentinel, and tramped out into the belt of ground between the French outposts and the Prussian field-watch. Now in this belt there stood a little village which Fevrier had held with skill and honour all the two days of the battle of Noisseville. Doubtless that recollection had something to do with his choice of the village. For in this martyrdom of shame he had fallen to wonder whether after all he had not deserved it, and any reassurance such as the gaping house-walls of Vaudere would bring to him was eagerly welcomed. There was another reason, however, in the position of the village.

It stood in an abrupt valley at the foot of a steep vine-hill, on the summit of which was the Prussian fore-post. The Prussian field-watch would be even nearer to Vaudere and dispersed amongst the vines on the slope. So he could get his ignominious work over quickly in the morning. The village would provide, too, safe quarters for the night, since it was well within range of the heavy guns in Fort St. Julien, and the Prussians on that account were unable to hold it.

He led his fifty soldiers then north-westward from his camp, skirted the Bois de Grimont, and marched into the village. The night was dark, and the sky so over-hung with clouds that not a star was visible. The one street of Vaudere was absolutely silent. The glimmering white cottages showed their black rents on either side, but never the light of a candle behind any shutter. Lieutenant Fevrier left his men at the western or Frenchward end of the street, and went forward alone.

The doors of the houses stood open. The path was encumbered with the wreckage of their contents, and every now and then he smelled a whiff of paraffin, as though lamps had been broken or cans overset. Vaudere had been looted, but there were no Prussians now in the village.

He made sure of this by walking as far as the large house at the head of the village. Then he went back to his men and led them forward, until he reached the general shop, which every village has.

"It is not likely," he said, "that we shall find even the makeshift of a supper. But courage, my friends, let us try!"

He could not have eaten a crust himself, but it had become an instinct with him to anticipate the needs of his privates, and he acted from habit. They crowded into the shop; one man shut the door. Fevrier lighted a match, and disclosed by its light staved-in barrels, empty canisters, broken boxes, fragments of lemonade bottles, but of food not so much as a stale biscuit.

"Go upstairs and search."

They went, and returned empty-handed.

"We have found nothing, monsieur," said they.

"But I have," replied Fevrier, and striking another match, he held up what he had found, dirty and crumpled in a corner of the shop. It was a little tricolour flag of painted linen upon a bamboo stick, a child's cheap and gaudy toy. But Fevrier held it up solemnly, and of the fifty deserters no one laughed.

"The flag of the *patrie*," said Fevrier, and with one accord the deserters uncovered.

The match burned down to Fevrier's fingers, he dropped it and trod upon it, and there was a moment's absolute stillness. Then in the darkness a ringing voice leapt out.

"*Vive la France?*"

It was not the lieutenant's voice, but the voice of a peasant from the south of the Loire, one of the deserters.

"Ah, but that is fine, that cry," said Fevrier.

He could have embraced that private on both cheeks. There was love in that cry, pain as well—it

234

could not be otherwise—but above all a very passion of confidence.

"Again!" said Fevrier; and this time all his men took it up, shouting it exultantly. The little ruined shop, in itself a contradiction of the cry, rang out, and clattered with the noise, until it seemed to Fevrier that it must surely pierce across the country into Metz and pluck the marshal in his headquarters from his diffidence. But they were only fifty deserters in a deserted village, lost in the darkness, and more likely to be overheard by the Prussian sentries than by any of their own blood.

It was Fevrier who first saw the danger of their ebullition. He cut it short by ordering them to seek quarters where they could sleep until daybreak. For himself, he thrust the little toy flag in his breast, and walked forward to the larger house at the end of the village beneath the vine-hill; and as he walked, again the smell of paraffin was forced upon his nostrils.

He walked more slowly. That odour of paraffin began to seem remarkable. The looting of the village had not occurred to-day, for there had been thick dust about the general shop. But the paraffin had surely been freshly spilt, or the odour would have evaporated.

Lieutenant Fevrier walked on, thinking this over. He found the broken door of the house, and, still thinking it over, mounted the stairs. There was a door fronting the stairs. He felt for the handle and opened it, and from a corner of the room a voice challenged him in German.

Fevrier was fairly startled. There were Germans in the village after all. He explained to himself now the smell of paraffin. Meanwhile he did not answer; neither did he move; neither did he hear any movement. He had forgotten for the moment that he was a deserter, and he stood holding his breath and listening. There was a tiny window opposite to the door, but it only declared itself a window, it gave no light. And illusions came to Lieutenant Fevrier, such as will come to the

235

bravest man so long as he listens hard enough in the dark—illusions of stealthy footsteps on the floor, of hands scraping and feeling along the walls, of a man's breathing upon his neck, of many infinitesimal noises and movements close by.

The challenge was repeated, and Fevrier remembered his orders.

"I am Lieutenant Fevrier of Montaudon's division."

"You are alone?"

Fevrier now distinguished that the voice came from the right-hand corner of the room, and that it was faint.

"I have fifty men with me. We are deserters," he blurted out, "and unarmed."

There followed silence, and a long silence. Then the voice spoke again, but in French, and the French of a native.

"My friend, your voice is not the voice of a deserter. There is too much humiliation in it. Come to my bedside here. I spoke in German, expecting Germans. But I am the curé of Vaudere. Why are you deserters?"

Fevrier had expected a scornful order to marshal his men as prisoners. The extraordinary gentleness of the curé's voice almost overcame him. He walked across to the bedside and told his story. The curé barely heard him out.

"It is right to obey," said he, "but here you can obey and disobey. You can relieve Metz of your appetites, my friend, but you need not desert." The curé reached up, and drawing Fevrier down, laid a hand upon his head. "I consecrate you to the service of your country. Do you understand?"

Fevrier leaned his mouth towards the curé's ear.

"The Prussians are coming to-night to burn the village."

"Yes, they came at dusk."

Just at the moment, in fact, when Fevrier had been summoned to Metz, the Prussians had crept down into

Vaudere and had been scared back to their *repli* by a false alarm.

"But they will come back, you may be sure," said the curé; and raising himself upon his elbow he said in a voice of suspense, "Listen!"

Fevrier went to the window and opened it. It faced the hillside, but no sounds came through it beyond the natural murmurs of the night. The curé sank back.

"After the fight here, there were dead soldiers in the streets—French soldiers and so French *chassepots*. Ah, my friend, the Prussians have found out which is the better rifle—the *chassepot* or the needle-gun. After your retreat they came down the hill for those *chassepots*. They could not find one. They searched every house. They came here and questioned me. Finally they caught one of the villagers hiding in a field, and he was afraid, and he told where the rifles had been buried. The Prussians dug for them, and the hole was empty. They believe they are still hidden somewhere in the village; they fancy, too, that there are secret stores of food; so they mean to burn the houses to the ground. They did not know that I was here this afternoon. I would have come into the French lines had it been possible, but I am tied here to my bed. No doubt God has sent you to me—you and your fifty men. You need not desert. You can make your last stand here for France."

"And perish," cried Fevrier, caught up from the depths of his humiliation, "as Frenchmen should, arms in hand." Then his voice dropped again. "But we have no arms."

The curé shook the lieutenant's arm gently.

"Did I not tell you the *chassepots* were not found? And why? Because too many knew where they were hidden. Because out of that many I feared there might be one to betray. There is always a Judas. So I took one man whom I knew, and he dug them up and hid them afresh!"

"Where, Father?"

237

The question was put with a feverish eagerness—it seemed to the curé with an eagerness too feverish. He drew his hand, his whole body away.

"You have matches? Light one!" he said, in a startled voice.

"But the window——"

"Light one!"

Every moment of time was now of value. Fevrier took the risk and lit the match, shading it from the window so far as he could with his hand.

"That will do."

Fevrier blew out the light. The curé had seen him, his uniform and his features. He, too, had seen the curé, had noticed his thin, emaciated face, and the eyes staring out of it feverishly bright and preternaturally large.

"Shall I tell you your malady, Father?" he said gently. "It is starvation."

"What will you, my son? I am alone. There is not a crust from one end of Vaudere to the other. You cannot help me. Help France! Go to the church, stand with your back to the door, turn left, and advance straight to the churchyard wall. You will find a new grave there, the rifles in the grave. Quick! There is a spade in the tower. Quick! The rifles are wrapped from the damp, the cartridges too. Quick! Quick!"

Fevrier hurried downstairs, roused three of his soldiers, bade one of them go from house to house and bring the soldiers in silence to the churchyard, and with the two he went thither himself. In groups of two and three the men crept through the street, and gathered about the grave. It was already open. The spade was driven hard and quick, deeper and deeper and at last rang upon metal. There were seventy *chassepots*, complete with bayonets and ammunition. Fifty-one were handed out, the remaining nineteen were hastily covered in again. Fevrier was immeasurably cheered to notice his men clutch at their weapons and fondle them, hold them to their shoulders taking aim, and work the breech-blocks.

"It is like meeting old friends, is it not, my children —or rather, new sweethearts?" said he. "Come! The Prussians may advance from the Brasserie at Lanvallier, from Servigny, from Montay, or from Noisseville, straight down the hill. The last direction is the most likely, but we must make no mistake. Ten men will watch on the Lanvallier road, ten on the Servigny, ten on the Montay, twenty will follow me. March!"

An hour ago Lieutenant Fevrier was in command of fifty men, who slouched along with their hands in their pockets, robbed even of self-respect. Now he had fifty armed and disciplined soldiers, men alert and inspired. So much difference a *chassepot* apiece had made. Lieutenant Fevrier was moved to the conception of another plan; and to prepare the way for its execution, he left his twenty men in a house at the Prussian end of Vaudere, and himself crept in among the vines and up the hill.

Somewhere near to him would be the sentries of the field-watch. He went down upon his hands and knees and crawled, parting the vine leaves, that the swish of them might not betray him. In a little while, high above his head he heard the cracking of wood, the sound of men stumbling. The Prussians were coming down to Vaudere. He lay flat upon the ground, waiting and waiting; and the sounds grew louder and approached. At last he heard that for which he waited— the challenge of the field-watch, the answer of the burning-party. It came down to him quiet clearly through the windless air: "Sadowa."

Lieutenant Fevrier turned about, chuckling. It seemed that in some respects the world after all was not going so ill with him that night. He crawled downwards as quickly as he could. But it was now more than ever requisite that he should not be detected. He dared not stand up and run; he must still keep upon his hands

and knees. His arms so ached that he was forced now
and then to stop and lie prone to give them ease; he
was soaked through and through with perspiration; his
blood hammered at his temples; he felt his spine weaken,
as though the marrow had melted into water; and his
heart throbbed until the effort to breathe was a pain.
But he reached the bottom of the hill, he was back
amongst his men, he even had time to give his orders
before the tread of the first Prussian was heard in the
street.

"They will make for the other end of Vaudere. They
will fire the village first at the point nearest to the
French lines and light the rest as they retreat. Let them
go forward! We will cut them off. And remember,
the bayonet! A shot would bring the Prussians down
in force. It would wake the French guns, too, so there
is just the chance we may find the enemy as silent as
ourselves."

But the plan was to undergo alteration. For as
Lieutenant Fevrier ended, the Prussians marched in
single file into the street and halted. Fevrier from the
corner within his doorway counted them; there were
twenty-three in all. Well, he had twenty besides himself, and the advantage of the surprise; and thirty more
upon the other roads, for whom, however, he had other
work in mind. The officer in command of the Prussians
carried a dark lantern, and he now turned the slide, so
that the light shone out.

His men fell out of their order, some to make a
cursory search, others to sprinkle yet more paraffin.
One man came close to Fevrier's doorway, and even
looked in, but he saw nothing, though Fevrier was
within six feet of him, holding his breath. Then the
officer closed his lantern, the men re-formed and marched
on. But they had left behind with Lieutenant Fevrier
—an idea.

He thought it quickly over. It pleased him, it was
feasible, and there was comedy in it. Lieutenant

240

Fevrier laughed again; his spirits were rising, and the world was not, after all, going so ill with him.

He had noticed by the lantern light that the Prussians had not re-formed in the same order. They were in single file again, but the man who marched last before the halt did not march last after it. Each soldier, as he came up, fell in in the rear of the file. Now Fevrier had in the darkness experienced some difficulty in counting the number of Prussians, although he had strained his eyes to that end.

He whispered accordingly some brief instructions to his men; he sent a message to the ten on the Servigny road, and when the Prussians marched on after their second halt, Lieutenant Fevrier and two Frenchmen fell in behind them. The same procedure was followed at the next halt, and at the next; so that when the Prussians reached the Frenchward end of Vaudere there were twenty-three Prussians and ten Frenchmen in the file. To Fevrier's thinking it was sufficiently comic. There was something artistic about it too.

Fevrier was pleased, but he had not counted on the quick Prussian step to which his soldiers were unaccustomed. At the fourth halt, the officer moved unsuspiciously first on one side of the street, then on the other, but gave no order to his men to fall out. It seemed that he had forgotten, until he came suddenly running down the file and flashed his lantern into Fevrier's face. He had been secretly counting his men.

"The French!" he cried. "Load!"

The one word quite compensated Fevrier for the detection. The Germans had come down into Vaudere with their rifles unloaded, lest an accidental discharge should betray their neighbourhood to the French.

"Load!" cried the German. And stepping back he tugged at the revolver in his belt. But before he could draw it out, Fevrier dashed his bayonet through the lantern, and hung it on the officer's heart. He whistled, and his other ten men came running down the street.

241

"*Vorwarts!*" shouted Fevrier derisively. "*Immer vorwarts!*"

The Prussians, surprised, and ignorant how many they had to face, fell back in disorder against a house-wall. The French soldiers dashed at them in the darkness, engaging them so that not a man had the chance to load.

That little fight in the dark street between the white ruined cottages made Fevrier's blood dance.

"Courage!" he cried. "*Ohé*, the paraffin!"

The combatants were well matched, and it was hand to hand and bayonet to bayonet. Fevrier loved his enemies at that moment. It even occurred to him that it was worth while to have deserted. After the sense of disgrace, the prospect of imprisonment and dishonour, it was all wonderful to him—the feel of the thick coat yielding to the bayonet point, the fatigue of the beaten opponent, the vigour of the new one, the feeling of injury and unfairness when a Prussian he had wounded let fall the butt of a rifle upon his toes.

Once he cried, "*Voilà pour la patrie!*" but for the rest he fought in silence, as did the others, having better uses for their breath. All that could be heard was a loud and laborious panting, as of wrestlers in a match, the clang of rifle crossing rifle, the rattle of bayonet guarding bayonet, and now and then a groan and a heavy fall. One Prussian escaped and ran; but the ten who had been stationed on the Servigny road were now guarding the entrance from Noisseville. Fevrier had no fears of him. He pressed upon a new man, drove him against the wall, and the man shouted in despair: "*A moi!*"

"You, Philippe?" exclaimed Fevrier. "That was a timely cry," and he sprang back. There were now six men standing, and the six saluted Fevrier; they were all Frenchmen. Fevrier mopped his forehead.

"But that was fine," said he, "though what's to come will be still better. Oh, but we will make this night

242

memorable to our friends. They shall talk of us by their firesides when they are grown old and France has had many years of peace—we shall not hear, but they will talk of us, the deserters from Metz."

Lieutenant Fevrier, in a word, was exalted, and had lost his sense of proportion. He did not, however, relax his activity. He sent off the six to gather the rest of his contingent. He made an examination of the Prussians, and found that sixteen had been killed outright, and eight were lying wounded. He removed their rifles and ammunition out of reach, and from dead and wounded alike took the coats and caps. To the wounded he gave instead French uniforms; and then, bidding twenty-three of his soldiers don the Prussian caps and coats, he snatched a moment wherein to run to the curé.

"It is over," said he. "The Prussians will not burn Vauderc to-night." And he jumped down the stairs again without waiting for any response. In the street he put on the cap and coat of the Prussian officer, buckled the sword about his waist, and thrust the revolver into his belt. He had now twenty-three men who at night might pass for Prussians, and thirteen others.

To these thirteen he gave general instructions. They were to spread out on the right and left, and make their way singly up through the vines, and past the field-watch if they could do so without risk of detection. They were to join him high up on the slope, and opposite to the bonfire which would be burning at the *repli*. His twenty-three he led boldly, following as nearly as possible the track by which the Prussians had descended. The party trampled down the vine poles, brushed through the leaves, and in a little were challenged.

"Sadowa," said Fevrier, in his best imitation of the German accent.

"Pass, Sadowa," returned the sentry.

Fevrier and his men filed upwards. He halted some two hundred yards farther on, and went down upon his knees. The soldiers behind him copied his example. They crept slowly and cautiously forward until the flames of the bonfire were visible through the screen of leaves, until the faces of the officers about the bonfire could be read.

Then Fevrier stopped and whispered to the soldier next to him. That soldier passed the whisper on, and from a file the Frenchmen crept into line. Fevrier had now nothing to do but to wait; and he waited without trepidation or excitement. The night from first to last had gone very well with him. He could even think of Marshal Bazaine without anger.

He waited for perhaps an hour, watching the faces round the fire increase in number and grow troubled with anxiety. The German officers talked in low tones, staring through their night-glasses down the hill to catch the first leaping flame from the roofs of Vaudere, pushing forward their heads to listen for any alarm. Fevrier watched them with the amusement of a spectator in a play-house. He was fully aware that he was shortly to step upon the stage himself. He was aware, too, that the play was to have a tragic ending. Meanwhile, however, here was very good comedy. He had a Frenchman's appreciation of the picturesque. The dark night, the glowing fire on the one broad level of grass, the French soldiers hidden in the vines within a stone's throw of the Germans, the Germans looking unconsciously over their heads for the return of those comrades who never would return! Lieutenant Fevrier was the dramatist who had created this striking and artistic situation. Lieutenant Fevrier could not but be pleased. Moreover, there were better effects to follow. One occurred to him at this very moment, an admirable one. He fumbled in his breast and took out the flag. A minute later he saw the colonel of the outpost join the group, hack nervously with his naked sword at a burning log, and despatch a subaltern down the hill to the field-watch.

The subaltern came crashing back through the vines. Fevrier did not need to hear his words in order to guess at his report. It could only be that the Prussian party had given the password and come safely back an hour since. Besides, the colonel's act was significant.

He sent four men at once in different directions, and the rest of his soldiers he withdrew into the darkness behind the bonfire. He did not follow them himself until he had picked up and tossed a fusee into the fire. The fusee flared and spat and spurted, and immediately it seemed to Fevrier—so short an interval of time was there—that the countryside was alive with the hum of a stirring camp, and the rattle of harness-chains, as horses were yoked to guns.

For the third time that evening Fevrier laughed softly. The deserters had roused the Prussian army round Metz to the expectation of an attack in force. He touched his neighbour on the shoulder.

"One volley when I give the word. Then charge. Pass the order on!" And the word went along the line like a ripple across a pond.

He had hardly given it, the fusee had barely ceased to sputter, before a company doubled out on the open space behind the bonfire. That company had barely formed in line, before another arrived to support it.

"Load!"

As the Prussian command was uttered, Fevrier was aware of a movement at his side. The soldier next to him was taking aim. Fevrier reached out his hand and stopped the man. Fevrier was going to die in five minutes, and meant to die chivalrously, like a gentleman. He waited until the German companies had loaded, until they were ordered to advance, and then he shouted;

"Fire!"

The little flames shot out and crackled among the vines. He saw gaps in the Prussian ranks, he saw the men waver, surprised at the proximity of the attack.

"Charge!" he shouted, and crashing through the

245

few yards of shelter, the deserters burst out upon the *repli*, and across the open space to the Prussian bayonets. But not one of the number reached the bayonets.

"Fire!" shouted the Prussian officer, in his turn.

The volley flashed out, the smoke cleared away, and showed a little heap of men silent between the bonfire and the Prussian ranks.

The Prussians loaded again and stood ready, waiting for the main attack. The morning was just breaking. They stood silent and motionless till the sky was flooded with light, and the hills one after another came into view, and the files of poplars were seen marching on the plains. Then the colonel approached the little heap. A rifle caught his eyes, and he picked it up. "They are all mad," said he. Fixed to the point of the bayonet was a gaudy little linen tricolour flag.

RAB AND HIS FRIENDS
by Dr. John Brown

BORN at Biggar, in 1810, Dr. John Brown was the grandson of another author, also John Brown, whose "self-interpreting Bible" was once widely read. The literary strain in the family appears to have been persistent, but the author of *Rab and His Friends* and *Marjorie Fleming and her Friends*, wrote rarely. He studied medicine under the famous surgeon Syme, graduated in 1823 and afterwards practiced in Edinburgh. His interests, however, lay in many directions and he did not make much progress in his profession. Nor was he ambitious for a literary career, holding the opinion that nobody should publish a work of literature, "unless he has something to say and has done his best to say it aright." Three small volumes contain all that this conscientious author thought worthy of publication. *Rab and His Friends* was originally delivered as a lecture and must have profoundly moved the audience who heard it, for it is one of the most beautiful stories of human endurance ever written.

RAB AND HIS FRIENDS

BY

Dr. John Brown

FOUR-AND-THIRTY years ago, Bob Ainslie and I were coming up Infirmary Street from the High School, our heads together, and our arms intertwisted, as only lovers and boys know how, or why.

When we got to the top of the street, and turned north, we espied a crowd at the Tron Church. "A dog-fight!" shouted Bob, and was off; and so was I, both of us all but praying that it might not be over before we got up! And is not this boy-nature? and human nature too? and don't we all wish a house on fire not to be out before we see it? Dogs like fighting; old Isaac says they "delight" in it, and for the best of all reasons; and boys are not cruel because they like to see the fight. They see three of the great cardinal virtues of dog or man—courage, endurance and skill—in intense action. This is very different from a love of making dogs fight, and enjoying, and aggravating, and making gain by their pluck. A boy—be he ever so fond himself of fighting—if he be a good boy, hates and despises all this; but he would have run off with Bob and me fast enough: it is a natural and a not wicked interest that all boys and men have in witnessing intense energy in action.

Does any curious and finely-ignorant woman wish to know how Bob's eye at a glance announced a dog-fight to his brain? He did not, he could not see the dogs fighting; it was a flash of an inference, a rapid induction. The crowd round a couple of dogs fighting is a crowd masculine mainly, with an occasional active, compassionate woman, fluttering wildly round the outside, and

251

using her tongue and her hands freely upon the men, as so many "brutes"; it is a crowd annular, compact, and mobile; a crowd centripetal, having its eyes and its heads all bent downwards and inwards, to one common focus.

Well, Bob and I are up, and find it is not over: a small thoroughbred white bull-terrier is busy throttling a large shepherd's dog, unaccustomed to war, but not to be trifled with. They are hard at it; the scientific little fellow doing his work in great style, his pastoral enemy fighting wildly, but with the sharpest of teeth and a great courage. Science and breeding, however, soon had their own; the Game Chicken, as the premature Bob called him, working his way up, took his final grip of poor Yarrow's throat—and he lay gasping and done for. His master, a brown, handsome, big young shepherd from Tweedsmuir, would have liked to have knocked down any man, would "drink up Esil, or eat a crocodile," for that part, if he had a chance: it was no use kicking the little dog; that would only make him hold the closer. Many were the means, shouted out in mouthfuls, of the best possible ways of ending it. "Water!"—but there was none near, and many cried for it who might have got it from the well at Blackfriar's Wynd. "Bite the tail!"—and a large, vague, benevolent, middle-aged man, more desirous than wise, with some struggle got the bushy end of *Yarrow's* tail into his ample mouth, and bit it with all his might. This was more than enough for the much-enduring, much-perspiring shepherd, who, with a gleam of joy over his broad visage, delivered a terrific facer upon our large, vague, benevolent, middle-aged friend—who went down like a shot.

Still the Chicken holds; death not far off. "Snuff! a pinch of snuff!" observed a calm, highly-dressed young buck, with an eyeglass in his eye. "Snuff, indeed!" growled the angry crowd, affronted and glaring. "Snuff! a pinch of snuff!" again observes the buck, but with more urgency; whereon were produced several open boxes, and from a mull which may have been at Culloden, he took a pinch, knelt down, and presented it to the nose of the Chicken. The laws of physiology and of snuff take their course; the Chicken sneezes, and Yarrow is free!

The young pastoral giant stalks off with Yarrow in his arms—comforting him.

But the bull-terrier's blood is up, and his soul unsatisfied; he grips the first dog he meets, and discovering she is not a dog, in Homeric phrase, he makes a brief sort of *amende*, and is off. The boys, with Bob and me at their head, are after him: down Niddry Street he goes, bent on mischief; up the Cowgate like an arrow —Bob and I, and our small men, panting behind.

There, under the single arch of the South Bridge, is a huge mastiff, sauntering down the middle of the causeway, as if with his hands in his pockets: he is old, grey, brindled, as big as a little Highland bull, and has the Shakespearan dewlaps shaking as he goes.

The Chicken makes straight at him, and fastens on his throat. To our astonishment, the great creature does nothing but stand still, hold himself up, and roar —yes, roar; a long, serious, remonstrative roar. How is this? Bob and I are up to them. *He is muzzled!* The bailies had proclaimed a general muzzling, and his master, studying strength and economy mainly, had encompassed his huge jaws in a home-made apparatus, constructed out of the leather of some ancient *breechin*. His mouth was open as far as it could; his lips curled up in rage—a sort of terrible grin; his teeth gleaming, ready, from out the darkness; the strap across his mouth tense as a bowstring; his whole frame stiff with indignation and surprise; his roar asking us all round, "Did you ever see the like of this?" He looked a statue of anger and astonishment, done in Aberdeen granite.

We soon had a crowd: the Chicken held on. "A knife!" cried Bob; and a cobbler gave him his knife: you know the kind of knife, worn away obliquely to a point, and always keen. I put its edge to the tense leather; it ran before it; and then!—one sudden jerk of that enormous head, a sort of dirty mist about his mouth, no noise—and the bright and fierce little fellow is dropped, limp and dead. A solemn pause: this was more than any of us had bargained for. I turned the little fellow over, and saw he was quite dead: the mastiff had taken him by the small of the back like a rat, and broken it.

He looked down at his victim appeased, ashamed, and amazed, snuffed him all over, stared at him, and, taking a sudden thought, turned round and trotted off. Bob took the dead dog up, and said, "John, we'll bury him after tea." "Yes," said I, and was off after the mastiff. He made up the Cowgate at a rapid swing; he had forgotten some engagement. He turned up the Candlemaker Row, and stopped at the Harrow Inn.

There was a carrier's cart ready to start, and a keen thin, impatient, black-avised little man, his hand at his grey horse's head, looking about angrily for something. "Rab, ye thief!" said he, aiming a kick at my great friend, who drew cringing up, and avoiding the heavy shoe with more agility than dignity, and watching his master's eye, slunk dismayed under the cart—his ears down, and as much as he had of tail down too.

What a man this must be—thought I—to whom my tremendous hero turns tail! The carrier saw the muzzle hanging, cut and useless, from his neck, and I eagerly told him the story, which Bob and I always thought, and still think, Homer, or King David, or Sir Walter alone were worthy to rehearse. The severe little man was mitigated, and condescended to say, "Rab, ma man, puir Rabbie"—whereupon the stump of a tail rose up, the ears were cocked, the eyes filled, and were comforted; the two friends were reconciled. "Hupp!" and a stroke of the whip were given to Jess; and off went the three.

Bob and I buried the Game Chicken that night (we had not much of a tea) in the back-green of his house, in Melville Street, No. 17, with considerable gravity and silence; and being at the time of the Iliad, and, like all boys, Trojans, we of course called him Hector.

Six years have passed—a long time for a boy and a dog: Bob Ainslie is off to the wars; I am a medical student, and clerk at Minto House Hospital.

Rab I saw almost every week, on the Wednesday; and we had much pleasant intimacy. I found the way to his heart by frequent scratching of his huge head, and an occasional bone. When I did not notice him he would plant himself straight before me, and stand wagging that bud of a tail, and looking up, with his head a little to the one side. His master I occasionally saw; he used to call me "Maister John," but was laconic as any Spartan.

One fine October afternoon I was leaving the hospital, when I saw the large gate open, and in walked Rab, with that great and easy saunter of his. He looked as if taking general possession of the place; like the Duke of Wellington entering a subdued city, satiated with victory and peace. After him came Jess, now white from age, with her cart; and in it a woman carefully wrapped up—the carrier leading the horse anxiously, and looking back. When he saw me, James (for his name was James Noble) made a curt and grotesque "boo," and said, "Maister John, this is the mistress; she's got a trouble in her breest—some kind o' an income we're thinkin'."

By this time I saw the woman's face; she was sitting on a sack filled with straw, with her husband's plaid round her, and his big coat, with its large white metal buttons, over her feet.

I never saw a more unforgettable face—pale, serious, *lonely* (it is not easy giving this look by one word; it was expressive of her being so much of her life alone),

255   s

delicate, sweet, without being at all what we call fine.
She looked sixty, and had on a mutch, white as a snow
with its black ribbon; her silvery, smooth hair setting
off her dark-grey eyes—eyes such as one sees only twice
or thrice in a lifetime, full of suffering, full also of the
overcoming of it: her eyebrows black and delicate, and
her mouth firm, patient, and contented, which few
mouths ever are.

As I have said, I never saw a more beautiful countenance, or one more subdued to settled quiet. "Ailie,"
said James, "this is Maister John, the young doctor;
Rab's freend, ye ken. We often speak aboot you,
Doctor." She smiled, and made a movement, but said
nothing; and prepared to come down, putting her plaid
aside and rising. Had Solomon, in all his glory, been
handing down the Queen of Sheba at his palace gate,
he could not have done it more daintily, more tenderly,
more like a gentleman, than did James the Howgate
carrier, when he lifted down Ailie, his wife. The
contrast of his small, swarthy, weather-beaten, keen,
worldly face to hers—pale, subdued, and beautiful—
was something wonderful. Rab looked on concerned and
puzzled, but ready for anything that might turn up—
were it to strangle the nurse, the porter, or even me.
Ailie and he seemed great friends.

"As I was sayin', she's got a kind o' trouble in her
breest, Doctor; wull ye tak' a look at it?" We walked
into the consulting-room, all four; Rab grim and comic,
willing to be happy and confidential if cause could be
shown, willing also to be the reverse, on the same terms.
Ailie sat down, undid her open gown and her lawn
handkerchief round her neck, and, without a word,
showed me her right breast. I looked at and examined
it carefully—she and James watching me, and Rab
eyeing all three. What could I say? there it was, that
had once been so soft, so shapely, so white, so gracious
and bountiful, so "full of all blessed conditions"—hard
a stone, a centre of horrid pain, making that pale

face, with its grey, lucid, reasonable eyes, and its sweet resolved mouth, express the full measure of suffering overcome. Why was that gentle, modest, sweet woman, clean and lovable, condemned by God to bear such a burden?

I got her away to bed. "May Rab and me bide?" said James. "*You* may; and Rab, if he will behave himself." "I'se warrant he's do that, Doctor;" and in slunk the faithful beast. I wish you could have seen him. There are no such dogs now. He belonged to a lost tribe. As I have said, he was brindled, and grey like Rubislaw granite; his hair short, hard, and close, like a lion's; his body thickset, like a little bull—a sort of compressed Hercules of a dog. He must have been ninety pounds weight, at the least; he had a large blunt head; his muzzle black as night, his mouth blacker than any night, a tooth or two—being all he had—gleaming out of his jaws of darkness. His head was scarred with the records of old wounds, a sort of series of fields of battle all over it; one eye out, one ear cropped as close as was Archbishop Leighton's father's; the remaining eye had the power of two; and above it, and in constant communication with it, was a tattered rag of an ear, which was for ever unfurling itself, like an old flag; and then that bud of a tail, about one inch long, if it could in any sense be said to be long, being as broad as long—the mobility, the instantaneousness of that bud were very funny and surprising, and its expressive twinklings and winkings, the intercommunications between the eye, the ear, and it, were of the oddest and swiftest.

Rab had the dignity and simplicity of great size; and having fought his way all along the road to absolute supremacy, he was as mighty in his own line as Julius Cæsar or the Duke of Wellington, and had the gravity of all great fighters.

You must have often observed the likeness of certain men to certain animals, and of certain dogs to men.

Now, I never looked at Rab without thinking of the great Baptist preacher, Andrew Fuller. The same large heavy, menacing, combative, sombre, honest countenance, the same deep inevitable eye, the same look, as of thunder asleep, but ready—neither a dog nor a man to be trifled with.

Next day, my master, the surgeon, examined Ailie. There was no doubt it must kill her, and soon. It could be removed—it might never return—it would give her speedy relief—she should have it done. She curtsied, looked at James, and said, "When?" "To-morrow," said the kind surgeon—a man of few words. She and James and Rab and I retired. I noticed that he and she spoke little, but seemed to anticipate everything in each other. The following day, at noon, the students came in, hurrying up the great stair. At the first landing-place, on a small, well-known black board, was a bit of paper fastened by wafers, and many remains of old wafers beside it. On the paper were the words:

"An operation to-day.—J. B., *Clerk*."

Up ran the youths, eager to secure good places: in they crowded, full of interest and talk. "What's the case?" "Which side is it?"

Don't think them heartless; they are neither better nor worse than you or I: they get over their professional horrors, and into their proper work; and in them pity, as an *emotion*, ending in itself or at best in tears and a long-drawn breath, lessens—while pity, as a *motive*, is quickened, and gains power and purpose. It is well for poor human nature that it is so.

The operating theatre is crowded; much talk and fun, and all the cordiality and stir of youth. The surgeon with his staff of assistants is there. In comes Ailie: one look at her quiets and abates the eager students. That beautiful old woman is too much for them; they sit down, and are dumb, and gaze at her. These rough

258

boys feel the power of her presence. She walks in quickly, but without haste; dressed in her mutch, her neckerchief, her white dimity short-gown, her black bombazeen petticoat, showing her white worsted stockings and her carpet shoes. Behind her was James with Rab. James sat down in the distance, and took that huge and noble head between his knees. Rab looked perplexed and dangerous; for ever cocking his ear and dropping it as fast.

Ailie stepped up on a seat, and laid herself on the table, as her friend the surgeon told her: arranged herself, gave a rapid look at James, shut her eyes, rested herself on me, and took my hand. The operation was at once begun; it was necessarily slow; and chloroform —one of God's best gifts to his suffering children—was then unknown. The surgeon did his work. The pale face showed its pain, but was still and silent. Rab's soul was working within him; he saw that something strange was going on—blood flowing from his mistress, and she suffering; his ragged ear was up, and importunate; he growled and gave now and then a sharp, impatient yelp; he would have liked to have done something to that man. But James had him firm, and gave him a *glower* from time to time, and an intimation of a possible kick; all the better for James, it kept his eye and his mind off Ailie.

It is over; she is dressed, steps gently and decently down from the table, looks for James; then, turning to the surgeon and the students, she curtsies—and, in a low, clear voice, begs their pardon if she has behaved ill. The students—all of us—wept like children; the surgeon happed her up carefully; and, resting on James and me, Ailie went to her room, Rab following. We put her to bed. James took off his heavy shoes, crammed with tackets, heel-capped and toe-capped, and put them carefully under the table, saying, "Maister John, I'm for nane o' yer strynge nurse-bodies for Ailie. I'll be her nurse, and I'll gang aboot on my stockin' soles

259

as canny as pussy." And so he did; and handy and clever, and swift and tender as any woman, was that horny-handed, snell, peremptory little man. Everything she got he gave her: he seldom slept; and often I saw his small shrewd eyes out of the darkness, fixed on her. As before, they spoke little.

Rab behaved well, never moving, showing us how meek and gentle he could be, and occasionally, in his sleep, letting us know that he was demolishing some adversary. He took a walk with me every day, generally to the Candlemaker Row; but he was sombre and mild; declined doing battle, though some fit cases offered, and indeed submitted to sundry indignities; and was always very ready to turn, and came faster back, and trotted up the stair with much lightness, and went straight to that door.

Jess, the mare, had been sent, with her weather-worn cart, to Howgate, and had doubtless her own dim and placid meditations and confusions on the absence of her master and Rab, and her unnatural freedom from the road and her cart.

For some days Ailie did well. The wound healed "by the first intention"; for, as James said, "Oor Ailie's skin's ower clean to heil." The students came in, quiet and anxious, and surrounded her bed. She said she liked to see their young, honest faces. The surgeon dressed her, and spoke to her in his own short, kind way, pitying her through his eyes, Rab and James outside the circle—Rab being now reconciled, and even cordial, and having made up his mind that as yet nobody required worrying, but, as you may suppose, *semper paratus*.

So far well: but, four days after the operation, my patient had a sudden and long shivering, a "groosin'," as she called it. I saw her soon after; her eyes were too bright, her cheek coloured; she was restless, and ashamed of being so; the balance was lost; mischief had begun.

On looking at the wound, a blush of red told the secret;
her pulse was rapid, her breathing anxious and quick,
she wasn't herself, as she said, and was vexed at her
restlessness. We tried what we could. James did
everything, was everywhere; never in the way, never
out of it; Rab subsided under the table into a dark
place, and was motionless, all but his eye, which followed everyone. Ailie got worse; began to wander in
her mind, gently, was more demonstrative in her ways
to James, rapid in her questions, and sharp at times.
He was vexed, and said, "She was never that way
afore; no, never." For a time she knew her head was
wrong, and was always asking our pardon—the dear,
gentle old woman: then delirium set in strong, without
pause. Her brain gave way, and then came that terrible
spectacle,

"The intellectual power, through words and things,
   Went sounding on, a dim and perilous way;

she sang bits of old songs and psalms, stopping suddenly,
mingling the Psalms of David, and the diviner words of
his Son and Lord, with homely odds and ends and scraps
of ballads.

Nothing more touching, or in a sense more strangely
beautiful, did I ever witness. Her tremulous, rapid,
affectionate, eager Scotch voice—the swift, aimless,
bewildered mind, the baffled utterance, the bright and
perilous eye; some wild words, some household cares,
something for James, the names of the dead, Rab called
rapidly and in a "fremyt" voice, and he starting up,
surprised, and slinking off as if he were to blame somehow, or had been dreaming he heard. Many eager
questions and beseechings which James and I could
make nothing if, and on which she seemed to set her
all, and then sink back misunderstood. It was very sad,
but better than many things that are not called sad.
James hovered about, put out and miserable, but active

261

and exact as ever; read to her, when there was a lull, short bits from the psalms, prose and metre, chanting the latter in his own rude and serious way, showing great knowledge of the fit words, bearing up like a man and doting over her as his "ain Ailie." "Ailie, ma woman!" "Ma ain bonnie wee dawtie!"

The end was drawing on: the golden bowl was breaking; the silver cord was fast being loosed—that *animula blandula, vagula, hospes, comesque* was about to flee. The body and the soul—companions for sixty years— were being sundered, and taking leave. She was walking, alone, through the valley of that shadow, into which one day we must all enter—and yet she was not alone, for we know whose rod and staff were comforting her.

One night she had fallen quiet, and, as we hoped, asleep; her eyes were shut. We put down the gas, and sat watching her. Suddenly she sat up in bed, and taking a bed-gown which was lying on it rolled up, she held it eagerly to her breast—to the right side. We could see her eyes bright with a surprising tenderness and joy, bending over this bundle of clothes. She held it as a woman holds her sucking child; opening out her night-gown impatiently, and holding it close, and brooding over it, and murmuring foolish little words, as over one whom his mother comforteth, and who sucks and is satisfied. It was pitiful and strange to see her wasted dying look, keen and yet vague—her immense love.

"Preserve me!" groaned James, giving way. And then she rocked back and forward, as if to make it sleep, hushing it, and wasting on it her infinite fondness. "Wae's me, Doctor; I declare she's thinkin' it's that bairn." "What bairn?" "The only bairn we ever had; our wee Mysie, and she's in the Kingdom forty years and mair." It was plainly true: the pain in the breast, telling its urgent story to a bewildered, ruined brain, was misread and mistaken; it suggested to her the uneasiness of a breast full of milk and then the child; and so again once more they were together, and she had her ain wee Mysie in her bosom.

This was the close. She sank rapidly: the delirium left her; but, as she whispered, she was "clean silly"; it was the lightening before the final darkness. After having for some time lain still—her eyes shut, she said, "James!" He came close to her, and lifting up her calm, clear, beautiful eyes, she gave him a long look, turned to me kindly but shortly, looked for Rab, but could not see him, then turned to her husband again, as if she would never leave off looking, shut her eyes and composed herself. She lay for some time breathing quick, and passed away so gently, that when we thought she was gone, James, in his old-fashioned way, held the mirror to her face. After a long pause, one small spot of dimness was breathed out; it vanished away, and never returned, leaving the blank clear darkness without a stain. "What is our life? it is even a vapour, which appeareth for a little time, and then vanisheth away."

Rab all this time had been full awake and motionless: he came forward beside us: Ailie's hand, which James had held, was hanging down; it was soaked with his tears; Rab licked it all over carefully, looked at her, and returned to his place under the table.

James and I sat, I don't know how long, but for some time, saying nothing; he started up abruptly, and with some noise went to the table, and putting his right fore and middle fingers each into a shoe, pulled them out, and put them on, breaking one of the leather latchets, and muttering in anger, "I did never the like o' that afore!"

I believe he never did; nor after either. "Rab!" he said roughly, and pointing with his thumb to the bottom of the bed. Rab leapt up, and settled himself, his head and eye to the dead face. "Maister John, ye'll wait for me," said the carrier; and disappeared in the darkness, thundering downstairs in his heavy shoes. I ran to a

263

front window: there he was, already round the house, and out at the gate, fleeing like a shadow.

I was afraid about him, and yet not afraid; so I sat down beside Rab, and, being wearied, fell asleep. I awoke from a sudden noise outside. It was November, and there had been a heavy fall of snow. Rab was *in statu quo;* he heard the noise too, and plainly knew it, but never moved. I looked out; and there, at the gate, in the dim morning, for the sun was not up, was Jess and the cart—a cloud of steam rising from the old mare. I did not see James; he was already at the door, and came up the stairs and met me. It was less than three hours since he left, and he must have posted out—who knows how?—to Howgate, full nine miles off; yoked Jess, and driven her astonished into town. He had an armful of blankets, and was streaming with perspiration. He nodded to me, spread out on the floor two pairs of clean old blankets having at their corners "A. G., 1794," in large letters in red worsted. These were the initials of Alison Græme, and James may have looked in at her from without—himself unseen but not unthought of—when he was "wat, wat, and weary," and after having walked many a mile over the hills, may have seen her sitting, while "a' the lave were sleeping'," and by the firelight working her name on the blankets, for her ain James's bed.

He motioned Rab down, and taking his wife in his arms, laid her in the blankets, and happed her carefully and firmly up, leaving the face uncovered; and then lifting her, he nodded again sharply to me, and, with a resolved but utterly miserable face, strode along the passage, and downstairs, followed by Rab. I followed with a light; but he didn't need it. I went out, holding stupidly the candle in my hand in the calm frosty air; we were soon at the gate. I could have helped him, but I saw he was not to be meddled with, and he was strong, and did not need it. He laid her down as tenderly, as safely, as he had lifted her out ten days before—as tenderly as when he had her first in his arms when she was only "A. G."—sorted her, leaving that beautiful sealed face open to the heavens; and then taking Jess by the head, he moved away. He did not notice me, neither did Rab, who presided behind the cart.

I stood till they passed through the long shadow of the College, and turned up Nicolson Street. I heard the solitary cart sound through the streets, and die away and come again; and I returned, thinking of that company going up Liberton Brae, then along Roslin Muir, the morning light touching the Pentlands, and making them like on-looking ghosts; then down the hill through Auchindinny woods, past "haunted Wood-houselee"; and as daybreak came sweeping up the bleak Lammermuirs, and fell on his own door, the company would stop, and James would take the key, and lift Ailie up again, laying her on her own bed, and, having put Jess up, would return with Rab and shut the door.

James buried his wife, with his neighbours mourning, Rab watching the proceedings from a distance. It was snow, and that black ragged hole would look strange in the midst of the swelling, spotless cushion of white. James looked after everything; then rather suddenly fell ill, and took to bed; was insensible when the doctor came, and soon died. A sort of low fever was prevailing in the village, and his want of sleep, his exhaustion, and his misery made him apt to take it. The grave was not difficult to re-open. A fresh fall of snow had again made all things white and smooth; Rab once more looked on, and slunk home to the stable.

And what of Rab? I asked for him next week at the new carrier who got the goodwill of James's business, and was now master of Jess and her cart. "How's Rab?" He put me off, and said rather rudely, "What's *your* business wi' the dowg?" I was not to be put off. "Where's Rab?" He, getting confused and red, and intermeddling with his hair, said, "'Deed, sir, Rab's deid." "Dead! what did he die of?" "Weel, sir," said he, getting redder, "he didna exactly dee; he was killed. I had to brain him wi' a rack-pin; there was nae doin' wi' him. He lay in the treviss wi' the mear, and wadna come oot. I tempit him wi' kail and meat, but he wad tak naething, and keepit me frae feedin' the beast, and he was aye gur gurrin', and grup gruppin' me by the legs. I was laith to mak' awa wi' the auld dowg, his like wasna atween this and Thornhill—but 'deed, sir, I could do naething else." I believed him. Fit end for Rab, quick and complete. His teeth and his friends gone, why should he keep the peace and be civil?

He was buried in the braeface, near the burn, the children of the village, his companions, who used to make very free with him and sit on his ample stomach as he lay half asleep at the door in the sun, watching the solemnity.

TOL'ABLE DAVID

by Joseph Hergesheimer

JOSEPH HERGESHEIMER was born in 1880 and wrote for many years before obtaining recognition with *The Three Black Pennys*, a fine novel of life in an American mining district. This was followed by *Gold and Iron* and *Java End* and many other novels of high distinction. Hergesheimer has been charged with obscurity and convolution of style; but the truth is he has the faculty of writing in almost any manner, and there are few masterpieces of fiction in which the style is so perfectly adapted to the matter as *Tol'able David*. A successful screen version of this excellent story has been made. Speaking of himself and his books Hergesheimer has said: "I always write about people, usually men, usually near forty, who are not happy. The story at bottom is nearly always the same—the struggle between what is called the spirit and what is called the flesh; the spirit is victorious, that is why it seems to me my books are happy books."

TOL'ABLE DAVID

BY

JOSEPH HERGESHEIMER

HE was the younger of two brothers, in his sixteenth year; and he had his father's eyes—a tender and idyllic blue. There, however, the obvious resemblance ended. The elder's azure gaze was set in a face scarred and riven by hardship, debauch and disease; he had been—before he had inevitably returned to the mountains where he was born—a brakeman in the lowest stratum of the corruption of small cities on big railroads; and his thin stooped body, his gaunt head and uncertain hands, all bore the stamp of ruinous years. But in the midst of this his eyes, like David's, retained their singularly tranquil colour of sweetness and innocence.

David was the youngest, the freshest thing imaginable; he was over tall and gawky, his cheeks were as delicately rosy as apple blossoms, and his smile was an epitome of ingenuous interest and frank wonder. It was as if some quality of especial fineness, lingering unspotted in Hunter Kinemon, had found complete expression in his son David. A great deal of this certainly was due to his mother, a thick, solid woman, who retained more than a trace of girlish beauty when she stood back, flushed from the heat of cooking, or, her bright eyes snapping, tramped with heavy pails from the milking shed on a winter morning.

Both the Kinemon boys were engaging. Allen, almost twenty-one, was, of course, the more conspicuous; he was called the strongest youth in Greenstream County. He had his mother's brown eyes; a deep bony box of a chest; rippling shoulders; and a broad peaceful coun-

tenance. He drove the Crabapple stage, between
Crabapple, the village just over the back mountain, and
Beaulings, in West Virginia.

It was twenty-six miles from point to point, a way that
crossed a towering range, hung above a far veil of
unbroken spruce, forded swift glittering streams, and
followed a road that passed rare isolated dwellings,
dominating rocky and precarious patches and hills of
cultivation. One night Allen slept in Beaulings; the
next he was home, rising at four o'clock in order to take
his stage out of Crabapple at seven sharp.

It was a splendid job, and brought them thirty-five
dollars a month; not in mere trade at the store, but actual
money. This, together with Hunter Kinemon's position
tending the rich bottom farm of State Senator Galt,
gave them a position of ease and comfort in Greenstream.
They were a very highly esteemed family.

Galt's farm was in grazing; it extended in deep green
pastures and sparkling water between two high moun-
tainous walls drawn across east and west. In the morning
the rising sun cast long delicate shadows on one side;
at evening the shadow troops lengthened across the
emerald valley from the other. The farm-house occupied
a fenced clearing on the eastern rise, with a grey huddle
of barn and sheds below, a garden patch of innumerable
bean poles, and an incessant stir of snowy chickens.
Beyond, the cattle moved in sleek chestnut-brown and
orange herds; and, farther out, flocks of sheep shifted like
grey-white clouds on a green-blue sky.

It was, Mrs. Kinemon occasionally complained,
powerful lonely, with the store two miles up the road,
Crabapple over a heft of a rise, and no personable
neighbours; and she kept a loaded rifle in an angle of
the kitchen when the men were all out in a distant
pasturage. But David liked it extremely well; he liked
riding an old horse after the steers, the all-night sap
boilings in spring groves, the rough path across a rib
of the mountain to school.

272

Nevertheless, he was glad when studying was over for the year. It finished early in May, on account of upland planting, and left David with a great many weeks filled only with work that seemed to him unadulterated play. Even that didn't last all the time; there were hours when he could fish for trout, plentiful in cool, rocky pools; or shoot grey squirrels in the towering maples. Then, of evenings, he could listen to Allen's thrilling tales of the road, of the gambling and fighting among the lumbermen in Beaulings, or of strange people that had taken passage in the Crabapple stage—drummers, for the most part, with impressive diamond rings and the doggonedest lies imaginable. But they couldn't fool Allen, however believing he might seem. . . . The Kinemons were listening to such a recital by their eldest son now.

They were gathered in a room of very general purpose. It had a rough board floor and crumbling plaster walls, and held a large scarred cherry bed with high posts and a gaily quilted cover; a long couch, covered with yellow untanned sheepskins; a primitive telephone; some painted wooden chairs; a wardrobe, lurching insecurely forward; and an empty iron stove with a pipe let into an original open hearth with a wide rugged stone. Beyond, a door opened into the kitchen, and behind the bed a raw unguarded flight of steps led up to the peaked space where Allen and David slept.

Hunter Kinemon was extended on the couch, his home-knitted socks comfortably free of shoes, smoking a sandstone pipe with a reed stem. Mrs. Kinemon was seated in a rocking-chair with a stained and torn red plush cushion, that moved with a thin complaint on a fixed base. Allen was over against the stove, his corduroy trousers thrust into greased laced boots, and a black cotton shirt open on a chest and throat like pink marble. And David supported his lanky length, in a careless and dust-coloured garb, with a capacious hand on the oak beam of the mantel.

273

It was May, school had stopped, and a door was open on a warm still dusk. Allen's tale had come to an end; he was pinching the ear of a diminutive dog—like a fat white sausage with wire-thin legs and a rat tail—that never left him. The smoke from the elder Kinemon's pipe rose in a tranquil cloud. Mrs. Kinemon rocked vigorously, with a prolonged wail of the chair springs. "I got to put some tallow to that chair," Kinemon proclaimed.

"The house on Elbow Barren's took," Allen told him suddenly—"the one just off the road. I saw smoke in the chimney this evening."

A revival of interest, a speculation, followed this announcement.

"Any women'll get to the church," Mr. Kinemon asserted. "I wonder? Did a person say who were they?"

"I asked; but they're strange to Crabapple. I heard this though; there weren't any women to them—just men—father and sons like. I drew up right slow going by; but nobody passed out a word. It's a middling bad farm place—rocks and berry-bushes. I wouldn't reckon much would be content there."

David walked out through the open doorway and stood on the small covered portico, that with a bench on each side hung to the face of the dwelling. The stars were brightening in the sky above the confining mountain-walls; there was a tremendous shrilling of frogs; the faint clamour of a sheep bell. He was absolutely, irresponsibly happy. He wished the time would hurry when he'd be big and strong like Allen and get out into the absorbing air of the world.

He was dimly roused by Allen's departure in the beginning brightness of the following morning. The road over which the stage ran drew by the rim of the farm; and later David saw the rigid three-seated surrey, the leather mail-bags strapped in the rear, trotted by under the swinging whip of his brother. He heard the faint sharp bark of Rocket, Allen's dog, braced at his side.

David spent the day with his father, repairing the fencing of the middle field, swinging a mall and digging post holes; and at evening his arms ached. But he assured himself he was not tired; any brother of Allen's couldn't give in before such insignificant effort. When Hunter Kinemon turned back toward house and supper David made a wide circle, ostensibly to see whether there was rock salt enough out for the cattle, but in reality to express his superabundant youth, staying qualities, and unquenchable vivid interest in every foot of the valley.

He saw the meanest kind of old fox, and marked what he thought might be its hole; his flashing gaze caught the obscure distant retreat of ground hogs; he threw a contemptuous clod at the woolly-brained sheep; and with a bent willow shoot neatly looped a trout out upon the grassy bank. As a consequence of all this he was late for supper, and sat at the table with his mother, who never took her place until the men—yes, and boys of her family—had satisfied their appetites. The dark came on and she lighted a lamp swinging under a tin reflector from the ceiling. The kitchen was an addition, and had a sloping shed roof, board sides, a polished stove, and a long table with a red cloth.

His father, David learned, attacking a plateful of brown chicken swimming with greens and gravy, was having another bad spell. He had the familiar sharp pain through his back and his arms hurt him.

"He can't be drove to a doctor," the woman told David, speaking, in her concern, as if to an equal in age and comprehension.

David had grown accustomed to the elder's periods of suffering; they came, twisted his father's face into deep lines, departed, and things were exactly as before —or very nearly the same. The boy saw that Hunter Kinemon couldn't support labour that only two or three years before he would have finished without conscious effort. David resolutely ignored this; he felt that it must be a cause of shame, unhappiness to his father; and he never mentioned it to Allen.

Kinemon lay very still on the couch; his pipe, beside him on the floor, had spilled its live core, burning into a length of rag-carpet. His face, hung with shadows like the marks of a sooty finger, was glistening with fine sweat. Not a whisper of complaint passed his dry lips. When his wife approached he attempted to smooth out his corrugated countenance. His eyes, as tenderly blue as flowers, gazed at her with a faint masking of humour.

"This is worse'n usual," she said sharply. "And I ain't going to have you fill yourself with any more of that patent trash. You don't spare me by not letting on. I can tell as soon as you're miserable. David can fetch the doctor from Crabapple to-night if you don't look better."

"But I am," he assured her. "It's just a comeback of an old ache. There was a power of heavy work to that fence."

"You'll have to get more to help you," she continued. "That Galt 'll let you kill yourself and not turn a hand. He can afford a dozen. I don't mind housing and cooking for them. David's only tol'able for lifting, too, while he's growing."

"Why," David protested, "it ain't just nothing what I do. I could do twice as much. I don't believe Allen could help more'n me when he was sixteen. It ain't just nothing at all."

He was disturbed by this insult upon his manhood; if his muscles were still a little stringy it was surprising what he could accomplish with them. He would show her to-morrow.

"And," he added impetuously, "I can shoot better than Allen right now. You ask him if I can't. You ask him what I did with that cranky twenty-two last Sunday up on the mountain."

276

His clear gaze sought her, his lean face quivered with anxiety to impress, convince her of his virility, skill. His jaw was as sharp as the blade of a hatchet. She studied him with a new surprised concern.

"David!" she exclaimed. "For a minute you had the look of a man. A real steady look, like your father. Don't you grow up too fast, David," she directed him in an irrepressible maternal solicitude. "I want a boy—something young—round a while yet."

Hunter Kinemon sat erect and reached for his pipe. The visible strain of his countenance had been largely relaxed. When his wife had left the room for a moment, he admitted to David:

"That was a hard one. I thought she had me that time."

The elder's voice was light, steady. The boy gazed at him with intense admiration. He felt instinctively that nothing mortal could shake the other's courage. And, on top of his mother's complimentary surprise, his father had confided in him, made an admission that, David realized, must be kept from fretting women. He couldn't have revealed more to Allen himself.

He pictured the latter swinging magnificently into Beaulings, cracking the whip over the horses' ears, putting on the grinding brake before the post office. No one, even in that town of reckless drinking, ever tried to down Allen; he was as ready as he was strong. He had charge of Government mail and of passengers; he carried a burnished revolver in a holster under the seat at his hand. Allen would kill anybody who interfered with him. So would he—David—if a man edged up on him or his family; if any one hurt even a dog of his, his own dog, he'd shoot him.

An inextinguishable hot pride, a deep sullen intolerance, rose in him at the thought of an assault on his personal liberty, his rights, or on his connections and belongings. A deeper red burned in his fresh young cheeks; his smiling lips were steady; his candid blue eyes,

277

ineffably gentle, gazed widely against the candle-lit gloom where he was making his simple preparations for bed. The last feeling of which he was conscious was a wave of sharp admiration, of love, for everything and everybody that constituted his home.

Allen, on his return the following evening, immediately opened an excited account of the new family, with no women, on the place by Elbow Barren.

"I heard they were from down hellwards on the Clinch," he repeated; "and then that they'd come from Kentucky. Anyway, they're bad. Ed Arbogast just stepped on their place for a pleasant howdy, and someone on the stoop hollered for him to move. Ed, he saw the shine on a rifle barrel, and went right along up to the store. Then they hired Simmons—the one that ain't good in his head—to cut out bush; and Simmons trailed home after a while with the side of his face all tore, where he'd been hit with a piece of board. Simmons' brother went and asked them what was it about; and one of the Hatburns—that's their name—said he'd busted the loony just because!"

"What did Simmons answer back?" Hunter Kinemon demanded, his coffee-cup suspended.

"Nothing much; he'd law them, or something like that. The Simmonses are right spindling: they don't belong in Greenstream either."

David commented: "I wouldn't have ate a thing till I'd got them!" In the ruddy reflection of the lamp his pink and blue charm, his shy lips, resembled a pastoral divinity of boyhood.

Allen laughed. "That family, the Hatburns—" He paused. "Why, they'd just mow you down with the field daisies."

David flushed with annoyance. He saw his mother studying him with the attentive concern she had first shown the day before yesterday.

"You have no call to mix in with them," Kinemon

told his elder son. "Drive stage and mind your business. I'd even step aside a little from folks like that."

A sense of surprised disappointment invaded David at his father's statement. It seemed to him out of keeping with the elder's courage and determination. It, too, appeared almost spindling. Perhaps he had said it because his wife, a mere woman, was there. He was certain that Allen would not agree with such mildness. The latter, lounging back from the table, narrowed his eyes; his fingers played with the ears of his dog, Rocket. Allen gave his father a cigar and lit one himself, a present from a passenger on the stage. David could see a third in Allen's shirt pocket, and he longed passionately for the day when he would be old enough to have a cigar offered him. He longed for the time when he, like Allen, would be swinging a whip over the horses of a stage, rumbling down a steep mountain, or walking up at the team's head to take off some weight.

Where the stage stopped in Beaulings the railroad began. Allen, he knew, intended in the fall to give up the stage for the infinitely wider world of freight cars; and David wondered whether Priest, the storekeeper in Crabapple who had charge of the awarding of the position, could be brought to see that he was as able a driver, almost, as Allen.

It was probable Priest would call him too young for the charge of the Government mail. But he wasn't; Allen had to admit that he, David, was the straighter shot. He wouldn't step aside for any Hatburn alive. And, he decided, he would smoke nothing but cigars. He considered whether he might light his small clay pipe, concealed under the stoop, before the family; but reluctantly concluded that the day had not yet arrived.

Allen passed, driving the next morning as usual, leaving a grey wreath of dust to settle back into the tranquil yellow sunshine; the sun moved from the east barrier to the west; a cool purple dusk filled the valley, and the shrilling of the frogs rose to meet the night. The following day was almost identical—the shadows swept out, shortened under the groves of trees and drew out again over the sheep on the western slope. Before Allen reached home he had to feed and bed his horses, and walk back the two miles over the mountain from Crabapple; and a full hour before the time for his brother's arrival, David was surprised to see the stage itself making its way over the precarious turf road that led up to the Kinemons' dwelling.

He was standing by the portico, and immediately his mother moved out to his side, as if subconsciously disturbed by the unusual occurrence. David saw, while the stage was still diminutive against the rolling pasture, that Allen was not driving; and there was an odd confusion of figures in a rear seat. Mrs. Kinemon said at once, in a shrill strange voice:

"Something has happened to Allen!"

She pressed her hands against her labouring breast; David ran forward and met the surrey as it came through the fence opening by the stable shed. Ed Arbogast was driving; and a stranger—a drummer evidently—in a white and black check suit, was holding Allen, crumpled in a dreadful bloody faint.

"Where's Hunter?" Arbogast asked the boy.

"There he comes now," David replied, his heart pounding wildly and dread constricting his throat.

Hunter Kinemon and his wife reached the stage at the same moment. Both were plaster-white; but the woman was shaking with frightened concern, while her husband was deliberate and still.

"Help me carry him in to our bed," he addressed Ed Arbogast.

They lifted Allen out and bore him toward the house, his limp fingers, David saw, trailing through the grass. At first the latter involuntarily turned away; but objurgating such cowardice, he forced himself to gaze at Allen. He recognized at once that his brother had not been shot; his hip was too smeared and muddy for that.

It was, he decided, an accident, as Arbogast and the drummer led Hunter Kinemon aside.

David Kinemon walked resolutely up to the little group. His father gestured for him to go away, but he ignored the elder's command. He must know what had happened to Allen. The stranger in the checked suit was speaking excitedly, waving trembling hands—a sharp contrast to the grim immobility of the Greenstream men:

"He'd been talking about that family, driving out of Beaulings and saying how they had done this and that; and when we came to where they lived he pointed out the house. A couple of dark-favoured men were working in a patch by the road, and he waved his whip at them, in a way of speaking; but they never made a sign. The horses were going slow then; and for some reason or other, his little dog jumped to the road and ran in on the patch. Sirs, one of those men spit, stepped up to the dog, and kicked it into Kingdom Come."

David's hands clenched; and he drew in a sharp sobbing breath.

"This Allen," the other continued, "pulled in the team and drawed a gun from under the seat before I could move a hand. You can hear me—I wouldn't have kicked any dog of his for all the gold there is! He got down from the stage and started forward, and his face was black; then he stopped, undecided. He stood studying, with the two men watching him, one leaning careless on a grub hoe. Then, by heaven, he turned and rested the gun on the seat, and walked up to where laid the last of his dog. He picked it up, and says he:

"Hatburn, I got Government mail on that stage to get in under contract, and there's a passenger too—paid to Crabapple; but when I get them two things done I'm coming back to kill you too dead to hear the last trumpet."

The one on the hoe laughed; but the other picked up a stone like my two fists and let Allen have it in the back.

281

It surprised him like; he stumbled forward, and the other stepped out and laid the hoe over his head. It missed him mostly, but enough landed to knock Allen over. He rolled into the ditch, like, by the road; and then Hatburn jumped down on him, deliberate, with lumbermen's irons in his shoes."

David was conscious of an icy flood pouring through him; a revulsion of grief and fury that blinded him. Tears welled over his fresh cheeks in an audible crying. But he was silenced by the aspect of his father. Hunter Kinemon's tender blue eyes had changed apparently into bits of polished steel; his mouth was pinched until it was only a line among the other lines and seaming of his worn face.

"I'd thank you to drive the stage into Crabapple, Ed," he said; "and if you see the doctor coming over the mountain—he's been rung up for—ask him, please, sir, will he hurry." He turned and walked abruptly away, followed by David.

Allen lay under the gay quilt in the Kinemons' big bed. His stained clothes drooped from a chair where Mrs. Kinemon had flung them. Allen's face was like white paper; suddenly it had grown as thin and sharp as an old man's. Only a slight quiver of his eyelids showed that he was not dead.

Hunter Kinemon sat on the couch, obviously waiting for the doctor. He, too, looked queer, David thought. He wished his father would break the dreadful silence gathering over them; but the only sound was the stirring of the woman in the kitchen, boiling a pot of water. Allen moved and cried out in a knife-like agony, and a flicker of suffering passed over his father's face.

An intolerable hour dragged out before the doctor arrived; and then David was driven from the room. He sat outside on the portico, listening to the passage of feet about Allen in a high shuddering protest. David's hands and feet were still cold, but he was conscious of an increasing stillness within, an attitude not unlike his father's. He held out an arm and saw that it was as steady as a beam of the stoop roof. He was without definite plan or knowledge of what must occur; but he told himself that any decision of Hunter Kinemon's must not exclude him.

There were four Hatburns; but two Kinemons were better; and he meant his father and himself, for he knew instinctively that Allen was badly hurt. Soon there would be no Hatburns at all. And then the law could do as it pleased. It seemed to David a long way from the valley, from Allen broken in bed, to the next term of court—September—in Crabapple. The Kinemons could protect, revenge, their own.

The doctor passed out, and David entered where his mother was bent above her elder son. Hunter Kinemon, with a blackened rag, was wiping the lock of an old but efficient repeating rifle. His motions were unhurried, careful. Mrs. Kinemon gazed at him with blanching lips, but she interposed no word. There was another rifle, David knew, in the long cupboard by the hearth; and he was moving to secure it when his father's voice halted him in the middle of the floor.

"You David," he said, "I want you to stop along here with your mother. It ain't fit for her to be left along with Allen, and there's a mess of little things for doing. I want those cows milked dry, and catch in those little Dominicker chickens before that old gander eats them up."

David was about to protest, to sob out a passionate refusal, when a glimpse of his father's expression silenced him. He realized that the slightest argument would be worse than futile. There wasn't a particle of familiar feeling in the elder's voice; suddenly David was afraid of him. Hunter Kinemon slipped a number of heavily greased cartridges into the rifle's magazine. Then he rose and said:

"Well, Mattie?"

His wife laid her hand on his shoulder.

"Hunter," she told him, "you've been a mighty sweet and good husband." He drew his hand slowly and lovingly across her cheek.

"I'm sorry about this, Mattie," he replied. "I've been powerful happy along with you and all of us. David, be a likely boy." He walked out of the room, across the grass to the stable shed.

"He's going to drive to Elbow Barren," David muttered; "and he hadn't ought to have left me to tend the cows and chickens. That's for a woman to do. I ought to be right along with him facing down those Hatburns. I can shoot, and my hand is steady as his."

He stood in the doorway, waiting for the reappearance of his father with the roan horse to hitch to their old buggy. It didn't occur to David to wonder at the fact that the other was going alone to confront four men. The Kinemons had a mort of friends who would have gladly accompanied, assisted Hunter; but this, the boy told himself, was their own affair—their own pride.

From within came the sound of his mother, crying softly, and of Allen murmuring in his pain. David was appalled by the swift change that had fallen over them —the breaking up of his entire world, the shifting of every hope and plan. He was appalled and confused; the thoughtless unquestioning security of his boyhood had been utterly destroyed. He looked about, dazed, at the surrounding scene, callous in its total carelessness of Allen's injury, his haggard father with the rifle. The valley was serenely beautiful; doves were calling from the eaves of the barn; a hen clucked excitedly. The western sky was a single expanse of primrose on which the mountains were jagged and blue.

He had never known the elder to be so long getting the bridle on the roan; the buggy was drawn up outside. An uneasy tension increased within him—a pressing necessity to see his father leading out their horse. He didn't come, and finally David was forced to walk over to the shed.

The roan had been untied, and turned as the boy entered; but David at first failed to find Hunter Kinemon; and then he almost stepped on his hand. His father lay across a corner of the earthen floor, with the bridle tangled in stiff fingers, and his blue eyes staring blankly up.

David stifled an exclamation of dread, and forced himself to bend forward and touch the grey face. Only then he realized that he was looking at death. The pain in his father's back had got him at last! The rifle had been carefully placed against the wall; and, without realizing the significance of his act, David picked it up and laid the cold barrel against his rigid young body.

On the evening after Hunter Kinemon's burial in the rocky steep graveyard above Crabapple, David and his mother sat, one on the couch, the other in her creaking rocking-chair, lost in heavy silence. Allen moved in a perpetual uneasy pain on the bed, his face drawn and fretful, and shadowed by a soft young beard. The wardrobe doors stood open, revealing a stripped interior; wooden chairs were tied back to back; and two trunks —one of mottled paper, the other of ancient leather— stood by the side of a willow basket filled with a miscellany of housekeeping objects.

What were left of the Kinemons were moving into a small house on the edge of Crabapple; Senator Galt had already secured another tenant for the care of his bottom acres and fat herds. The night swept into the room, fragrant and blue, powdered with stars; the sheep bells sounded in a faintly distant clashing; a whip-poor-will beat its throat out against the piny dark.

An overpowering melancholy surged through David; though his youth responded to the dramatic, the tragic change that had enveloped them, at the same time he was reluctant to leave the farm, the valley with its trout and ground hogs, its fox holes and sap boilings. These feelings mingled in the back of his consciousness; his

285

active thoughts were all directed towards the time when, with the rifle, the obligation that he had picked up practically from his dead father's hand, he would walk up to the Hatburn place and take full payment for Allen's injury and their paternal loss.

He felt uneasy that he should have gone before this —at once; but there had been a multitude of small duties connected with the funeral, intimate things that could not be turned over to the kindest neighbours; and the ceremony itself, it seemed to him, should be attended by dignity and repose.

Now, however, it was over; and only his great duty remained, filling the entire threshold of his existence. He had no plan; only a necessity to perform. It was possible that he would fail—there were four Hatburns; and that chance depressed him. If he were killed there was no one else, for Allen could never take another step. That had been disclosed by the most casual examination of his injury. Only himself, David, remained to uphold the pride of the Kinemons.

He gazed covertly at his mother; she must not, certainly, be warned of his course; she was a woman, to be spared the responsibility borne by man. A feeling of her being under his protection, even advice, had grown within him since he had discovered the death in the stable shed. This had not changed his aspect of blossoming youth, the intense blue candour of his gaze; he sat with his knees bent boyishly, his immature hands locked behind his head.

An open wagon, piled with blankets, carried Allen to Crabapple, and Mrs. Kinemon and David followed in the buggy, a great bundle, folded in the bright quilt, roped behind. They soon crossed the range, and dropped into a broader valley. Crabapple lay on a road leading from mountain wall to wall, the houses quickly thinning out into meadow at each end.

A cross-roads was occupied by three stores and the court-house, a square red-brick edifice with a classic
286

white portico and high lantern; and it was out from
that, where the highway had degenerated into a sod-cut
trail, that the future home of the Kinemons lay. It was
a small sombre frame dwelling, immediately on the
road, with a rain-washed patch rising abruptly at the
back. A dilapidated shed on the left provided a meagre
shelter for the roan; and there was an aged and twisted
apple tree over the broken pump.

"You'll have to get at that shed, David," his mother
told him; "the first rain would drown anything inside."

She was settling Allen on the couch with the ragged
sheep-skin. So he would; but there was something else
to attend to first. He would walk over to Elbow Barren
to-morrow. He involuntarily laid his hand on the
barrel of the rifle, temporarily leaned against a table,
when his mother spoke sharply from an inner doorway.

"You David," she said; "come right out into the
kitchen."

There he stood before her, with his gaze stubbornly
fixed on the bare floor, his mouth tight shut.

"David," she continued, her voice now lowered,
fluctuating with anxiety, "you weren't reckoning on
paying off them Hatburns? You never?" She halted,
gazing at him intently. "Why, they'd shoot you up in
no time! You're nothing but a——"

"You can call me a boy if you've a mind to," he
interrupted; "and maybe the Hatburns'll kill me—and
maybe they won't. But there's no one can hurt Allen
like that and go plumb, sniggering free; not while I can
move and hold a gun."

"I saw a look to you that was right manlike a week
or two back," she replied; "and I said to myself: 'There's
David growing up overnight.' I favoured it, too, though
I didn't want to lose you that way so soon. And only
last night I said again: 'Thank God, David's a man in
his heart, for all his pretty cheeks!' I thought I could
build on you, with me getting old and Allen never
taking a mortal step. Priest would give you a place,

and glad, in the store—the Kinemons are mighty good people. I had it all fixed up like that, how we'd live here and pay regular.

"Oh, I didn't say nothing to your father when he started out—he was too old to change; but I hoped you would be different. I hoped you would forget your own feeling, and see Allen there on his back, and me . . . getting along. You're all we got, David. It's no use, I reckon; you'll go like Allen and Hunter, full up with your own pride and never——" She broke off, gazing bitterly at her hands folded in her calico lap.

A new trouble filled David's heart. Through the open doorway he could see Allen, twisting on the couch; his mother was older, more worn, than he had realized. She had failed a great deal in the past few days. She was suddenly stripped of her aspect of authority, force; suddenly she appeared negative, dependent. A sharp pity for her arose through his other contending emotions.

"I don't know how you figure you will be helping Allen by stepping off to be shot instead of putting food in his mouth," she spoke again. "He's got nobody at all but you, David."

That was so; and yet——

"How can I let those skunks set their hell on us?" he demanded passionately. "Why, all Greenstream will think I'm afraid, that I let the Hatburns bust Allen and kill my father. I couldn't stand up in Priest's store; I couldn't bear to look at anybody. Don't you understand how men are about those things?"

She nodded.

"I can see, right enough—with Hunter in the graveyard and Allen with both hips broke. What I can't see is what we'll do next winter; how we'll keep Allen warm and fed. I suppose we can go to the County Home."

But that, David knew, was as disgraceful as the other —his own mother, Allen, objects of public charity! His face was clouded, his hands clenched. It was only a chance that he would be killed; there were four Hatburns though. His heart, he thought, would burst with misery; every instinct fought for the expression, the upholding of the family prestige, honour. A hatred for the Hatburns was like a strangling hand at his throat.

"I got to!" he said; but his voice was wavering; the dull conviction seized him that his mother was right.

All the mountains would think of him as a coward— that Kinemon who wouldn't stand up to the men who had destroyed Allen and his father!

A sob heaved in his chest; rebellious tears streamed over his thin cheeks. He was crying like a baby. He threw an arm up across his eyes and stumbled from the room.

However, he had no intention of clerking back of a counter, of getting down rolls of muslin, papers of buttons, for women, if it could be avoided. Priest's store was a long wooden structure with a painted façade and a high platform before it where the mountain wagons unloaded their various merchandise teamed from the railroad, fifty miles distant. The owner had a small glass-enclosed office on the left as you entered the store; and there David found him. He turned, gazing over his glasses, as the other entered.

"How's Allen?" he asked pleasantly. "I heard he was bad; but we certainly look to have him back driving stage."

"I came to see you about that," David replied. "Allen can't never drive again; but, Mr. Priest, sir, I can. Will you give me a try?"

The elder ignored the question in the concern he exhibited for Allen's injury.

"It is a cursed outrage!" he declared. "Those Hatburns will be got up, or my name's not Priest! We'd have them now, but the jail wouldn't keep them overnight and court three months off."

David preserved a stony silence—the only attitude possible, had decided, in the face of his patent dereliction.

"Will you try me on the Beaulings stage?" he repeated.

"I've been round horses all my life; and I can hold a gun straighter than Allen."

Priest shook his head negatively.

"You are too light—too young," he explained; "you have to be above a certain age for the responsibility of the mail. There are some rough customers to handle. If you only had five more years now. We are having a hard time finding a suitable man. A damned shame about Allen! Splendid man!"

"Can't you give it to me for a week?" David persisted, "and see how I do?"

They would have awarded him the position immediately, he felt, if he had properly attended to the Hatburns. He wanted desperately to explain his failure to Priest, but a dogged pride prevented. The storekeeper was tapping on an open ledger with a pen, gazing doubtfully at David.

"You couldn't be worse than the drunken object we have now," he admitted. "You couldn't hold the job permanent yet, but I might let you drive extra—a day or so—till we find a man. I'd like to do what I could for Mrs. Kinemon. Your father was a good man, a good customer. . . . Come and see me again—say, day after to-morrow."

This half-promise partly rehabilitated his fallen pride. There was no sign of the men he passed that they held him in contempt for neglecting to kill the Hatburns; and his mother wisely avoided the subject. She wondered a little at Priest's considering him, even temporarily, for the stage; but confined her wonder to a species of compliment. David sat beside Allen, while the latter, between silent spaces of suffering, advised him of the individual characters and attributes of the horses that might come under his guiding reins.

It seemed incredible that he should actually be seated in the driver's place on the stage, swinging the heavy whip out over a team trotting briskly into the early morning; but there he was. There were no passengers, and the stage rode roughly over a small bridge of loose boards beyond the village. He pulled the horses into a walk on the mountain beyond, and was soon skirting the Galt farm, with its broad fields, where he had lived as a mere boy.

David slipped his hand under the leather seat and felt the smooth handle of the revolver. Then, on an even reach, he wrapped the rains about the whipstock, and publicly filled and lighted his clay pipe. The smoke drifted back in a fragrant cloud; the stage moved forwards steadily and easily; folded in momentary forgetfulness, lifted by a feeling of mature responsibility, he was almost happy. But he swung down the mountain beyond his familiar valley, crossed a smaller ridge, and turned into a stony sweep rising on the left.

It was Elbow Barren. In an instant a tide of bitterness, of passionate regret, swept over him. He saw the Hatburns' house, a rectangular bleak structure crowning a grey prominence, with the tender green of young pole beans on one hand, and a disorderly barn on the other, and a blue plume of smoke rising from an unsteady stone chimney against an end of the dwelling. No one was visible.

Hot tears filled his eyes as the stage rolled along past the muddy ditch into which Allen had fallen. The mangy curs! His grip tightened on the reins and the team broke into a clattering trot, speedily leaving the Barren behind. But the day had been robbed of its sparkle, his position of its pleasurable pride. He saw again his father's body on the earthen floor of the stable, the bridle in his stiff fingers; Allen carried into the house. And he, David Kinemon, had had to step back, like a coward or a woman, and let the Hatburns triumph.

The stage drew up before the Beaulings post office in the middle of the afternoon. David delivered the mail-bags, and then led the team back to a stable on the grassy verge of the houses clustered at the end of tracks laid precariously over a green plain to a box-like station.

Beaulings had a short row of unpainted, two-storey
structures, the single street cut into deep muddy scars;
stores with small dusty windows; eating-houses elevated
on piles; an insignificant mission chapel with a tar-
papered roof; and a number of obviously masked depots
for the illicit sale of liquor.

A hotel, neatly painted white and green, stood
detached from the main activity. There, washing his
face in a tin basin on a back porch, David had his
fried supper, sat for a while outside in the gathering
dusk, gazing at the crude-oil flares, the passing dark
figures beyond, the still obscured immensity of mountain
and forest. And then he went up to a pine-ceiled room,
like the heated interior of a packing-box, where he
partly undressed for bed.

The next mid-morning, descending the sharp grade
towards Elbow Barren, there was no lessening of David's
bitterness against the Hatburns. The flavour of tobacco
died in his mouth, he grew unconscious of the lurching
heavy stage, the responsibility of the mail, all committed
to his care. A man was standing by the ditch on the
reach of scrubby grass that fell to the road; and David
pulled his team into the slowest walk possible. It was
his first actual sight of a Hatburn. He saw a man,
middling tall, with narrow, high shoulders, and a clay-
yellow countenance, extraordinarily pitched through the
temples, with minute restless black eyes. The latter were
the only mobile feature of his slouching indolent pose,
his sullen regard. He might have been a scarecrow,
David thought, but for that glittering gaze.

The latter leaned forward, the stage barely moving,
and looked unwaveringly at the Hatburn beyond. He
wondered whether the man knew him—David Kinemon. But of course he did; all the small details of
mountain living circulated with the utmost rapidity from
clearing to clearing. He was now directly opposite the
other; he could take out the revolver and kill that

Hatburn, where he stood, with one precise shot. His hand instinctively reached under the seat. Then he remembered Allen, for ever dependent on the couch; his mother, who had lately seemed so old. The stage was passing the motionless figure. David drew a deep painful breath, and swung out his whip with a vicious sweep.

His pride, however, returned when he drove into Crabapple, down the familiar street, past the familiar men and women turning to watch him, with a new automatic measure of attention; in his elevated position. He walked back to his dwelling with a slight swagger of hips and shoulders, and, with something of a flourish, laid down the two dollars he had been paid for the trip to Beaulings.

"I'm to drive again to-morrow," he stated to his mother and Allen; "after that Priest has a regular man. I suppose, then, I'll have to go into the store."

The last seemed doubly difficult now, since he had driven stage. As he disposed of supper, eating half a pie with his cracklings and greens, his mother moved from the stove to the table, refilled his plate, waved the paper streamers of the fly-brush above his head, exactly as she had for his father. Already, he assured himself, he had become a man.

The journey to Beaulings the following day was an unremarkable replica of the one before. He saw no Hatburns; the sun wheeled from east to west at apparently the same speed as the stage; and Beaulings held its inevitable surge of turbulent lumbermen, the oil flares made their lurid note on the vast unbroken starry canopy of night.

The morning of his return was heavy with a wet low vapour. The mail-bags, as he strapped them to the rear rack, were slippery; the dawn was a slow monotonous widening of dull light. There were no passengers for Crabapple, and David, with his coat collar turned up about his throat, urged the horses to a faster gait through the watery cold.

The brake set up a shrill grinding, and then the stage passed Elbow Barren in a smart rattle and bumping. After that David slowed down to light his pipe. The horses willingly lingered, almost stopping; and the memory of the slippery bags at the back of his head, David dismounted, walked to the rear of the stage.

A chilling dread swept through him as he saw, realized, that one of the Government sacks was missing. The straps were loose about the remaining two; in a minute or more they would have gone. Panic seized him, utter misery, at the thought of what Priest, Crab-apple, would say. He would be disgraced, contemptuously dismissed—failure in the trust laid on him.

He collected his faculties by a violent effort; the bags, he was sure, had been safe coming down the last mountain; he had walked part of the way, and he was certain that he would have noticed anything wrong. The road was powerful bad through the Barren.

He got up into the stage, backed the team abruptly on its haunches, and slowly retraced his way to the foot of the descent. There was no mail lying on the empty road. David turned again, his heart pounding against his ribs, tears of mortification, of apprehension, blurring his vision. The bag must have fallen here in Elbow Barren. Subconsciously, he stopped the stage. On the right the dwelling of the Hatburns showed vaguely through the mist. No one else could have been on the road. A troubled expression settled on his glowing countenance, a pondering doubt; then his mouth drew into a determined line.

"I'll have to go right up and ask," he said aloud.

He jumped down to the road, led the horses to a convenient sapling, where he hitched them. Then he drew his belt tighter about his slender waist and took a step forward. A swift frown scarred his brow, and he turned and transferred the revolver to a pocket in his trousers.

The approach to the house was rough with stones and

muddy clumps of grass. A track, he saw, circled the dwelling to the back; but he walked steadily and directly up to the shallow portico between windows with hanging, partly slatted shutters. The house had been painted dark brown a long while before; the paint had weathered and blistered into a depressing harmony with the broken and mossy shingles of the roof, the rust-eaten and sagging gutters festooning the ragged eaves.

David proceeded up the steps, hesitated, and then, his mouth firm and hand steady, knocked. He waited for an apparently interminable space, and then knocked again, more sharply. Now he heard voices within. He waited rigidly for steps to approach, the door to open, but in vain. They had heard, but chose to ignore his summons; and a swift cold anger mounted in him. He could follow the path round to the back; but, he told himself, he—David Kinemon—wouldn't walk to the Hatburns' kitchen door. They should meet him at the front. He beat again on the scarred wood, waited; and then, in an irrepressible flare of temper, kicked the door open.

He was conscious of a slight gasping surprise at the dark mouldy-smelling hall open before him. A narrow bare stairway mounted above, with a passage at one side, and on each hand entrances were shut on farther interiors. The scraping of a chair, talking came from the left; the door, he saw, was not latched. He pushed it open and entered. There was a movement in the room still beyond, and he walked evenly into what evidently was a kitchen.

The first thing he saw was the mail-bag, lying intact on a table. Then he was meeting the concerted stare of four men. One of two, so similar that he could not have distinguished between them, he had seen before at the edge of the road. Another was very much older, taller, more sallow. The fourth was strangely fat, with a great red hanging mouth. The latter laughed uproariously, a jangling mirthless sound followed by a

295

mumble of words without connective sense. David moved towards the mail-bag.

"I'm driving stage and lost those letters. I'll take them right along."

The oldest Hatburn, with a pail in his hand, was standing by an opening, obviously at the point of departure on a small errand. He looked towards the two similar men nearer David.

"Boy," he demanded, "did you kick in my front door?"

"I'm the Government's agent," David replied. "I've got to have the mail. I'm David Kinemon too; and I wouldn't step round to your back door, Hatburn—not if there was a boiling of you!"

"You'll learn you this," one of the others broke in: "it will be the sweetest breath you ever draw'd when you get out that back door!"

The elder moved on to the pounded earth beyond. Here, in their presence, David felt the loathing for the Hatburns a snake inspires—dusty brown rattlers and silent cotton-mouths. His hatred obliterated every other feeling but a dim consciousness of the necessity to recover the mail-bag. He was filled with an overpowering longing to revenge Allen; to mark them with the payment of his father, dead in the stable shed.

His objective senses were abnormally clear, cold; he saw every detail of the Hatburns' garb—the soiled shirts with buttoned pockets on their left breasts; the stained baggy breeches in heavy boots—such boots as had stamped Allen into nothingness; dull yellow faces and beady eyes; the long black hair about their dark ears.

The idiot thrust his fingers into his loose mouth, his shirt open on a hairy pendulous chest. The Hatburn who had not yet spoken showed a row of tobacco-brown broken teeth.

"He mightn't get a heave on that breath," he asserted.

The latter lounged over against a set of open shelves where, David saw, lay a heavy rusted revolver. Hatburn picked up the weapon and turned it slowly in his thin grasp.

"I'm carrying the mail," David repeated, his hand on the bag. "You've got no call on this or on me."

He added the last with tremendous effort. It seemed unspeakable that he should be there, the Hatburns before him, and merely depart.

"What do you think of putting the stage under a soft little strawberry like that?" the other enquired.

For answer there was a stunning report, a stinging odour of saltpetre; and David felt a sharp burning on his shoulder, followed by a slow warmish wet, spreading.

"I didn't go to do just that there!" the Hatburn who had fired explained. "I wanted to clip his ear, but he twitched like."

David picked up the mail-bag and took a step backwards in the direction he had come. The other moved between him and the door.

"If you get out," he said, "it'll be through the hog-wash."

David placed the bag on the floor, stirred by a sudden realization—he had charge of the stage, official responsibility for the mail. He was no longer a private individual; what his mother had commanded, entreated had no force here and now. The Hatburns were unlawfully detaining him.

As this swept over him, a smile lighted his fresh young cheeks, his frank mouth, his eyes like innocent flowers. Hatburn shot again, this time the bullet flicked at David's old felt hat. With his smile lingering he smoothly levelled the revolver from his pocket and shot the mocking figure in the exact centre of the pocket patched on his left breast.

David wheeled instantly before the other Hatburn running for him, and stopped him with a bullet as remorselessly placed as the first. The two men on the floor stiffened grotesquely and the idiot crouched in a corner, whimpering.

David passed his hand across his brow; then he bent and grasped the mail-bag. His was still pausing when the remaining Hatburn strode into the kitchen. The latter whispered a sharp oath, David shifted the bag; but the elder had him before he could bring the revolver up. A battering blow fell, knocked the pistol clattering over the floor, and David instinctively caught the other's wrist.

The blows multiplied, beating David into a daze, through which a single realization persisted—he must not lose his grip upon the arm that was swinging him about the room, knocking over chairs, crashing against the table, even drawing him across the hot iron of the stove. He must hold on.

He saw the face above him dimly through the deepening mist—it seemed demoniacal, inhuman, reaching up to the ceiling—a yellow giant bent on his destruction.

His mother, years ago, lives away, had read to them —to his father and Allen and himself—about a giant, a giant and David, and in the end——

He lost all sense of the entity of the man striving to break him against the wooden angles of the room; he had been caught, was twisting, in a great storm; a storm with thunder and cruel flashes of lightning, a storm hammering and hammering at him.

. . . Must not lose his hold on—on life! He must stay fast against everything! It wasn't his hand gripping the destructive force towering above him, but a strange quality within him, at once within him and aside, burning his heart and directing him from without.

The storm subsided; out of it emerged the livid face of Hatburn; and then, quite easily, he pitched David back across the floor. He lay there a moment and then stirred, partly rose, beside the mail-bag. His pistol was lying before him; he picked it up.

The other was deliberately moving the dull barrel of a revolver up over his body. A sharp sense of victory possessed David and he whispered his brother's name.

Hatburn fired—uselessly. The other's battered lips smiled. Goliath, that was the giant's name. He shot easily, securely—once.

Outside, the mail-bag seemed weighted with lead. He swayed and staggered over the rough declivity to the road. It required a superhuman effort to heave the pack into the stage. The strap with which he had hitched the horses had turned into iron. At last it was untied. He clambered up to the enormous height of the driver's seat, unwrapped the reins from the whipstock, and the team started forward.

He swung to the lurching of the stage like an inverted pendulum; darkness continually thickened before his vision; waves of sickness swept up to his head. He must keep the horses on the road, he must forward the Government mail!

A grim struggle began between his beaten flesh, a terrible weariness, and that spirit which seemed to be at once a part of him and a voice. He wiped the blood from his young brow; from his eyes miraculously blue like an ineffable May sky.

"Just a tol'able David," he muttered weakly—"only just tol'able!"

STAFF-CAPTAIN RIBNIKOV
by Alexandre Kuprin

ALEXANDRE KUPRIN, whose *Staff-Captain Ribnikov* is one of the most remarkable short stories of the modern era, was born at Narovtchak, Penza, in 1870. He began life as a soldier, becoming second lieutenant in a Dnieper regiment. After a few years he left the army in order to devote himself to a writing career. His first success, *The Duel*, was regarded as a trenchant criticism of pre-revolution Russian military life. Subsequently, Kuprin wrote stories with less deliberate purpose, but his knowledge of Russian army methods in the days of the last of the Tsars served him in good stead when writing what is probably the most dramatic "spy" story ever written, as well as a great story of human courage.

STAFF-CAPTAIN RIBNIKOV

BY

ALEXANDRE KUPRIN

I

ON the very day when the terrible defeat of the Russian fleet at Tshushima was being consummated and when the first timid, whispered rumours of that bloody Japanese victory began to spread over Europe —on that very same day Staff-Captain Ribnikov, who lived in a nameless alley in the Piesky quarter, got a telegram from Irkutsk: "Send papers immediately watch invalid pay expenses."

Staff-Captain Ribnikov at once told his landlady that business summoned him away for a day—or perhaps two—from Petersburg, and that therefore she mustn't be anxious at his absence. Then he dressed, went out, and never more returned.

Only five days afterwards the landlady was summoned to the police station to have her evidence about her late lodger taken down. The honest, stout, forty-five years old woman, widow of an official attached to an ecclesiastical court, told frankly everything she knew. Her former lodger had been a quiet, poor man, rather stupid, a moderate eater, civil. He hadn't drunk or smoked, he'd seldom left the house and he'd received no visitors.

She could say nothing more, in spite of all her respectful terror of the gendarme captain, who moved his magnificent moustache ferociously and hadn't to search in his pocket for ugly words.

During that intervening five days, Staff-Captain Ribnikov hurried on foot and drove, all over St. Petersburg, far and wide. He was in the streets, in the

305

restaurants, in the theatres in the trams, in the railway stations—that little, swarthy, lame officer, curiously garrulous, untidy, and not particularly sober, dressed in an infantry uniform with a turned-over red collar—a veritable type of the rats that haunt military hospitals or offices, or commissariats. He also made his appearance time and again at headquarters, at the offices of the Committee for the Care of the Wounded, at police stations, in the office of the general commanding the garrison, in the Cossack Command, and in dozens more of government offices and court-rooms, scattering his servile, absurd complaints and claims, his humble petitions, with rugged, soldierly speech and noisy patriotism. Everyone already knew by heart that he had served in the Transport Corps, that he had got a blow on the head at Liao-Yang, and that he had been wounded in the leg during the retreat from Mukden. Why the devil hadn't he got a gratuity till now? Why hadn't he been given his daily maintenance money and his fare home? And then his pay for two months that was due? He was perfectly ready to shed his last drop of blood, confound it all, for the Tsar, the altar and his country, and he'd go back to the Far East as soon as ever his wounded leg was cured. But, the devil take it all, that accursed leg wouldn't heal! Just imagine, it had gangrened! Yes, indeed, they might look themselves! And he would put the wounded leg on a chair and eagerly turn up his trousers, but each time he was stopped, with squeamish, compassionate shame. His bustling, nervous familiarity of manner, his timidity, strangely bordering on impudence, his stupidity and nagging, idle curiosity annoyed people who were engaged in important and terribly responsible clerical work.

It was no use explaining to him, with the greatest possible kindness, that he'd come to the wrong place, that he should apply somewhere else, that he ought to submit such and such documents, that they'd let him know. . . . He understood nothing, simply nothing at all, but one couldn't get into a rage with him. He was so defenceless, timid and simple, and if one turned round on him crossly he only smiled, baring his gums with an idiotic look, bowed quickly and repeatedly and rubbed his hands agitatedly; or again he would say, in a hoarse, ingratiating voice:

"Please, won't you oblige me with a cigarette? I'm just dying for a smoke and I haven't enough to buy any. . . . It's blessed to have nothing . . . poverty, so they say, isn't a crime, but it's horrid!"

Thus did he disarm even the most irritable and gloomy officials. They gave him cigarettes and let him sit at the corner of the table. Involuntarily and negligently they replied to his tiresome questions about the course of military events. There was, too, something very touching, childishly sincere, in the painful curiosity with which the unfortunate, shabby, impoverished soldier followed the course of the war. Quite simply, out of sheer humanity, they wanted to satisfy him, inform him and encourage him, and so they spoke more openly to him than to others.

He was so interested in anything touching the Russo-Japanese war that while some involved technical matter was being inquired into he would stroll from room to room, from table to table, and whenever he caught a word or two about the war, he came up close and listened, with his strained and rather stupid smile.

When at last he went away, he left behind him, together with a feeling of relief, a sort of sad, burdensome, fearful regret. Often very neat, dandified officers, belonging to the Headquarters Staff, spoke of him with a kind of lofty bitterness.

"And that's a Russian officer!" they would say. "Just look at that type! Now isn't it clear why we're losing battle after battle? Dullness, stupidity, complete lack of a sense of his own dignity! Poor Russia!"

During those troublous days Staff-Captain Ribnikov took a room in a grubby hostelry near the main station.

Though he always had with him a reserve-officer's passport, for some reason or other he deemed it necessary to disclose the fact that his papers were in the Governor's office. To the hotel he brought his traps—a hold-all containing his blanket and pillow, a valise and a cheap, new trunk, in which was linen and a complete suit of mufti.

Afterwards the hotel servants declared that he used to come in late and slightly the worse for drink, that he always punctiliously gave the porter who opened the door the him, a tip to buy himself tea with. He slept no more than three or four hours, and sometimes he didn't undress when he lay down. He rose early and sometimes for a long time would walk up and down the room. He went out at noon.

Sometimes the staff-captain sent telegrams from various post offices, and all these telegrams expressed great anxiety about some person who was wounded and seriously ill, probably somebody very dear to the staff-captain.

It was just this strange busy, half-baked fellow that Vladimir Ivanovitch Shchavinsky, a journalist on the staff of a big St. Petersburg paper, happened to meet.

II

Before going to the races, Shchavinsky turned into a little dark restaurant: "The Glory of Petersburg," where newspaper reporters generally assembled about two o'clock, for the exchange of thought and news. It was a rather daring, gay, cynical, omniscient and hungry assembly, and Shchavinsky, to a certain extent an aristocrat of the journalistic world, didn't, of course, belong to it. His Sunday articles, brilliant and amusing, though not deep, had considerable success with the public. He earned very well, dressed perfectly, and had a wide circle of acquaintances. So he was cordially received at "The Glory of Petersburg" as well as in other places, for his free, acute speech and for the pleasant open-handedness with which he lent small gold coins to his brother writers. On this particular day the reporters had promised to get him a programme of the race meeting, with mysterious notes from the stables written on it. Basil, the porter, with a respectful and friendly smile, took Shchavinsky's overcoat, saying:

"Please, Vladimir Ivanovitch, everyone's here. They're in the largest private room, with Prochov."

And stout, close-cropped Prochov, with his carroty moustache, smiled kindly and familiarly, as usual not looking into the eyes but over the head of a respected guest.

"It's ages since you honoured us with your company, Vladimir Ivanovitch. Come this way, please! All the company's here."

As usual, his brother writers were sitting round a long table and, hastily dipping their pens in inkpots, were scribbling swiftly on long strips of paper. Simultaneously they went on, without interrupting that occupation, swallowing pasty and fried sausages with chipped potatoes, and drinking vodka and beer, smoking and exchanging the newest news of the town, and unprintable editorial-room gossip. One slept soundly on a sofa, with his pocket-handkerchief under his head. The air in the room was blue and thick, and there were clouds of tobacco smoke floating in it.

Having greeted the reporters, Shchavinsky noticed among them a staff-captain in an infantry uniform. He was sitting with his legs apart, leaning his arms and chin on the hilt of an immense sword. Shchavinsky didn't wonder at the sight of him, having grown accustomed to wonder at nothing in journalistic life. He was aware that in that mixed and careless company there got merged for weeks at a time—provincial land-owners, jewellers, musicians, teachers of dancing, actors, owners of menageries, fishmongers, managers of café-chantants, club-gamblers and others, with the faces of people of no definite profession.

When Shchavinsky came to the officer, the latter

stood up, straightened his back, stuck his elbows out and introduced himself in the hoarse, drink-sodden voice of an officer of the line.

"Ahem—Staff-Captain Ribnikov. Pleased to meet you! Are you a writer too? Very, very pleased! I respect writers. The Press—is the sixth Great Power, isn't it? Eh?"

With that he smiled, brought his heels together, shook Shchavinsky's hand heartily, and the whole time kept bowing in a most absurd manner, quickly bending and raising the upper part of his body.

"Where have I seen him?"

An uneasy thought flashed through Shchavinsky's mind: "He's strangely like somebody. Who's he like?"

Here in the room were all the notabilities of the Petersburg journalistic world. There were the Three Musketeers—Kodlubtzov, Riazhkin and Popov. Nobody ever saw them apart, even their surnames, if you pronounced them one after the other, went very slickly into an iambic tetrameter. This didn't prevent them from perpetually squabbling and inventing tales about the most incredible extortion, criminal fraud, slander and blackmail, against each other. Serge Kondrashov, too, was there, who, on account of his unbridled sensuality was called "not a man but a pathological case." There was one whose surname time had effaced—only his usual nickname, Matanya, remained, and by that all Petersburg knew him. Of gloomy Svishchev, who wrote paragraphs about the police courts they said, by way of a friendly joke: "Svishchev is a great blackmailer, he won't take less than three roubles." On the sofa slept the long-haired poet, Piestruchin, who kept his fragile, drunken self alive by writing lyric poems in honour of the birthdays of the members of the imperial family, and of the twelve church holidays. There were others with names that were no less great: specialists in municipal affairs, in fire-brigade matters, in the opening and closing of public gardens.

Tall, pimply, tousled headed Matanya said:

"They'll bring you the menu in a minute, Vladimir Ivanovitch. Meanwhile I would recommend the brave staff-captain to your attention. He's but just back from the Far East, where, it may be said, he's been reducing to powder our yellow-faced squint-eyed, crafty enemy. Now, then, general, get on!"

The officer cleared his throat and spat on the floor to one side.

"Boor!" thought Shchavinsky, frowning.

"The Russian soldier, brother, isn't just a pound of raisins," cried Ribnikov hoarsely, clanking his sword. "He's a marvellous hero, as immortal Suvorov said. What? Am I lying? In a word. . . . Well, I'll tell you frankly, our generals in the East aren't worth a damn. No doubt you know our proverb: "Like priest, like people.' Eh what? They thieve, they play cards, they run after women . . . and you know, 'Where the devil can't go, he sends a woman.'"

"You began something about maps, General," Matanya reminded him.

"Aha, about maps! Merci! What a head I have! I've been drinking all day." Ribnikov cast a quick penetrating glance at Shchavinsky. "Yes, that's it! They ordered a certain colonel on the General Staff to carry out a reconnaissance of the route to be followed. He took a platoon of Cossacks with him, bold lads, devil take them! Eh? What? He took a guide and he went. He came to a village. 'What's its name?' asked he. The guide said nothing. 'Now, then, my children!'— The Cossacks at once went for the guide with their whips. The guide said: 'Butundu.' Now 'Butundu' is the Chinese for 'I don't understand.' 'Aha, the son of a dog has spoken!' said the colonel, and wrote on the map: 'Butundu village.' They started again. They came to another village. Its name? 'Butundu.' 'What, Butundu again?' 'Butundu.' The colonel wrote 'Butundu' once more. So he marked ten villages

311 W

as 'Butundu,' and was like the fellow in Tchekov: 'Though you,' says he, 'are Ivanov the seventh, you're a fool all the same.' "

"Oh! Oh! So you know Tchekov?" asked Shchavinsky.

"Who? Tchekov? Anton? Why, of course! He's a friend of mine. We've had fine drinks together. "Although,' he said, 'you're the seventh, still you're a fool.' "

While he was talking Shchavinsky looked at him hard. Everything about him was typical of the infantry soldier, his voice, his manners, his threadbare uniform, his vulgar, coarse language. Shchavinsky had come across hundreds of drink-sodden captains like him. They had smiled just in his way, cursed like he did, twirled their moustaches with the same daring flourish, shrugged their shoulders, stuck out their elbows, leaned picturesquely on their swords and clinked imaginary spurs. Still, there was something peculiar about him, something mysterious that Shchavinsky had never seen before and couldn't define; some inward, intense nervous force. It was rather as if Shchavinsky wouldn't have been surprised if suddenly this hoarse, drunken soldier of fortune had spoken about fine and intellectual things, easily and clearly, in cultivated language; but he wouldn't have been surprised either, at some mad, unexpected, hasty, nay even bloody, outburst on the staff-captain's part.

Looking at his face, Shchavinsky was struck by the fact that it looked so different full-face and in profile. Seen from the side, it was an ordinary Russian face, with something slightly Tartar about it: the little, protuberant forehead, beneath a pointed skull, the formless, Russian nose, plum-shaped, the thin, bristly, black moustache and the little beard, the close-shaven head with grizzled hair, the complexion tanned to dark yellow by the sun. But when for the first time Ribnikov turned his full face towards Shchavinsky, he at once recalled somebody to him. There was something extraordinarily familiar about him, though what it was Shchavinsky couldn't tell. He perceived it in those narrow, bright, slanting, eagle eyes, in the alarming angle of the black eyebrows, which sloped upwards from above the nose, in the energetic dryness of the skin, tightly stretched over the big cheek-bones; but particularly in the expression of the whole face—sardonic, mocking, intelligent—perhaps even arrogant, but not human, rather animal, or, rather, the face of some inhabitant of another planet.

"I must have seen him in a dream," thought Shchavinsky. Looking at Ribnikov, he involuntarily screwed up his eyes and put his head on one side. At once Ribnikov turned round on him and chuckled nervously and loudly:

"Why, have you taken a fancy to me, Mr. Author? Are you interested in me? I—" He raised his voice and, with comical pride hit his chest with his fist. "I'm Staff-Captain Ribnikov. Rib-ni-kov! 'The orthodox Russian warrior slaughters enemies unnumbered'—thus runs the Russian soldier's song. Eh? What?"

Kodlubtzov, running his pen over the paper and not looking up, said lightly:

"And, unnumbered, surrenders!"

Ribnikov glanced swiftly at Kodlubtzov and Shchavinsky observed that in his tawny eyes gleaned queer, greenish-yellow fires. But it was only for a moment. Immediately Staff-Captain Ribnikov chuckled, extended his arms and then resoundingly smacked his thighs.

"It can't be helped," he said. "It's the will of the Lord! It's not for nothing that they say: 'The scythe hit a stone.' Eh? What?"

He turned again to Shchavinsky, tapped him lightly on his knee, and from his lips issued a sound expressive of hopelessness: "Pfit! We do everything at random, anyhow, anyway, to get done with it. We don't know how to adapt ourselves to the terrain, the shells won't

313

fit the guns: the men at the front don't get anything to eat for four days and nights together. And the Japanese, the devil take them, work like machines. Yellow monkeys—but there's civilization on their side, damn them! Eh? What?"

"Do you think they may beat us?" asked Shchavinsky.

Ribnikov's lips twitched again. Shchavinsky had already noted this habit. All through the conversation, specially when the staff-captain asked a question and, on his guard, awaited the answer, or nervously turned round to meet somebody's stare, his mouth twitched quickly, first at one side, then at the other, making a strange grimace, rather like a spasmodic, sardonic smile. And then he would hastily lick his cracked, dry lips with the end of his tongue—thin, bluish lips, like those of a monkey or a goat.

"Who knows?" answered the staff-captain. "God alone! You can't cross your own threshold without the help of God, so they say. Eh? What? The campaign's not finished yet. Everything's in the future. We Russians have got used to victory. Remember Poltava, the unforgettable Suvorov . . . and Sebastopol! And how, in 1812, we chased away the greatest leader in the world, Napoleon! The God of Russia is great, eh?"

He spoke, and the corners of his mouth twitched queerly, with a sardonic, mocking, inhuman smile, and a sardonic, yellow gleam played in his eyes, under those black, severe brows of his.

At that moment Shchavinsky's coffee was brought in.

"Wouldn't you like a glass of brandy?" said he to the staff-captain.

Ribnikov again tapped him lightly on the knee.

"No thank you, my dear fellow. The devil alone knows how much I've drunk to-day. My head's splitting. Damn it all, I've been at it since the morning! Russia's delight's in the bottle—Eh? What?" he exclaimed suddenly, with a mischievous glance and a suddenly drunken sound in his voice.

314

"He's pretending," thought Shchavinsky. For some reason or other he wouldn't leave it at that, and went on pressing the staff-captain to drink.

"Perhaps you'd like some beer, or some red wine?"

"No, thank you very much. I'm drunk without them. Gran' merci!"

"Soda water then?"

The staff-captain accepted cheerfully.

"Oh yes! Oh yes! That's just what I want. Just soda water! I won't refuse a glass."

A siphon was brought. Ribnikov drank a glass with great, greedy gulps. His hand trembled with avidity, and he at once poured himself out a second glass. It was evident that he had been very thirsty for a long time.

"He's pretending," thought Shchavinsky again. "What a strange man! He's agitated, he's tired, but not a bit drunk."

"Damn it all, how hot it is," said Ribnikov hoarsely. "But, gentlemen, I think I'm interfering with your work."

"No, not at all, we're used to that," growled Riazhkin.

"But haven't you any news of the war?" asked Ribnikov. "Eh, sirs?" he exclaimed, and clanked his sword again. "What interesting material I could give you about the war! If you like I'll dictate it to you, and you only write it down. Put at the top: 'Memoirs of Staff-Captain Ribnikov, back from the war.' No, don't think that! I'll do it without payment—for nothing! For nothing! What do you think of that, gentlemen authors?"

"Well, it might be done," growled Matanya lazily. "Somehow or other we might manage a little interview for you. Listen, Vladimir Ivanovitch, you don't know anything about our fleet, do you?"

"No, nothing. Why, is there anything up?"

"There was an incredible tale going round. Kondrashov heard from an acquaintance on the Admiralty Staff. Hi there, Pathological Case, tell Shchavinsky!"

The "Pathological Case," a man with a dark beard, like the hero of a tragedy, and a screwed-up face said through his nose:

"I can't vouch for it, Vladimir Ivanovitch, but the source is fairly dependable. There was a dark rumour going the rounds at headquarters that the greater part of our squadron had surrendered without fighting. It would seem that the sailors bound their officers and hoisted the white flag. Something like twenty ships!"

"That's really terrible," said Shchavinsky, in a low voice. "Perhaps, however, it isn't true. Still, the times are such that the most impossible things have become possible. By the way, do you know what's happening in our naval ports? A terrible, mysterious ferment, is spreading through all the crews. Naval officers on shore fear to meet their subordinates."

The conversation became general. That subtle, ubiquitous, cynical assembly was in the nature of a sensitive receiver for every kind of gossip and rumour of the city, which often reached the private rooms of "The Glory of Petrograd" sooner than the offices of Ministers. . . . Everyone had his own news. It was so interesting that even the Three Musketeers, for whom, people said, nothing in the world was sacred, entered into the conversation with unusual fervour.

"There's a story that the reservists in the rear of the army are refusing to fulfil their duties. It's said that the soldiers are shooting the officers with their own revolvers."

"I heard that the commander-in-chief hanged fifty nursing sisters. But of course, they were only apparently nursing sisters."

Shchavinsky looked round at Ribnikov. The loquacious staff-captain kept silence now. With narrowed eyes, leaning his chest on the hilt of his sword, he watched intently each speaker in turn, and under the tightly-stretched skin on his cheek-bones, the muscles twitched quickly, and his lips moved as if he was repeating each word to himself.

"Lord, whoever is it that he reminds me of?" the journalist thought impatiently for the tenth time. It worried him so that he tried having recourse to an old trick of his: To imagine to himself that he had somehow or other quite forgotten about the staff-captain, and then again suddenly to look at him. As a rule this method helped him fairly quickly to remember the surname or place of meeting required. But this time it proved quite ineffective.

Beneath his persistent gaze, Ribnikov turned round again, sighed deeply and shook his head regretfully:

"Terrible news!" he said. "Do you believe it? Eh? Even if it were true, we mustn't despair; you know what we Russians say: 'Whom God doesn't forsake, the pigs won't eat!' That is, I mean by pigs of course, the Japanese."

He held his own obstinately against Shchavinsky's persistent gaze, and in his tawny, animal eyes, the journalist saw the fire of an infinite and inhuman hatred.

At that moment Piestruchin, the poet, who had been asleep on the sofa, woke up suddenly, smacked his lips and fixed a dazed look on the officer.

"Oh, you Jap mug, aren't you gone yet?" he said in a drunken voice, scarcely moving his mouth, and he fell back on to the sofa, turning round on to his other side.

"A Japanese!" thought Shchavinsky, with fearful curiosity. "That's what he's like!" And Shchavinsky drawled, accenting his words significantly:

"You're a caution, Mr. Staff-Captain, you are indeed!"

"I?" cried the captain. The fire had gone out of his eyes but his lips still twitched nervously. "I'm Staff-Captain Rib-ni-kov." Again with ridiculous pride he hit his chest with his fist. "My Russian heart is pained. Give me your right hand. I was hit on the head at Liao-Yang, and wounded in the head at Mukden.

317

What? You don't believe me? I'll show you here, at once."

He put his leg on the chair and began to turn up his trousers.

"Stop, stop, Captain, we believe you," said Shchavinsky, frowning. Yet with his usual curiosity he managed to glance quickly at Ribnikov's leg and noticed that this infantry captain wore white underclothing of fine spun silk.

At that moment a messenger came into the room with a letter for Matanya.

"That's for you, Vladimir Ivanovitch," said Matanya, when he had opened the envelope. "The race card from the stable! Please put a rouble for me on Zenith, both ways. I'll give it back to you on Tuesday."

"Come along with me to the races, Captain," proposed Shchavinsky.

"Where to? To the races? With pleasure!" Ribnikov stood up boisterously, overturning his chair. "That's where the horses jump. Staff-Captain Ribnikov at your service, to the fight, to the front line, to the devil's dam. Ha, ha, ha! That's the way! Eh? What?"

When they had got into the cab and were driving along Kabinetsky Street, Shchavinsky put his arm through the officer's, leaned over and said, in a scarcely audible voice; close into Ribnikov's ear:

"Don't be afraid, I won't betray you. You're just as much Ribnikov as I'm Vanderbilt. You're an officer of the Japanese General Staff, I should think of no lesser rank than that of a colonel, and now—you're a military agent in Russia."

Either Ribnikov didn't hear his words because of the noise of the wheels, or he didn't understand him. Swaying slightly from side to side, he said hoarsely, with renewed drunken enthusiasm:

"You and I are out for a spree, so we are! Damn it

318

all, I love it! I shouldn't be Staff-Captain Ribnikov if I didn't like Russian authors! Fine fellows they are! They drink heartily and they know life through and through. Russia's joy's in the bottle, and I, old man, have been drinking all day."

III

Shchavinsky, both by reason of his profession and of his disposition, was a collector of human documents, a fancier in rare and strange phenomena of the human soul. Often for weeks, sometimes for whole months, he observed an interesting specimen, keeping on the track with the obstinacy of a passionate hunter or an amateur detective. Sometimes it turned out that the tracked one was, as Shchavinsky was wont to express it, "a knight born under a dark star"—a gambler, a notorious plagiarist, a pander, a souteneur, a graphomaniac (the horror of all editorial offices), an absconding cashier or mess-caterer, prowling round the restaurants, race meetings and gaming halls, spending money with the folly of men rushing towards the precipice. Seasonal celebrities, pianists, singers, literati, specially lucky gamblers, jockeys, athletes, fashionable cocottes, were also the objects of his sporting passion. Making their acquaintance one way or the other, Shchavinsky gently and endearingly, with a kind of enveloping, spiderish manœuvre, secured the attention of his prey. Then he was ready for anything. He sat for whole nights without any sleep, with commonplace, stupid people, devoid of intellectual equipment, except, like Bushmen, a few dozen animal conceptions and trite phrases. He treated, in restaurants, arrant fools and rascals, patiently waiting till, in their cups, they disclosed the fine, full-blown flower of their depravity; he flattered people to the top of their bent, knowing what they were, giving them flattery in huge doses, for he firmly believed it to be universally effective. He lent money freely, knowing beforehand that he would never get it back. When defending this dangerous sport of his, he was used to say that its inward, psychological interest had considerably more value for him than the profit which he afterwards derived from it in his profession as a realistic writer. It yielded him a mysterious, uneasy delight to make his way into the secret, remote recesses of the human soul, to see the hidden, the sometimes trifling, sometimes disgraceful, more often absurd than pathetic motives of external actions—as it were, to grasp the living, hot human heart in his hand, and to feel its beating. Often in the course of that strange work of his it seemed to him that he was completely losing his own individuality, to such a degree did he come to think and feel with the soul of the other man, nay, even to speak with his tongue and use his characteristic expressions; till finally he even caught himself making use of the other man's gestures and speaking with his intonation. But when he had had enough of a man, he threw him away. Of course, he sometimes had to pay for a long time and dearly for the fancy of a moment.

It was a long time since he had been so deeply interested in, nay, even excited about, anyone as he was now. This boisterous, hoarse, drunken infantry captain absorbed him. Shchavinsky kept him by him the whole day. At times, sitting by his side in a cab and covertly watching him, he thought positively:

"No, I can't possibly be mistaken! We have the yellow, slant-eyed face, the high cheek-bones, those continual, quick bowings, and rubbings of the hands, besides that strained, nervous, painful familiarity of bearing. Well, if it's true and Staff-Captain Ribnikov is really a Japanese spy, what an unimaginable presence of mind must be his, to give with splendid temerity, in broad daylight, in the capital of a hostile nation, this malicious yet faithful impersonation of a debauched Russian soldier! What dreadful sensations he must have,

balanced all day, every minute of the day, on the brink
of an unavoidable death!"

Here was a courage quite incomprehensible to Shchavinsky—fascinating, insensate but cool—perhaps the
highest possible patriotic heroism. Acute curiosity,
together with a kind of awe, drew the journalist's mind
ever more strongly towards the soul of that astonishing
staff-captain.

But sometimes he pulled his thoughts up.

"What if an absurd, preconceived idea has got hold
of me? What if I, the inquisitive searcher of hearts,
have made a fool of myself about a drunken, strutting
infantry captain? Aren't there in the Ural and Oren-
burg Cossack districts, any number of similar Mongol,
saffron-coloured faces?"

Then he looked still more fixedly at every gesture and
expression of the staff-captain, listened more attentively
to the sound of his voice.

Ribnikov didn't omit to return the salute of a single
soldier who saluted him. He put his hand to his forage-
cap with prolonged and exaggerated carefulness. When
they drove past an orthodox church he invariably took
off his cap and crossed himself widely and accurately.
Doing so, he just glanced sideways at his neighbour:
Had he seen or not?

Once Shchavinsky couldn't restrain himself from
saying:

"Anyhow, you're pious, Captain."

Ribnikov spread his arms, shrugged his shoulders
comically and cried:

"Can't be helped, my dear sir! I got used to doing
it at the front. 'Who hasn't been to the wars doesn't
know God'—it's a beautiful Russian proverb. Out
there, old fellow, a man learns to pray in spite of himself.
Maybe you're off to the front line of trenches. Bullets
whizz, shrapnel, grenades explode—and there's nothing
to be done but to go forward. It's your duty, you've
sworn, and you go. And you say to yourself: 'Our

Father Who art in Heaven, hallowed be Thy name, Thy kingdom come, Thy will be done, on earth as it is Heaven. . . .'"

He said the whole prayer down to the very end, most carefully pronouncing every sound.

"Shy!" decided Shchavinsky.

But he wouldn't leave his suspicion half-confirmed. For several hours on end he kept on questioning and worrying the staff-captain. In a private room, at dinner, he talked, bending over the table and the glasses of wine that were on it, looking Ribnikov in the very pupils of his eyes.

"Listen, Captain," he said, "nobody hears us and . . . I don't know what word of honour to give you that nobody in the world shall know of our conversation. I'm completely and deeply convinced that you're a—Japanese."

Again Ribnikov hit his chest with his fist.

"I'm Staff——"

Shchavinsky interrupted him.

"No, no," he said, "let's leave those subterfuges alone. However clever you may be, you can't hide your face. The line of your cheek-bones, the shape of your eyes, that characteristic skull of yours, the thin, bristly hair on your face—everything, everything unfailingly shows that you belong to the yellow race. I won't betray you whatever they offer me, however they threaten me for silence. In the first place, I'll do you no harm because my whole heart is full of respect for your marvellous boldness—I'll say even more, it's full of reverence—of awe, if you like! I—and I'm a writer, hence a man with imagination and fancy, I can't imagine how a fellow can make up his mind to do it. Tens of thousands of versts from his country, in a town full of his mortal enemies, risking his life every minute—why, they'd hang you without a trial if you fell into their hands! You know that, don't you? And then to walk about in an officer's uniform and to mix indiscriminately with any kind of company, and enter into the most dangerous conversations! Why, just a tiny mistake could ruin in you in one second. Listen now—just half an hour ago you said 'holograph' instead of 'manuscript.' It's a trifling thing, but very characteristic. No army staff-captain would use that word when talking of a present-day manuscript. He'd only use it when referring to a record, or some very important document. He wouldn't even say 'manuscript,' but 'work.' But that's a trifle. The chief thing is that I can't imagine that perpetual strain of the intellect and will, that diabolical waste of the powers of the soul. To unlearn to think in Japanese, to forget your name completely, to identify yourself wholly with another personality! No, no! It's positively greater heroism than any we heard of at school. My dear fellow, don't try to deceive me. I'm not your enemy."

He spoke in absolutely good faith, all roused and excited by the heroic picture his imagination had limned. But even flattery couldn't get over the staff-captain! He listened to Shchavinsky, blinking a little, looking at a tumbler which he kept moving quietly about on the table-cloth. The corners of his bluish lips twitched nervously. And Shchavinsky perceived on his face all the hidden mockery, all the obstinate, deep, inextinguishable hatred, peculiar perhaps, never to be comprehended by a European, which a clever, well-mannered, man-like beast can feel for a being of another species than his own.

"Oh, stop playing the kind friend!" replied Ribnikov. "To the devil with your kindness! They were always teasing me in our regiment, calling me Japanese. Japanese indeed! I'm Staff-Captain Ribnikov. You know the Russian proverb: 'A sheep's mug, but a man's soul.' But I tell you, in our regiment we used to——"

"And what was your regiment?" asked Shchavinsky suddenly.

But the staff-captain seemed not to have heard him.

He began to tell those old, time-worn, ribald stories that are told in camp, on manœuvres, in barracks. Shchavinsky involuntarily felt affronted.

Once, when the evening had already come and they were sitting in a cab, Shchavinsky put his arm round Ribnikov's waist, drew him towards him, and said softly:

"Captain . . . no, not captain but really colonel, for otherwise they wouldn't have entrusted you with such an important mission—then, let us say, colonel, I bow to the earth before your courage—that is, I would say, before the infinite valour of the Japanese nation. Sometimes when I read or think about individual instances of your diabolical bravery, about that infinite self-sacrifice and scorn of death, I feel a shiver of rapture. What immortal beauty there is, what divine audacity, in the conduct of that commander of a ship that had been shattered by a shell when, summoned to surrender, he could light a cigarette and, with the cigarette between his teeth, go to the bottom. What immense strength and what admirable contempt for the enemy! And then, the naval cadets, who, on fire-ships, went to certain death with such joy as that with which a man sets out for a ball. And do you remember that lieutenant —alone, quite alone—who by night, in a boat, towed a torpedo to the end of the Port Arthur mole? Search-lights were turned upon him, and all that remained of him and his torpedo was a big, bloody spot on the concrete wall; but on the next day all the midshipmen and lieutenants of the Japanese fleet overwhelmed Admiral Togo with petitions, in which they offered to repeat that frantic deed. What heroes! But even more splendid is Togo's order that the officers under his command should not dare thus to risk their lives, which belonged not to themselves, but to their country. Oh, damn it all, it's splendid!"

"What street are we in?" interrupted Ribnikov, yawning. "After the Manchurian trenches, I've completely forgotten my way about the streets. When we were at Harbin . . ."

But the enthusiastic Shchavinsky went on, without listening to him:

"Do you remember the case where an officer, having been captured by the enemy, dashed his head against a rock? But the most marvellous thing of all is the signatures of the Samurai. Of course you've never heard of that, Mr. Staff-Captain Ribnikov," said Shchavinsky, with sarcastic emphasis. "It's quite comprehensible, naturally, that you shouldn't have. . . . General Nogi, you know, asked for volunteers to march in the first column, to storm the Port Arthur forts by night. Nearly a whole division offered for that service, for that honourable death. As there were too many of them, and they pushed forward, one before another, towards death, they were asked to petition in writing, and some of them, in accordance with an ancient custom, cut off the first finger of their left hands, and affixed it to their signature, like a bloody seal. The Samurai did that!"

"The Samurai!" repeated Ribnikov, swallowing the wrong way. It was as if something broke and spread in his throat. Shchavinsky looked quickly at his side-face. A sudden expression such as he had never seen before, of tender gentleness played about the staff-captain's mouth, and his chin quivered and his eyes began to shine with that warm, tremulous light which shines through unshed tears. But at once he controlled himself, shut his eyes for a second, then turned a simple, inane face to Shchavinsky, and suddenly swore a long and obscene Russian oath.

"Captain, Captain, what's the matter with you?" cried Schchavinsky, almost alarmed.

"Those are all newspaper lies," said Ribnikov carelessly. "Our little Russian soldier isn't a whit worse. Of course, you know, there's a difference. They're defending their lives—fighting for glory, for independence—and why did we mix ourselves up in it all? Nobody knows. The devil knows why. 'There was no trouble, and the devil pumped it up,' as the Russian proverb says. Eh? What? Ha, ha, ha!"

Shchavinsky was a little distracted by the races, and he couldn't keep an eye on the staff-captain the whole time. But in the intervals between the races he saw his rare specimen on one stand or the other, high up, low down, at the buffet, and near the cash office. On that day the word "Tshushima" was on all lips—those of betters and riders and bookmakers, even on the lips of all those mysterious, tattered individuals not generally absent from races. That word was even converted into a jibe at a defeated horse, was used in vexation by those who lost with careless laughter, and those who lost with bitterness. Here and there it was spoken passionately, and Shchavinsky saw from afar how the staff-captain, with his confident, careless, half-drunken ways, picked a quarrel with one, shook another by the hand, clapped yet another on the back. His little, lame figure flitted about everywhere.

From the races they went to a restaurant, and thence to Shchavinsky's home. The journalist was rather ashamed of his part of volunteer detective, but hadn't strength of mind to relinquish it, though already he began to be weary and his head began to ache from that secret, strained fight with another soul.

Having found that flattery was no use, he now tried to draw the staff-captain into candour by teasing him and awakening his patriotic sentiment.

"All the same I'm sorry for the yellow monkeys," he said with ironical sympathy. "Whatever they say, Japan has expended all her national genius in the course of this war. In my opinion she's like a thin, puny man who in a state of excitement or intoxication, or from mere boastfulness, has lifted a ton on his back and has strained himself internally and begun to die a lingering death. Russia, you see, is quite a different country.

To her the Manchurian rout doesn't matter a bit—it's like cupping to a full-blooded man. You'll see how she'll recover and flourish after the war. But Japan will fade and die. She's overstrained herself. Don't tell me they have culture, general knowledge, European technique! Your Japanese is, when all's said and done, an Asiatic, half human, half simian. Even in his type he's akin to the apes, like the Bushman, the Touareg, or the Australian native. You have only to note his facial angle. In a word, he's just—a yellow monkey! It wasn't your culture or political youth that beat us, but just simply a fit of madness or epilepsy. You know what a seizure is, a fit of fury? In a fit like that a weak woman will break chains and throw healthy men about like straws. Next day she won't be able to lift her hand. That's how it is with Japan. Believe me, after her fit of heroism will come feebleness and decay. But of course before that ensues she'll pass through a zone of national greediness, of offensive militarism, and of foolish chauvinism."

"Re-al-ly!" cried Staff-Captain Ribnikov, with stupid ecstasy, in reply. "What's true's true! Your hand, Mr. Author. You can tell a clever man at once!"

He chuckled hoarsely, spit all round, tapped Shchavinsky on the knees, shook him by the hand, and Shchavinsky suddenly got ashamed of himself and of his secret manœuvres in the character of a penetrating searcher of hearts.

"And what if I've made a mistake and this Ribnikov is really and truly a typical drunken infantryman? No, the devil take it all, it's impossible! But if it *is* possible, what a fool I'm making of myself!"

At his own place he showed Ribnikov his library, his collection of old china, his rare engravings and two thoroughbred Siberian dogs. His wife—a little operatic artiste—was out of town.

Ribnikov looked at it all with civil but detached curiosity, in which his host discerned something like boredom, or even cold disdain. Among other things, Ribnikov happened to open a magazine and read aloud a few lines from it.

"That's a mistake on his part, anyhow," thought Shchavinsky when he heard his reading, which was extraordinarily correct but wooden, with the exaggeratedly exact pronunciation of every letter which one would expect from the head pupil of a language class, displaying his knowledge of a foreign tongue. At last Ribnikov himself noticed this and quickly closed the magazine and said:

"You write yourself, don't you?"

"Yes . . . a little."

"And what newspapers do you write for?"

Shchavinsky named them. Ribnikov had asked him the same question six times already that day.

"Oh yes, oh yes! I forgot, I asked you that before. Do you know what, Mr. Author?"

"Well?"

"We'll do this: You write and I'll dictate. . . . That is, not dictate. Oh, I'd never dare to!' Ribnikov rubbed his hands and bowed hastily. "You, of course, would compose, and I'd only give you ideas and a few . . . how *shall* I say it? . . . memories of the war. Oh, what interesting materal I have!"

Shchavinsky sat down with his side to the table and looked at the staff-captain cunningly, half closing one eye.

"And, of course, I'd mention your name."

"Why, of course you may! I've no objection to that. Put it down this way: 'This information was kindly supplied by Staff-Captain Ribnikov, only just back from the theatre of military operations.' "

"All right, fine! But why do you want it like that?"

"What do you say?"

"Why do you want your name mentioned? Will it be needful to you in the future as evidence that you inspired the Russian papers? 'What a cunning chap am I !' eh?"

But the staff-captain, as usual, evaded a straight answer.

"But maybe," he said, "you haven't time? You're busy with other work? If so—damn those reminiscences of mine! How goes it? 'Living your life isn't crossing a field!' Eh? What? Ha, ha, ha!"

Just then something interesting came into Shchavinsky's head. There was a big, white table in his study, made of unstained ash. On the clean, virgin surface of this table all Shchavinsky's acquaintances had written their autographs, with aphorisms, verses, sketches and even musical notes. He said to Ribnikov:

"Look, here's my autograph album, Mr. Captain. Won't you write something in it for me, in honour of our acquaintance?'—Shchavinsky bowed courteously— "which, I dare to cherish the hope, won't be a short one."

"Why not? With pleasure!" agreed Ribnikov readily. "Something out of Pushkin or Gogol?"

"No, better something of your own."

"Of my own? Fine!"

He took a pen, dipped it in the ink, thought and made ready to write. But Shchavinsky suddenly stopped him.

"We'll do something better than that! Here's a bit of paper for you, and here, in that box, are drawing-pins. Please write something particularly interesting and then cover it with the paper and fasten the corners down with drawing-pins. I give you my word of honour, as a writer, that for two months I won't touch that paper and won't look what you've written there. Agreed? Well, then, write! I'll go away, so as not to embarrass you."

At the end of five minutes Ribnikov called him.

"Please come in!"

"Ready?" asked Shchavinsky, entering.

Ribnikov drew himself up, put his hand to his head as if saluting and bawled like a soldier:

"Yes, sir!"

"Thank you! Now we'll go to 'The Buff' or somewhere like that," said Shchavinsky. "When we get

329

there we'll see what else there is to do. I won't let you away from me the whole day to-morrow, Captain!"

"With the greatest pleasure," said Ribnikov, in a hoarse, bass voice, clicking his heels together; and he raised his shoulders and gave his moustache a mischievous twist at both sides.

But Shchavinsky involuntarily cheated the staff-captain, and didn't keep his word. The very moment before he left the house, the journalist perceived that he had forgotten his cigarette-case, and went to get it, leaving Ribnikov in the hall. The white sheet of paper, accurately fastened down with drawing-pins, awoke his curiosity. He couldn't resist the temptation. Turning stealthily back, he raised the corner of the paper and read the following words; written in a fine, legible, unusually elegant hand:

"Though you're Ivanov the seventh, you're a fool."

IV

They came out of a suburban café-chantant long after midnight, in the company of the well-known musical comedy actor; Zenin-Lirsky, the young Assistant-Crown Prosecutor, Sasha Strahlmann, who was known everywhere in Petersburg for his incomparable power of telling funny stories about the topic of the day, and a patron of the arts—Karyukov, a merchant's son.

It was neither light nor dark. It was a warm, white, transparent night, with softly changing colours, with mother-of-pearl-like water in the quiet canals, which clearly reflected the grey stone of the embankments and the motionless verdure of the trees, with a pale sky, weary as though from sleeplessness, and there were numberless clouds in that sky, long, thin, feathery, like scattered tufts of cotton-wool.

"Where shall we go to?" asked Shchavinsky, standing still at the gate of the garden. "Marshal Oyama, let us have your enlightened opinion."

330

The whole five of them tarried on the pavement. They were in the power of that usual moment of indecision which comes before daybreak, when, in revellers, physical lassitude fights with the irresistible, irritating longing for new and pleasant sensations. Out of the garden there came a continuous stream of its guests, laughing, singing, shuffling their feet noisily on the dry, white paving-stones. Music-hall artistes came out with a bold rustle of their silken petticoats, in huge hats, with quivering diamonds in their ears, escorted by elegant men in fashionable attire, with flowers in their buttonholes. These ladies, respectfully conducted by the porters, got into their carriages or into panting automobiles, unconstrainedly arranged their dresses about their legs and drove quickly off, holding the front part of their hat-brims. The chorus-girls and "garden-girls," of the better class, drove away in ordinary cabs, alone or in pairs, with a man accompanying them. The others—ordinary, registered prostitutes, pushed their way everywhere, round about the wooden fence, following the men who went away on foot, particularly those that were drunk. They ran beside the men for a long time and offered themselves in a low voice, with brazen submissiveness naming that profession of theirs, with plain, coarse, terrible words. Their faces, in the light, white twilight of a May night, looked like coarse masks, blue with white paint, red with crimson blushes, and one's eyes were struck with the blackness and thickness of their unusually arched eyebrows. The yellow tint of their wrinkled faces, the meagreness of their veiny necks and the flabbiness of their retreating chins showed the more pitiably for this glaring adornment. Two mounted policemen, swearing coarsely, rode at them from time to time, their horses' mouths foaming, and then the girls shrieked, scattered and caught at the sleeves of passers-by. Near the canal railing some twenty men had assembled—the usual early morning scandal was taking its usual course. A beardless, young officer was

as drunk as a piper, and was making a row. He wanted
to draw his sword, and a policeman was begging him
persuasively, with his hand on his heart, to do something or other else. A lively, suspicious-looking drunken
fellow, wearing a cap with a torn peak, was speaking in
a honeyed, flattering tone:

"Spit on them, sir! It's beneath your dignity even
to turn round and look at them. You'd do better to
give *me* a blow on the mug. Let me kiss your hand,
sir!"

A lean, severe gentleman, somewhere at the back,
whose bowler hat, tilted over his nose, let nothing be
seen except his black whiskers, droned in an indistinct,
bass voice:

"Why do you keep looking at him? Throw him into
the water, that's all!"

"Really, Major Fukushima," said the actor, "we
must give a proper ending to this day of pleasant
acquaintanceship. Let's go to the girls. Where shall
we go, Sasha?"

"To Bertha's," replied Strahlmann.

Ribnikov giggled and rubbed his hands with joyful
eagerness.

"To the women? Why, as the Russian proverb says:
'For a lady even a Jew hanged himself!' Eh, what?
'If we're going let's go!' said the parrot. Eh? Ha,
ha, ha!"

Shchavinsky had introduced him to these young men,
and they had all been supping in the café-chantant,
listening to Rumanian singers and drinking champagne
and liqueurs. In the course of supper they thought it
funny to call Ribnikov by the names of various Japanese
colonels, the more so that the staff-captain's good nature
seemed to be inexhaustible. Shchavinsky, began this
rough, vulgar game. It is true that at times he felt that
he was behaving in an ugly way towards Ribnikov, nay,
even treacherously. But he quietened his reason by
the fact that not even once had he said a single word

about his suspicions, and his acquaintances had no idea of anything.

At the beginning of the evening he kept his eye on Ribnikov. The staff-captain was the noisiest and most loquacious of all the company. He kept clinking glasses every minute, jumping up, sitting down again, upsetting wine onto the table-cloth, smoking cigarettes from the wrong end. Nevertheless Shchavinsky noticed that he was drinking very little.

Again, Ribnikov happened to drive in the same cab as Shchavinsky, who was hardly drunk at all. He was generally known to hold his liquor well when out for a spree, but there was a singing in his ears and his head was light, for the champagne was fizzing in it. He looked sideways at the staff-captain. In the uncertain, slumberous light of the white night, Ribnikov's face had a dark, earthy tint. All the hollows in it were sharply defined and dark, the wrinkles on his temples and the deep lines near his nose and on his throat looked deeper; and the staff-captain himself sat humped up, bent, his hands hidden in the sleeves of his uniform coat. He breathed heavily through his open mouth. All this made him look exhausted and as if he was suffering. Shchavinsky also smelt his breath, and reflected that gamblers after several nights of hazard have just the same, stale, sour breath as men worn out by sleeplessness or intense brain-work. A wave of kindly emotion and compassion flowed into Shchavinsky's heart. The staff-captain suddenly seemed to him little, worn out, touchingly pitiable. He put his arm round Ribnikov, drew him towards him and said kindly:

"All right, Captain, I surrender! I can't do anything with you and I apologize if I've caused you some unpleasant moments. Give me your hand!"

He took from his buttonhole a holder with a rose in it, which a flower-girl had inveigled him into buying in the garden, and put it into the captain's buttonhole.

333

"That's a sign of peace between us, Captain. We won't tease each other any more."

The driver drew up before a two-storied stone house, detached, with a decorous approach, with closely-shuttered windows. The others had arrived before and were awaiting them. They weren't admitted at once. A little square, barred window in the heavy door was opened from within, and somebody's cold, menacing grey eyes appeared in it. Then the door was opened.

The establishment was something between an expensive hotel and a luxurious club. The entrance was elegant, there was a stuffed bear in the hall, there were carpets, silk hangings, mirrors, footmen in evening dress, wearing gloves. From all parts men came there to finish the night, when the restaurants were shut. Cards were played, expensive wine was drunk, and there were a large number of beautiful women, who were frequently arriving.

The new arrivals had to go upstairs to the first floor. Up there there was a wide landing, with plants in tubs and little sofas, separated from the staircase by a balustrade.

Shchavinsky took Ribnikov's arm. Although he had inwardly vowed not to tease him any more, he couldn't now restrain himself from saying:

"Let's mount the scaffold, Captain!"

"I'm not afraid," drawled Ribnikov. "I walk up to death every day of my life."

Ribnikov waved his hand slightly and smiled a forced smile. As he smiled, his face grew suddenly tired, grey-looking and old.

Shchavinsky looked at him in silent surprise. He was ashamed of himself for his tiresomeness; but Ribnikov turned to him and continued at once:

"Yes, yes, to death! A soldier should always be ready for it. What can one do! Death—it's just a little inconvenience attached to our profession."

In that house Shchavinsky and Karyukov were

familiar guests and honoured patrons. They were received with joyful smiles and deep bows.

They were assigned a large, warm, private room, decorated in red and gold, with a thick, bright-green carpet covering the floor, with candelabra in the corners and on the table. They were served with champagne, fruit and sweets. Women came—at first three of them, then another two—then the whole time some kept coming and others going, and one and all they were very pretty, very much powdered, with bare, white arms, neck and chest; were clothed in glittering, bright, costly clothes, some with skirts to the knee only, one in the brown uniform of a schoolgirl, one in tight riding-breeches and a jockey-cap. There came, too, a stout, oldish lady, dressed in black, something like a landlady or a housekeeper, very respectable-looking, with a lemon-yellow, flabby face, which kept smiling the whole time, in an agreeable, elderly way. She was coughing every minute and never stopped smoking. She behaved towards Shchavinsky, the actor, and the art critic with the pleasant, unforced coquetry of a lady who might be their mother, flicking their hands with her handkerchief, and Strahlmann, evidently a favourite, she called "Sashka."

"Now, then, General Kuroki, let's drink to the brilliant success of the famous Manchurian army. You'll get mouldy sitting over there!" said Karyukov.

Shchavinsky interrupted him, yawning.

"That's enough, gentlemen. Wouldn't any more of it bore you? You're abusing the captain's good nature."

"No, I'm not offended," declared Ribnikov. "Let's drink, sirs, to the health of our charming ladies!"

"Lirsky, sing something," said Shchavinsky.

The actor willingly sat down to the piano and sang a gipsy ballad. He didn't actually sing it, he rather recited it, without taking his cigar out of his mouth, his eyes gazing at the ceiling, swinging affectedly backwards and forwards. The women joined in loudly and out of tune.

335

Each of them tried to get the words out before the others. Then Sashka Strahlmann imitated a phonograph most beautifully, impersonated the characters in an Italian opera, and imitated animals. Karyukov danced a fandango and kept on calling for further bottles of wine.

He was the first to slip out of the room with a red-haired, taciturn, Polish girl. Strahlmann and the actor went next. Shchavinsky alone remained, with a slender, white-toothed Hungarian girl sitting on his knees, and Ribnikov beside a fair, plump woman in a blue satin blouse, cut low and square to almost half-way down her chest.

"Well, Captain, let's say farewell for a while," said Shchavinsky, rising and stretching himself. "It's late, or rather, I should say, early. Come to me at breakfast-time, Captain. Mamma, put the wine down to Karyukov, if he likes holy art, let him pay for the honour of supping with its priests. My compliments!"

The fair woman put her bare arm round the captain's neck and said simply:

"Let's go too, darling. It really is late."

V

Her room was a cheerful, little one with blue paper on the walls and a pale, blue shade on the lamp. On the dressing-table stood a round looking-glass framed in blue muslin. On one wall was an oleograph: "Girls Bathing" and another: "The Royal Bridegroom." On the opposite wall there was a hanging, beneath which stood a broad, brass bed.

The woman took off her coat, and with a feeling of relief and satisfaction, stroked her sides where her chemise had been wrinkled under her corset. Then she turned down the wick of the lamp, and sitting down on the bed, began quietly to unlace her boots.

Ribnikov sat by the table, his elbows apart, supported

by his knees, and dropped his head into his hands. He kept on looking at her.

"Why don't you undress yourself?" asked the woman. "Tell me, darling, why they kept calling you a Japanese general?"

Ribnikov laughed, not looking up.

"It's just—nonsense. They were just simply joking. You know the verse:

> "I laugh (in that no sin I see)
> At what doth seem a joke to me."

"You'll treat me to some more champagne, or if you're too stingy for that, I'll ask you for some oranges.

She lay down beside him, hastily threw the cigarette she had lit on to the floor, and wriggled down under the coverlet.

"Do you like to be near the wall?" she asked. "All right, if you do. Oof, how cold you are! You know, I adore military men. What's your name?"

"Mine?" He coughed and answered uncertainly: "I —I'm Staff-Captain Ribnikov—Vassili Alexandrovitch Ribnikov."

"Oh, Vasya! I've a friend called Vasya—a boy from school. Charming! What a nice fellow he is!

> 'Vasya, Vasya, now I see
> What a tale you're telling me!'

But do you know, you *are* like a Japanese. And do you know who you're like? You're exactly like the Mikado. We subscribe to 'Neva' and there's a picture of him there. It's a pity it's late now, for I'd have shown it to you. Yes, indeed, you're as like as two drops of water."

"Well, that's very nice," said Ribnikov, and quietly put his arm round her smooth, plump shoulders.

"But perhaps you're really a Japanese? They said

337

you were at the war. Is it true? Oh, love, I'm afraid to be tickled. . . . Well, was it terrible at the war?"

"Terrible? No, not particularly. . . . Let's leave that alone," he said wearily. "What's your name?"

"Clotilda. No, I'll tell you a secret. My name is Nastya. It's only here that they gave me the name of Clotilda, because my name's so ugly—Nastya, Natasha, like a cook!"

"Nastya?" he repeated, reflectively, and carefully kissed her on the breast. "No, it's nice. Nas-tya!" he repeated slowly.

"What is there nice in it? Malvina, Vanya, Xenia are nice names, for instance, and perhaps Irma. Oh, darling"—she pressed close to him—"You're nice—so dark . . . I like dark men. You're married, I suppose?"

"No, I'm not married."

"What a story! They all pretend to be bachelors here. I'm sure you've got six children."

As the window was shuttered and the lamp very low, it was dark in the room. Her face, lying quite close to his head, looked quite fantastic and changing, on the dim whiteness of the pillow. It had now become something unlike the face it was before—the simple, pretty, round, wide-eyed Russian face. Now it looked quite thin, and strangely changing its expression every minute, looked tender, sweet, mysterious and reminded Ribnikov of the face of someone infinitely well-known, loved long ago, fascinating, most beautiful.

"How beautiful you are!" he whispered. "I love you. I love you."

Suddenly he uttered some incomprehensible word, quite strange to the woman's ears.

"What are you saying?" she asked, surprised.

"No . . . nothing. Just nothing at all! Beloved—you're a woman. . . . I love you!"

He kissed her arms, her neck, her hair, quivering with an impatience, the restraint of which yielded him a strange delight.

338

A stormy yet tender passion possessed him for this well-fed, childless female, for her big, young, perfumed, beautiful body. The desire for woman, suppressed up to then by his severe, ascetic life, his constant physical fatigue, the intensive working of his mind and will, suddenly flared up in him in a consuming, unbearable flame.

"How cold your hands are!" said she shyly. There was in this man something surprising and terrible, completely incomprehensible to her. Cold hands—warm heart!

"Yes—yes—yes, heart!" he declared senselessly, panting and trembling. "My heart is warm—my heart!"

She had got accustomed long ago to the outward rites and disgusting details of passion, and conformed to them every day several times, mechanically, calmly, often with silent aversion.

Hundreds of men, from old fellows who put their false teeth in a glass of water, to boys in whose voice bass was mingled with treble, civilians, military men, and disguised orthodox priests, bald pates, and men hairy as apes from head to foot; emotionally excited and impotent; drug fiends who didn't hide their vice from her; handsome men, cripples, depraved men, whom she sometimes loathed, boys crying in the distress of their first fall!—they all embraced her with shameless words, with long kisses, breathed in her face, groaned in paroxysms of animal passion which —she knew it beforehand—within that very minute would change into open, invincible disgust. Long ago now all men's faces had lost in her eyes all individual features—and had merged into one repugnant, inevitable, goatish, male face, bending lasciviously towards her, with bristling, slobbering mouth, with dim eyes, clouded like muffed glass, distorted and disfigured by the grimace of a voluptuousness which was revolting to her because she never shared it.

Besides, they were all rough, exacting and lacking in the most simple feeling of shame—they were for the most part as unimaginably ridiculous as only the modern man in his underclothing can be. But this little, elderly officer made some kind of a peculiar, new, attractive impression upon her. Every movement of his was distinguished by quiet, insinuating delicacy. His caresses, his kisses and his touch, were unwontedly gentle. With all that, he unobtrusively surrounded her with that nervous atmosphere of real, intense, animal passion which, even at a distance, even against her will, compels a woman's emotions, makes her submissive, subdues her to the will of the male. But her poor, little understanding, not perceiving anything without the precincts of that house of infamy, couldn't recognize or perceive that strange, compelling charm. She could only whisper, shy, happy and amazed; the usual trite words:

"What a nice man you are! You're my sweetheart, aren't you?"

She got up, extinguished the lamp and again lay down by him. Through the chinks between the shutters and the wall dawn sent streaks of whiteness, filled the room with a blue-clouded twilight. Somewhere behind a partition an alarm clock rang. Somebody sang suddenly in the distance.

"When will you come again?" asked the woman.

"What?" asked Ribnikov, sleepily opening his eyes.

"When will I come? Quickly. . . .To-morrow . . ."

"Oh, of course you're deceiving me. . . . No, tell me the very truth, when? I shall be longing for you."

"M-m! We'll come, we'll be longing. We'll write to them. . . . They'll stay in the mountains. . . ." He muttered disjointedly. Heavy slumber chained and weighed down his body. But, as it always is with people who have for a long time denied themselves sleep, he couldn't go to sleep at once. As soon as ever his consciousness began to be clouded over with the dark, gentle, pleasant veil of forgetfulness, a fearful, inward shock suddenly shook his body. He groaned and shivered, opened his eyes wide in wild terror, and then sank again into an uneasy, transitory state, between sleep and waking, like delirium, full of menacing, confused phantoms.

The woman wasn't sleepy. She sat up in the bed in her chemise alone, clasping her bent knees with her naked arms, and with awed curiosity she looked upon Ribnikov. In the bluish twilight his face looked still yellower, was sharper and like the face of a dead man. His mouth was open, but she didn't hear his breathing, and all over his face—specially round his eyes and mouth, was an expression of such weariness, such deep, human suffering, as she had never seen in all her life before. She softly stroked his bristling hair. His skin was cold and all covered with sticky sweat. At the contact of her hand Ribnikov quivered, shouted in alarm and, with a swift movement, sat up.

"Ah, who is it? Who?" he said disjointedly, wiping his face with his shirt sleeve.

"What is it, darling?" asked the woman sympathetically. "Do you feel ill? Perhaps you'd like me to get you some water?"

But Ribnikov had already controlled himself, and he lay down again.

"No, thank you. I'm all right now. I was dreaming. Lie down to sleep, dear girl. Please do!"

"When shall I wake you, darling?" she asked.

"Wake me? . . . To-morrow. . . . The sun will rise early and the cavalry will ride up. . . . We'll sail over. . . . Do you know? We'll sail across the river."

He fell silent, and for some minutes he lay still. But suddenly his moveless, dead face was distorted as by a convulsive movement of terrible pain. He turned over on to his back with a groan, and strange, wild-sounding, mysterious words in a foreign language flowed swiftly from his lips.

The woman listened, holding her breath, taken with that superstitious terror which is always aroused by the ravings of a sleeper. His face wasn't more than two

341

inches from her, and she didn't take her eyes from it. He was silent again for a minute, and then spoke again, at length, and incomprehensively. Yet again he was silent, as if listening hard to somebody's words. Then suddenly the woman heard, spoken loudly in a clear, hard voice the one and only Japanese word she knew, having seen it in the papers:

"Banzai!"

Her heart beat so hard that from its beating the velvet coverlet rose and fell frequently. She remembered how that evening, in the red private room, they had called Ribnikov by the names of Japanese generals, and a slight, far-off suspicion now began to form in her dark understanding.

Somebody tapped very softly on the door. She got up and opened it.

"Clotilda, darling, is that you?" she heard in a soft, woman's whisper. "You're not asleep? Come to my room for half a minute. Leonka is with me. He's treating us to some apricot wine. Come along, darling!"

That was Sonia, the Karaim, Clotilda's neighbour, bound to her by the bonds of that hysterical and honeyed sentimentality which always unites women in couples in such establishments.

"All right, I'll come in a minute. Oh, I'll tell you something very interesting. Wait till I dress myself."

"Nonsense, you needn't. You needn't mind Leonka, anyhow. Come as you are."

She began to put on her petticoat. Ribnikov awakened.

"Where are you?" he asked sleepily.

"I'll be back at once, I must go," she replied, hastily tying the string round her waist. "Go to sleep, I'll be back in a minute."

But he didn't hear her last words. A dense, dark sleep suddenly drowned his consciousness.

VI

Leonka was the darling of the whole house, beginning with Mamma, and ending with the lowest servant-maid. In those surroundings, where boredom, idleness and bad literature encouraged exaggerated romantic tastes, the greatest adoration is given to thieves and detectives, because of their heroic lives, full of enchanting adventures, dangers and risks. Leonka appeared there in the most varied costumes, almost in make-up! At times he preserved a significant and mysterious silence, but the chief thing, which everyone kept well in mind was that he frequently asserted that the local police had an unlimited respect for him, and would blindly obey his orders. There had been an occasion when he, with three or four words spoken in a mysterious jargon, had put an end in an instant to a terrible row begun by some drunken thieves, and had made them go humbly off the premises. Besides this, he sometimes had plenty of money at his disposal. For these reasons it isn't difficult to understand that Henrietta or, as he called her, Genka, with whom he was having a rather prolonged affair, was treated in Bertha's establishment with envious respect.

He was a swarthy, young man, with a dark moustache, twisted upwards, with a firm, short, broad chin, and with dark, fine bold eyes. He now sat on a sofa with his coat off, with his waistcoat unbottoned and his neck-tie loosened. He was well-proportioned if short, but his well-developed chest and his muscles that seemed ready to tear his blouse apart at the shoulders, witnessed to his great strength. Beside him, with her feet on the sofa, sat Genka, opposite him Clotilda. Slowly sipping his liqueur with his red lips, he was carelessly narrating, with an artificially elegant tone:

"They brought him to the police station. His passport was made out for Korney Sapietov, a townsman from Kolpin, or something like that. Well, of course, he was properly drunk, the rascal. 'Put him into a cold cell to sober him down!'—The usual procedure! But just at that very moment I happened to drop into the inspector's office. I looked. . . . Bah, bah, bah! An old acquaintance, Sanka, the butcher! Triple homicide and sacrilege! At once I winked from a distance to the constable on duty, and he, just like that, came out into the corridor. He came up to me: 'What is it, Leonti Spiridonovitch?' 'Just send that beauty round for a minute to the detective bureau!' He was brought there. Not a muscle of the villain's face quivered. I just looked him straight in the eyes and said: (Leonka here rapped the table significantly with his knuckles) 'Is it long, little Sanka, since you deigned to leave Odessa and come to us?' He, of course, kept his indifferent demeanour, pretending to be dense. He'd let nothing out. He's a caution. 'I know nothing at all about Sanka, the butcher, I'm so and so,' he said. Then I went up to him and took hold of his beard, and there —the beard came off in my hand A false one! 'Will you confess, son of a bitch!' I shouted. 'I know nothing at all.' Then I seized him, gave him a blow on the nose—once—twice. Blood all over his face. 'Will you confess,' I shouted again. 'I know nothing at all.' 'Oh, that's the way with you, is it? I've been humanely sparing you up to this, but now blame yourself for what happens. Call Arsene, The Flea!' There was in our place a convict who hated Sanka, the butcher, like poison. Of course, my dears, you know, I know quite well what's going on among them. . . . The Flea was brought in. 'You, there, Flea,' I said, 'who's that fellow there?' 'Oh, that's none other than Sanka, the butcher. How are you, Sanka? It's a long time since you honoured us with your presence, isn't it? How did you get on in Odessa?' So then, of course, the butcher gave in. 'All right, Leonti Spiridonovitch,' he said, 'it's your cop. Nobody can escape you. Give me a cigarette.' Well, of course, I gave him a cigarette. Out

344

of sheer altruism I never refuse a thing like that. The fellow was led away! He just looked at The Flea, and I thought: 'Well, now, I should think The Flea won't get any good from that! The butcher'll surely do for him.'"

"Do for him?" whispered Genka with horror in her voice—with flattering awe and confidence

"Absolutely do for him, of course! That's the kind of chap he is."

He sipped complacently from his glass. Genka, who was looking at him with staring, terrified eyes, so fixedly that her mouth even opened and she began to dribble, clapped her hands to her mouth.

"Oh, my God, how dreadful," she cried. "Just think now, Clotilda dear! And you weren't afraid, Lenya!"

"Oh, there—how should I be afraid of every rascal?"

The ecstatic attention with which the women listened to him stirred Leonti up, and he began to tell lying tales about students making bombs somewhere on Vassilevski Island, and how the Governor of the town had ordered him to arrest those evil-thinking ones, and how there were found to be twelve thousand bombs there. If they had all gone off, not only this house but most likely the whole of Petersburg would have been blown to bits.

Then came an extraordinary account of Leonka's extraordinary heroism. Disguised as a student, he had penetrated to the infernal laboratory, had made some kind of a sign through the window, and, in a minute, had disarmed the rascals. One of them he caught by the sleeve at the very moment when he was about to explode a pile of bombs.

Genka groaned, got into a fright, slapped her legs and kept on turning to Clotilda and crying:

"Oh, Lord, what a terrible thing! . . . Just only think, Clotilda, how wicked those students are! But there, I never did care for them much."

Finally, completely upset, but charmed by her lover's courage, she hung round his neck and began to kiss him loudly.

345

"Leonka, my sweetheart, it's terrible even to hear of it. And how is it that you fear nothing?"

He complacently twisted the left side of his moustache upwards and carelessly let fall the words: "Why be afraid? We die only once. That's what I'm paid for."

The whole time Clotilda was tormented by envy of her comrade, who had won such a splendid lover. She dimly suspected that there was a good deal of lying in Leonka's stories, and meantime she had in her own hands something quite unusual, that had never happened to anyone yet, and which would at once dim the brightness of Leonka's exploits. For a few minutes she hesitated. A little echo of her tender pity for Ribnikov still held her back. But a hysterical desire to share in the brilliance of a romantic event, got the upper hand, and she said, in a quiet, low voice:

"Do you know, Lenya, I wanted to tell you something. I have a strange guest to-day."

"M-m! Do you think he's a swindler?" asked Lenya patronizingly

Genka was affronted.

"What?" she cried. "A swindler, indeed! What a story! Some little, drunken officer!"

"Oh, don't talk like that," interrupted Leonka, with official dignity. "It sometimes happens that a swindler dresses up as an officer. What was it you wanted to tell me, Clotilda?"

Then she told in detail, displaying a purely feminine talent for observation, the whole story about Ribnikov —how he had been called General Kuroki, about his Japanese face, about his strangely tender passion, about his ravings and finally about his shouting: 'Banzai!' "

"Here—you're not lying?" asked Leonka quickly, and bright sparks began to shimmer in his dark eyes.

"By God, it's true! May I be rooted to the ground if it isn't! You can look through the keyhole. I'll open the shutter so that you can see. There—he's as like a Japanese as one drop of water to another!"

346

Leonka got up. Deliberately, with a grave look, he put on his coat and carefully felt in his left, inner pocket. "Let's go!" he said firmly. "Who did he come with?"

Karyukov and Strahlmann alone remained of the party, but Karyukov couldn't be roused, and Strahlmann, with watery, red eyes, still half drunk, growled indistinctly:

"What officer? Yes, the devil take him! He came up to us at Buff's. . . . Where he came from nobody knows."

He began to dress immediately, snorting wrathfully. Leonka apologized and went out of the room. He had already managed to look at Ribnikov's face through the keyhole, and though he still had his doubts, he was a good patriot, noted for his boldness, and not wanting in imagination. He determined to act on his own hand. In a minute he was on the staircase and had whistled an alarm.

VII

Ribnikov suddenly awakened as if some powerful voice had cried within him: "Get up!" Half an hour's sleep had quite freshened him up. First of all he gazed suspiciously at the door. He had a feeling that somebody was watching him thence, with a fixed gaze. Then he looked about him. A shutter was half-open, and every detail in the room could be seen. The woman was sitting opposite the bed, near the table, silent and pale, looking at him with great shining eyes.

"What's the matter?" asked Ribnikov, alarmed. "Listen, tell me what's been happening here?"

She made no reply, but her chin trembled and her teeth were chattering.

A suspicious, fierce gleam came into the officer's eyes. He bent right over from the bed and put his ear to the door. Numerous footsteps, obviously those of people not accustomed to caution, were approaching

347

along the corridor, and then they were quiet before the door.

Ribnikov, with a soft, noiseless movement, jumped from the bed and double-locked the door. Then somebody knocked at it, The woman, with a cry, dropped her head on to the table, covering her face with the palms of her hands.

In a few seconds the staff-captain had dressed. . . . Again came the knocking at the door. He had only his cap with him, having left his sword and his coat downstairs. He was pale, but quite calm, his hand didn't even tremble as he dressed, and every movement of his was absolutely unhurried and skilful. Having buttoned the last button of his coat, he went up to the woman and suddenly squeezed her arm above the wrist with such terrible force that in a moment her face flushed purple with the blood that rushed to her head.

"You!" he said quietly, in an angry whisper, without moving his jaws. "If you stir or cry out I'll kill you!"

Again there was a knocking and a gruff voice said: "Please open the door, sir!"

Now the staff-captain limped no more. He ran quickly and noiselessly to the window, with a soft, cat-like leap jumped on to the sill, opening the shutters wide with one wide movement of his arms. Down below him gleamed whitely the pavement of the yard, with dry grass among the stones and the branches of a few trees sticking up. He didn't hesitate a second, but at the very moment when he, sitting sideways on the iron facing of the window-sill, leaning his left hand on it and with one foot already hanging over, prepared to jump with the whole of his body—the woman, with a piercing cry, rushed towards him and seized him by the right arm. In tearing himself away he made an awkward movement and suddenly, with a slight, rather surprised cry, fell in a heap on to the stones below.

Almost simultaneously the frail door fell inwards into the room. First of all, Leonka ran in, panting, with

348

bared teeth and burning eyes. Behind him came, clutching drawn swords in their left hands, several immense policemen. Seeing the open window and the woman, who, clutching the frame, shrieked continuously, Leonka quickly took in everything that had happened. He was undoubtedly a very daring fellow, and so, without hesitating or saying a word, as if he had planned it beforehand, he took a running jump through the window.

He came down two paces from Ribnikov, who lay motionless on his side. In spite of the throbbing in his head from the impact, and the terrible pain which he felt in his stomach and heels, Leonka didn't lose his presence of mind, and in a moment threw the full weight of his body on to the staff-captain.

"Ah, I have you!" he cried hoarsely, pressing on his victim, with frantic fury.

The staff-captain made no resistance. His eyes burned with an infinite hatred, but he was as pale as death and pink foam bubbled at the corners of his lips.

"Don't crush me," he said in a whisper. "I've broken my leg."

THE HEART OF THE PAGAN
by Ernest Bramah

ERNEST BRAMAH began life as a farmer and signalized his failure in that career by writing his first book, *English Farming and Why I Turned it Up*. In 1901 he won fame as the author of *The Wallett of Kai Lung*, a remarkable "tour de force," extracting the utmost humour from the mingled wisdom and absurdity of Chinese Mandarism as seen through European eyes. Bramah then achieved another reputation as a writer of brilliant crime stories, and his blind detective, Max Carrados, has become one of the accepted heroes of modern dectivism in fiction. In *The Heart of the Pagan* Bramah gives us a serious study of a Chinaman; it is impossible to feel anything but admiration for the exile in this story, who, against all the warnings of his strange gods, performs an act of pathetic bravery.

THE HEART OF THE PAGAN

BY

ERNEST BRAMAH

"AS a matter of fact," said young Holt, "I was coming up to your place if I had not seen you. We are most desperately short of men this harvest, and my father thought that perhaps you could lend him one or two until you started cutting your oats."

Andrew Garstang, senior, the burly, shrewd, independent yeoman of Stonecroft Farm, leaning over one of his fieldgates, looked at Andrew Garstang, junior, who stood in the road by his horse's side. Both were amused so much that half a minute passed before either made reply.

"Why, Harold," said the younger Andrew, "where do you think I've been to get my horse in this state? Scouring the whole countryside for five blessed hours trying to pick up a few tramps or dead-beats to make shift with ourselves."

"Got hungry, that's all. And now I'm going up to have my tea. You may as well come with us, Harold."

"I should much like to," said Harold, with every appearance of sincerity, "but I must go somewhere else, if only to make a decent show."

The two Garstangs had already turned away, when along the road a strange and unfamiliar figure was seen approaching.

"What outlandish kind of foreigner is that, now?" demanded the farmer, staring down the road.

"A gipsy?" suggested his son, as the stranger got nearer. "I saw some of their vans down Sprostock way."

"Why, I do believe," exclaimed Harold suddenly, "it's an infernal Chinee! What on earth can one of those reptiles be doing in Overbury?"

It was a speculation that might well excite curiosity. Yen Sung himself could have supplied a very meagre outline of his journeyings, and even that he would have thought it prudent to withhold in the face of every inducement, not including actual torture. The beginning of the story would have gone back more than a single year, and as far as the township of Lien-Ning, on the banks of the Pei-kiang. It would have exhibited a wide range of Oriental nature and disclosed a little jealousy, some high-handed official tyranny, bloodshed, a fixed belief in the virtue of revenge and in the inexorable demands of the spirits of the dead, more bloodshed, the insidious implication of the Triad League, and the final outcome of a tribal feud. It involved Yen Sung—whose interest in the original cause of the strife was of the slightest—and by wave after wave of development it finally cast him, under a new name and with a highly fictitious account of himself, among his countrymen in Limehouse.

His object was to lose all association with the past, and doubtless he might have succeeded had not another family matter requiring adjustment (not in the remotest degree connected with Yen Sung) called for the assassination of an amiable Shanghai merchant, in London on business. The Chinese abroad have the strongest objection to invoking the assistance of the police, possibly as a result of their experience of the official classes at home, so that the remains of the Shanghai gentleman were sent back to his family in a crate bearing a label "Photographic Accessories. To be opened only in a ruby light. Perishable" and went through in the most correct manner. But, as the merchant was a person of some importance, an informal tribune considered the case, and discreet inquiries about the newcomer Yen Sung were set afoot with the object of ascertaining whether he was sufficiently friendless to be suffocated quietly and sent on in a crate by the next boat as a peace-offering to the outraged relations at Shanghai. A casual act of charity towards a poor countryman, on Yen Sung's part, was the means of saving him. The decision of the committee went against him, but before anything could be done a little block of wood, shaped into the semblance of a miniature coffin and bearing his own name, appeared miraculously in the fold of his sleeve as he walked along the Causeway.

Before the incident took place Yen Sung's expression was that of a person who gazes into futurity in a contemplation of the Confucian Analects. Without varying a single line of his preoccupation, without apparently withdrawing his eyes and mind from a sublime engrossment in the Beyond, Yen Sung saw the symbol, read the name, and perfectly understood the warning.

He continued to saunter on; presently he was out of the district which he knew, but Confucius and the North-West appeared to draw him on. By evening he had passed through Watford, and when night fell he entered a wood and slept there.

The next morning he resumed his journey without a word of inquiry about the route, believing that in a blind and unreasoning course lay his only hope. But, sparely as he lived, the little money he had was soon exhausted, and he found himself face to face with the necessity of seeking some unfamiliar employment.

The three men stood curiously at the gate as he approached. A foreigner might have been excused if, in search of authority, he had addressed the dapper Harold or the man who bestrode a horse; but it was the elder Garstang whom Yen Sung saluted with grave courtesy.

"I seek one," he said, with an air of perfect self-possession, "bearing the illustrious name Ga-tang. A

357

wayfarer, following the sun, spoke of the rider upon a horse who offered a just reward to all who would labour in his fields."

Surprise held them for a moment, but it was plain beyond all mistake that this strange being was offering his services as a harvester.

"I don't think that it's work you would care about, unless you've been used to it," said Garstang doubtfully, his conservative ideas of the fixed order of things not quite at ease.

"Try," replied Yen Sung laconically. "Not work honourably, not pay honourably."

"I am giving half a crown a day, overtime and bagging," remarked Garstang technically.

"It is sufficient," replied Yen Sung with the dignity of a Mandarin of the Sapphire Button. Why should he admit to these barbarians that he had not the remotest idea of what any of the three inducements comprised?

"But, Mr. Garstang," interposed Harold, "surely you are not going to engage him?"

"Yea," replied Garstang, regarding the young man with his shrewd, placid gaze. "May as well, Harold. We can't pick and choose now."

"But just think what sort of a man you are bringing into the neighbourhood, sir," urged Harold. "One of the most degraded races on the face of the earth—a pagan and an idol worshipper."

Garstang opened his eyes in gentle surprise. He was a staunch churchman, but it was not the custom—to state the case mildly—to carry religious tests into the harvest-fields. Nor, unless innuendo missed its mark, did Holt, senior, invariably regulate his business during the last six days of the week by the sentiments to which he gave open profession on the first.

"I mean," continued Harold, "that, being a heathen, he will have no ideas of right and wrong. A friend who has been in Australia tells me that they are the most treacherous, bloodthirsty and revengeful creatures in existence—more like animals, in fact. I hope that you understand me, sir, when I say that you are really taking very grave risks."

"They eat birds' nests, don't they?" remarked the younger Andrew with a well-meaning effort to include himself in the conversation.

"They eat anything that is filthy," said Harold, with elegant disdain. "Rats and mice and cattle that have died of disease."

So far this frank exposition of his national qualities had been carried on within Yen Sung's hearing, despite the fact that he could probably understand at least the essentials of every sentence, although nothing animate could have more successfully preserved an expression of absolute vacuity. But now Harold stepped nearer to the Garstangs, and in spite of the contemptuous intensity of his tone nothing could be heard of his words beyond an occasional disconnected phrase . . . " . . . Really too horrible to . . . dozens of cases . . . and then murdered . . rather commit suicide . . for Miss Edith's sake. . . . You cannot warn . . ."

"What is that about 'Miss Edith'?"

The three men turned quickly at the voice. A very fair young girl, not rustic, but wearing the grace and freedom that spring from the English soil had approached unseen by the field-path and stood smiling by the gate.

"The proverb has no terrors for you, Miss Edith," said Harold with easy gallantry. "*You* need never fear hearing ill of yourself."

"I was not listening," she replied; "but I did hear my name."

"The simple fact," volunteered Harold lightly, "is that a very undesirable alien wanted to be taken on for harvesting, and I was endeavouring to persuade your father to harden his naturally benevolent heart. Is her exacting ladyship satisfied?"

359

"But what have I to do with it?" she persisted.

"I was merely reminding your father of the many valuable articles lying about which might excite the cupidity of a covetous stranger."

She laughed, still unsatisfied : but another step brought her to the gate, and then the patient figure of the await-ing Celestial fell upon her surprised gaze and drove every other thought from her mind. With a curiosity quite free from shyness or alarm she approached Yen Sung with a friendly smile, as one who seeks to make a strange guest feel more at home.

"Do you speak English?" she asked.

"Most imperfectly, honourable lady," he replied.

She started a little at the quaint form of address, but there could be no doubting the perfect courtesy of Yen Sung's manner.

"You have come a very long way," she continued. It was a strange, new thing for her to stand face to face with this queerly-clad wanderer. She would have liked to ask him many things about his far-off home.

"A dead leaf is easily carried by the wind," replied Yen Sung, who smiled also. It was a very faint smile, scarcely worth the name, but it was the first sign of the lighter emotion he had shown for many months.

"But you must have seen a great many wonderful places; and of course to us your own country is the most wonderful of all." His presence conjured up a thousand bright visions within her eager mind—of sun-flashing, burnished temples and graceful pagodas, rice-fields greener than any English meadow in the spring, palm-dotted deserts, forests of bamboo, and azalea-covered hills; rivers and canals crowded with junks, sampans, and motley craft; stockaded towns, their fantastic streets filled with strange types or full of silent mystery beneath the moon. Doubtless the picture was quite unreal, but it was none the less fascinating, and the knowledge of it seemed all to be centred in Yen Sung.

To her remark, however, he only bowed acquiescently. Limited as his experience of English custom might be, he possessed both the quick intuition and the keen observation of his race, and he divined that the interest of this barbarian maiden would not be to his immediate advantage.

"I think that you are possibly under a misapprehension, Miss Garstang," suggested Harold, coming forward with an expression that was a little awry in its smiling effort. "This fellow is not an educated traveller who will be able to gratify your thirst for information, but a common tramp asking your father to take him on as a harvester—doubtless some seaman or stoker who has deserted from his ship and is now anxious to keep out of the way."

"It must be very hard to be friendless in a foreign country and to have to ask for work among strangers," observed Edith sympathetically, pointedly addressing herself to Yen Sung, "but I am sure that you will have no more trouble, because my father never refuses work to anyone who really wants it. Then if you like to come up to the farm you can have some tea." She nodded to Harold quite graciously, reminded her father that it was nearly six o'clock, and disappeared along the field-path.

"Well, Harold, it's no use; we can't help ourselves, you see," declared Garstang with an air of amused resignation which only half disguised an equally amused satisfaction.

"Oh, I don't mind," said Harold quickly, "only, knowing what I do, I thought it was my duty to warn you. I suppose you have a proverb applicable to the occasion, eh, Ah-John?"

"We have a saying, 'When the road bends we cannot see what lies before us,'" admitted Yen Sung indifferently.

"A very safe assertion to make, too," replied Harold, turning to resume his way; "but we can often guess, my pagan friend." He smiled frequently to himself on the journey, but it was not a pleasant smile, and a good many wayside flowers and overhanging boughs were prematurely cut off by his vindictive cane.

The following day marked the opening of the oat harvest, and Yen Sung took his place among the half-dozen men whose task consisted in tying up the sheaves and throwing them aside out of the path of the horses before the reaping machine made its round again. Garstang initiated him into all that there was to learn in the process—the peculiar knot by which the band is secured. "You may find it to be a little orkard at first, but you'll soon pick it up," he remarked kindly; but with the fatal imitative genius of his countrymen Yen Sung had already picked it up and was reproducing the knot, even down to the minute and accidental detail of a tuft of broken ends protruding at a certain point. The farmer was turning away satisfied when a thought occurred to him. "By the way," he added, taking out his wage-book, "I don't think I have asked you your name yet."

"Claude!" replied Yen Sung with transparent simplicity. He had noticed the name over a shop window as he passed through the village, and he now adopted it as a pleasant little compliment to the neighbourhood.

"Any other?" asked the farmer, whose knowledge of the ways of the Central Kingdom was not extensive.

"Of the obscure house of Kiu," replied Yen Sung for no particular reason, and as Claude Kiu he remained in the annals of Stonecroft Farm.

The days and weeks passed by; all the harvesting was over, but Yen Sung still remained. Why, on his part, it might be hard to say, for he had enough money now to take him safely out of the country, and had he been a human being instead of a mere yellow man it would have to be written that at Stonecroft Farm he suffered

much. The men early discovered that he never returned
a blow, so, to confess the shameful truth, to prove their
manliness or to impress their moral superiority, some
frequently struck and kicked him. Dead mice and other
carrion were thrown into his food as he ate, in exquisite
drollery. Whenever Harold Holt visited the farm he
never failed to drop upon good ground a few light-
hearted suggestions for turning Yen Sung's eccentricities
to humorous account. Garstang rather liked the
impassive pagan, but there was much taking place that
he could not see.

If he might be judged by his works, Yen Sung out-
shone all his associates in the Christian virtues. To the
blow on the right cheek he returned the left; he was
patient, industrious, long-suffering; he bore the burdens
of others. Only, it should be recorded that in moments
of solitude, especially after suffering an indignity, Yen
Sung sometimes took a very bright knife from beneath
his tunic and proceeded to whet it quietly and systemati-
cally upon his leather belt, although it was always keen
enough to split a hair. This might have given some
colour to Harold's warning were it not that the Oriental
mind remains an insoluble riddle, and it would be as
reasonable and more charitable to assume that Yen
Sung's formidable blade was intended for no more
desperate purpose than that of smoothing its owner's
chin. There is even a more amiable possibility, for one
morning about this time Edith Garstang found upon her
plate at the breakfast-table a little box of wood and
inlaid straw, which proved to contain a variety of
figures carved with taste and untiring skill in bone and
fruit stones, and one or two in ivory. There were mandarins in official robes: trees of gnarled, fantastic growth;
tigers, elephants, and serpents; a wonderful street scene,
with stalls, merchants, beggars, a procession of priests,
and all the details of a busy thoroughfare: a child-bride
in her ornamental wedding-chair; and a number of
fearsome objects which could only be accounted for as

evil demons, though more probably in Yen Sung's mind they stood as the embodiment of beneficent spirits. It was a collection which must have occupied all his spare hours almost from the day of his arrival.

Edith was enchanted with the grace and delicacy of the pretty things, but Garstang remained thoughtfully silent, and when the story came to Harold's ears he vowed softly between smiling lips that Yen Sung should presently suffer somewhat for his presumption. The immediate settlement arrived at by Garstang was to take the box in one hand and a pound in the other, and to tell Yen Sung kindly but definitely, that he must take back the toys or be paid with the money. It furnished fresh proof of the sordid nature of the Chinaman's instincts, for he took the note without a word of protest, and when alone cheerfully added it to his secret store.

Thenceforth he carved no more, occupying himself with the composition of sundry notices in his own tortuous language, which he afterwards fastened to the branches of the largest trees or to buildings, and even cast into the streams. A local wit affected to regard these documents as Boxer proclamations; in reality they were invocations addressed to the tutelary spirit residing within the tree or building or stream committing "the most honourable sun-haired maiden" to its unceasing protection; recommending a benevolent interest in the general affairs of the "large-bodied earth-tiller Garstang"; and requesting as a personal favour to Yen Sung that the tree or building would fall upon, or the stream engulf, "the rat-lipped outcast whose polluted ancestral altar lies beyond the hill-top."

The "most honourable maiden" herself was never without a smile and a word of greeting for Yen Sung when she passed him at his work. She cross-examined him out of his polite dissimulation on the subject of food and obtained some small concessions to provide a simple

364

fare more suited to his tastes. His oblique eyes took her up at the earliest possible point of vision, and, still intent upon his work, he continued to watch her stealthily until the last glimpse of her white dress was hidden from his sight; but by no interest or encouragement could he be induced to cease work during his working hours. Amused, half-piqued, and curious to learn, she was driven to approach him at a more convenient time, when, in the monotonous tone and passionless narration of his race, he told her all she asked. About himself he lied without the least consciousness of shame or ingratitude, painting for her benefit a purely imaginary picture of his home, his life, his kinspeople, and all that pertained to Yen Sung; but the picture, though individually deceptive, was typically correct, so that in time Edith Garstang in her remote English home began to raise a little of the veil of the mysterious land and even to find some slight foothold among the shifting complexities of the Celestial mind.

It was a continual matter for self-reproach to her that she did not bring about Yen Sung's conversion to a better faith; but, with surprise, she found an increasing difficulty in urging her own religion upon this courteous, high-minded pagan. She shrank from the shameful justice of the reproach in case Yen Sung should indicate the blasphemers, the Commandment-breakers, the thieves and the persecutors, by whom he was surrounded, and ask in a voice requiring no irony of tone, "Are these, too, Christians?"

In his own land Yen Sung burned joss-sticks to many deities, including one, blind and inexorable, whom we might call Destiny. Being at so great a distance from home, and therefore almost out of the sphere of influence of these deities, he had perhaps grown lax in his observances, or it may be that a supply of the proper worshipping materials was not obtainable in Overbury. Whatever the cause, this same Destiny determined to render Yen Sung a sharp account of her presence, he having no beneficent deities to intervene, and the spirits of his ancestors presumably being all engaged in China. The visible outcome was that on a raw November afternoon two of the labourers returned to the house assisting Yen Sung, who walked very uncertainly between them.

It then appeared that there had been a very unfortunate accident. Six men in all were concerned, including Harold, who had walked across the field on his way up to the house, and there were five different and occasionally conflicting accounts, Yen Sung himself contributing nothing. The five Stonecroft men had been engaged in collecting, carting, and burning the dried potato-tops when Harold appeared. Someone had playfully thrown a potato (the accepted version), which someone else had caught and returned. Then someone threw another, and in a minute a game was in progress, with all engaged except Yen Sung, who continued his duty of replenishing the fires. Unfortunately, someone threw the potato in the direction of Yen Sung, and the someone whose turn it was to catch it, with no eyes except for the missile, had run in and precipitated the unfortunate Chinaman into the heart of the fire. Everyone was sorry.

There chanced to be a decent room over a loose-box empty at that time, and here, on a pallet, Yen Sung was made as comfortable as possible. Harold himself rode for a doctor, and everyone was much relieved to learn that although severely burned here and there, Yen Sung was in no danger of dying.

With the cloud of a possible inquest lifted, a lighter vein prevailed. Harold declared that they need not have worried as it was impossible to kill a Chinee—they all died natural deaths; and before night it came to be agreed that it was Yen Sung's own fault and the result of his persistent habit of getting into people's way.

He made an ideal patient. He never complained, and seemed to find no difficulty in remaining quiescent, bodily and mentally, for days together. He accepted the doctor as "benevolently intentioned," and did as he was told in spite of a little private incredulity as to the efficacy of remedies applied without incantations or even coloured lights.

Yen Sung celebrated the beginning of his third week in the loft by sitting up for the first time.

"But on no account must he go out yet," reiterated the doctor for the sixth time to Miss Garstang. "I sometimes wonder most poignantly whether it's the sublimest philosophy or merely a lacquered mask over absolute vacuity that the fellow wears. Does he understand?"

"Oh, yes; only he is very patient," replied Edith, who generally took the instructions. "I am sure he will do as you say."

"Well, Kiu, my friend," he continued, turning again to Yen Sung, "let the prosaic but sincere work of the barbarian medicine-man sink into your retentive Oriental mind. Although you are on the mend, you are for that reason to take all the more care. Shun the insidious delight of potato-top burning or any other outdoor exercise until I give you leave to stir. If you go out and get cold or wet you will most certainly join the spirits of your illustrious ancestors."

"It is as the all-seeing Buddha ordains," replied Yen Sung imperturbably, but he quite accepted the warning.

Edith accompanied the doctor to the yard and then returned to the loft.

"I am going to Overbury now," she remarked, after she had made up the fire and given a glance round the room. "Is there anything that you would like: anything that I could get you?"

Yen Sung shook his head. There was nothing that he required.

"I am going to buy my Christmas cards," she continued, lingering. "You know what Christmas is, Kiu?"

"The Season of Much Gladness," replied Yen Sung from his couch.

Two pitiful tears formed suddenly in Edith's eyes. "We say, 'Peace on earth and goodwill to men,' " she said in a low voice.

"Peace on earth and goodwill to men," repeated the pagan. Fifty years ago, he was remembering, his father's house had been shelled to the ground by the navies of two most Christian nations at this very same season of "Peace on earth and goodwill to men."

"You have perhaps read some part of the little book I brought?" she asked timidly after a moment's pause. On a table within his reach lay a copy of the New Testament.

"I have read somewhat of the words, honourable lady Edith," he replied, his usual impassiveness cloaking any feelings he might have of interest or indifference.

She could venture no further. "I must go now," she announced, glancing at the window. "It is coming dark already."

It was, indeed, very dark, even for a December afternoon, and as she spoke a roll of distant thunder told the cause. Yen Sung glanced through the window also, and into his face there came an expression more indicative of emotion than anything he had yet betrayed.

"If it be permitted me to speak unasked, might not the venture of this journey be put off to a more auspicious day?" he said earnestly. "Very soon the rain will descend in torrents, the lightning will tear open the sky, and doubtful powers will then be able to launch their thunderbolts even against the most virtuous."

"I am not afraid of the thunder and lightning," replied Edith with a smile; "and as for the rain, see, I am well provided against it."

"But the omen—even as you declared your purpose the thunder spoke," he persisted. "Furthermore, by a most unpropitious chain of events, the road you must take lies to the north, while at this season the high heavens are situate directly in the south."

Suddenly a look almost of terror came into his eyes. "Stay, most honourable," he gasped; "what day of your twelfth moon do you call this?"

"It is the eleventh day of the twelfth month—our December," she replied.

Yen Sung made a rapid calculation in his mind, converting the date into its equivalent in his own system of time. Twice, three times he repeated the process in his anxiety, and then, as the unevadable fact was driven home to him, he leaned forward in trembling anxiety.

"You must not go forth to-day, lady Edith; you cannot go," he whispered fearfully. "It is a day of the blackest omen and the direct possibilities. It is the one day of an entire cycle when all the diverging lines of evil, from whatever cause arising, meet in one irresistible concentration. Demons, foul dragons, and the malevolent shadows of all the unworthy dead are abroad and supreme to-day, while the benevolent forces stand powerless. So far back as last New Year's Day a special Imperial edict went forth warning all that they should give no feast, go on no journey, nor engage in any new enterprise upon this most abandoned day. Even I, in the obscurity of this hidden chamber, would not have ventured to leave my couch to-day had I not most incapably forgotten. How, then, shall you take a journey directly away from the high heavens and after the portent of the thunder?"

It was so real to him as he spoke—one who all his life had walked with evil spirits on the one side and good spirits on the other; surrounded by demons whose supposed prejudices had to be conformed to in every action—that Edith listened half in pity, half in despair. It would have seemed cruel to her to leave him abruptly in his real distress. With an inspiration a means

369

occurred to her not only of reassuring him but even of turning the incident to good account.

"I am not afraid," she replied serenely, "for I carry a safeguard against which no power of evil can prevail." A little gold cross, plain save for the three initials which it bore, hung by a slender chain about her neck. She touched it as she spoke.

Here was something that Yen Sung could fully understand; it appealed, naturally and convincingly, to one whose religion was steeped in idolatry, witchcraft and geomancy. Suspended about *his* neck there also hung a powerful charm, a square of parchment inscribed with mystic characters, drawn out by one of the most successful necromancers of the age. It was an infallible specific against leprosy and shipwreck, and, in token, Yen Sung had never contracted leprosy or been shipwrecked. If only he had provided himself with a similar protection against the perils of fire he would certainly have escaped his present plight; but one cannot foresee everything. A charm of universal potency excited his wonder and admiration. It did not occur to him that Edith might not be speaking quite literally—that her geometrical device was a symbol more efficacious when carried in the heart than when worn among the garments.

"Is there, indeed, no possible contingency against which this talisman might fail?" he asked, scarcely yet fully reassured.

"If I believe in its power and wear it faithfully there is nothing in the whole world that can harm me. Are you not satisfied, Kiu?"

"Your lips are incapable of guile, nor can alloy pass for gold before the touch of a pure heart," replied Yen Sung.

He watched her cross the yard; he marked the clang of the iron gate as she turned into the narrow lane beyond; then for five minutes he sat motionless—so unbreathingly still that not one of the grotesque idols in his far-off ancestral temple could have seemed more devoid of being.

A vivid flash of lightning recalled him from his thoughts and lit up the room with an electric brilliance for one moment. It brought out every detail as the sun had never done, and picked up in that short second, and seemed to fling it back to meet Yen's staring eyes, one bright object lying by the door. Then darkness.

In the overwhelming shock of the discovery Yen Sung's mind was momentarily eclipsed by a blow that stunned —a feeling of irreparable disaster that closed round his heart like a grasp of ice. He shook himself free, and, falling upon hands and knees, swiftly sought the spot. The half-light had returned after the darkness, sufficient, with face bent to the floor, for him to verify the worst. The little magic talisman that the most gracious lady Edith had wholly and implicitly relied upon to guard her on her perilous way lay beneath his eyes. And she had gone!

His mind, freed from its numbness, leapt now. She had gone forth, unconscious of her loss, into that most evil day when the unrestrained powers of darkness, loose from ten thousand unchained hells, would surround her in every form. She had gone out heralded by the most ill-destined omens from the skies. She had gone where her very direction cut her off from the slenderest possibility of relief.

At all cost she must be overtaken and the safeguard restored to her at once. Every second was precious, every step she took was full of danger. He had no means of communicating with the house; the yard beneath his window was deserted. In spite of the honourable doctor's warning, Yen Sung himself must set in motion the means for her deliverance.

He moved quickly, feverishly, but with due caution, or he might utterly defeat his end; for who could say but that his unworthy touch might destroy the virtue of the charm or immediate death be the fruit of his presumption? A half-burned twig lay on his hearth;

deftly, in spite of his bandaged hands, Yen Sung wound the chain about it; then, as fast as his weak limbs would carry him, he sought the house.

"See!" he exclaimed, bursting into the great kitchen where Edith's mother chanced to be engaged alone; "the fair one of your house has gone forth on a most perilous journey and the charm upon which she alone relied for protection has escaped her unperceived. Let a speedy messenger be sent before harm reaches her."

"Whatever are you doing out on a day like this?" exclaimed Mrs. Garstang without paying any attention to his excited words. She was a woman of sound practical common sense, and had found it simpler in her dealings with Yen Sung to regard him as quite irresponsible. "After what the doctor said, too! Go back this very minute."

"But the charm?" he protested blankly. "The safeguard upon which the most kind of heart depends?"

"Oh, Edith's little cross?" she said without concern, noticing it for the first time. "Yes, I'll give it her when she comes back. Now, do make haste, Kiu. Here, I'd better get Andrew to you."

She left the kitchen to call her husband, and in the impotence of his position a despair more hideous than before fell on Yen Sung.

Blind! Mad! He knew they were not cruel; some fatal obliquity of vision hid his view from them, their view from him; but was the gentlest and fairest to be sacrificed? He remembered the tone in which she had spoken of the power of the charm—the soft touch by which she had assured herself that it hung about her neck, and something that was the nearest to a sob that he had ever known strangled his breath.

Twenty seconds later, from a bank behind the buildings, Yen Sung dropped stealthily into the narrow lane and began to run. One possible hope had flashed across his mind. In following the road to Overbury, Edith would have to make a detour of half a mile in order to cross the River Aish by the bridge at Rockford; there was, indeed, no other way. By taking to the fields, wading the Aish, and striking the high road at its nearest point, Yen Sung hoped just to intercept her.

He was under no delusion. To the plain warning of the doctor he added—or perhaps took them as inter-mingling in the scheme of destiny—the supernatural terrors of the day, and with dispassionate fatalism he bowed acquiescently. The extent of his hopes was that he might be permitted to reach his revered one before the vengeance of the furies caught him or his earthly powers failed. Under ordinary conditions the race was not a hopeless one—three fields, the river, and beyond, a strip of meadow lay between him and the high road; but his heroic heart was chained to a slight and crippled frame. Already the rain, now descending in torrents, had soaked him to the skin and the sodden clay of the ploughed land hung in great clods about his feet.

He beat his way through the hedges, but the thorns and brambles tore him through his thin clothes as though with hooks, and very soon he found with dismay that he could only stumble blindly forward with half-bent knees. All his life he had believed in demons, and now to justify his faith, they came in their legions to mock and thwart him. Some drove barbs into every tingling joint, tore his unhealed burns with their talons, or turned the beating rain that fell upon his face into alternate ice and fire. Others, riding the wind like drifts of smoke, surrounded him in their endless circlings shrieking in his ears as they swept by.

They made the earth heavy in his path, directed the rain into a denser volume where he was, knit the brambles together before him at each hedge, and impeded him in every way to an unending accompaniment of swirling, shrieking, riotous devilry. There were earth spirits, wind spirits, water spirits, fire spirits, and the outcast band. The accusing shadows of his ancestors walked by his side, desirous of arguing with him on many

373

subjects, while the Great Dragon, floating above all, wrote unmoved with an iron pen upon a marble slate.

At the last hedge before the river he was blinded for the moment by a branch which slipped from his feeble grasp, and groping through he fell into a deep and thorny ditch. The myriads of spirits shrieked their mirth, and in his half-stunned confusion Yen Sung began painfully to climb back again up to the hedge through which he had just come. A little precious time was lost before he discovered his mistake and the fall had crippled him still further. The most gallant effort he could now call up was nothing but a shambling walk.

He reached the river, and would have stepped in, when the chain slipped from the twig upon which he had so far carried it, and fell into the grass. A few more steps and it would have been lost beneath the muddy waters of the Aish. At the cost of another delay he broke a willow branch and with a thread of linen from his hand he tied the cross to the thin end of the wand. Then using the butt to feel his way among the rock-strewn icy water, he stumbled to the other bank.

There was nothing now but the narrow strip of meadow, beyond which the highway marked his goal. Had his "high deities" determined to be kind? Perhaps; for suddenly the heavens opened above his head, the leaping flame caught the glittering emblem which he held aloft, and, without the knowledge of a failure —grotesque but for its climax—to mock his eyes, Yen Sung sank straightway to the ground and reached a farther goal.

There is very little to add to the story of his end.

The effect of lightning upon the object which it strikes is curious and diverse. Yen Sung supplied another instance of this purely scientific phenomenon, for when his body came to be unrobed, those who stood by were startled for the moment to see the perfect outline of a cross charged with three letters imprinted with unmistakable clearness upon his breast.

At first it was intended that he should be buried in a secluded corner of the old churchyard at Overbury; but to many influential parishioners the thought of a pagan finding a resting-place within their hallowed "God's Acre" was repugnant. In the end a site deemed more suitable was found in a neighbouring cemetery, where he sleeps in an unconsecrated plot set apart for suicides and the unbaptized.

THE VICTOR
by Dale Collins

DALE COLLINS was born in Sydney, in 1897, and is one of the most promising of the younger Australian authors. His first published work, *The Story of the First Motor-Boat Voyage Round the World*, told the story of a youthful enterprise. On the publication of his novel, *Ordeal*, a story of the sea which invited comparison with the work of Joseph Conrad, Collins immediately stepped into the front rank of modern novelists. *The Victor* is a story O. Henry would have admired; it is ingenious, yet of unquestionable sincerity.

THE VICTOR

BY

DALE COLLINS

ARCHIPELAGO RUBBER, with the best intentions in the world, sent all its brightest young men to the East to study production on the plantations. When these bright young men returned they knew a great deal about the business and other things, and were of increased value to the Company. When they did not return the East had taken them, but Archipelago Rubber did not understand that.

In accordance with the dispensation of his board, Peter Burney had stepped ashore at Maccalengleng three hours before, and as he walked between the grey-blue trees he told Sam Reid, the plantation manager, many things with the candour and confidence of twenty-two years. He talked of a girl with eyes as blue as the sea, of England, of System, of Big Business, of his Dad, and of the East.

"The way I size up the East is, it needs waking up and some life put into it," said Peter Burney. "There's labour in any quantity—cheap and good; the natural conditions are fine; there's any amount of room for increased production. The only catch is that the East's grown dull and sleepy through the centuries. It's like a worn-out old man—wants a dose of monkey gland, I'd say."

Sam Reid—grizzled, slovenly and drink-warped—heard him and gave a snort. He was not impressed. This was another of the bright young men. They left him cold, after a quarter of a century in the East. They came out full of this kind of stuff, and presently they went away again and he stayed on at Maccalengleng,

381

where every mosquito carried fever and every bottle a more perilous disease. They came and went—these smart young men—but he remained, like part of the plantation, absorbed by it, as if the rubber had congealed about him. And they held him in contempt because he was of the East and didn't care what they thought, and knew them for young fools. Also, they didn't like him because he had forgotten how to part his hair and how to be polite and tactful and make pretty speeches.

But he got the rubber out of Maccalengleng, and that was more than they could have done.

"So——!" said Reid, and shrugged contemptuously.

This talk riled him, as did the cocksure young man, who was weak as a babe. Well, the fool would learn presently. With grim and bitter satisfaction the elder man looked forward into the long months of disillusionment.

And Peter Burney said his say with youth's cheerful arrogance, seeing Sam Reid as a wreck who didn't amount to anything.

Presently they went up to the veranda, where Reid drank a gin and Burney a lime-squash, the one sprawled out and comatose, the other alert and upright.

Before their eyes the grey-blue rows of rubber trees marched down to the glassy sea, flanked on either hand by the living jungle. Two Malays drowsed in the shadow of the house; insects burred; lizards stared with jewelled eyes; the sun blazed down upon the world with intense, palpitating light.

"It fairly gets my goat, this East!" said Burney. "It's numb and lifeless and crusted with age. For all its fertility it's barren. Nothing happens here. Life doesn't get along. If a man were big enough he could shake up this East."

Reid took another gin.

"Yes," he said dryly, "if he was big enough!"

A flush stole into Burney's smooth face, his amiable mouth hardened and his eyes were aglow with the reflections of youth's dreams. He was vaguely aware of conflict with an intangible but powerful presence, and he rejoiced in the sensation. In a flaccid and exhausted world, too occupied with birth and decay to live, he, at least, was vigorous and virile.

The night was heavy on Maccalengleng, the darkness being so deep and thick that it had a substantial quality. A flare on a drifting sampan out on the unseen water gained the effect of burning in the heart of solid gloom. It was very quiet because the noises of the jungle seemed to weave into the silence and become part of it, so that the ear was not conscious of any sound at all. The stars were as holes in the night's mass, letting in hints of glory from a place beyond.

For two years and eleven months in the evenings Peter Burney and Sam Reid had sat in their chairs on either side of the table on the veranda, and in that time nothing had happened—nothing of which they were actively conscious, nothing that had borne the appearance of importance. Through the days they had worked in broiling heat, slept after luncheon, risen and worked again, bathed and had the evening meal. Reid had been following this routine for as long as he could remember, and he had not changed. The sea, the rubber trees, the jungle, the sweep of sky, and the steaming heat had not changed either; the Malays and the stone gods looking down on the village had not changed. But Peter Burney had.

He spoke no more of putting life into the East, nor of England, nor of the girl with eyes like the sea, nor of his Dad. He had come to the knowledge that letter-writing was a trial when the sweating arms stuck to the table. He did not drink lime-squash. Youth's dreams and enthusiasms and appetites had been his enemies and had betrayed him into the grasp of the East.

Reid had the satisfaction of seeing that he had been right on that first day when he had snorted. The

degeneration had been rapid. Without lifting a hand
he had been avenged upon the young man whose first
quick glance had judged him to be a waster and good-
for-nothing, and with justice.

Burney lifted his glass, lapped at the gin, shivered
because there was still fever in him, and spoke, his
mouth softer now and weaker, less likeable.

"Hell, why should I go back?" he asked, continuing
their discussion. "There's something in all this gets a
man." He waved his hand out at the mystery of the
night. "There's colour and glamour in this—it's the
life I was cut out for. They told me I'd be glad enough
to get home! Rot! This is the little place I've been
looking for—out here, out East. A man lives out here,
takes his time, dreams along. It's warm here—like hell
at times—but I don't know—it's a miracle. Supposing I
went home to an office desk—could I stick it after this?
Sleet and cold and snow—motor-cars, hustle—I wasn't
planned for that. Out here a man's a king over subjects
—back home I'd be a slave! I'd be chased round and
on the run every day and all day just to earn a crust.
It isn't worth it, Sam, and that's God's truth."

The manager made no comment beyond smiling
darkly while he gloated over the completeness of his
vindication. But Burney did not need an answer. He
was thinking aloud. How the old wreck judged things
did not matter.

"Go home——?" he swept on. "Go home to what?
To slave, to moil, to strive, to kill myself! And out
here I've got everything I want—peace, quiet, pros-
perity, power. A man could live to be a hundred out
here, and never know what the misery of life meant after
he'd beaten the fever. A little bit of trading or planting
—I've got enough of that—and he could live in luxury.
To the devil with Archipelago Rubber! Why should I
kill myself for them?"

"That's right," Reid agreed carelessly, "why should
you?"

"Let's have a drink on it!"

Burney tipped the bottle dexterously, despite the fact that his hand trembled. His face was flushed, for he had had more gin than was good for him—more that night and more on previous nights. The tropics had sapped him, the monotony had blunted him. He was not the same young man who had landed at Maccalengleng. There were moments when he was dimly aware of this, but consolation and a means of quietening these qualms were available in the bottles on the store-room shelves.

"Well, you'll have to be sure positive before three weeks are up and the steamer comes," said the man who did not care, triumphing over his critic of yester-year.

"I'm all that now," was the answer.

They lay in silence which was broken only by the drumming of Burney's fingers upon the arm of his chair. Reid was inert, being twenty, twenty-five years past that stage.

"You were over at Njo-Angat's kampong again to-day?" he questioned at last.

The younger man stretched with elaborate unconcern.

"What if I was?" he countered, and then abruptly, because it was lonely on Maccalengleng and a man had to have a confidant, the truth came tumbling out in a torrent: "Tell you, Sam, I've fallen for that daughter of his, Sali. Yes, she's wonderful! She's like a little golden saint. She doesn't seem coloured. I put no account to coloured girls, but this one—well, she's different. All said and done, her skin's no darker than yours, and her heart's clear white. She's—oh, hell what's the use of trying to express these things?—she's the living symbol of all that's most fascinating in the East. She's calm and grave and quiet and polished; she's incomprehensible; she's the lovely riddle of all woman; she's still and sweet and soft. I want that girl like I never wanted anything before." He broke off, panting. "She loves me," he resumed, his voice falling into an odd sing-song, "and I'm going over to Panjoeng with her when my time's up here, and I'm going to trade there, and we'll be happy and forget the world, forget everything except our joy. There's no escape from these things. They happen. It would be folly, and worse than folly, to run away. It is Fate!"

He made a gesture of acceptance, which was Oriental in its resignation. Burney had gone East when he was young and fluid, and his soul had been easily shaped by the mould of his environment.

"That's so," Reid agreed, sucking his moustache and then: "You'll be happy at Panjoeng, eh?"

"Yes!" said Burney, and swore, to emphasize the statement, for he had experienced a sudden twinge of doubt before the dry question, as if he were sliding down an inclined plane to he knew not what, and yet was powerless to stop his descent, and careless of its consequences. Memories flooded to him, and fears assailed him.

To clear his brain and steady his nerves he took a stiff gin. The effect was magical. Doubt died. He saw with crystal clarity that he was right and that it was a mercy of Fate that had shown him his path. There was no sense in fighting and struggling. Life was a stream, and humanity no more than troubled flotsam upon its surface.

He thought of Sali, and she was as a star—distant, unreadable, almost beyond attainment, and yet brought within his grasp by this magical chance of love which broke down barriers of race and creed. He felt exhilarated, and was possessed by the fancy that he was one with the whole living night.

The man on the other side of the table drank again, and smiled bitterly, and yet as he looked out at the East a strange expression passed across his face, a look of respect and dread.

The triumph was so complete, so easily gained.

Thought was not a good occupation for Sam Reid. He was nearly fifty and had nothing much to look back on, and nothing to which he could look forward. And yet he found thought hard to escape from, and it was for this reason that he was devoting his concentrated attention to the liquid contents of the store-room.

Reid was often drunk, but he went on a proper spree about once in twelve months, and always when he had been thinking. These debauches of his were lonely and terrible festivities, embarked upon deliberately and viciously, not enjoyed, but terribly thorough.

He stood in the dimly-lit store-room, wearing only his pyjama trousers. A lantern flung upon the wall a shadow caricature of the caricature of a man. His grey moustache, his grey hair, emphasized the pity of him. Swaying, he drank from a bottle and flung it to one side. It struck the wall and shattered into tinkling fragments. What remained of its contents made a dark smudge on the split-bamboo floor.

Sam Reid swung about and faced out through the open door which gave on to the veranda. With the stupid dignity of a drunken man he raised a thin fist and shook it at the night.

"You——!" he snarled. "You——!"

Wrath, hatred and fear were in his eyes.

Reeling away from whatever he saw in the darkness, and spitting oaths, he dragged down another bottle. Two more fell with it, and his feet were wet with liquor. To and fro he swayed, a ghastly figure of licence, with his black shadow for company and his mind swamped in a sea of spirits. He sang, he shouted, he danced—now out on the veranda, now in the store-room.

The sensation of escape filled him with pride in his strength. He smashed and kicked and wrought havoc in a paroxysm of destruction, as if seeking to accomplish the ruination of his surroundings that they might match himself.

Two hours later Peter Burney returned from the

kampong of Njo-Angat, where no white man should have been. He was surprised to see that the veranda was in darkness, and as he drew nearer he became aware of an atmosphere of calamity and collapse, so that his heart throbbed uneasily beneath the fingers of foreboding.

"Reid," he called, "Reid!" and broke into a run. There was no answer, and the black house crouched against the stars like a sulky monster.

At the head of the steps leading up to the veranda he struck a match. The light blazed brightly in the still air, revealing, with impish delight, the aftermath of Sam Reid's party. The manager lay at full length upon the floor, and about him was scattered an amazing array of bottles, some broken though still uncorked, but all empty. The boards were dark with stains, and the air reeked. Reid lay like a dead man, his arms flung out above his head, and each hand clutching a bottle.

For a second Burney stood aghast, an oath taking shape on his lips, and then he realized that Reid was not dead but drunk, for his shoulders were moving in the heavy breathing of intoxication.

A wave of wrath swept the younger man. Falling on his knees he gripped the manager with rough hands, and shook him this way and that, maddened by the thought of the reckless waste which had been involved in the orgy.

The sharp motion brought Reid to his senses, and he sat upright in the darkness.

"Here—here——" he mumbled. "What you mean heh?—wake me up middle of night——!"

"I'll wake you up, you hog! What have you been doing? Tell me that, will you?"

Reid coughed and snorted, and then answered with dignity: "Certainly, m'boy, I tell you, yesh! I've helped meself to party while you were out courting— every man hish own amusement! I like the liquor,

388

yesh! I've drunk and I've drunk, and I'd be drinking still if there was so much as another drop to drink in thish house!"

"*What?*" gasped Burney, astounded and appalled.

But having made his announcement, Reid had collapsed again.

The other rose to his feet, his hands clenched and the blood pumping through his head. He wanted to break things, and most of all to break the head of the greedy old sot. Drink—that vital part of the East's life!—there wasn't a drop of drink left, and there he was marooned on Maccalengleng with no prospect of getting any more. The thought was unbearable and murder was in his heart. He had been pillaged, plundered, and the thief lay before him too drunken to fight.

"You——!" said Peter Burney, and expressed his candid opinion of Reid. But Reid did not hear him, being deep in heavy slumber.

"In the morning—boss or no boss—I'll punch you into jelly!" vowed the young man.

For the first night in more than two years Peter Burney drank plain water, and it failed lamentably to quench his thirst. His nerves missed the accustomed stimulant, and he lay wide awake for hours on his bed looking out through the mosquito netting at the great stars. No one, he argued with himself, could say that he was a drunkard—not like that swine Reid—but a man got into the way of taking alcohol in the East, and it hurt to be without it. He was wretched. The sentinel palms against the sky maddened him, the drone of the mosquitoes was like the chanting of fiends, and the glamour of the tropical night was not for him.

Sam Reid had not dwelt twenty-five years in the archipelago without acquiring certain powers, and one of these was the capacity for making a rapid recovery. With dawn stealing over the Eastern sea he was astir, and the first thing he saw by the pink and pearl light was that he had gained his junior's hatred. This did not trouble him—for the hatred of one held in contempt is a slight thing—but he had no desire to have life made uncomfortable. Accordingly he was busy.

His task was accomplished and he was toying with a breakfast of a mangosteen and a banana when Burney appeared on the veranda.

The young man's face was grim, and there was no greeting on his lips for the touselled, untidy wreck who sat at the table.

Reid met his angry eyes calmly.

"I got off the chain last night," he said. "I suppose you figure I shouldn't have been so liberal with myself?"

Burney's face portended the coming storm.

"You're sober now, and I'm going to make you pay for last night."

But Reid sat at ease in his chair after one quick movement—a movement which resulted in the appearance of an automatic pistol, the chilly eye of which regarded Burney with cold disfavour. Beneath its scrutiny his advance was checked.

"If I hadn't been twenty years in the East I'd fight you with my fists," said Reid with a little gesture of apology, "but as I have been, I'm not much of a man and so I've got to windward of you. I've cleansed this house of fire-arms this morning—all save this one. You'd better behave yourself, or I'll fill you that full of lead you'll sink into the ground. I'm a peaceful man, but I'm tired of you. For three years I've stuck it, but I'll not stand it any more. I'll have no jumped-up kid talking to me. I'm boss here, and I'll drink as much as I want. Twenty-five years I've been on Maccalengleng, and what's life got for me if I can't have a burst when I feel so inclined? I tell you, I forgot the empty misery of life last night, and that's a relief I'll not forgo out of consideration for you or anyone. When you've been East as long as me maybe you'll understand!"

He spoke with an air of finality, and Burney knew

that he was mastered by reason of the weapon and the bitter experience which was the lot of his opponent.

His anger was displaced by an unanalysable feeling of hopelessness and despair. The night had sapped his energies, and the morning reviver which he needed so badly was not to be had. A shiver ran through him as he looked at Reid and understood how little life meant to him.

Burney was nauseated by Reid's presence, hating him because he was a wreck, a waster, a drunkard, and a thief of other men's rights.

And Reid looked at him with open dislike, because he was a smart young man out from the home office and no stronger than a kitten.

For twenty days and twenty nights the two lonely men dwelt on the raw edge of hatred, speaking but little and brooding in the company of their own thoughts. The danger of violence had passed, for the heat and the absence of stimulants had left them without energy, so that all they wished to do was to avoid each other.

In Burney's heart remained gnawing anger which spread like a canker worm, so that the peace went out of his life and the lotus was bitter in his mouth. He found himself at war with everything in the sunny world, from the suave Malays to the green things of the jungle. There was nothing to which he could turn for aid to recapture that rosy glow which once had dimmed his eyes to the fact that he was a stranger in a strange land of which he was a little afraid. His eyes, seeing clearly now, discovered the truth, and he sickened for home. Even Sali seemed less delicious.

But when the steamer came in it would be all right, he told himself. The steamer would replenish the store-room, and the dream would be resumed, effortless and soothing.

Upon the evening of the twentieth day, with the steamer due upon the morrow, calamity overtook Peter

Burney in the form of a second act of baser pillage by the man who hated him because he was young and better educated and had not learnt the East at the cost of twenty-five years of life.

Having broken the nose of the grave Njo-Angat, who told him the news of this event, Peter Burney set out for the plantation house to slay his boss.

But as he tramped back between the hot walls of jungle, with the calm stars looking down on him, and the presence of Asia breathing from the purple hills and from the purple sea—something snapped in his brain. He felt suddenly helpless and hopeless, cold and lost; he felt like a child that has strayed into a dark place and is beset by the knowledge of evil.

The beauty of the night disgusted him, as the beauty of something diseased and unclean. He was miserable and disillusioned, but even while he blamed Reid for his state he walked the more swiftly, fearing lest his just wrath should be swallowed up in other emotions, the causes of which he did not comprehend.

The manager sat upon the veranda, but he rose as his junior entered, for he saw by the whiteness of his face that he had discovered the position. Reid's hand rested on the pistol butt, and he smiled beneath his draggled moustache because now his victory was finally won, and the jeerer had been reduced to an object pitiable and to be mocked by all the world; the man who had failed in love.

"If I said what I think of you," said Burney, crouched on the topmost step, "it'd burn you up! You—you call yourself a man—and you'd go behind my back and steal the heart of the girl you know I love—you——!"

But the night was hot and the elder had no desire for a scene or prolonged argument.

"I'm boss here," he said, "because I know the East. I want to tell you something—I've got that girl because she's the cutest Malay I've ever seen, and there's not much in life for me. But I don't make the mistake you

did—I don't figure I've got her heart. I've bought her
—that's all. She was going to the highest bidder; one
white man or another meant nothing to her. She's a
low caste Malay. Great stars, man, you don't think
you're dealing with something white? I know the East,
I tell you, and I know how much of her love Sali is
going to give to me, to you, or to any other *tuan*. But
there's not much in life for me, and so I shall be
content!"

He broke off, sucking his moustache, and Burney, who
had intended to be so fierce, stood silent, because he saw
Reid as a poor prisoner in a dark gaol—in a gaol to
which he clamoured to be admitted, insanely and without understanding.

"You're young," Reid said slowly, "but me—I've
been twenty-five years out here, and I'm entitled to all
I can get!"

He taunted the young man who was his enemy because
he saw that the pride had gone out of him and that he
was in the dust. He smiled, but although Burney saw
all this he found no protest because he was broken.

Reid shouted the girl's name, and she came out of
the night from around the corner of the veranda, and
at a word from him in her own language sat down
beside him cross-legged upon the floor, not looking at
the boy who had been her lover, not looking at her
master, not looking at anything their eyes could see, but
at something in the night invisible to them.

Peter Burney stared at her, and for the first time
noticed the flatness of her features, the childish smallness
of her body, and the brownness of her feet. But his
most vital discovery was that he saw her as if she sat a
long way off in another world in which he had no
existence.

A flush of shame and chagrin stole into his tanned
cheeks, and he hastily averted his eyes. Then a savage
laugh choked his throat, and his hands opened limply.

"Take her—Reid—take her!" he cried, and went

unsteadily across the veranda to his room like a man who had been stunned and suffers all the pains of rebirth. And after an interval there came from within the sound of trunks being dragged about.

Sam Reid nodded his grizzled head as he gloated on the vanquishing of the self-righteous.

"That's taught the puppy!" he said to his pipe.

The big Dutch steamer lying off Maccalengleng flung up a plume of steam against the sunset sky, and a breath later a grunting hoot reached the beach, urging the boat to be quick since darkness stalked the world and there was a channel to be negotiated before the highway of the sea was reached.

"Now, sir!" said the officer in the stern.

Peter Burney hesitated, and suddenly extended his hand to his late manager.

"No ill-feeling, Sam," he said, jerkily. "I guess I'm not much fitted for this life out here." His face darkened. "I'm glad to see the last of the vile place!" With one comprehensive glance he swept the rising slopes.

"I know," said Sam Reid without emotion. "I been here twenty-five years!"

Their hands clasped, and a moment later the boat was clear of the beach, and Burney, had started on his long voyage home to the offices of Archipelago Rubber. Every fibre of his being was a-thrill with relief, joy and anticipation, as if he went out to high adventure. His mind—freed from the oppression which had been upon it—was working clearly now, and the first effect of this was to cause him to strike his knee and shout an oath. The boat was a hundred yards from the shore, and the light was fading.

"Say, I've got another word to speak to Mr. Reid," he cried. "I've just got on to something—something I should have seen long ago—I've got to go back. I've got to thank him!" His voice rose excitedly.

394

But the phlegmatic Hollander in charge shook his head. "It is not possible," he grunted.

Burney sprang to his feet and looked back over the stern. Along the beach the shrunken, white figure was receding into the shadows.

"Sam—I understand now—I see it now, Sam!" Burney yelled. "They won't let me come back to tell you, but thanks! thanks!—thanks!"

The cry was heavily burdened with feeling, but the distance between boat and shore had widened, and it seemed that the lonely figure on the beach had not heard. And yet Burney fancied that he had seen a hand raised in acknowledgment, though he could not be certain, because, for some reason, his eyes had misted over and his head was spinning. He continued to shout his gratitude, and the boat went on.

Sam Reid had heard right enough.

"What's he understand?—nothing, the puppy!" He snorted.

The quick night had come before he reached the house. On the veranda sat Sali and her father. Reid nodded to the old Malay, and passing into the office returned with a roll of guilder notes, which he handed to him.

"Take her away, O Father," he said in Malay, "and marry her to one of thine own people!"

Njo-Angat rose obediently, his daughter's hand in his, and mumbled that the *tuan* was great and wise and good, that the peace of Allah would be upon him, and that there was no other god.

Sam Reid paid no attention, but when he was alone he raised his clenched fist and shook it at the night of the East which possessed the world with wanton witchery.

"Bah!" he cried. "Bah! That time I beat you— just that time I beat you!"

A smile of triumph was born on his face, and he stood erect, a proud man, a victor though for twenty-five years he had been enslaved.

THE RAID
by Leo Tolstoi

LEO NIKOLAVITCH TOLSTOI, the greatest of Russian writers, was born at Yasnaya Polyana, his father's impoverished estate, in 1828. The Tolstoi family were of German origin and had migrated to Muscovy early in the seventeenth century. Tolstoi's mother, Princess Volkhonskaya, was a lineal descendant of the Muscovite Tsars, and there was thus an aristocratic strain in Tolstoi's blood, although his sympathies were always with the Russian peasant, in whose cause he worked unceasingly from early manhood to extreme old age. He was educated at the comparatively unimportant university of Kazan, but rejected most careers open to him on the grounds that the practice of them was inconsistent with his ideals. He joined the army and fought in the Crimean war, and was attached to the staff of the commander-in-chief at Sebastopol. His military experiences form the background of his greatest work, *War and Peace*, and also of *The Raid* which describes his own initiation into the horrors of warfare. Tolstoi believed in the possibility of human perfection and strove to achieve it in his personal conduct, even sacrificing his personal belongings and living the life, and wearing the garb, of a peasant.

THE RAID

BY

LEO TOLSTOI

A Volunteer's Story

CHAPTER I

WAR always interested me : not war in the sense of manœuvres devised by great generals—my imagination refused to follow such immense movements, I did not understand them—but the reality of war—the actual killing.

I was more interested to know in what way and under the influence of what feeling one soldier kills another than to know how the armies were arranged at Austerlitz and Borodinó.

I had long passed the time when, pacing the room alone and waving my arms, I imagined myself a hero instantaneously slaughtering an immense number of men and receiving a generalship as well as imperishable glory for so doing.

The question now occupying me was different: under the influence of what feeling does a man, with no apparent advantage to himself, decide to subject himself to danger and, what is more surprising still, to kill his fellow men? I always wished to think that this is done under the influence of anger, but we cannot suppose that all those who fight are angry all the time, and I had to postulate feelings of self-preservation and duty.

What is courage—that quality respected in all ages and among all nations? Why is this good quality—contrary to all others—sometimes met with in vicious

401

men? Can it be that to endure danger calmly is merely a physical capacity and that people respect it in the same way that they do a man's tall stature or robust frame? Can a horse be called brave, which fearing the whip throws itself down a steep place where it will be smashed to pieces; or a child who fearing to be punished runs into a forest where it will lose itself; or a woman who for fear of shame kills her baby and has to endure penal prosecution; or a man who from vanity resolves to kill a fellow creature and exposes himself to the danger of being killed?

In every danger there is a choice. Does it not depend on whether the choice is prompted by a noble feeling or a base one whether it should be called courage or cowardice? These were the questions and the doubts that occupied my mind and to decide which I intended to avail myself of the first opportunity to go into action.

In the summer of 184– I was living in the Caucasus at the small fortified post of N——.

On the twelfth of July Captain Khlópov entered the low door of my earth-hut. He was wearing epaulettes and carrying a sword, which I had never before seen him do since I had reached the Caucasus.

"I come straight from the colonel's," he said in answer to my questioning look. "To-morrow our battalion is to march."

"Where to?" I asked.

"To M. The forces are to assemble there."

"And from there I suppose they will go into action?"

"I expect so."

"In what direction? What do you think?"

"What is there to think about? I am telling you what I know. A Tartar galloped here last night and brought orders from the general for the battalion to march with two days' rations of rusks. But where to, why, and for how long, we do not ask my friend. We are told to go—and that's enough."

"But if you are to take only two days' rations of rusks it proves that the troops won't be out longer than that."

"It proves nothing at all!"

"How is that?" I asked with surprise.

"Because it is so. We went to Dargo and took one week's rations of rusks, but we stayed there nearly a month."

"Can I go with you?" I asked after a pause.

"You could, no doubt, but my advice is, don't. Why run risks?"

"Oh, but you must allow me not to take your advice. I have been here a whole month solely on the chance of seeing an action, and you wish me to miss it!"

"Well, you must please yourself. But really you had better stay behind. You could wait for us here and might go hunting—and we would go our way, and it would be splendid," he said with such conviction that for a moment it really seemed to me too that it would be "splendid." However, I told him decidedly that nothing would induce me to stay behind.

"But what is there for you to see?" the captain went on, still trying to dissuade me. "Do you want to know what battles are like? Read Mikháylovski Danilevski's *Description of War*. It's a fine book, it gives a detailed account of everything. It gives the position of every corps and describes how battles are fought."

"All that does not interest me," I replied.

"What is it then? Do you simply wish to see how people are killed?—In 1832 we had a fellow here, also a civilian, a Spaniard I think he was. He took part with us in two campaigns, wearing some kind of blue mantle. Well, they did for the fine fellow. You won't astonish anyone here, friend!"

Humiliating though it was that the captain so misjudged my motives, I did not try to disabuse him.

"Was he brave?" I asked.

"Heaven only knows: he always used to ride in front, and where there was firing there he always was."

"Then he must have been brave," said I.

"No. Pushing oneself in where one is not needed does not prove one to be brave."

"Then what do you call brave?"

"Brave? . . . Brave?" repeated the captain with the air of one to whom such a question presents itself for the first time. "He who does what he ought to do is brave," he said after thinking awhile.

I remembered that Plato defines courage as "The knowledge of what should and what should not be feared," and despite the looseness and vagueness of the captain's definition I thought that the fundamental ideas of the two were not so different as they might appear, and that the captain's definition was even more correct than that of the Greek philosopher. For if the captain had been able to express himself like Plato he would no doubt have said that, "He is brave who fears only what should be feared and not what should not be feared."

I wished to explain my idea to the captain.

"Yes," said I, "it seems to me that in every danger there is a choice, and a choice made under the influence of a sense of duty is courage, but a choice made under the influence of a base motive is cowardice. Therefore a man who risks his life from vanity, curiosity, or greed, cannot be called brave; while on the other hand he who avoids a danger from honest consideration for his family, or simply from conviction, cannot be called a coward."

The captain looked at me with a curious expression while I was speaking.

"Well, that I cannot prove to you," he said, filling his pipe, "but we have a cadet here who is fond of philosophising. You should have a talk with him. He also writes verses."

I had known of the captain before I left Russia, but I had only made his acquaintance in the Caucasus. His mother, Mary Ivánovna Khlópova, a small and poor landowner, lives within two miles of my estate. Before I left for the Caucasus I had called on her. The old lady was very glad to hear that I should see her "Páshenka," by which pet name she called the grey-haired elderly captain, and that I, "a living letter," could tell him all about her and take him a small parcel from her. Having treated me to excellent pie and smoked goose, Mary Ivánovna went into her bedroom and returned with a black bag to which a black silk ribbon was attached.

"Here, this is the icon of our Mother Mediatress of the Burning Bush," said she, crossing herself and kissing the icon of the Virgin and placing it in my hands. "Please let him have it. You see, when he went to the Caucasus I had a Mass said for him and promised, if he remained alive and safe, to order this icon of the Mother of God for him. And now for eighteen years the Mediatress and the Holy Saints have had mercy on him, he has not been wounded once, and yet in what battles has he not taken part? . . . What Michael, who went with him, told me was enough, believe me, to make one's hair stand on end. You see, what I know about him is only from others. He, my pet, never writes me about his campaigns for fear of frightening me."

After I reached the Caucasus I learnt, and then not from the captain himself, that he had been severely wounded four times and of course never wrote to his mother either about his wounds or his campaigns.

"So let him now wear this holy image," she continued. "I give it him with my blessing. May the Most Holy Mediatress guard him. Especially when going to battle let him wear it. Tell him so, dear friend. Say 'Your mother wishes it.'"

I promised to carry out her instructions carefully.

"I know you will grow fond of my Páshenka," continued the old lady. "He is such a splendid fellow. Will you believe it, he never lets a year pass without sending me some money, and he also helps my daughter Annushka a good deal, and all out of his pay! I thank God for having given me such a child," she continued with tears in her eyes.

"Does he often write to you?" I asked.

"Seldom, my dear: perhaps once a year. Only when he sends the money, not otherwise. He says, 'If I don't write to you, mother, that means I am alive and well. Should anything befall me, which God forbid, they'll tell you without me.'"

When I handed his mother's present to the captain (it was in my own quarters) he asked for a bit of paper, carefully wrapped it up, and then put it away. I told him many things about his mother's life. He remained silent, and when I had finished speaking he went to a corner of the room and busied himself for what seemed a long time, filling his pipe.

"Yes, she's a splendid old woman!" he said from there in a rather muffled voice. "Will God ever let me see her again?"

These simple words expressed much love and sadness.

"Why do you serve here?" I asked.

"One has to serve," he answered with conviction.

"You should transfer to Russia. You would then be nearer to her."

"To Russia? To Russia?" repeated the captain, dubiously swaying his head and smiling mournfully. "Here I am still of some use, but there I should be the least of the officers. And besides, the double pay we get here also means something to a poor man."

"Can it be, Pável Ivánovich, that living as you do the ordinary pay would not suffice?"

"And does the double pay suffice?" interjected the captain. "Look at our officers. Have any of them a brass farthing? They all go on tick at the sutler's, and are all up to their ears in debt. You say 'living as I do. . . .' Do you really think that living as I do I have anything over out of my salary? Not a farthing!

You don't yet know what prices are like here; everything is three times dearer. . . ."

The captain lived economically, did not play cards, rarely went carousing, and smoked the cheapest tobacco (which for some reason he called home-grown tobacco). I had liked him before—he had one of those simple, calm, Russian faces which are easy and pleasant to look straight in the eyes—and after this talk I felt a sincere regard for him.

CHAPTER II

Next morning at four o'clock the captain came for me. He wore an old threadbare coat without epaulettes, wide Caucasian trousers, a white sheepskin cap the wool of which had grown yellow and limp, and had a shabby Asiatic sword strapped round his shoulders. The small white horse he rode ambled along with short strides, hanging its head down and swinging its thin tail. Although the worthy captain's figure was not very martial or even good-looking, it expressed such equanimity towards everything around him that it involuntarily inspired respect.

I did not keep him waiting a single moment, but mounted my horse at once, and we rode together through the gates of the fort.

The battalion was some five hundred yards ahead of us and looked like a dense, oscillating, black mass. It was only possible to guess that it was an infantry battalion by the bayonets which looked like needles standing close together, and by the sound of the soldiers' songs which occasionally reached us, the beating of a drum, and the delightful voice of the Sixth Company's second tenor, which had often charmed me at the fort. The road lay along the middle of a deep and broad ravine by the side of a stream which had overflowed its banks. Flocks of wild pigeons whirled above it, now alighting on the rocky banks, now turning in the air in rapid circles and vanishing out of sight. The sun was not yet visible, but the crest of the right side of the ravine was just beginning to be lit up. The grey and whitish rock, the yellowish-green moss, the dew-covered bushes of Christ's Thorn, dogberry, and dwarf elm, appeared extraordinarily distinct and salient in the golden morning light, but the other side and the valley, wrapped in thick mist which floated in uneven layers, were damp and gloomy and presented an indefinite mingling of colours: pale purple, almost black, dark green, and white. Right in front of us, strikingly distinct against the dark-blue horizon, rose the bright, dead-white masses of the snowy mountains, with their shadows and outlines fantastic and yet exquisite in every detail. Crickets, grasshoppers, and thousands of other insects, awoke in the tall grasses and filled the air with their clear and ceaseless sounds: it was as if innumerable tiny bells were ringing inside our very ears. The air was full of the scent of water, grass, and mist: the scent of a lovely early summer morning. The captain struck a light and lit his pipe, and the smell of his cheap tobacco and of the tinder seemed to me extraordinarily pleasant.

To overtake the infantry more quickly we left the road. The captain appeared more thoughtful than usual, did not take his Daghestan pipe from his mouth, and at every step touched with his heels his horse, which swaying from side to side left a scarcely perceptible green track in the tall wet grass. From under its very feet, with the cry and the whirr of wings which involuntarily sends a thrill through every sportsman, a pheasant rose, and flew slowly upwards. The captain did not take the least notice of it.

We had nearly overtaken the battalion when we heard the thud of a horse galloping behind us, and that same moment a good-looking youth in an officer's uniform and white sheepskin cap galloped past us.

He smiled in passing, nodded to the captain, and flourished his whip. I only had time to notice that he sat his horse and held his reins with peculiar grace, that he had beautiful black eyes, a fine nose, and only the first indications of a moustache. What specially pleased me about him was that he could not repress a smile when he noticed our admiration. This smile alone showed him to be very young.

"Where is he galloping to?" muttered the captain with a dissatisfied air, without taking the pipe from his mouth.

"Who is he?" I replied.

"Ensign Alánin, a subaltern in my company. He came from the Cadet Corps only a month ago."

"I suppose he is going into action for the first time," I said.

"That's why he is so delighted," answered the captain, thoughtfully shaking his head. "Youth!"

"But how could he help being pleased? I can fancy how interesting it must be for a young officer."

The captain remained silent for a minute or two.

"That is just why I say 'Youth'," he added in a deep voice. "What is there to be pleased at without ever having seen the thing? When one has seen it many times one is not so pleased. There are now, let us say, twenty of us officers here: one or other is sure to be killed or wounded, that is quite certain. To-day it may be I, to-morrow he, the next day a third. So what is there to be pleased about?"

CHAPTER III

As soon as the bright sun appeared above the hill and lit up the valley along which we were marching, the wavy clouds of mist cleared and it grew hot. The soldiers, with muskets and sacks on their shoulders, marched slowly along the dusty road. Now and then Ukrainian words and laughter could be heard in their ranks. Several old soldiers in white blouses (most of them non-commissioned officers) walked together by the roadside, smoking their pipes and conversing gravely. Heavily-laden wagons drawn by three horses moved steadily along, raising thick clouds of dust that hung motionless in the air. The officers rode in front: some of them caracoled—whipping their horses, making them take three or four leaps and then, pulling their heads round, stopping abruptly. Others were occupied with the singers, who in spite of the heat and sultriness sang song after song.

With the mounted Tartars, about two hundred yards ahead of the infantry, rode a tall handsome lieutenant in Asiatic costume on a large white horse. He was known in the regiment as a desperate dare-devil who would spit the truth out at anybody. He wore a black tunic trimmed with gold braid, leggings to match, soft closely-fitting gold-braided oriental shoes, a yellow coat and tall sheepskin cap pushed back from his forehead. Fastened to the silver strap that lay across his chest and back, he carried a powder-flask, and a pistol behind him. Another pistol and a silver-mounted dagger hung from his girdle, and above these a sword in a red leather sheath, and a musket in a black cover, were slung over his shoulder. By his clothing, by the way he sat his horse, by his general bearing, in fact by his every movement, one could see that he tried to resemble a Tartar. He even spoke to the Tartars with whom he was riding in a language I did not know, and from the bewildered and amused looks with which they glanced at one another I surmised that they did not understand him either. He was one of your young officers, dare-devil braves who shape their lives on the model of Lermontov's and Marlínsky's heroes. These officers see the Caucasus only through the prism of such books as *A Hero of our Time*, and

Mullah-Nur, and are guided in their actions not by their own inclinations but by the examples of their models.

The lieutenant, for instance, may perhaps have liked the company of well-bred women and men of rank: generals, colonels, and aides-de-camp (it is even my conviction that he liked such society very much, for he was exceedingly ambitious), but he considered it his imperative duty to turn his roughest side to all important men, though he was strictly moderate in his rudeness to them; and when any lady came to the fort he considered it his duty to walk before her window with his bosom friends, in a red shirt and with slippers on his bare feet, and shout and swear at the top of his voice. But all this he did not so much with the intention of offending her as to let her see what beautiful white feet he had, and how easy it would be to fall in love with him should he desire it. Or he would often go with two or three friendly Tartars to the hills at night to lie in ambush by the roadside to watch for passing hostile Tartars and kill them: and though his heart told him more than once that there was nothing valiant in this, he considered himself bound to cause suffering to people with whom he affected to be disillusioned and whom he chose to hate and despise. He always carried two things: a large icon hanging round his neck, and a dagger which he wore over his shirt even when in bed. He sincerely believed that he had enemies. To persuade himself that he must avenge himself on someone and wash away some insult with blood was his greatest enjoyment. He was convinced that hatred, vengeance, and contempt for the human race were the noblest and most poetic of emotions. But his mistress (a Circassian of course) whom I happened to meet subsequently, used to say that he was the kindest and mildest of men, and that every evening he wrote down his dismal thoughts in his diary, as well as his accounts on ruled paper, and prayed to God on his knees. And how much he suffered merely to appear in his own eyes what he wished to be! For his comrades and the soldiers could never see him as he wished to appear. Once on one of his nocturnal expeditions on the road with his bosom friends he happened to wound a hostile Chechen with a bullet in the leg, and took him prisoner. After that the Chechen lived for seven weeks with the lieutenant, who attended to him and nursed him as he would have nursed his dearest friend, and when the Chechen recovered he gave him presents and set him free. After that, during one of our expeditions when the lieutenant was retreating with the soldiers of the cordon and firing to keep back the foe, he heard someone among the enemy call him by name, and the man he had wounded rode forward and made signs to the lieutenant to do the same. The lieutenant rode up to his friend and pressed his hand. The hillsmen stood some way back and did not fire, but scarcely had the lieutenant turned his horse to return before several men shot at him and a bullet grazed the small of his back. Another time, at night, when a fire had broken out in the fort and two companies of soldiers were putting it out, I myself saw how the tall figure of a man mounted on a black horse and lit up by the red glow of the fire suddenly appeared among the crowd and, pushing through, rode up to the very flames. When quite close the lieutenant jumped from his horse and rushed into the house, one side of which was burning. Five minutes later he came out with singed hair and scorched elbow, carrying in his bosom two pigeons he had rescued from the flames.

His name was Rosenkranz, yet he often spoke of his descent, deducing it somehow from the Varangians (the first rulers of Russia), and clearly demonstrated that he and his ancestors were pure Russians.

CHAPTER IV

The sun had done half its journey and cast its hot rays through the glowing air on to the dry earth. The dark blue sky was perfectly clear, and only the base of the snowy mountains began to clothe itself in lilac-tinged white clouds. The motionless air seemed full of transparent dust, the heat was becoming unbearable.

Half-way on their march the troops reached a small stream and halted. The soldiers stacked their muskets and rushed to the stream; the commander of the battalion sat down in the shade on a drum, his full face assuming the correct expression denoting the greatness of his rank. He, together with some other officers, prepared to have a snack. The captain lay down on the grass under his company's wagon. The brave Lieutenant Rosenkranz and some other young officers disposed themselves on their outspread cloaks and got ready for a drinking-bout, as could be gathered from the bottles and flasks arranged round them, as well as from the peculiar animation of the singers who, standing before them in a semicircle, sang a Caucasian dance-song with a whistling obbligato interjected:

> "Shamyl, he began to riot
> In the days gone by,
> Try-ry-rataty,
> In the days gone by!"

Among these officers was the young ensign who had overtaken us in the morning. He was very amusing: his eyes shone, he spoke rather thickly, and he wished to kiss and declare his love to everyone. Poor boy! He did not know that he might appear funny in such a situation, that the frankness and tenderness with which he assailed everyone predisposed them not to the affection he so longed for, but to ridicule; nor did

413

he know that when, quite heated, he at last threw himself down on the cloak and rested on his elbow with his thick black hair thrown back, he looked uncommonly charming.

In a word, everyone was cheerful, except perhaps one officer who, sitting under his company's cart, had lost the horse he was riding to another officer at cards and had agreed to hand it over when they reached headquarters. He was vainly trying to induce the other to play again, offering to stake a casket which everyone could confirm he had bought for thirty roubles from a Jew, but which—merely because he was in difficulties—he was now willing to stake for fifteen. His opponent looked casually into the distance and persistently remained silent, till at last he remarked that he was terribly anxious to have a doze.

I confess that from the time I started from the fort and decided to take part in this action, gloomy reflections involuntarily rose in my mind, and so— since one has a tendency to judge of others by oneself I listened with curiosity to the conversation of the soldiers and officers and attentively watched the expression of their faces, but could find absolutely no trace of the anxiety I myself experienced: jokes, laughter and anecdotes, gambling and drunkenness, expressed the general carelessness and indifference to the impending danger as if all these people had long ago finished their affairs in this world. What was this— firmness, habituation to danger, or carelessness and indifference to life? Or was it all these things together as well as others I did not know, forming a complex but powerful moral motive of human nature termed *esprit de corps*—a subtle code embracing within itself a general expression of all the virtues and vices of men banded together in any permanent condition, a code each new member involuntarily submits to unmurmuringly and which does not change with the individuals, since whoever they may be the sum total of human tendencies everywhere and always remains the same?

CHAPTER V

Towards seven that evening, dusty and tired, we entered the wide fortified gate of Fort M. The sun was already setting and threw its rosy slanting rays on the picturesque little batteries, on the gardens with their tall poplars which surrounded the fortress, on the yellow gleaming cultivated fields, and on the white clouds that crowding round the snowy peaks had, as if trying to imitate them, formed a range not less fantastic and beautiful. On the horizon the new moon appeared delicate as a little cloud. In the Tartar village, from the roof of a hut, a Tartar was calling the faithful to prayer, and our singers raised their voices with renewed energy and vigour.

After a rest and after tidying myself up a bit, I went to an adjutant of my acquaintance to ask him to let the general know of my intention. On my way from the suburb where I had put up I noticed in Fort M. something I did not at all expect : a pretty little brougham overtook me, in which I caught sight of a fashionable bonnet and from which I overheard some French words. The sounds of some "Lizzie" or "Kátenka" polka, played on a bad ramshackle piano, reached me through the windows of the commander's house. In a little grocery and wine shop which I passed some clerks with cigarettes in their fingers sat drinking wine, and I heard one of them say to another, "No, excuse me, as to politics, Mary Gregórevna is first of our ladies." A Jew in a worn-out coat, with a bent back and sickly countenance, was dragging along a wheezy barrel-organ and the whole suburb resounded to the tones of the finale of "Lucia." Two women in rustling dresses with silk kerchiefs on their heads and carrying bright-coloured parasols passed by along the planks that did duty for a pavement. Two girls, one in a pink, the other in a blue dress, stood bareheaded beside the earth-embankments of a low-roofed house, and shrieked with high-pitched, forced laughter, evidently to attract the attention of passing officers. Officers, dressed in new uniforms with glittering epaulettes and white gloves, flaunted along the street and on the boulevard.

I found my acquaintance on the ground floor of the general's house. I had scarcely had time to explain my wish to him and to get his reply that it could easily be fulfilled, when the pretty little brougham I had noticed outside rattled past the window we were sitting at. A tall well-built man in an infantry major's uniform and epaulettes got out and entered the house.

"Oh, please excuse me," said the adjutant rising, "I must go and announce them to the general."

"Who is it?" I asked.

"The countess," he replied, and buttoning his uniform he rushed upstairs.

A few minutes later a very handsome man in a frock coat without epaulettes and with a white cross in his buttonhole went out into the porch. He was not tall but remarkably good-looking. He was followed by the major, an adjutant, and a couple of other officers. The general's gait, voice, and all his movements, showed him to be a man well aware of his own value.

"*Bonsoir, madame la comtesse,*" he said, offering his hand through the carriage window.

A small hand in a kid glove pressed his, and a pretty smiling face in a yellow bonnet appeared at the carriage window.

Of the conversation which lasted several minutes, I only overheard the general say laughingly as I passed by:

416

"*Vous savez que j'ai fait vœu de combattre les infideles; prenez donc garde de la devenir.*"[1]

A laugh replied from inside the carriage.

"*Adieu donc, cher general!*[2]"

"*Non, au revoir,*" said the general, ascending the steps of the porch. "*N'oubliez pas, que je m'invite pour la soirée de demain.*"[3]

The carriage rattled off and the general went into the sitting-room with the major. Passing by the open window of the adjutant's room, he noticed my uniformed figure and turned his kind attention to me. Having heard my request he announced his complete agreement with it, and passed on into his room.

"There again," I thought as I walked home, "is a man who possesses all that Russians strive after: rank, riches, distinction; and this man, the day before an engagement, the outcome of which is known only to God, jokes with a pretty woman and promises to have tea with her next day, just as if they had met at a ball!"

I remembered a reflection I had heard a Tartar utter, to the effect that only a pauper can be brave. "*Become rich, become a coward,*" said he, not at all to offend his comrade but as a common and unquestionable rule. But the general could lose together with his life much more than anyone else I had had an opportunity of observing and, contrary to the Tartar's rule, no one had shown such a pleasant, graceful indifference and confidence as he. My conceptions of courage became completely confused.

At that same adjutant's I met a young man who surprised me even more. He was a young lieutenant of the K. regiment who was noted for his almost feminine meekness and timidity and who had come to the adjutant to pour out his vexation and resentment against those who, he said, had intrigued against him to keep

---

[1] "You know I have sworn to fight the infidels (the unfaithful), so beware of becoming one."

[2] "Good-bye then, dear General."

[3] "No, *au revoir*. Don't forget that I am inviting myself for to-morrow's soirée."

417

him from taking part in the impending action. He said it was mean to behave in that way, that it was unfriendly, that he would not forget it, and so forth. Intently as I watched the expression of his face and listened to the sound of his voice, I could not help feeling convinced that he was not pretending but was genuinely filled with indignation and grief at not being allowed to go and shoot Circassians and expose himself to their fire. He was grieving like a little child who has been unjustly birched . . . I could make nothing at all of it.

CHAPTER VI

The troops were to start at ten in the evening. At half-past eight I mounted and rode to the general's, but thinking that he and his adjutant were busy I tied my horse to the fence and sat down on an earth-bank intending to catch the general when he came out.

The heat and glare of the sun were now replaced by the coolness of night and the soft light of the young moon, which had formed a pale glimmering semi-circle around itself on the deep blue of the starry sky and was already setting. Lights appeared in the windows of the houses and shone through cracks in the shutters of the earth huts. The stately poplars, beyond the white moonlit earth huts with their rush-thatched roofs, looked darker and taller than ever against the horizon.

The long shadows of the houses, the trees, and the fences, stretched out daintily on the dusty road. . . . From the river came the ringing voices of frogs;[1] along the street came the sound of hurried steps and voices talking, or the gallop of a horse, and from the suburb the tones of a barrel-organ playing now "The Winds are blowing," now some "Aurora Waltz."

[1] Frogs in the Caucasus make a noise quite different from the croaking of frogs elsewhere. L.T.

I will not say in what meditations I was absorbed: first, because I should be ashamed to confess the gloomy waves of thought that insistently flooded my soul while around me I noticed nothing but gaiety and joy, and secondly, because it would not suit my story. I was so absorbed in thought that I did not even notice the bell strike eleven and the general with his suite ride past me.

Hastily mounting my horse I set out to overtake the detachment.

The rear-guard was still within the gates of the fort. I had great difficulty in making my way across the bridge among the guns, ammunition wagons, carts of different companies, and officers noisily giving orders. Once outside the gates I trotted past the troops who, stretching out over nearly three-quarters of a mile, were silently moving on amid the darkness, and I overtook the general. As I rode past the guns drawn out in single file, and the officers who rode between them, I was hurt as by a discord in the quiet and solemn harmony by the German accents of a voice shouting, "A linstock, you devil!" and the voice of a soldier hurriedly exclaiming, "Shévchenko, the lieutenant wants a light!"

The greater part of the sky was now overcast by long strips of dark grey clouds; it was only here and there that a few stars twinkled dimly among them. The moon had already sunk behind the near horizon of the black hills visible to the right and threw a faint trembling light on their peaks, in sharp contrast to the impenetrable darkness enveloping their base. The air was so warm and still that it seemed as if not a single blade of grass, not a single cloudlet, was moving. It was so dark that even objects close at hand could not be distinguished. By the sides of the road I seemed to see now rocks, now animals, now some strange kind of men, and I discovered that they were merely bushes only when I heard them rustle, or felt the dew with which they were sprinkled.

419

Before me I saw a dense heaving wall followed by some dark moving spots; this was the cavalry vanguard and the general with his suite. Another similar dark mass, only lower, moved beside us; this was the infantry.

The silence that reigned over the whole division was so great that all the mingling sounds of night with their mysterious charm were distinctly audible: the far-off mournful howling of jackals, now like agonized weeping, now like chuckling; the monotonous resounding song of crickets, frogs, and quails; a sort of rumbling I could not at all account for but which seemed to draw nearer; and all those scarcely audible motions of Nature which can neither be understood nor defined, mingled into one beautiful harmony, which we call the stillness of night. This stillness was interrupted by, or rather combined with, the dull thud of hoofs and the rustling of the tall grass caused by the slowly advancing detachment.

Only very occasionally could the clang of a heavy gun, the sound of bayonets touching one another, hushed voices, or the snorting of a horse, be heard. By the scent of the wet juicy grass which sank under our horses' feet, by the light steam rising from the ground and by the horizons seen on two sides of us, it was evident that we were moving across a wide, luxuriant meadow. Nature seemed to breathe with pacifying beauty and power.

Can it be that there is not room for all men on this beautiful earth under those immeasurable starry heavens? Can it be possible that in the midst of this entrancing Nature, feelings of hatred, vengeance, or the desire to exterminate their fellows, can endure in the souls of men? All that is unkind in the hearts of men should, one would think, vanish at contact with Nature—that most direct expression of beauty and goodness.

War! What an incomprehensible phenomenon! When one's reason asks: "Is it just, is it necessary?" an inner voice always replies "No." Only the persistence of this unnatural occurrence makes it seem natural and a feeling of self-preservation makes it seem just.

Who will doubt that in the war of the Russians against the mountain-tribes, justice—resulting from a feeling of self-preservation—is on our side? Were it not for this war, what would secure the neighbouring rich and cultured Russian territories from robbery, murder, and raids by wild and warlike tribes? But consider two private persons. On whose side is the feeling of self-preservation and consequently of justice? Is it on the side of this ragamuffin—some Djemi or other—who hearing of the approach of the Russians snatches down his old gun from the wall, puts three or four charges (which he will only reluctantly discharge) in his pouch, and runs to meet the giaours, and on seeing that the Russians still advance, approaching the fields he has sown which they will tread down and his hut which they will burn, and the ravine where his mother, his wife, and his children have hidden themselves, shaking with fear—seeing that he will be deprived of all that constitutes his happiness—in impotent anger and with a cry of despair tears off his tattered jacket, flings down his gun, and drawing his sheepskin cap over his eyes sings his death-song and flings himself headlong onto the Russian bayonets with only a dagger in his hand? Is justice on his side or on that of this officer on the general's staff who is singing French chansonettes so well just as he rides past us? He has a family in Russia, relations, friends, serfs, and obligations towards them, but has no reason or desire to be at enmity with the hillsmen and has come to the Caucasus just by chance and to show his courage. Or is it on the side of my acquaintance the adjutant, who only wishes to obtain a captaincy and a comfortable position as soon as possible and for that reason has become the hillsmen's enemy? Or is it on the side of this young German who, with a strong

German accent, is demanding a linstock from the artillerymen? What devil has brought him from his fatherland and set him down in this distant region? Why should this Saxon, Kaspar Lavréntich, mix himself up in our blood-thirsty conflict with these turbulent neighbours?

CHAPTER VII

We had been riding for more than two hours. I was beginning to shiver and feel drowsy. Through the gloom I still seemed to see the same indefinite forms; a little way in front the same black wall and the moving spots. Close in front of me I could see the crupper of a white horse which swung its tail and threw its hind legs wide apart, the back of a white Circassian coat on which could be discerned a musket in a black case, and the glimmering butt of a pistol in an embroidered holster; the glow of a cigarette lit up a fair moustache, a beaver collar and a hand in a chamois glove. Every now and then I leant over my horse's neck, shutting my eyes and forgetting myself for a few minutes, then startled by the familiar tramping and rustling I glanced round, and felt as if I were standing still and the black wall in front was moving towards me, or that it had stopped and I should in a moment ride into it. At one such moment the rumbling which increased and seemed to approach, and the cause of which I could not guess, struck me forcibly: it was the sound of water. We were entering a deep gorge and approaching a mountain-stream that was overflowing its banks.[1] The rumbling increased, the damp grass became thicker and taller and the bushes closer, while the horizon gradually narrowed. Now and then bright lights appeared here and there against the dark background of the hills and vanished instantly.

[1] In the Caucasus rivers are apt to overflow in July. L.T.

"Tell me, please, what are those lights?" I asked in a whisper of a Tartar riding beside me.

"Don't you know?" he replied.

"No."

"The hillsmen have tied straw to poles and are waving it about alight."

"Why are they doing that?"

"So that everyone should know that the Russians have come. Oh, oh! What a bustle is going on now in the *aouls!* Everybody's dragging his belongings into the ravine," he said laughing.

"Why, do they already know in the mountains that a detachment is on its way?" I asked him.

"How can they help knowing? They always know. Our people are like that."

"Then Shamyl[1] too is preparing for action?" I asked.

"No," he answered, shaking his head, "Shamyl won't go into action; Shamyl will send his *naibs*,[2] and he himself will look on through a telescope from above."

"Does he live far away?"

"Not far. Some eight miles to the left."

"How do you know?" I asked. "Have you been there?"

"I have. Our people have all been."

"Have you seen Shamyl?"

"Such as we don't see Shamyl! There are a hundred, three hundred, a thousand *murids*[3] all round him, and Shamyl is in the centre," he said, with an expression of servile admiration.

Looking up, it was possible to discern that the sky, now cleared, was beginning to grow lighter in the east and the pleiades to sink towards the horizon, but

---

[1] Shamyl was the leader (in 1834-59) of the Caucasian hill-tribes in their resistance to Russia.

[2] A *naib* was a man to whom Shamyl had entrusted some administrative office. L.T.

[3] The word *murid* has several meanings, but here it denotes something between an adjutant and a bodyguard.

the ravine through which we were marching was still damp and gloomy.

Suddenly a little way in front of us several lights flashed through the darkness; at the same moment some bullets flew whizzing past, and amid the surrounding silence sharp abrupt firing could be heard and loud cries, as piercing as cries of despair but expressing instead of fear such a passion of brutal audacity and rage that one could not but shudder at hearing it. It was the enemy's advanced picket. The Tartars who composed it whooped, fired at random, and then ran in different directions.

All became silent again. The general called up an interpreter. A Tartar in a white Circassian coat rode up to him and, gesticulating and whispering, talked with him for some time.

"Colonel Khasánov! Order the cordon to take open order," commanded the general with a quiet but distinct drawl.

The detachment advanced to the river, the black hills and gorges were left behind, the dawn appeared. The vault of the heavens, in which a few pale stars were still dimly visible, seemed higher; the sunrise glow beyond shone brightly in the east, a fresh penetrating breeze blew from the west and the white mists rose like steam above the rushing stream.

CHAPTER VIII

Our guide pointed out a ford and the cavalry vanguard, followed by the general, began crossing the stream. The water which reached to the horses' chests rushed with tremendous force between the white boulders which here and there appeared on a level with its surface, and formed foaming and gurgling ripples around the horses' legs. The horses, surprised by the noise of the water, lifted their heads and pricked

424

their ears, but stepped evenly and carefully against the current on the uneven bottom of the stream. Their riders lifted their feet and their weapons. The infantry, literally in nothing but their shirts, linked arm in arm by twenties, and holding above the water their muskets, to which their bundles of clothing were fastened, made great efforts (as the strained expression of their faces showed) to resist the force of the current. The mounted artillerymen with loud shouts drove their horses into the water at a trot. The guns and green ammunition-wagons, over which the water occasionally splashed, rang against the stony bottom, but the sturdy little horses, churning the water, pulled at the traces in unison and with dripping manes and tails clambered out on the opposite bank.

As soon as the crossing was accomplished the general's face suddenly assumed a meditative and serious look and he turned his horse, and, followed by the cavalry, rode at a trot down a broad glade which opened out before us in the midst of the forest. A cordon of mounted Cossacks was scattered along the skirts of the forest.

In the woods we noticed a man on foot dressed in a Circassian coat and wearing a tall cap—then a second and a third. One of the officers said: "Those are Tartars." Then a puff of smoke appeared from behind a tree, a shot, and another. . . . Our rapid fire drowns the enemy's. Only now and then a bullet, with a slow sound like the buzzing of a bee's wings, passes by and proves that the firing is not all ours. Now the infantry at a run and the guns at a trot pass into the cordon. You can hear the boom of the guns, the metallic sounds of flying grape-shot, the hissing of rockets, and the crackle of musketry. Over the wide glade on all sides you can see cavalry, infantry, and artillery. Puffs of smoke mingle with the dew-covered verdure and the mist. Colonel Khasánov, approaching the general at full gallop, suddenly reins in his horse.

"Your Excellency, shall we order the cavalry to

charge?" he says, raising his hand to his cap. "The enemy's colours[1] are in sight," and he points with his whip to some mounted Tartars in front of whom ride two men on white horses with bits of blue and red stuff fastened to poles in their hands.

"Go, and God be with you, Iván Mikháylovich!" says the general.

The colonel turns his horse sharply round, draws his sword, and shouts "Hurrah!"

"Hurrah! Hurrah! Hurrah!" comes from the ranks, and the cavalry gallop after him. . . .

Everyone looks on with interest: there is a colour, another, a third and a fourth. . . .

The enemy, not waiting for the attack, hides in the wood and thence opens a small-arms fire. Bullets come flying more and more frequently.

"*Quel charmant coup d'œil!*"[2] says the general rising slightly, English fashion, in his saddle on his slim-legged black horse.

"*Charmant!*" answers the major, rolling his r's, and striking his horse he rides up to the general: "*C'est un vrai plaisir que la guerre dans un aussi beau pays,*"[3] he says.

"*Et surtout en bonne compagnie,*"[4] replied the general with a pleasant smile.

The major bows.

At that moment a hostile cannon-ball with a disagreeable whiz flies past and strikes something. We hear behind us the moan of a wounded man.

This moaning strikes me so strangely that the warlike scene instantly loses all its charm for me. But no one except myself seems to notice it: the major laughs with apparently greater gusto, another officer repeats with perfect calm the first words of a sentence he had

[1] The colours among the hillsmen correspond to those of our troops, except that every *dzhigit* or "brave" among them may make his own colours and carry them. L.T.
[2] "What a charming view."
[3] "Charming! . . . War in such beautiful country is a real pleasure."
[4] "Especially in good company."

just been saying, the general looks the other way and with the quietest smile says something in French.

"Shall we reply to their fire?" asks the commander of the artillery, galloping up.

"Yes, frighten them a bit!" carelessly replies the general, lighting a cigar.

The battery takes up its position and the firing begins. The earth groans under the shots, the discharges flash out incessantly, and smoke, through which it is scarcely possible to distinguish the artillerymen moving round their guns, veils your sight.

The *aoul* has been bombarded. Colonel Khasánov rides up again, and at the general's command gallops towards the *aoul*. The war-cry is again heard and the cavalry disappears in the cloud of dust it has raised.

The spectacle was truly magnificent. The one thing that spoilt the general impression for me—who took no part in the affair and was unaccustomed to it—was that this movement and the animation and the shouting appeared unnecessary. The comparison involuntarily suggested itself to me of a man swinging his arms vigorously to cut the air with an axe.

CHAPTER IX

Our troops had taken possession of the village and not a single soul of the enemy remained in it when the general and his suite, to which I had attached myself, rode up to it.

The long clean huts, with their flat earthen roofs and shapely chimneys, stood on irregular stony mounds between which flowed a small stream. On one side were green gardens with enormous pear and small plum trees brightly lit up by the sun, on the other strange upright shadows, the perpendicular stones of the cemetery, and long poles with balls and many-coloured

427

flags fastened to their ends. (These marked the graves of *dzhigits*.)

The troops were drawn up outside the gates.

"Well, how about it, Colonel?" said the general. "Let them loot. I see they are terribly anxious to," he added with a smile, pointing at the Cossacks.

You cannot imagine how striking was the contrast between the carelessness with which the general uttered these words, and their import and the military surroundings.

A moment later, dragoons, Cossacks, and infantry spread with evident delight through the crooked lanes and in an instant the empty village was animated again. Here a roof crashes, an axe rings against the hard wood of a door that is being forced open, here a stack of hay, a fence, a hut, is set on fire and a pillar of thick smoke rises up in the clear air. Here is a Cossack dragging along a sack of flour and a carpet, there a soldier, with a delighted look on his face, brings a tin basin and some rag out of a hut, another is trying with outstretched arms to catch two hens that struggle and cackle beside a fence, a third has somewhere discovered an enormous pot of milk and after drinking some of it throws the rest on the ground with a loud laugh.

The battalion with which I had come from Fort N. was also in the *aoul*. The captain sat on the roof of a hut and sent thin whiffs of cheap tobacco smoke through his short pipe with such an expression of indifference on his face that on seeing him I forgot that I was in a hostile *aoul* and felt quite at home.

"Ah, you are here too?" he said when he noticed me.

The tall figure of Lieutenant Rosenkranz flitted here and there in the village. He gave orders unceasingly and appeared exceedingly engrossed in his task. I saw him emerge with a triumphant air from a hut, followed by two soldiers leading an old Tartar. The old man, whose only clothing consisted of a mottled

428

tunic all in rags and patchwork trousers, was so frail
that his arms, tightly bound behind his bent back,
seemed scarcely to hold onto his shoulders, and he
could scarcely drag his bare crooked legs along. His
face and even part of his shaven head were deeply
furrowed. His wry toothless mouth kept moving
beneath his close-cut moustache and beard, as if he
were chewing something; but a gleam still sparkled
in his red lashless eyes which clearly expressed an old
man's indifference to life.

Rosenkranz asked him, through an interpreter, why
he had not gone away with the others.

"Where should I go?" he answered, looking quietly
away.

"Where the others have gone," someone remarked.

"The *dzhigits* have gone to fight the Russians, but
I am an old man."

"Are you not afraid of the Russians?"

"What will the Russians do to me? I am old," he
repeated, again glancing carelessly round the circle
that had formed about him.

Later, as I was returning, I saw that old man bare-
headed, with his arms tied, being jolted along behind
the saddle of a Cossack and he was looking round
with the same expression of indifference on his face.
He was needed for the exchange of prisoners.

I climbed onto the roof and sat down beside he
captain.

A bugler who had vodka and provisions was sent
for. The captain's calmness and equanimity involuntarily produced an effect on me. We ate roasted
pheasant and chatted, without at all reflecting that
the owners of that hut had not merely no desire to see
us there but could hardly have imagined our existence.

"There don't seem to have been many of the enemy,"
I said, wishing to know his opinion of the action that
had taken place.

"The enemy?" he repeated with surprise. "The

enemy was not there at all! Do you call those the enemy? . . . Wait till the evening when we go back and you will see how they will speed us on our way: what a lot of them will pour out from there," he said, pointing to a thicket we had passed in the morning.

"What is that?" I asked anxiously, interrupting the captain and pointing to a group of Don Cossacks who had collected round something not far from us.

A sound of something like a child's cry came from there, and the words:

"Stop . . . don't hack it . . . you'll be seen. . . . Have you a knife, Evstignéich. . . . Lend me a knife. . . ."

"They are up to something, the scoundrels . . ." replied the captain calmly.

But at that moment the young ensign, his comely face flushed and frightened, came suddenly running from behind a corner and rushed towards the Cossacks waving his arms.

"Don't touch it! Don't kill it!" he cried in a childish voice.

Seeing the officer, the Cossacks stepped apart and released a little white kid. The young ensign was quite abashed, muttered something, and stopped before us with a confused face. Seeing the captain and me on the roof he blushed still more and ran leaping towards us.

"I thought they were killing a child," he said with a bashful smile.

CHAPTER X

The general went ahead with the cavalry. The battalion with which I had come from Fort N. remained in the rear-guard. Captain Khlópov's and Lieutenant Rosenkranz's battalions retired together.

The captain's prediction was fully justified. No sooner had we entered the narrow thicket he had mentioned, than on both sides of us we caught glimpses of hillsmen mounted and on foot, and so near were they that I could distinctly see how some of them ran stooping, rifle in hand, from one tree to another.

The captain took off his cap and piously crossed himself, some of the older soldiers did the same. From the wood were heard war-cries and the words "*Iay giaour*," "*Urus! iay!*" Sharp short rifle-shots, following one another fast, whizzed on both sides of us. Our men answered silently with a running fire, and only now and then remarks like the following were made in the ranks: "See where he[1] fires from! It's all right for him inside the wood. We ought to use cannon," and so forth.

Our ordnance was brought out, and after some grape-shot had been fired the enemy seemed to grow weaker, but a moment later and at every step taken by our troops, the enemy's fire again grew hotter and the shouting louder.

We had hardly gone seven hundred yards from the village before enemy cannon-balls began whistling over our heads. I saw a soldier killed by one. . . . But why should I describe the details of that terrible picture which I would myself give much to be able to forget!

Lieutenant Rosenkranz kept firing, and incessantly shouted in a hoarse voice at the soldiers and galloped from one end of the cordon to the other. He was rather pale and this suited his martial countenance very well.

The good-looking young ensign was in raptures: his beautiful dark eyes shone with daring, his lips were slightly smiling, and he kept riding up to the captain and begging permission to charge.

"We will repel them," he said persuasively, "we certainly will."

"It's not necessary," replied the captain abruptly. "We must retreat."

---

[1] *He* is a collective pronoun by which the soldiers indicate the enemy. L.T.

The captain's company held the skirts of the wood, the men lying down and replying to the enemy's fire. The captain in his shabby coat and shabby cap sat silent and on his white horse, with loose reins, bent knees, his feet in the stirrups, and did not stir from his place. The soldiers knew and did their work so well that there was no need to give them any orders. Only at rare intervals he raised his voice to shout at those who exposed their heads. There was nothing at all martial about the captain's appearance, but there was something so sincere and simple in it that I was unusually struck by it. "It is he who is really brave," I involuntarily said to myself.

He was just the same as I had always seen him: the same calm movements, the same guileless expression on his plain but frank face, only his eyes, which were brighter than usual, showed the concentration of one quietly engaged on his duties. "As I had always seen him" is easily said, but how many different shades have I noticed in the behaviour of others; one wishing to appear quieter, another sterner, a third merrier, than usual, but the captain's face showed that he did not even see why he should appear anything but what he was.

The Frenchman at Waterloo who said, "*La garde meurt, mais ne se rend pas,*"[1] and other, particularly French, heroes who uttered memorable sayings were brave, and really uttered remarkable words, but between their courage and the captain's there was this difference, that even if a great saying had in any circumstance stirred in the soul of my hero, I am convinced that he would not have uttered it: first because by uttering a great saying he would have feared to spoil a great deed, and secondly because when a man feels within himself the capacity to perform a great deed no talk of any kind is needed. That, I think, is a peculiar and a lofty characteristic of Russian courage, and that being so, how can a Russian heart

[1] "The Guard dies, but does not surrender."

432

help aching when our young Russian warriors utter trivial French phrases intended to imitate antiquated French chivalry?

Suddenly from the side where our young ensign stood with his platoon we heard a not very hearty or loud "Hurrah!" Looking round to where the shout came from, I saw some thirty soldiers with sacks on their shoulders and muskets in their hands managing with very great difficulty to run across a ploughed field. They kept stumbling, but nevertheless ran on and shouted. In front of them, sword in hand, galloped the young ensign.

They all disappeared into the wood. . . .

After a few minutes of whooping and clatter a frightened horse ran out of the wood, and soldiers appeared bringing back the dead and wounded. Among the latter was the young ensign. Two soldiers supported him under his arms. He was as pale as a sheet, and his pretty head, on which only a shadow remained of the warlike enthusiasm that had animated him a few minutes before, was dreadfully sunk between his shoulders and drooped on his chest. There was a small spot of blood on the white shirt beneath his unbuttoned coat.

"Ah, what a pity!" I said, involuntarily turning away from this sad spectacle.

"Of course it's a pity," said an old soldier, who stood leaning on his musket beside me with a gloomy expression on his face. "He's not afraid of anything. How can one do such things?" he added, looking intently at the wounded lad. "He was still foolish and now he has paid for it!"

"And you?" I asked. "Are you afraid?"

"What do you expect?"

433

CHAPTER XI

Four soldiers were carrying the ensign on a stretcher and behind them an ambulance soldier was leading a thin, broken-winded horse with two green boxes on its back containing surgical appliances. They waited for the doctor. Some officers rode up to the stretcher and tried to cheer and comfort the wounded lad.

"Well, friend Alanin, it will be some time before you will dance again with castanets," said Lieutenant Rosenkranz, riding up to the stretcher with a smile.

He probably supposed that these words would raise the young ensign's spirits, but as far as one could judge by the latter's coldly sad look the words had not the desired effect.

The captain rode up too. He looked intently at the wounded man and his usually calm and cold face expressed sincere sympathy. "Well, my dear Anatol Ivanich," he said, in a voice of tender sympathy such as I never expected from him, "evidently it is God's will."

The wounded lad looked round and his pale face lit up with a sad smile. "Yes, I disobeyed you."

"Say rather, it was God's will," repeated the captain.

The doctor when he arrived, as far as could be judged by the shakiness of his legs and the redness of his eyes, was in no fit condition to bandage the patient: however, he took from his assistant bandages, a probe, and another instrument, rolled up his sleeves and stepped up to the ensign with an encouraging smile.

"So it seems they have made a hole in a sound spot for you too," he said in a carelessly playful tone. "Let me see."

The ensign obeyed, but the look he gave the merry doctor expressed astonishment and reproof which the inebriated practitioner did not notice. He touched the wound so awkwardly, quite unnecessarily pressing on it with his unsteady fingers, that the wounded ensign driven beyond the limits of endurance pushed away his hand with a deep groan.

"Let me alone!" he said in a scarcely audible voice. "I shall die anyway."

Then, addressing the captain, he said with difficulty: "Please, Captain . . . yesterday I lost . . . twenty roubles to Dronov. . . . When my things are sold . . . let him be paid."

With those words he fell back, and five minutes later when I passed the group that had formed around him, and asked a soldier, "How is the ensign?" the answer was, "Passing away."

CHAPTER XII

It was late in the day when the detachment, formed into a broad column and singing, approached the Fort.

The general rode in front and by his merry countenance one could see that the raid had been successful. In fact, with little loss, we had that day been in Mukay *aoul*—where from immemorial times no Russian foot had trod.

The Saxon, Kaspar Lavréntich, narrated to another officer that he had himself seen how three Chechens had aimed straight at his breast. In the mind of Ensign Rosenkranz a complete story of the day's action had formulated itself. Captain Khlópov walked with thoughtful face in front of his company, leading his little white horse by its bridle.

The sun had hidden behind the snowy mountain range and threw its last rosy beams on a long thin cloud stretching motionless across the clear horizon. The snow peaks began to disappear in purple mist and only their top outline was visible, wonderfully distinct in the crimson sunset glow. The delicate

435

moon, which had risen long since, began to grow pale against the deep azure. The green of the grass and trees was turning black and becoming covered with dew. The dark masses of troops moved with measured sounds over the luxuriant meadows. Tambourines, drums, and merry songs were heard from various sides. The voice of the second tenor of the Sixth Company rang out with full force and the sounds of his clear chest-notes, full of feeling and power, floated through the clear evening air.

THE ESSENCE OF A MAN
by Alan Sullivan

A CANADIAN by birth, Alan Sullivan spent many years of an active, wandering life in the Far North, being, by turns, railway engineer, mining engineer and explorer. He was educated in Scotland, and he passed so much of his early life in England that he may well be described an an Anglo-Canadian author. He graduated, however, at Toronto University. His best tales are those that tell of the dying races of Indians in the wildest parts of Canada. One of his best stories *M. Portofino*, was included in the *Best Stories of 1927*, edited by E. J. O'Brien. Sullivan was born in 1868.

EE

THE ESSENCE OF A MAN

BY
ALAN SULLIVAN

THROUGH level lines of streaming snow, a huge
figure loomed large and portentous. Vanishing in
blinding gusts, it ever and ever appeared again, thrusting itself onward with dogged persistence. Across flat
and frozen plains forged the great piston-like legs,
driving down his snow-shoes with a clock-like regularity
that suggested, rather than told, of enormous muscular
strength. Behind him, knee-deep, toiled five yellow-
coated, black-muzzled dogs, their shoulders jammed
tight into their collars, their tawny sides rippling with
the play of straining tendons; and, last of all, a long
low toboggan lurched indomitably on, the trampled
trail breaking into a surge of powdered snow under its
curving bow.

Into the teeth of the gale pushed this pigmy caravan
—a gale that was born on the flat shores of Hudson
Bay, that breasted the slopes of the Height of Land,
that raged across the blank white expanse of Lac Seul,
and was now shrieking down, dire and desolate, to the
ice-bound and battlemented borders of Lake Superior.
It was a wind that had weight. Tom Moore felt its
vast and impalpable force, as he leaned against it, when
he stopped for breath. It assaulted him—it tore steadily,
relentlessly, at him, as if seeking to devour—it lashed the
stinging grains into his face, and into the open mouths
of his panting dogs—it smoothed out the crumpled trail
as the wake of a ship is obliterated by closing waters—
till, a moment after his passing, the snow ridges lay
trackless and unruffled. Still, however insignificant
in these formless wastes, that silent progress held steadily

441

on; and so it had held from early morn. These black specks on a measureless counterpane, guided by some unfailing instinct that lurked far back in the big half-breed's brain, were making an unswerving line for a wooded point that thrust out a faint and purple finger, far ahead in the gathering dusk. As they drew slowly in, the wind began to abate its force, and Tom, peering out from the mass of ice that was cemented to his mouth and eyes, looked for some sheltering haven. The dogs smelled the land, and more eagerly flung themselves into the taut traces, while over them gathered the shadows of the welcome woods.

Peter Anderson, the Hudson Bay factor at Lac Seul, was low in provisions, and had sent to the Ignace post a curt suggestion that the deficiency be supplied; and Tom Moore's laden toboggan was the brief but practical answer to his letter. The three-hundred-pound load was made up of the bare necessities of life—pork, flour and the like; these, delivered, would be worth seventy-five cents a pound and thirty dollars a sack respectively; and Tom was the arbiter of transportation. In summer his canoe thrust its delicate bows through the waterways that interlaced the two posts, and in winter his snow-shoes threaded the stark and frozen wilderness. He had always travelled alone on the ice. Nature had moulded him with such a titan frame, so huge and powerful a body, so indomitable and fearless a soul, that he had become accustomed to laughing at the fate that overtook many of his tribe. They disappeared every now and then, utterly, silently, and mysteriously; but ever Big Tom moved on, the incarnation of force and of life that mocked at death.

When, two days before, MacPherson had summoned him to the Ignace Post, and pointed to the pile of provisions, and said laconically: "For Anderson, at Lac Seul," Tom had merely grunted, "How," and set out to harness his dogs. But the last day had brought him more serious reflection. By the flight of the goose it was two hundred miles and by the winter trail perhaps two hundred and fifteen; and of these forty now lay behind him.

He made his camp, he lit his fire, he flung to each ravenous dog a frozen white fish, and ate, himself, almost as sparingly; then, rolled in his rabbit-skin blanket, he lay down on his back, and looked up at the winking stars.

About midnight the wind changed and veered into the south-east, bringing with it a clammy drizzle, half snow, half rain, that plastered the trees with a transparent enamel, and spread over the surface of the earth a sheet of ice, half an inch thick, and exceeding sharp.

In that shivering hour which heralds the dawn, a branch cracked sharply a little distance from the camp. One of the dogs twitched an ear, and Tom was too deep in sleep to notice it. The five huskies were buried in snow beneath a tree, from a branch of which swung a sheaf of rigid fish, suspended in the air for security. But, in the half light, something moved, a something that turned upon the smouldering fire great luminous eyes—globes that seemed to receive the glow of dull coals, and give it out again in a vivid iridescence. Around the eyes was a white-grey mask, crowned by short, black-pointed ears; behind the ears moved noiselessly a tawny body, with heavy legs and broad, soft pads. It slipped from tree to tree, touching the ground lightly here and there, till the great lynx hung, motionless and menacing, above the sleeping camp. It stopped, sniffed the tainted air, and then stared, fascinated, at the sheaf of fish which hung, slowly revolving, in tantalizing proximity. Silently, with dainty and delicate caution, the lynx laid itself out on the branch, and, clinging tight, stretched out a curved forepaw; it just touched its object, and set it swaying. Again the paw went out, and again fell short. A quicker thrust, and the big pads slipped on the frozen wood, and, with a scream, the great cat fell fair on the sleeping dogs.

In an instant the air split with a frenzy of noise.

443

Tom sprang up, and saw a maelstrom of yellow forms, from which came the vicious snap of locking jaws, the yelp of agonized animals, and the short, coughing bark of the lynx. Around and in and out they rolled, buried in fur and snow. The wolf was born again in the huskies, and, with all their primal ferocity, they assailed each other and a common enemy. Two of them crawled away, licking great wounds from deadly claws; and then gradually the battle waned, till it died in a fugue of howls, and the marauder escaped torn and bleeding, into the silence from which he came.

Tom stood helpless, and then, when the three came limping home, went over to where his two best dogs lay, licking great gashes—for the lynx had literally torn them open. As he approached, they lifted their black lips, till the long fangs shone, ivory white; and death and defiance gurgled in their throbbing throats. A glance told him that nothing could be done; the frost was already nipping the raw flesh till they snapped at their own vitals in desperation. He raised his axe, once, twice—and his two best huskies lay on a blanket of blood-stained snow, with twitching bodies and glazing eyes.

Then, very soberly, he examined the others. They were still fit for harness; so, in the yellow light that began to flood the world, he shortened his traces, twisted his feet into his toe-straps, and, with never a look behind, faced again the burden of the day.

The trail was hard to break. The crust, that would not carry the dogs, was smashed down, and tilted cakes of ice fell over on his shoes, a deck load that made them a weariness to lift. Behind floundered the toiling huskies, the leader's nose glued to the tail of the trailing shoes. What vast reserve of strength did man and beast then draw upon, Tom could not have told you; but, hour after hour, the small indomitable train went on. As the day lengthened, Tom shortened his stride; for the dogs were evidently giving out, and his thigh muscles were burning like hot wires. At four o'clock the team stopped dead, the leader swaying in his tracks. The big half-breed, running his hands over the shaking body, suddenly found one of them warm and wet—it was sticky with blood. Then he saw blood on the trail; looking back, he saw crimson spots as far as the eye could distinguish them; lifting the matted hide, he revealed a gash from which oozed great, slow drops. The valiant brute had drained his life out in a gory baptism of that killing trail. Then Tom sat down in dumb despair, took the lean yellow head upon his knees, smoothed the tawny fur back from those clouding eyes, and set his teeth hard as the dying beast licked his caressing hand in mute fidelity.

The great frame grew rigid as he watched, and slowly into the man's mind, for the first time in all his life, came doubt. Perhaps it was more of wonderment. It was not any suggestion of failing powers, imminent danger, or impending hardships; it was rather a mute questioning of things which he had always heretofore accepted, as he did the rising and sinking of the sun —things which began and ended with the day. His reasonings were slow and laborious; his mind creaked, as it were, with the effort—like an unused muscle, it responded with difficulty. Then, finally, he saw it all.

Long ago, when his mother died, she had warned him against the false new gods which the white man had brought from the big sea water, and in her old faith had turned her face to the wall of her teepee. She had been buried in a tree-top, near a bend of the Albany River, where it turns north from Nepigon and runs through the spruce forests that slope down to Hudson's Bay. But Tom had listened to the new story—more than that, he had hewed square timber for the mission church at Ignace; and now—retribution had come, at last. No sooner had the idea formulated itself, than it seized upon him; and then there rose to meet it— defiance. Grimly, he slacked the collar from the dead

445

husky, and laid the empty traces across his own breast; savagely he thrust forward, and started the toboggan, and the diminished company stayed and stopped not till, once again, the darkness came.

That night the two surviving dogs eyed him furtively, when he flung them their food. They did not devour it ravenously, as was their custom; but crouched, with the fish under their paws, and followed, with shifting look, every move he made. He was too weary to care; but, had he watched them an hour later, the sight would have convinced him that there was an evil spirit abroad in those frosty woods.

Noiselessly, they approached his sleeping form, sniffing intently at everything in the camp. He lay, massive and motionless, wrapped in an immense rabbit-skin blanket, one fold of which was thrown over the bag that held his provisions; his giant body was slack, and full of great weariness.

The dogs moved without a sound, till they stood over the sleeping man. The long hair rose in ridges along their spines, as they put their noses to his robe, and sniffed at their unconscious master: for, whether it was the fight with the lynx, or that yellow body out on the ice, some new and strange thing had come into their blood; they had reverted to the primal dog, and no longer felt the burden of the collar or the trace—the labour of the trail had passed from them.

At first, the smell of man repelled them, but it was only for a moment; their lean shoulders swayed as their twitching noses ran over his outline, and then a new scent assailed them. It was the provision bag. Gently, and with infinite precaution, they pulled it. Tom stirred, but only stirred. The sack was trailed out over the snow, and the tough canvas soon gave way before those murderous teeth. In silence, and in hunger, they gorged; what they could not eat was destroyed, till, finally, with bulging sides, they lay down and slept, in utter repletion.

It was the sun on his face that woke Tom to a consciousness of what had happened. He felt for the bag, and, finding it not, looked at the dogs, and, on seeing them, raised his hand in anger. Now, this was a mistake; few dogs will wait for punishment, least of all a half-savage husky who expects it. He approached, they retreated; he stopped, they squatted on their haunches and eyed him suspiciously; he retreated, they did not move; he held out a fish, they were supremely indifferent. They had entered a new world, which was none of his; they suddenly found that they did not have to obey—and when man or beast reasons thus, it spells ruin. All his arts were exhausted and proved fruitless, and then Tom knew that an evil spirit—a Wendigo—was on his trail.

To push forward was his first instinct. Slowly, he rolled up the blanket, and laced it to the toboggan; and, as the sun topped the rim of the land, the unconquerable breed struck out across the ice, the traces tugging at his shoulders. A few yards behind followed the enfranchised team, drunk with the intoxication of their new-found liberty. Never did he get within striking distance, but ever he was conscious of those soft, padding sounds; he felt as if they were always about to spring at his defenceless back, but all through the weary day they followed, elusive, mysteriously threatening.

He pulled up, faint with anger, in mid-afternoon, and went into a thicket of cedar to set rabbit snares; but no sooner had he turned than the dogs were at the toboggan. A ripping of canvas caught his ear, and he rushed back in fury. They fled at his approach, and lay, flat on the snow, their heads between their paws; so Tom pulled up his load, built a fire beside it, and watched the huskies till morning. He had now one hundred miles to go; he had three hundred pounds to pull, and no dogs; he could not, dare not, sleep; and he had no food, but—Anderson was waiting at Lac Seul.

Who can enter into those next days? Through the

447   FF

storms—and they were many—moved a gigantic figure, and after it crawled a long, coffin-like shape; and behind the shape trotted two wolfish forms, with lean flanks and ravenous jaws. Across the crystalline plains plodded the grim procession, and, at night, the red eye of a camp-fire flung its flickering gleam on those same threatening forms, as they moved restlessly and noiselessly about, watching and waiting, waiting and watching. As his strength diminished with the miles, Tom began to see strange things, and hear curious and pleasant sounds. Then he got very sleepy; the snow was just the colour of the twenty-dollar blankets in the H.B. post; it was not cold now; he experienced a delicious languor; and people began to talk all around him; only they wouldn't answer when he shouted at them. Then the Wendigo came, and told him to lie down and rest, and, as he was taking off his shoes, another spirit called out:

"*Kago, kago—nebowah neepah panemah.*" (Don't, don't, —you will find rest by and by.)

At noon, on the eighth day after Tom left Ignace Post, Peter Anderson looked across the drifts of Lac Seul, and shook his head. The horizon was blotted out in a blizzard that whipped the flakes into his face like needle points, and the distance dissolved in a whirling view. The bush had been cleared away around his buildings and, in the bare space, a mighty wind swooped and shrieked. As he turned, the gale lifted for a moment, and, infinitely remote, something appeared to break the snow-line at the end of a long white lane of dancing wreaths; then the storm closed down, and the vision was lost. Keenly, he strained through half-closed lids; once more something stirred, and, suddenly, the wind began to slacken. In the heart of it was staggering a giant shape, that swayed and tottered, but doggedly, almost unconsciously, moved on into the shelter of the land; behind trailed a formless mass, and, last of all, the apparitions of two, lank, limping dogs.

448

Drunkenly and unseeingly, but with blind, indomitable purpose, the man won every agonizing step. His snow-shoes were smashed to a shapeless tangle of wood and sinew; his face was gaunt, patched with grey blots of frost-bite; and, through his sunken cheeks, the high bones stood out like knuckles on a clenched fist. Ice was plastered on his cap, and lay fringed on brow and lids, but beneath them burned eyes that glowed with dull fires, quenchless and abysmal. By infinitesimal degrees he drew in, with not a wave of the hand, not a sign of recognition. Up the path, from shore to trading post, shouldered the titan figure, till it reached the door. At the latch, stiff, frozen fingers were fumbling, as Anderson flung it open; and then a vast bulk darkened the threshold, swung in helpless hesitation for a fraction of time, and pitched, face foremost, on the rough pine floor.

A few hours later, he looked up from the pile of skins upon which Anderson had rolled him. His eyes wandered to the figure of the trader, who sat, serenely smoking, regarding with silent satisfaction a small mountain of provisions.

"All here, boss?"

"Ay, Tom, all here, and I'm muckle obliged to ye; are ye hungry, Tom? Will ye hae a bit sup?"

"No eat for five days; pull toboggan. No dogs."

Anderson stiffened where he sat. "What's that? Haulin' three hunder' of grub, and ye were starving? Ye big copper-coloured fule!"

"No packer's grub, boss; Hudson Bay grub!"

It was almost a groan, for Tom was far spent.

Involuntarily the quiet Scot lifted his hands in amazement, and then hurried into his kitchen, murmuring, as he disappeared:

"Man, man, it's with the likes of ye that the Hudson Bay keeps its word."

449

EL VERDUGO

by Honoré de Balzac

HONORÉ DE BALZAC, whom the French critic, Saint Beuve, described as "the greatest Frenchman who ever lived," was born at Tours, in 1799. His literary output, begun at an early age, was colossal. He planned, in a sequence of novels and tales under the title of *The Human Comedy*, and which was to record "the history of the human heart traced thread by thread and social history made by all its parts," a work consisting of one hundred and twenty-three separate volumes. Many of these were never completed, but Balzac, burdened by debt and inspired by the desire to make a home for the woman he loved, for years toiled unceasingly at his ambitious task. It has been said that Balzac created "realism"; his tales are full of authentic historical detail and observation of the society in which he lived. *El Verdugo* is one of his most dramatic stories and breathes the spirit of sublime courage. Prematurely worn out by over-work, Balzac died at the age of fifty-one, in 1850.

EL VERDUGO

BY

Honoré de Balzac

THE town clock of Menda had just struck midnight. The young French officer, leaning against the château wall that overlooked the rocky parapet, seemed to be sunk in a deeper meditation than his military calling warranted; but, on the other hand, both the hour and the surroundings evoked a reverie. The blue vault of the Spanish sky was sown with stars, and the moon lit up the enchanting valley. As he stood by an orange tree, the commander of the battalion could see the houses of Menda huddled together a hundred feet below at the foot of the rock on which the castle was built, out of reach of the icy north winds. When he turned round, he could see the sea, whose shining waters girdled the shore like a ribbon of silver. The windows of the castle were illuminated, and the sounds of merry-making, the strains of an orchestra, the laughter of officers and their partners, mingled with the distant murmur of the waves. The cool night air invigorated his body, lax with the heat of day, and the fragrance of flowers and sweet-scented herbs was diffused around him.

The castle of Menda belonged to a grandee of Spain who, with his family, was then in residence. During the whole of that evening, Clara, the eldest daughter, had gazed at the young officer with an absorption that was filled with such sorrow that it had plunged him into thought. She was beautiful, and although she had three brothers and a sister, the Marquis de Leganes was so rich that Victor Marchand had grounds for believing that her dowry would be considerable. Yet he scarcely dared hope that the daughter of one of the proudest families in Spain should be given in marriage to the son of a Paris pastry-cook. Moreover, the French were anathema. General X suspected that the marquis was intending to engineer a rising in favour of Ferdinand VII, and for this reason the battalion under Victor Marchand had been quartered on Menda to suppress any signs of insurrection.

A recent despatch from Marshal Ney had given warning that the English troops might land at any moment, and further indicated that the Marquis had been holding secret communication with the British Cabinet. Thus, in spite of the cordial welcome which the Spaniard had given him, Victor was continually on his guard. As he stood now on the terrace, from which he could command an uninterrupted view of the town, he was wondering yet again how to interpret the apparent friendliness and why the peaceful country-side had aroused his general's uneasiness.

Soon, however, these thoughts gave way to curiosity and speculation of another and more legitimate nature. It was St. John's Eve, but that morning he had given orders that all lights and fires were to be extinguished at the usual hour, the only exception being in favour of the castle. In spite of this, he now noticed the glimmer of a considerable number of lights. He could see the glitter of the bayonets of his men at their usual posts; the silence was unbroken, and there was nothing to indicate that the Spaniards were celebrating the feast. The forbidden illuminations struck him as being particularly mysterious in view of the fact that he had left certain of his officers on duty with the night patrols.

With the rashness of youth, he squeezed through an opening in the wall, and had reached the sentry-box on the road below by a short cut when a stealthy noise brought him to a full stop. He thought he heard the slight sound of sand slipping beneath the light footsteps of a woman, but looking round, he could distinguish

nothing. His eyes rested with amazement on the
brilliantly glittering sea, and the sinister sight that met
him riveted him to the spot even though he told himself
he must be dreaming. Black against the moonlight, he
saw the silhouette of distant sails. He started violently,
and tried to assure himself that what he saw was no
more than the play of moonbeams on the dancing waves.
At that moment, however, a hoarse voice uttered his
name, and turning, Victor recognized the soldier who
had accompanied him to the castle.

"Is that you, sir?"

"Yes—what is the matter?" asked Victor, instinctively
lowering his voice.

"Them Spaniards are as restless as a heap of worms,
and I thought I'd better let you know what I've seen,
sir."

"Speak up, man," said Victor.

"I've been following someone from the castle. He
came this way with a lantern. Very suspicious, that
lantern. He may be a good Christian all right, thinks
I, but what does he want to go lighting tapers for at
this hour of night? So I followed him, and, not a dozen
yards from here, I found a pile of wood."

Suddenly he stopped short. A series of frightful
screams rang out from the town. There was a blaze of
light, and Victor saw that the soldier had been shot
through the head. A few paces away, a beacon of
straw and dry wood was burning furiously. The sounds
of music and laughter in the ballroom at the castle
ceased. Instead of the light-hearted strains of the
music, there was a deathly silence, broken by groans.
The boom of a cannon echoed over the translucent
water.

Beads of moisture dewed the young man's forehead.
He was unarmed; he understood that his men had been
massacred, and that the English were about to land.
He saw himself dishonoured if he survived, saw himself
being sentenced by court-martial; he gazed at the valley

457

spread out before him, and was about to fly when a
hand touched his.

It was Clara.

"Quick! Escape while you can!" she whispered
urgently. "My brothers intend to kill you. At the foot
of the rock you will find Juanito's horse. . . . There is
not a moment to lose."

As she spoke, she impelled him forward. For a second
he stared at her wildly; then, driven by that instinct of
self-preservation that is common to both weak and
strong, he broke into a run, making his way over rocky
boulders that only the nimble goats were used to climb.
He heard Clara urging her brothers to overtake him,
heard the footsteps of his pursuers, heard the whistle of
bullets that sang past his head. But he managed to
reach the valley in safety, found the horse awaiting
him, mounted and rode off like the wind.

In a few hours' time he arrived at headquarters,
where the general was dining with his staff-major.

"I've come to give myself up!" stammered Victor,
exhausted and deadly pale.

He dropped into a chair, and told them what had
happened. His story was followed by a terrifying silence.

"You have been more unfortunate than guilty,"
said the redoubtable general, at length. "You are not
responsible for the treachery of the Spaniards, and,
unless Marshal Ney decides otherwise, I absolve you
from blame."

These words evoked only a faint glimmer of consolation in Victor.

"But when the Emperor learns what has happened—?"
he exclaimed.

"He will sentence you to be shot," replied the general.
"But we will see. Let us talk no more of the consequences
to *you* of this affair," he added sternly, "let us rather
devise some fitting punishment that will serve as a
salutary lesson to a country where men make war like
brute beasts."

An hour later, an infantry regiment, a cavalry platoon and a gun corps were on their way to Menda. The general and Victor rode at the head of the column, and the men, who had been told of the butchery of their comrades, were thirsting for revenge. They stopped only to surround the wretched wayside villages, whose armed inhabitants they mowed down, and the distance to Menda was covered in record time.

By one of those strange mischances, the English ships still lay far out at sea; it was discovered later that they carried artillery only, and had somehow outsailed the troop-ships. The sight of the billowing canvas, however, had assured the population of Menda that their allies would shortly land; but their expectations had come to nothing, and they were now overcome by the French after a brief struggle. With a heroism that was not rare during the Peninsular War, the actual murderers of the soldiers offered to surrender themselves, for the general's cruelty was notorious, and it was feared that he would set fire to the town and massacre its inhabitants. The general agreed to their terms provided that every inmate of the castle, from the family of Leganes down to the least scullion, were delivered up to him. He also stipulated that a large sum of money should be paid over to him, and, in order to ensure payment, he held the leading citizens of Menda prisoners as security.

He then took every step to ensure the safety of his men, and a camp was pitched. He made a formal entrance into the castle, and the entire household, the family and their servants alike, were bound hand and foot and kept under arrest in the ballroom, where, so short a while ago, the dance had been in full swing. From the windows, the rocky parapet that overhung the town could be seen. The general and the staff-major held counsel in an adjacent room as to how the English could be prevented from landing. An aide-de-camp was sent to Marshal Ney, and a cannon was trained towards the sea. The matter of the prisoners was next discussed. The

459

two hundred Spaniards who had given themselves up were shot on the terrace, and when there was no single survivor left, the general ordered the executioner of Menda to be summoned, and as many scaffolds as there were captives to be erected.

Victor, who had been in the ballroom, came hurriedly into the general's presence.

"I have come to ask you a favour, sir," he said in a shaking voice.

"*You* ask *me* a favour!" said the general, with bitter irony.

"It's a sorry enough favour," replied the young man. "The marquis has seen the scaffold, and hopes that you will grant his family the privilege of dying by the sword."

"So be it," said the general.

"He also asks that they may be allowed to have the consolation of religion, and that they may be freed of their bonds. They have given me their promise not to escape."

"So be it," said the general again. "But I hold you responsible for their safety."

"The marquis offers you all his possessions if you will spare the life of his little son."

"Indeed!" exclaimed the general. "The marquis' possessions are already the property of King Joseph."

He stopped. An ugly thought betrayed itself by the expression of his face, as he added:

"I will do more than the marquis asks. I understand the full meaning of his last request. Let him carry on his race to eternity, but let Spain remember for ever its betrayal and agony. The possessions of the marquis shall be given, and life granted, to whichever of his sons will undertake the rôle of executioner. That is my final word—let us speak no more of the matter."

Dinner was served. The officers, seated round the table, satisfied the hunger that weariness had sharpened. Only one of them—Victor Marchand—was missing. After several minutes of hesitation, he had entered the ballroom where the proud family of Leganes were now suffering humiliation. He looked sorrowfully round the great room where, only the night before, he had seen the dark heads of two girls and three young men amongst those of the other dancers; he shuddered as he thought how soon those heads would be rolling in the dust— severed by the executioner's knife. Bound in their gilded chairs, father, mother, and their five children sat motionless. Eight servants stood before them, their hands tied behind their backs; and these fifteen people gazed at each other steadily with no sign of the emotion that filled them. On some of the faces Victor could read acceptance of the fate that waited them, mingled with anguish at the failure of their attempt. The soldiers who had been detailed to guard them paid a tribute of respect to the sorrow of their cruel enemies.

There was a rustle of curiosity when Victor entered. He gave orders that the noble family were to be freed from their bonds, and himself cut the thongs that were knotted round Clara's wrists. She smiled mournfully, and Victor could not refrian from pressing her arm lightly as his gaze dwelt on her dark curls and slender shoulders. She was a true daughter of Spain; her skin had a golden tinge, and her velvety eyes were blacker than the raven's wing beneath their long, curling lashes.

"Have you succeeded?" she asked him, still with that heart-breaking smile.

Victor could not repress a groan. He glanced at the three brothers, and back again at Clara. The eldest son was thirty years old. Short, somewhat ill-made, with a proud and disdainful air, there was yet something noble about his bearing that showed him possessed of that quality which once blazoned forth the fame of Spanish chivalry. His name was Juanito. Philip, the second son, was just out of his 'teens; he resembled Clara. The third and youngest brother was eight years old. In little Manuel's features a painter would have distinguished something of that look which David put

461

into the face of his Republican pages. The old marquis with his white head might have stepped straight from some canvas of Murillo.

As Victor gazed at each of them in turn, he made a movement of despair, convinced that one and all would refuse the general's offer. Nevertheless, he whispered it to Clara. She shuddered as she listened, then suddenly grew calm, and knelt at her father's feet.

"Make Juanito swear to obey the order you are going to give him," she said. "Make him swear to carry it out, and we shall die happy."

The marquise quivered with hope, but when she bent forward to hear what Clara was saying, she fainted. Juanito suddenly grasped the meaning of his sister's words, and sprang to his feet with animal rage. Victor took it upon himself to dismiss the soldiers, the marquis having given him the assurance that there would be no attempt at escape. The servants were dragged away to the terrace and hanged.

When none but Victor was present, the father arose.

"Juanito," he began.

Juanito shook his head in silence, then fell back in his chair, and regarded his parents with anguish and despair. Clara approached him, sat on his knee, and put her arms round his neck.

"Dear Juanito," she said softly, kissing him on the eye-lids, "dear Juanito, if only you knew how sweet it would be to die at your hand. I tremble when I think of the hateful touch of the executioner. You will deliver me from the sorrows the future may have held—you could never bear to think I might one day leave you . . . So. . . ."

Her velvety eyes flung a burning glance at Victor as though to awaken in her brother's breast hatred of the French.

"Courage, Juanito!" said Philip. "On you depends the future of our race."

Suddenly Clara rose, the group that had formed

462

round Juanito broke up, and the old marquis confronted his son.

"Juanito, I *command* you to obey me."

Juanito remained motionless, and the father fell on his knees. Involuntarily, Clara, Philip and Manuel followed his example. They stretched out their arms to him who must ensure the continuance of their line, as the marquis continued:

"My son, are you lacking in the courage and devotion of a Spaniard? How long must I kneel to you? Why do you brood over *your* future life and *your* future sufferings? Is this a son of *my* begetting?" he asked, turning to his wife.

"He *will* do it!" cried the mother despairingly, as Juanito's lashes flickered in a way whose meaning was known only to herself.

Mariquita, the second daughter, held her mother in a close embrace. She was weeping uncontrollably, and little Manuel chided her tears. Victor could endure no more; he made a sign to Clara, and hurried to the general to beseech him to be merciful. He found his superior in high good humour, eating and drinking with his officers, who were at the height of merriment.

An hour later, a hundred of the leading citizens of Menda were made to take up their stand on the terrace to witness the execution of the family of Leganes. They were placed beneath the scaffolds from which the dead men dangled, their feet barely swinging clear of the watchers' heads. A body of soldiers was on guard. A dozen yards away was a block and a shining knife. The executioner was present in case Juanito's courage should fail.

Approaching footsteps were heard above the gay laughter of the hilarious officers; the night before, music had drowned the rumour of bloody treachery. All looks were turned towards the castle, and the spectators watched the doomed family issue forth with calm and unshakable courage. Their faces bore no mark of fear

—they were serene and still. Only one man amongst them was pale and undone; he staggered beside the priest who was murmuring the consolations of religion to him who was condemned to live. The executioner understood, the whole assembly understood that Juanito had consented to act as headsman.

The marquis, his wife, Clara, Mariquita and the two young brothers stopped a few paces from the block. Juanito was led thither by the priest; and as he drew near, the executioner led him aside and whispered instructions to him. The priest then arranged the victims in such a manner that they could not witness one another's suffering. But they were true Spaniards, and held themselves erect without a quiver.

Clara ran lightly to her brother.

"Juanito," she said, "be pitiful to my weakness. Let me be the first."

At that moment the sound of running feet was heard. It was Victor. Clara was already kneeling, her white throat stretched towards the knife. The young officer turned livid, but he stumbled on.

"The general says he will spare your life if you will marry me," he said in a low voice.

The Spanish girl cast on him a glance full of loathing and contempt.

"Strike, Juanito!" she cried in a ringing voice.

Her severed head rolled at Victor's feet. The Marquis de Leganes started convulsively at the sound—it was his only betrayal of grief.

"Am I kneeling properly, darling Juanito?" asked the little Manuel of his brother.

"You are weeping, Mariquita," said Juanito to his second sister.

"Yes, I am weeping for you," she murmured. "Poor Juanito—you will be so unhappy without us."

Proudly the old marquis stepped to the block. He looked at the spilt blood of his children, turned to the onlookers who stood silent and motionless, stretched out his hands to Juanito, and said, in a loud, clear voice:

"Spaniards, I give my son his father's blessing. Now, *marquis*, strike without fear, for you are without reproach."

But when Juanito saw his mother draw near, leaning on the priest, he cried in agony:

"She suckled me at her breast."

His words drew a shriek of horror from the crowd. At that terrible cry the laughter of the officers suddenly ceased. The mother understood that her son's courage had failed him. Instantly she flung herself over the rocky parapet and was dashed to pieces far below. Again a cry arose—a cry of wonder at such heroism. Juanito fell fainting to the ground.

"I say, sir," said a half-tipsy officer to the general, "Marshand's been telling me something about this execution, but I swear it was never by your order that——"

"You forget that in a month five hundred families in France will be mourning their dead," said the general sternly. "You forget we are in Spain. Do you wish us to leave our bones on this alien soil?"

When he had spoken, no single man dared raise his glass to his lips.

THE CHIEF OF THE GOLDEN HOPE
by Captain Frank H. Shaw

CAPTAIN FRANK H. SHAW is a story-teller by nature, often irresistible and certainly irrepressible. Born in 1877, he took to the sea at an early age, and he had piloted liners across the Atlantic for some years before finally discovering in writing stories an even more interesting and profitable occupation. He has written countless stories, and will write countless more; believing as he does that there are as many good stories in the sea as ever came out of it. *The Chief of the Golden Hope* is an exceptionally fine human story as well as an exciting yarn of the sea.

THE CHIEF OF THE GOLDEN HOPE

BY
CAPTAIN FRANK H. SHAW

A ROLLING expanse of greasy sea stretched from horizon to horizon in one unbroken plane, save that, far to southward, breaking the immaculate curve, there showed a few dark fangs, like a wolf's teeth. The Solomon Islands, notorious for the cannibalistic proclivities of their inhabitants, lay under the lee of the *Golden Hope*, and even at that illimitable distance, the dull moan of the far-flung surf could be heard stealing through the heavy air, like the rolling thunder of another world. The sun was glooming through a yellowish haze, and far to the north, like a dark line, there was a great cloud-bank. A sense as of impending events hung over the tramp steamer, and Captain Sheerpole gnawed his fingers with a new nervousness. He was frankly uneasy, for the falling mercury in the barometer had a queer concave curve on its surface and long experience told the skipper that a typhoon was mustering up its forces for a savage onslaught. The subtle undersea current set resistlessly towards those ugly spikes of rock; but, given a full head of steam and plenty of sea-room, there was no reason why the *Golden Hope* should not weather the impending storm as well as she had weathered a thousand others.

"Losh, but ye have fine times, ye o' the deck staff," said the chief engineer of the steamer as he hove himself up to the bridge deck and left the imprint of his greasy hands on the white rails of the ladder. "Mon, ye'd no believe me, but it's stewin' hot doon ablaw there in the engine-room. A hunner and thirty-five Fahrenheit, as I'm a fully certificated chief."

"Wind and steam can never mix" is the proverb at sea, which means in plain prose, that the deck staff and those of the engine-room are never inclined to fraternize to any alarming extent. Therefore it is no wonder that Captain Sheerpole smiled somewhat caustically as he replied:

"That's all you greasers can think of, Mac, us of the deck and our soft times. Why, man, you don't know the rudimentary elements of work yet. Never a wet stitch on your backs, never a chill in your marrow, no headwork, nothing to do but sit on the spare crank with your pipe in your mouth and watch the wheels go round! That's what an engineer has to do."

"Ay? So ye think yersel', dootless. Weel, I wouldna mind sayin' ye're a bit off the straight line. No, dinna let yer bearin's get overhet; it's no worth. It's maist fatiguin' tae argle-bargle wi' a man o' the deck staff on a hot day." Sheerpole's face had crimsoned somewhat and he just bit back a sharp retort in time. But the coolness and patronage of the chief galled him.

"As a fair comparison," resumed the imperturbable chief with a slow smile, "I wouldna mind assertin' that the average engineer does mair on ane day than an officer does in a month. To say nothin' o' keepin' fractious stokers up tae the mark and cloutin' the ears o' third engineers, who tell ye there's a hot bearin' when it's only the shine o' a hand-lamp on the hot steel, there's mony a calculation that has tae be worked oot tae a far greater nicety than ye o' the deck ever dae it. For instance——"

"Look here, Mac," said the skipper, "what have you come up here for? I like to see you occasionally, but I'm a bit worried at present. The typhoon is working up like a high-press cylinder; and if the current gets any stronger we'll need to fight for it before morning."

"As I was sayin', an engineer must be a man o' pairts. He maun hae the courage o' a Nelson and the determination of a Nelson. He maun hae the wit o' Harry

472

Lauder and the gravity o' the Archbishop o' Canterbury, for-bye I'm a member o' the Free Kirk. The reason o' my promiscuous call on ye, sir, is no tae swap opeenions on the distinctions atween the taw departments, so much as tae tell ye the high-press cylinder's leakin' badly, an' it'll be necessary tae stop the ship for six hours at least while we effect the necessary repairs. Ye'll understand me diffidence, but it's a fact, and we maun look facts in the face."

"Confound you for a long-winded, dissolute mechanic," cried Sheerpole savagely. "Why ever couldn't you have told me that before? The high-press cylinder out of gear! Why, man, we can't stop. The ship needs all the power that we can muster to weather this howler that's coming up. Here, look here." He took the chief by the elbow and led him to the chart-house, where the barometer hung. Tapping the glass, Sheerpole pointed out its lowness and also drew attention to that ominous curve of the mercury's surface.

"Now, tell me whether you think it's possible to stop her at the present moment."

Mr. Macphee shook his head dubiously. He wiped his black hands on the cotton-waste which he invariably carried in lieu of a handkerchief, and then, searching in his pockets, he produced a plug of "Lucky Hit," from which he thoughtfully shredded a pipeful. When the pipe was charged to his liking, he looked up.

"Ye'll no happen to have a match, will ye?" he asked calmly.

"Oh, damn your Scotch callousness!" roared Sheer-pole. "Let's have an understanding at once, Mac. You say the ship's got to be stopped; and I say she can't be stopped. It's more than all our lives are worth to let her lose her way now. She's not making more than four knots ahead at present and the current's setting her four knots south each hour, too; so it's touch and go whether we'll make our way past those blasted rocks even as we are, without that cursed typhoon and the

473

rotten engines to add to our difficulties. My word is the ship's got to keep going for all she's worth. If you say another word about stopping her I'll log you for insubordination."

"Ay, ye'll dae that, I've no doot. But, Captain Sheerpole, apart frae merely professional jealousies, ye're a man I've a great admiration for. Ye're cool in emergency and ye've got yer heid screwed on the right way. Here's ma final word: gin ye drive thae engines anither thirty minutes, ye'll hae naething in the engine-room but a mass o' twisted shoddy. She'll no stand it."

Sheerpole tore his hair and called upon his gods. The low mutter of the gathering storm sounded like the voice of an angry Jove and the lashing diapason of the surf on the distant rocks sounded like the hissing expectation of a waiting multitude.

"See what you can do in an hour," he said finally. "I'll give you that, but not another minute. If you've not got her to rights in that time, she must blow herself to bits; but I'm going to have way on her."

There was a sudden crash from the engine-room and both the good men started simultaneously. Then the telegraph on the bridge rang rapidly to stop and the thud of the propeller died away. The ship went along a little distance by her own impetus, but before the captain had time to open his mouth she had stopped and only the greasy lap of water against the motionless side answered his thoughts.

"Ay, she's done it," said the chief. "I was expectin' it. Ye will say the engine-room staff's no gude, sir; but ye'll acknowledge a highly skilled mechanic's a vera handy man tae have aboard at this time." And he went on a tour of inspection.

"Sax hours at the vera least, wi' safety," said he, when he returned. "Ye didna gie me yon match I was askin' after. She's stripped the packing completely away; and she's damaged otherwise, tae. She's needin' dry-dockin' maistly, but we maun dae as we can wi' the

474

materials at oor disposal. Ye'll need tae lend me the whole o' the deck staff, I'm thinking."

Sheerpole summoned the mate and gave his orders. Soon there arose from the engine-room the sound of furious hammerings on solid metal, the dull clang of a dropped implement, the screeching yell of a rusty bolt as the great spanners bit home and twisted it from its holding. Spurts of hot oil sizzled up through the open skylight and the sounds of violent cursings rang loudly above the sullen day. And all the time the threatening growl to windward increased in violence and dull flashes of lightning whirled wildly to and fro over the dark, cloudy sky.

Leaving the bridge in charge of a mate, the captain hung agonizedly over the engine-room skylight, only breaking off at times to race to the chart-room and watch the downward-trending barometer. He came back from every observation with a face that grew blacker and blacker, and the strained appearance of his eyes told his mate that the danger impending was only too real. The steamer lay like a log in the vast expanse. The sun was dropping down its western path and showed a distorted, danger-impending disc. It was flattened to a queer oval and was the colour of a P. & O. liner's boat. The sea was growing troubled now. A long heave from the north had set in and it lifted the ship in its embracing arms, setting her back with a dull squelch; and once a great wave raced madly onwards, rose up the sides of the motionless craft and half-buried her. It was only one, there was no other; but somewhere at the back of that sulphurous curtain to the north there was waiting a whole army of similar waves.

Forgetting the sacredness of the engine-room, Captain Sheerpole raced below and confronted the chief, who was waving a spanner with grim majesty. He had just felled an offending seaman who had complained that he wasn't a minutely particularized artificer and was waiting to see what would come of the action.

"You'll have to get way on her," yelled Sheerpole, snatching at the chief's arm as a drowning man at a straw. "The typhoon 'll be down in another twenty minutes and she'll never live. Can't you run her on two cylinders?"

"Can a man twist a universe upside doon?" asked the chief grimly. "We're daein' all we can an' we canna dae more. There's mair damage than I thought for at the first sicht, but we're gettin' on. Anither hour or twa 'll mak' a big difference."

Captain Sheerpole let go his frenzied hold and simply sobbed. He was madly in love with his calling, but he was vouchsafed a vision in which he saw the pitying sneers of fellow master-mariners, who would comment on his accident in no measured terms.

Macphee heard that sob and his hard face softened. "Gin it's as bad as a' that," he said emphatically, "we'll dae oor best. Spare me anither thirty minutes an' I'll get way on the bit shippie or—bust!"

He made no boast about what he would do, for, as he said, he was only an engineer. But for the remaining thirty minutes he worked like a dozen men, worked with the sweat hopping down his face like hailstones, till his back seemed breaking at the hips, till his fingers were raw and bleeding with slipped spanners and rusted bars. On and on he toiled, inspiring his men with word and blow, doing as much as they all were doing together; and yet, as the time allotted drew to its close, he looked at his work and shook his head. Nothing but a miracle could bring the engines to a fit condition in time to save the ship, and without the necessary repairs it would be positive madness to make any attempt to drive them. Positive madness—or sublime heroism!

As his heavy hammer dealt blow after sounding blow at implacable masses of chilled steel, Mr. Macphee's brain kept time to the strokes; and the words that sang through his mind were those same words spoken by the captain a little while before: "The average engineer is

476

no earthly use aboard ship." He was showing his utility now if ever a man did and he was wondering if Sheerpole knew it.

"I'm dootin' he'll tak' credit for onything we dae himsel'," muttered the chief, as a wedge fell across his foot with a painful thud. "Sheerpole's aye forrit at takin' credit, forbye he's no blate tae share the blame wi' ony that comes handy. Well, I'll no mind. I ken masel' who's who an' what's what; and I'll dae may best notwithstandin'."

The storm broke suddenly in spite of the long warning. It seemed as if a sudden vacuum had been created in the sky and a high pillar of water leaped up bodily to fill the void. Then, the whole sea rose boisterously and swept down upon the *Golden Hope* and she staggered at the awful shock.

Those who worked in the engine-room, or held on, with white faces and gripping hands, to anything that would support a man's weight, saw a sudden vision. The skipper, his eyes bloodshot and starting, the blood streaming down his beard where he had bitten through his underlip, tore down the slippery ladder and fairly flung himself on the chief engineer.

"At all costs give us steam!" he yelled loudly, and yet above the frenzied scream of the typhoon his words might have been whispered.

"We're all dead men if you don't," he cried again.

And the chief engineer, understanding the gestures if not the words, looked at him for a moment in stern silence. Then he waved his hand around the dismantled engine-room. The motion was self-explanatory and the captain turned away with a groan. Apparently nothing could save the ship.

With a weird shake of his head, he staggered up the dizzy ladder again, warped himself along the decks hand over hand until he gained the bridge and then, on all fours, crept to the weather-cloth at the front and peered over. The wind flattened him back against the wheel-house, with the breath knocked clean out of his body. The mate and second mate had disappeared, but a sharp glance showed him them flattened against the funnel, insensible. They had been caught up by the giant hand of the gale and flung like feathers against the iron stack.

The sea was shut out from sight now in a fog of seething foam. It was only made apparent by the low, groaning note that beat through the mad strife, as the typhoon bit off the tops of the waves and flung them sky-high in mad abandon. And the steamer herself was labouring hard, her decks clean-swept, the life-boats smashed to matchwood, save that one remained, with the after-tackle carried away, so that the boat streamed out to leeward like a flag, until the remaining tackle chafed through and the boat vanished into the inferno overside.

But the *Golden Hope* was safe still. A magnificent sea-boat, she kept her bluff stem up into the eye of the wind and refused to be overwhelmed by the massed might of her opponent. With plenty of sea-room the chances were in her favour still, but there were the fangs of the Solomons to leeward and they were drawing nearer with every slow second that passed. The ship was drifting bodily down upon them and presently, so Sheerpole said, as he lay flat on the bridge planks and peered through a hole he had cut in the weather-cloth, presently she would be lifted like a toy and flung upon those cruel ridges to her unavoidable doom.

A sharp tinkling came to Sheerpole's ears, rising even above the elemental thunder. He could hardly believe his ears, but a sharp look at the engine telegraph told him that the engines were rung to full speed ahead. Then the familiar vibration of the clashing machinery shook the ship from stem to stern. She was moving ahead, she was under steam once more—there was a fragment of hope that she might be saved still.

478

Understanding nothing of what the chief was doing, but with a great prayer of thankfulness in his heart, Sheerpole wormed his way to the wheel-house and grasped the deserted wheel. He scanned the compass with narrowed eyes and fixed on a course that would take him soonest out of danger; then, with muscles of steel and eyes of fire, he held the kicking helm true.

The men who had been at work in the engine-room were clustered, a wonderful group, in the alley-ways on deck. They were still half-dazed, for they had met with a mighty surprise. Ten minutes before, as they groaned and panted below, now holding like grim death to a rail, now making a fitful dash with a hammer or spanner at some work, they had been driven in a body on deck by the chief engineer, whose eyes were afire with a new light.

"On deck, every mother's son of ye!" he had screamed "Get oot o' the engine-room, ye gowks! Up wi' ye, wull ye no gang? Firemen, intae the stokehold wi' ye like ane man. Gie me every ounce o' steam ye can muster and gie it me quick!"

They had fled before his looks and words, while men muttered that the old Scot was "fey." The second and third engineers had endeavoured to reason with him, to point out the utter futility of his staying in the engine-room, but he drove them from him with harsh words —ay, and with blows—bidding them to the stokehold, to keep the firemen up to their work. They went sadly, for they loved the stern old man who had taught them most of what they knew about their trade.

The great room, filled with shining steel, was deserted by all save Macphee now, and he set himself to do the most heroic thing in his life. He knew that to turn the power into the engines would fill the place with blinding, scalding steam, and that, if the ship were to be driven at all, it was at the cost of the driver's life. But his knotted hands never trembled as he rang the telegraph to the bridge and opened the throttle valve slowly.

479   HH

There was a hiss of escaping steam that drowned the
tumult from above. A smoky cloud dripped out from
the leaking cylinders and filled every corner of the vast
apartment, impinging cruelly on the man's flesh as he
stood resolutely at his post. Little by little he turned
the throttle, until the sweeping pistons began their work.
The engines were working again. With many a gasp
and splutter, with many a wheeze and shudder, they
were going round. The ship was surging unevenly
through the awful seas that had been lashed up in a
moment; the propeller was more often out of water than
under and it was necessary—for Macphee knew well that
the keying of the screw was untrustworthy—to stand by
the throttle without a break, in order that the mad
racing of the shaft might be checked as the steamer's
stern lifted to the 'scend of the sea.

Alone in the oscillating room, with the ray of the lamp
clattering gauges and sweeping pistons, he stood at his
post without a complaint. The skipper's words were
forgotten now—he was borne up by a strange mental
exaltation that comes to some men at the time of their
greatest peril. He was pitting his own feeble strength
against the strength of the elusive vapour that he had
enslaved for so many years—and he said that he would
win the fight or die at his post.

Hot oil and blinding steam were everywhere. The
whirling cranks revolved in zoetrope circles of dazzling
light, a loosened gauge on the fore-column of the engine
danced a mad witches' dance to the play of the thrusting
monsters; the plates underfoot hove and shook as the
Golden Hope gathered her way upon her, and breasted
the storm with pugnacious courage. And the sound of
the hissing steam was deafening. It came sweeping out
in vast scalding clouds. It whistled through tiny aper-
tures; it volleyed through open crevices in the loosened
packing. It smote with the force of a hammer on the
chief's smarting skin, and when he released his grasp of
the throttle for a minute to tear away the loose collar

that threatened to choke him, strips of his parboiled skin came away with it, leaving the raw and smarting flesh exposed.

He was more than half-blinded now; and a strange, dizzy feeling made him reel. But he never lost his presence of mind and for long hour after long hour he worked the heated throttle, now lessening the steam and now increasing it, as the vessel pitched and wallowed madly. His old face was unrecognizable. He was dully aware that a stream of blood was coursing down his cheeks, where a loosened bolt had flown from its holding and cut him to the bone; but he took no heed. His fingers retained their grasp on the throttle more by instinct than by will-power, for his senses were reeling and he staggered like a drunken man to the lurch of the struggling fabric around him. But he stuck to his post, with a grim courage that defied the end.

On deck chaos reigned supreme. The captain was alone on the bridge, for the mates had not yet recovered from their stunning fall and no man had ventured to ascend the clattering ladders to bear a hand. At the helm, peering through the salt-rimmed glass in front of the wheel-house, with his every nerve tensed to the awful strain, Sheerpole, his brain torn with dread and confused with the ceaseless strife of the wind, kept the ship's head unalterably on her course and prayed silently that he might yet win through.

Once, a sudden lift in the salt fog that hung like a mantle over the sea, showed him the tooth-like rocks to leeward, and they were very near. But the ship was gallantly holding her own at last and, when the next clearance came in that curtain of gloom, he saw that the vessel was making slow headway past the danger. If only the engines would hold out another hour, the danger would be past.

Using every ounce of his strength and every fraction of his skill, Sheerpole kept her to her course. After his second glance to leeward he never looked in that direction again, for he said that the issue was in Higher Hands than his.

The insidious current took her by the keel and urged her to her immediate destruction, the thunderous gale lifted her bodily and swept her down towards her fate; but the engines never stopped—they lifted her to her thrust and sent her swirling ahead into the very heart of the storm. She was little better than a wreck now. She had been swept of everything that could be moved; huge rents gaped in her bulwarks and the bent and twisted rails of the bridge showed the awful might of the crashing seas. Still she struggled on. She lifted her bow to the rolling combers and trod them underfoot with a remnant of her old saucy pride. She swept her decks of every shuddering roll, but the hurtling water leaped through the gaping bulwarks as soon as it came aboard and did not bear her down.

It was almost dark now. For three long hours the storm had raged with such awful fury that the captain could not believe his own ears when that constant drumming ceased. For a moment he stood dazed in the sudden calm that followed the awful riot; and then, as the mist rolled bodily away and showed a clear and smiling sky, showed, too, the cruel rocks astern and out of reach with ordinary care, he let go the wheel and flung himself down on the deck, sobbing like a woman.

The engine still rumbled on and, in the lull, their pitiful wheezing was plainly to be heard. Recovering himself, Sheerpole rang the telegraph to stop and went along the fiddley to where his officers lay. They were coming back to life slowly. He carried the mate to the bridge and left him there, noticing, as he did so, that in spite of his signal to the engineer below, the machinery was still rotating at undiminished speed. Suddenly, the clatter died away.

Sheerpole, looking like a man who had fought a bout with Death, went off the bridge and down to the engine-room. The place was full of blinding steam still; but, as his eyes grew accustomed to the haze, the skipper saw the place was empty. But when he cautiously crept across the swirling floor, ankle deep in oil and water, he stumbled over something that lay at the foot of the main column. Then, with a cry, he put down his hand.

Macphee, the chief engineer, had been faithful unto death. The titanic task well done, he had fallen dead, and his lifeless hand had closed the throttle as he fell.

NACH VERDUN!

by F. Britten Austin

FRANCIS BRITTEN AUSTIN achieved a reputation as a writer of dramatic military stories long before the outbreak of the European War in 1914, when *Action*, which title he had given to his first volume, was for the time being forgotten in the stress of distinguished active service. He joined the army as a private in a rifle battalion, and soon became a commissioned officer. He was born in London, in 1885, and attended the Grocer's Company School. During the War he conceived the idea of writing a series of tales dramatizing the experiences of German soldiers. *Nach Verdun!* was the most successful of these, and it is also one of the most powerful and convincing war stories of modern times. A great traveller, Britten Austin has contributed much useful journalism to periodicals on both sides of the Atlantic, including a complete study of post-War civil and military aviation.

NACH VERDUN!

BY

F. BRITTEN AUSTIN

IN the long, luxuriously furnished saloon car of the
special train an officer clad in the field-service
uniform of a South-Eastern Power sat in conversation
with a colonel of the German General Staff. The
deference shown to him made it immediately obvious that
he was a distinguished personage representing a neutral
whose friendliness was important. His dark, clever eyes
rested thoughtfully upon the groups of officers with
whom the car was overcrowded. All round was a buzz
of talk, of suppressed excitement. The air was thick with
cigar smoke.

"*Ja, Excellenz,*" said the German colonel, podgy little
fingers drumming the table between them. "The secret
is out. You have rightly guessed our objective." His
eyes were those of a rather clumsy and not too scrupulous
diplomat. His smile was deliberate flattery. "Allow me
to congratulate you upon your good fortune. You will
see the machinery of our *Kriegswirtschaftlichkeit*[1] "—he
throated the word impressively, "at the moment when
it works at its highest power to shape for Germany her
final victory."

The distinguished neutral smiled also, perfectly courteous. He spoke with a faint Austrian accent.

"I can understand your desire for the final"—he
stressed the word ever so slightly—"victory, Herr
Oberst."

The German stared at him, suspicious of the nimbler
brain.

"Who would not desire it, Excellenz? This awful

[1] War economy.

489

slaughter—" he waved a deprecating hand. "It is terrible that our adversaries do not recognize they are already beaten."

The neutral nodded.

"Bar-le-Duc and the Upper Marne, I suppose—Paris?"

The German colonel's eyes went dead. "Excellenz, I believe the supreme command reserves to itself the honour of enlightening you on its plans."

The conversation languished. The train rolled on, heavily comfortable. The staff officers talked earnestly among themselves, the word *Majestät* oft repeated. Orderlies, garbed as soldiers but obviously royal *Kammerdiener*, stole noiselessly in and out of the car, went frequently into the car beyond. On those occasions the distinguished neutral had a glimpse of a world-familiar figure, upturned moustaches on a tired face, a uniform of grey hung with many decorations.

The train rolled into a station, stopped. The blare of a military band started on the precise instant of its arrival. The platform was thronged with officers, bright with the red of the general staff.

The distinguished neutral took little interest in the ceremony outside. He busied himself with collecting the small articles of his kit. Through the large windows he glimpsed the salutes of the rigidly erect officers. Above the noise of the band he heard the repeated, "*Hoch! Hoch! Hoch!*" of soldiers who cheered as they drilled, exactly synchronous.

He stepped on to the platform, followed by the colonel appointed to be his conductor. "*Majestät*" had already departed. Officers went thronging to the exit laughing and talking, much excited, revealing, despite the grey and red of the staff uniform, the essential childishness of the crowd mind. "*Nach Verdun!*" said one of them, very close to the distinguished neutral, nudging another in the ribs. "*Nach Verdun!*" He repeated the just-given watchword of victory as a schoolboy repeats the latest smart expression. The officers around him laughed. The crowd buzzed with high spirits.

Outside the station the roadway was choked with waiting motor-cars, lined with soldiers readjusting their helmets after tumultuous *"Hochs!"* Some cars—those containing the highest personages—had already departed. One after the other, those remaining were filled, swerved out and sped away. The distinguished neutral and his companion found a vehicle reserved for them. The colonel led him to it with an air that suggested: "See how the smallest details are thought out!" They too, sped away through the walls of infantry.

Behind the soldiers were a few listless French inhabitants; from the windows of that French town hung German flags, but no French faces looked out. The shops were open, but their owners stood not at the doors. The neutral noted these things. The complete apathy of the population was in contrast to stories his companion had related in the train. In many of the side streets long convoys of ammunition and ration wagons were halted to allow them passage. On one of those foremost wagons was scrawled in big chalk letters *"Nach Verdun!"*

"Nach Verdun!" That was the *Leitmotiv* underlying all the intense military activity that filled the town, and as they shot out beyond the houses, the countryside also. Every road was choked with columns of marching infantry, with endless trains of wagons, of limbers, of ambulances. Even cavalry was in evidence, riding with tall lances and saddle-hung rifles on wretched-looking horses. *"Nach Verdun!"* The German colonel, though he warily gave no information, could talk of nothing else. Under that grey February sky pulsed and boomed the distant detonations of artillery. The neutral listened to it with a professional ear, was puzzled. It was persistent enough, but it was certainly not the prolonged roar of a preparatory bombardment.

The car swung into the drive of a park. A tunnel of

winter-stripped trees, brown above, green streaking the bark, and then a large château drew itself across the vista. Thither the other cars had preceded them. They stood now ranked in a mass. There was a throng of officers round the great doors, the buzz awakened by the recent passage of the All Highest. The neutral was shown to his room, the German colonel volubly regretting that the exigencies of space forced him to share it.

Some hours later the neutral was ushered into a vast, lofty apartment whose tapestried walls were almost completely rehung with the huge maps pinned upon them. On easels stood other maps, strange diagrams in curves and slants of red, green, and black ink. On a large table was a horizontal relief model of hills and woods, a river with tributary streams, a splash of red in the valley, thin lines of red converging upon it, passing through, opening out again. On all these maps, on the splash of red in the relief model, the name "Verdun" was repeated again and again.

All these things the neutral officer noticed with the corner of his eye—the large writing-tables behind which sat officers of high rank, other officers grouped in a corner. His direct gaze was held by the figure he saluted. Spare, of medium height, in the grey, field-service uniform of a general, gold cord looping across his right breast, a star upon the left above the Iron Cross, gilt epaulettes, gilt leaves upon the red gorgets of his collar, the would-be conqueror of the world stood stiffly erect, graciously acknowledged his salute. The brushed-up moustache was still dark, though the short hair on the head was grey, almost white. The face was deeply furrowed with endless anxieties, but the blue eyes—pouched though were their under lids—gleamed with excitement. He spoke in a jerky but distinct manner that betrayed a temperament of long ill-controlled impulses.

"*Guten Abend, Herr General!* Welcome to Germany's greatest hour! You shall see our sun mount triumphantly

492

to its zenith, breaking through the dark clouds of foes who cluster over against us in vain!" The tone was that of a rhetoric practised until it has become a habit. The right hand gesticulated with quick motions, the left arm was conspicuously still. "General!" he turned to one of the officers sitting at the tables, "be so good as to explain everything to our friend here."

It was to be clearly understood that the All Highest was flatteringly gracious.

The neutral officer bowed, expressed his thanks courteously, ventured a request: "That I may be allowed to admire your War Machine in all its work, *Majestät*—go where I will."

"By all means, General. We have nothing to hide. You will find much to interest you, much to relate to our well-wishers in your country. General! see that a pass is given to our friend that will give him the fullest freedom." The All Highest answered the neutral's salute in a manner that terminated the conversation.

Seated at the huge carved writing-table with the officer to whom he had been addressed, the neutral found himself looking at a pair of keen grey eyes that peered through pince-nez under bushy white eyebrows. The German spread out maps, indicated positions. He drew notice to the fact that all roads squeezed through a bottle-neck over the river at Verdun, spread out in a fan on the east bank to a long line of positions that climbed from the river over the Heights of the Meuse and fell into the plain of the Woevre across which they bent southward.

"Die sache is asserst einfach!" ("The thing is absolutely simple!") he said, with the air of a man explaining a chess problem. "The French have three divisions of territorials in front of us to hold the entire sector. That force is not strong enough to defend it, and certainly too weak to have kept the trench systems in good repair. In fact, we know that they have been allowed to fall into ruin. We have fifteen divisions in front line, fifteen divisions in reserve. We do not intend to fling those divisions away. No. Step by step our artillery will blast a passage for them—see, here are our artillery positions." He showed concentric lines one within the other on the map, round the doomed sector. "It is the greatest artillery concentration the world has ever seen. Even our concentration on the Donajetz last year is surpassed. We shall obliterate the positions in front of us—other batteries will drench the only avenues of supplies with shells, they must all go through the town —our infantry will merely march into the devastated position, wait for the clearance of the next step. I may tell you that the French have only one small branch railway line which is safe from our fire. We have built fourteen new lines, besides those already existing. In the great problem of supply we have an overwhelming superiority. We believe we have the advantage of surprise. Certainly the French have no concentration within easy reach. In four days we shall be in Verdun. The Western Front will have been broken."

"In four days?" The neutral officer looked at the map as a chess player looks at the board. "And—if I might ask the question—supposing you do not take Verdun in four days? There is said to be an enormous Allied force somewhere in France."

"We have yet another day," said the German, a little wearily, as though resenting the effort to explain the unnecessary. "We have five clear days before any reinforcements can be brought up against us—all the chances have been calculated, you see. If we are not in Verdun by the evening of the fifth day—well, the battle will continue. But, I repeat, we shall be in Verdun within four days. The thing is certain!"

"Of course it is, General," said another voice above their heads. Both officers looked up, rose to their feet. "In four days we shall be in Verdun. In a fortnight —Paris!"

The speaker was a youngish man, with a long nose in

494

a long face, somewhat bald upon the brow, a clipped moustache above a long thin mouth. There was something in his manner which suggested not too reputable finance doubled with Monte Carlo and the *coulisses*. He repeated, smacking his hand familiarly upon the back of the distinguished neutral: "In a fortnight— Paris!" He named the famous city with a smack of the lips.

"Undoubtedly, Highness," said the German general, his professional manner replaced by the obsequiousness of the courtier. "The army led by your Highness cannot fail to conquer."

"Verdun—Paris! This time it will not fail, General." He walked across the room, smacking a riding-switch on his tall, patent leather hussar boots, and chanting, "*Nach Verdun. Nach Verdun—Paris!*" [1]

The morning of the 21st February, 1916, opened damp and bleak. Over the heavy clay fields of the Woevre plain the mist hung persistently, enclosing all vision in a few hundred yards. Through the obscurity the poplars lining the roads loomed up like ghosts, dripping moisture from each bare twig. In the copses and the larger stretch of woodland known as the Forêt de Spincourt the conglobulated mist fell like rain. From either of the high knolls known as the Twins of Ornes, just south-west of the Forêt de Spincourt, the wooded slopes of the Heights of the Meuse—Merbebois and the Bois de Wavrille—rose dark and indefinite, discernible only when a little puff of the raw east wind, coming up the valley of the Orne, broke a rift in the fog.

The neutral and the German Oberst who was his inseparable companion stood on the more southerly of the twin heights. About them was a group of artillery officers. In their immediate front was the deep dug-out, sod-roofed, where telephonists sat and waited. It was

[1] *Nach* means "to, toward," and also "after." "To Verdun! *After* Verdun—Paris!"

an artillery observation post. The light was yet dim'
though the wet fog was white. It had been quite dark
when the two spectators had made their way over roads
deep in mud to this position of vantage.

The journey had been long, for their car had had to
squeeze, lurching and slithering, past endless columns
of infantry plodding over the atrocious roads. In the
darkness those thousands of men had been scarcely
more visible than phantoms who sang continuously as
they marched, chorusing to the tune set by picked
singers at the head of each company. Those who were
merely the chorus broke off frequently to shout wit-
ticisms at the labouring motor-car. In high spirits, they
wagered that they would be the first, after all, to arrive
in Verdun.

On the hill-top of the Twin of Ornes, where the
officers clustered, was tense expectation. The fog did
not lift. Only at rare intervals was there a faint glimpse
of the wooded heights towards which all gazed with
thrilling foreknowledge. As yet all was a quiet broken
only by an occasional isolated detonation that rolled
heavily down the Ornes valley. It echoed in a dull
repercussion from the mist-filled woods upon the great
scarp that was the far-flung rampart of the doomed city.
An officer looked at his watch. The example was in-
fectious. The seconds, the minutes, passed slowly. It
was like waiting for the curtain to go up. The watches
marked 8.13 (German time)—8.14—8.15!

There was one simultaneous vast roar that leaped from
an arc stretching from far in the north-west and passing
round behind them to the south. It did not cease.
Minute after minute it continued, unabated, prolonged.
In the first sudden shock it appeared one colossal bellow
of sound, evenly maintained. But as the ear became
accustomed to it, instinctively analysed it, it was possible
to distinguish spasms of even fiercer sound than the
general welter; the ponderous concussion of especially
heavy ordnance; the frenzied hammering of the quick-

firing field-guns. The sense of hearing was overwrought, but the view changed not. The mist still hung over the landscape, was a curtain before the straining eye. Only down below them to the right a howitzer battery, adventurously pushed forward, rent the fog with stabs of orange-red flame.

It seemed, in the overpowering blast of the German guns, that the French artillery was making no general reply. From time to time a shell came whining over toward them, finished in an ugly rush and a crash somewhere upon the knoll. They scarcely noticed these occasional djinns of death, so ineffective were they by contrast to the whirlwind of destruction that swept the other way. The habituated ear could now pick out the rumbling tram-car-like progress of the heavy shells overhead, the fierce rushing drone of the missiles from lighter guns, mingling interwoven with the uninterrupted sheet of sound.

What was happening over there among the dank, wooded hills? Nothing could be seen, but the experienced imagination sketched, conscious that it fell below the reality, fearful havoc distant in the fog. Trees suddenly blasted, toppling; parapets leaping into the air—horrors among the spout of earth that had been a sheltered dug-out; trenches whose walls fell in; men who cowered, fear-paralysed, in a shambles; overhead a ceaseless cracking that rained down death; shock upon shock; chaos—such flitted through the minds of those who strained their eyes at the fog. An artillery observation officer turned to the neutral.

"Five hours of this, Excellenz," he said with a smile, "and then, the first step to Verdun!"

The Oberst expatiated on the wonderful German system for supplying all these batteries indefinitely at this intensity of fire. "Who can resist us?" was the implied corollary to his dissertation. The neutral was duly impressed, his dark clever eyes serious.

The bombardment continued, became monotonous.

497

The fog thinned somewhat but permitted no clear vision. The batteries were firing by the map, according to a pre-arranged programme. The Oberst suggested to his distinguished guest that further stay was useless.

"I would like to see your guns at work, Herr Oberst," said the neutral, and the colonel saw himself forced to put aside his hopes of returning to Corps Headquarters for *Mittagessen*. He speculated on the Divisional Messes in the vicinity as he replied:

"By all means, Excellenz."

They scrambled down the rough path of the knoll, through a thin growth of birch, passed into the denser mist below.

They found themselves suddenly among long ranks of resting infantry squatting and lying in close proximity to their piled arms. The *feld-grau* uniforms merged, were lost in the fog, but there was an indefinable suggestion of the presence of many thousands. The Oberst and his guest might walk where they would, the shadowy grey forms still loomed up out of the mist. All were cheerful and confident. The officers in little groups smiling as they conversed, bent over a map. The men grinning. They were waiting for the guns to level the path for their "promenade."

At last the ranks of infantry ceased. They came upon a field-battery that was firing furiously. The guns were in the open, their upturned caissons—lid upright to form a shield, exposing the pigeon-holed bases of the cartridges —close against the left wheel. Grouped behind each were the busy gunners, in rapid movement of arms and torso, crouching, labouring with swift concentrated intensity as they passed the long, gleaming projectile from hand to hand, thrust it into the breech, closed and fired. Behind them was a heap of brass cartridge-cases, the flat compartmented baskets that had held three rounds. The watching officers, helmeted, in long, closely-buttoned coats, stood behind their sections. The battery hurled out its stream of death in absolute immunity. No enemy shell came to seek it. The fog veiled its target.

Beyond that battery was another, in the open like the first, almost wheel to wheel with it. And beyond that, another and yet others, an endless chain of them, all scorning concealment, all firing as fast as sweating, straining men could load and pull the lever. From behind came the prolonged, heavy, linked detonations of yet other batteries of more weighty metal. Overhead the rumble and rush of hurrying shells was as the sound of heavy traffic.

The neutral and his guide turned eastward toward the zone of the three great howitzers. Once more they were entangled in waiting masses of grey-clad infantry. The mist had thinned, permitted quite long vistas. Everywhere there was infantry, battalion upon battalion, regiment on regiment, brigade after brigade. The time had passed almost unnoticed—by the neutral, at least, so much was there for his brain to register—it was now almost noon. The infantry was standing to its ranks, forming into column of route, marching forward with songs and shouts, their spiked helmets decorated with sprigs of fir. "*Vorwärts!*" came the sharp, barking commands of the officer. "*Nach Verdun!*" shouted the excited men, drunk with the prospect of superbly easy victory.

And ever the indefatigable batteries hammered and crashed, spewing forth death in volumes that the men they served might live. From behind every hedge, every hillock; in long lines across the open—so many that they could afford to neglect the enemy's reply; their tongues of flame shot out, flickered indefinitely repeated into the distance. Their infinitely reiterated detonations smote splittingly upon the ear, were gathered into one overpowering roar.

The dark mass of the Forêt de Spincourt was riven by red flame that lit and was gone momentarily in every

499

part of its recesses. As the two officers approached it, they saw a faint film of smoke hanging over the tree-tops, saw the quick flashes gleaming through the undergrowth of the verge. They entered its obscurity. The air choked one with the fumes of burnt explosive, beat against the face in gusts with the disturbance of the multiplied discharges. The wood was a nest of howitzer batteries. On platforms of concrete and timber the monsters squatted, bowed their heads to receive yet another shell, raised it again with slow, determined movement, the great round jaws gazing upward to the sky, belched with a sudden eructation of vivid flame, a tremendous shock of which the stunning noise was only part. The spectator behind the gun, looking upward, saw a black object speeding high into the air, rapidly diminishing, the while a rain of twigs pattered down upon his face. As the barrel was lowered again, the breech opened, slow curling tongues of flame licked round the muzzle. Behind each weapon were great stacks of shells. Hurrying men, two at a time, a tray supported on two short poles between them, carried more food to the iron monster, fed its fuming breech for yet another roar.

Farther within the wood were still greater monsters, so huge that their aliment was trundled to them on light rails, swung into their maw by overhanging cranes. The earth shook, the trees rocked with the vehemence of their discharge.

"Frau Bertha has a most persuasive voice, *nicht wahr?*" said the Oberst to his guest. The neutral agreed as courteously as was possible in this chaos of bludgeoning noise. His dark eyes rested a little contemptuously on the dapper, somewhat podgy colonel whose soul, even in this crisis of nations, was still essentially the soul of a commercial traveller. The order to Krupp's was not yet given.

It was one o'clock—noon to the anxious general far over there in the terrible distance. As suddenly as it had commenced, the vast bombardment ceased. There was an uncanny silence. All knew its significance. The German infantry was advancing to the assault. With what resistance would it be met? Every ear was at strain—machine-guns? There was no sound. Suddenly the bombardment opened again, as violent as before. The German guns were putting a screen of death behind the doomed positions, barring off all help. Far away huge shells were crashing down from a curve that was four miles high at its zenith, making an inferno of a once quiet cathedral town, wrecking the bridges across a flooded river, blocking every avenue of supply to the defenders agonizing on the plateau.

That night in the Army Headquarters was a night of jubilation. Courtier soldiers—who none the less laboured into the small hours at the intricate calculations and orders that would improve the victory on the morrow —glanced at a youngish, very exalted personage and murmured platitudes about the pardonable intoxication of success. An even more exalted personage strode from general to general in the great tapestried, map-hung apartment and gave instructions that were received as the inspiration of genius and then merged, lost sight of, nullified in the mass of orders that emanated from those fiercely toiling brains.

The distinguished guest seated at the table with the keen-eyed, white-browed general, had everything patiently explained to him.

"All has gone exactly to schedule," said the German. "The first-line positions are ours. There has been a counter-attack in the Bois de Caures, but we have stemmed it. Elsewhere there has been no serious opposition. The first day has been a brilliant success. We have pierced the line where we intended to pierce it. If the French maintain their flank position their disaster is certain. The battle will be developed to-morrow. We shall drive right through to the Ornes-Louvemont road. The French defence is dead, was

501

annihilated by our bombardment. To-morrow disintegration will set in and our progress will be rapid. On the third day we shall take Fort Douaumont—the key to Verdun."

"And on the fourth day?" queried the neutral, his dark eyes gazing at the map in front of him.

"We shall be in Verdun!" said the German.

"*Verdun! Verdun! Nach Verdun—Paris!*" chanted an unsteady voice across the room, finished in a suspicious resemblance to a hiccup. There was a moment of tense awkward silence in the great apartment, and then a buzz of low voices earnestly discussing technicalities.

Day followed day, surcharged with fateful issues. Men who flung themselves down, utterly wearied, to snatch a brief sleep, woke from it with an oppression of the breast, a tremor of the nerves. Their fiercely excited brains begrudged an instant's unconsciousness where every minute was a vehicle of destiny, once ahead never to be overtaken. Strenuously, night and day, laboured the staffs in the Army Headquarters, in the Corps, Divisions, Artillery Groups—desperately, for after the second day they were behind their time-table. On that second day the French defence they had fondly thought annihilated woke to sternly resisting life. There had been terrific fighting on the whole front Brabant to Ornes. Once more a frightful bombardment had opened with the dawn. Once more the German infantry had advanced in masses. They found the trenches in front of them weakly held, had occupied them. But en route a storm of shells had rained down on the swarming columns, had strewn the ground with dead and dying. Further advance was barred by sheets of rifle fire, torrents of machine-gun bullets. There were ugly rumours as to losses. The day's objective had not been reached. Counter-attacks had flung the grey infantry out of positions already conquered.

During the black night of the 22nd-23rd, while the

gun teams of the German batteries strained and stumbled forward over a shell-torn ground to new positions, the French left flank had fallen back from Brabant. The German guns hurled an avalanche of projectiles blindly upon the new lines of defence, more or less at hazard, since no longer did they have them accurately marked upon the map. Once more the grey masses swept forward, once more the hail of shells beat them down. The end of that day saw the centre pushed in with wild confusion, but the French resistance still alive, determined to perish rather than break. Once more the objective had not been attained. Douaumont was not even menaced. The time-table was hopelessly out. That night the French fell back on both flanks, withdrew from Ornes.

The fourth day dawned—the appointed day for final victory—and still the struggle continued fiercer than ever. Slowly, slowly, the German infantry pressed forward, leaving behind them a sea of helpless bodies— a grey carpet as perceived from a distance. The artillery fire swelled and mounted in paroxysms of incredible violence, the German guns hammering in savage persistence, the French batteries lurking for their target, overwhelming it in a deluge. On and on pressed the grey infantry, thrust dangerously, as night fell, straight at the heart, towards Fort Douaumont. A fierce conflict—body to body, rifles that flashed in the face of the victim, bayonets perforce shortened for the thrust, gripping fingers clutched at the throat as men wrestled and swayed—raved and roared in an indescribable tumult on the Ornes-Louvemont road. The defenders had made a supreme rally. The Germans fought like men who grasp at victory, maddened that it is withheld. The French fought like heroes, desperately outnumbered, who know their duty is to die. When night fell the defence was still intact, but the French had withdrawn to their last line, covering Douaumont.

"We have still one more day," said the German

general to the distinguished neutral that night in the great map-hung apartment. "We allowed that margin of time. To-morrow will see our greatest effort, Douaumont in our hands, Verdun untenable." The dark eyes of the neutral read a certain nervousness in the German's face, despite the confident tone.

"It has proved rather more difficult than you expected?"

"The French field-guns have been terrible—terrible," replied the German. "Without them——" He waved an expressive hand. "But to-morrow we shall deliver the *coup de grâce*. We have not boasted idly, Excellenz." His eyes looked searchingly through their pince-nez on the calmly interested face of the neutral. "When Germany threatens she performs."

On the morning of the 25th the German guns roared over white fields of snow, through veils of the softly falling flakes that fluttered inexhaustibly from the leaden sky. Their thunder swelled louder and ever louder as the batteries which had changed position consequently upon the French withdrawal during the night, got to work, searching for their target, more or less accurately finding it despite the difficulty of observation. Not a minute was to be lost. The anxious German staff knew that the reinforcements of their foes must be hurrying —hurrying. Some perhaps had already arrived. If night fell without definite victory, the morrow would surely see fresh masses against them re-invigorating the defence. Victory to-day—complete victory—Douaumont captured, the pursuit pressed into the streets of Verdun—meant victory indeed. Mighty, therefore, was the effort. By noon every German battery was firing at its maximum. Under the leaden sky, over the white ground, in the still cold of a bitter frost, their thunder swelled and crashed, roaring in a never-ending frenzy. Eighteen German divisions were massed to break down all opposition. Already they had attacked—again and

again. Again and again the rapid detonations of the
French guns had leaped into the din, smiting desperately, frantically, to stay them. Over there, in the
mist-hung gullies of the plateau, on its bare open spaces
between the woods, the snow had ceased to be white
—save where it fell freshly upon the huddled bodies of
the fallen.

In the afternoon the weather cleared somewhat.
More distant views were possible. On the higher of
the Twins of Ornes, the knolls just south-west of the
Forêt de Spincourt, stood the figure who more than any
other individual would have to dare the answer for all
the agony rolled out there before him, spread over
continents, crying to strange stars. Spiked helmet on
his head, long grey cavalry cloak wrapped about him
his field-glasses held to his eyes by the right hand only,
he gazed upon the now distant conflict. At his side
stood a younger figure, his face masked also by binoculars. Behind them was a group of dignitaries, generals
of high position, the distinguished neutral and the
Oberst who never quitted him. All gazed to the wooded
scarp of the Heights of the Meuse, their glasses pointing
south-south-west.

The great masses of woodland rose dark from the
snow of the plain—a long stretch of undulating, climbing
tree-tops. Beyond them the bare bulk of the plateau
humped itself yet higher, dirty grey against the sky.
It rose to a culminating knoll—Douaumont! All that
bare plateau was whelmed in a drifting reek, but the
highest point was like a volcano in eruption. Great
founts of smoke shot up from it incessantly, spread in
the air in heavy plumes that overhung. It was the
objective of the Third Corps (Brandenburgers), attacking under the eye of the Kaiser so particularly their chief.
Their orders were that Douaumont was to be taken at
all costs. On the Twin of Ornes operators from Army
Headquarters had taken over the telephone dug-out.
Behind them the line was clear to Berlin—waiting—

waiting for the triumphant announcement that should thrill the world.

Somewhat impatiently the neutral scanned the lofty distances where the great drama was being enacted. Innumerable puffs of bursting shells indicated the conflict but gave no hint of its varying fortunes. The professional instinct was strong within him, the report to his government an ideal to which it strove. To perfect that report he must see the fight at closer quarters, must describe the effects of the French fire as a complement to the already written minute on the German batteries. His keen eye picked out a position of vantage on the Heights. Then he waited for an opportunity, alert for a moment when the eye of majesty should rest itself from the distant view, should fall upon him. The opportunity occurred. The glance of the All Highest swept over him, preoccupied. The neutral stepped forward, saluted, indicated the far-off point.

"*Ich bitte um Erlaubnis, Majestät*" ("I beg permission, your Majesty"), he said.

A frowning glance rested upon him for an instant, intolerant of aught save the mighty contest whose issue was the fate of nations.

"*Gestattet*" ("Granted"), was the curt, indifferent reply.

The German Oberst, standing behind the neutral, changed colour. He had no option but to accompany this damnable foreigner in his mad adventure into unnecessary danger. He, too, saluted *Majestät*, followed the neutral to the spot where a number of orderlies stood at the heads of saddled horses. They had been sent forward in case the dignitaries should require them.

In a few moments the two officers, followed by mounted attendants, were slithering down the snowy side of the knoll, were cantering across the valley toward Ornes.

High above them towered the dark Bois de la Chaume

as they threaded the debris-covered street of the wrecked
village. It was packed with Brandenburger infantry
waiting to advance. They followed the road southward,
at the foot of the hills, toward Bezonvaux. Everywhere
the infantry stood thick, waiting. The cannonade
mounted to a frightful intensity, appalling even the ears
now habituated to it, bewildering the senses, troubling
the sight. French shells came whining, screaming
rushing, to burst with loud crashes in the woodland
rising on their right hand, on the road and the fields
through which it passed. Domes of dark smoke leaped
upward from the earth, preceding the stunning, metallic
detonation. White shrapnel puffs clustered thickly
above the trees. Bezonvaux was a ruin. They turned
off from it to the right, up a rough track that climbed
into the woods. The snow on the track had been
trampled into a dirty slush. All about them lay bodies,
grey and blue; weapons pell-mell as they had fallen
from a suddenly opened grasp. Their horses shuddered,
whinnied, jerked nervous ears, moved disconcertingly
sideways from red stains soaking deep into the snow.

Just under the edge of the plateau the neutral stopped,
dismounted, threw his reins to an orderly. The Oberst
followed his example. His face was blotchy white, he
trembled in every limb.

"We shall see nothing, Excellenz—absolutely nothing," he asseverated, appealingly.

"We can at least try," replied his guest. "Something
is happening over there."

Above them, some distance ahead, was a tremendous
uproar, a chaos of violent thudding slams, splitting
crashes, a faint troublous murmur of human voices.
Behind them, up the rough track, a column of infantry
was advancing, overtaking them. They ascended with
a steady progress, splashing through the slush; officers
waving swords, shouting; rank upon rank of tense faces
that had lost their humanity in the tremulous brute;
glazed, staring eyes under the spiked helmets; singing,

507

singing like drugged, doomed gladiators marching to the arena. They passed upward.

The neutral, to whom his conductor had nervelessly surrendered the initiative, led the way. They left their horses behind them, struck off at a tangent to the right, through the woods, climbing always. They emerged upon the plateau, in a clearing. Across the open space, from a whelm of smoke and noise in the distance, groups of grey men were running swiftly toward them, shouting inarticulately. Along the edge of the woods was a line of pickets. Their weapons rose to the shoulder. Sternly, every fugitive but those wounded was driven again into the fight. Those who hesitated, screaming under the menace of the rifle, dropped shot.

The neutral hurried along the verge of the wood, scanning every tall tree carefully, expectantly. "Ah!" He had found what he sought. Against the green bark of a lofty beech dangled a rope ladder. It was an abandoned French artillery observation post. He scrambled up the ladder, followed by the trembling, shivering Oberst. High up among the topmost branches was a little platform.

The neutral settled himself, adjusted his binoculars, pushed aside the twigs. He looked out over an undulating terrain, dark with woods that ceased raggedly in deep indentations short of a bare hog's back that gathered itself into a hump. That bare ground was smothered in a turmoil of smoke that fumed to the grey sky, far to right and left. But through it, in chance rifts, his glasses revealed a dark mass upon the highest point. A reek of white smoke drifted away from it as from burning buildings, mingling with the darker clouds of incessant explosions. He had a glimpse of a rounded cupola. It was Douaumont!

The snow on the open space between the fort and the woods was grey. It was moving with crawling life like the festering of a stagnant pool. Over it burst occasional puffs of shrapnel.

"Ah!" The cry was involuntary from both the watching men. From the woods emerged masses of running tiny grey figures, running, running toward the fort. The open space was covered with them. A moment of tense expectation when the heart seemed to stop—and then, as by a terrible magic, great fountains of dark smoke and darker objects leaped up among those running figures, countless explosions. A canopy of vicious little shrapnel bursts in thousands spread itself over them. Under it men sprawled in great patches, seemed to be fighting the air ere they tumbled and fell. A horrid screaming, faint through the uproar. More masses rushed out, were beaten down. There was a running to and fro of men bewildered—a headlong flight.

The storm of fire did not cease. It rolled over the plateau toward the woods, remorselessly following the fugitives. Louder and louder, nearer and nearer, the crashes, the fountains, the puffs—the great mingled reek of the inferno—rolled toward the two men in the observation post.

The Oberst clutched the neutral's arm.

"Excellenz!" he shouted, stammeringly. "We must go. I insist. I have superior authority—written authority—my discretion—I insist!" he almost screamed. His hand groped for a scrap of paper which he waved. "Arrest!" he cried, like a maniac. "Arrest if you do not come!"

The storm of French shells was a very near menace. The neutral acquiesced with a shrug of his shoulders. Nimbly they descended the ladder.

On the ground they found themselves among a swarm of slightly wounded, terror-stricken men. One of them, a tall, bearded Brandenburger, his clothes torn to rags, was shrieking and laughing in a manner horrible to hear. His comrades drew away from him as he clutched at them. He was insane.

509

"Only I am left!" he cried. "Only I! They are all dead—dead—out there. They were meant to be dead. They were dead men before we attacked—all dead men running on—I could see it in their faces—only I was alive! And now they are still crawling—crawling—dead men!" His tone emphasized the horror of his words, struck a chill. A sentry lowered his rifle, irresolutely.

The maniac turned, waved a hand to the westward. The sun, on the point of setting, showed itself in a rift of the threatening snow clouds, sank, a great ball of glowing fire, over the rim of the plateau. Its last rays were lurid on the face of the madman, as he stood, arm, outstretched, his eyes flaming, his tangled beard falling upon his rags, like some antique prophet of the wilderness.

"Woe! Woe!" he shrieked. "*Nach Verdun! Nach Verdun—Verdunkelung!*" ("To Verdun. After Verdun eclipse!") He finished in a scream of maniac laughter, glorying in the crazy assonance of the words. "*Nach Verdun—Verdunkelung!*"

The neutral and the Oberst hurried through the woods to their horses.

A rapid ride with the German always in front, and once more they ascended the Twin of Ornes. As they arrived at the summit they found themselves among wildly cheering men. "*Douaumont! Douaumont is taken!*" Far away to the south-south-west, rocket after rocket shot up into the darkening sky. Already the great news had gone—electrical—to Berlin.

The crowd of dignitaries descended the steep path in the gloom to where the motor-cars were ranked in waiting. Along the road passed streams of wounded who could walk, phantoms half-distinguished in the dim light. Joyous were the voices of the War Lords. One, a familiar tone, chanted, "*Nach Verdun! Nach Verdun—Paris!*"

Out of the darkness came a screamed reply, a burst of insane laughter.

510

"*Nach Verdun—Verdunkelung! Nach Verdun—Verdunkelung!*"

It was the voice of the crazed Brandenburger. There was a scuffle, the sound of a man hurried away, resisting.

All through that dark journey, as the car bumped and lurched over the atrocious roads, the words beat in a refrain through the mind of the neutral. "*Nach Verdun —Verdunkelung!*" He wondered, Eclipse? Was it the sun of Germany that set on the French position? The Oberst was loquaciously cheerful.

That night, in the great map-hung apartment, the War Lords received the news that their further advance was barred.

Next morning a furious counter-attack surrounded a handful of defenders in the fort for which they had paid so much. The French reinforcements had arrived.

by W. W. Jacobs

THREE AT TABLE
by W. W. Jacobs

A NATIONAL institution is embodied in the quiet personality of W. W. Jacobs. It is not too much to say that such droll characters as Bob Pretty, Sam Small and Ginger Dick, and even many of the "walking-on" parts in the Jacobean human comedy, are as real in the imagination of the British public, as are the characters of Dickens. But that Jacobs is also a master of the grim and the dramatic is shown in *Three at Table*, which immortalizes a brave act with extraordinary art. Creatively, Jacobs is akin to the exuberant mirth-makers of English fiction: but in the discipline which he exercises as a writer he is a veritable Flaubert. He never begins to write a story until he has thought it out in every detail to the end. Jacobs was born in London, in 1863, and educated at private schools. Entering the civil service, he was a clerk in the Savings Bank department for sixteen years.

THREE AT TABLE

BY

W. W. Jacobs

THE talk in the coffee-room had been of ghosts and apparitions, and nearly everybody present had contributed his mite to the stock of information upon a hazy and somewhat threadbare subject. Opinions ranged from rank incredulity to childlike faith, one believer going so far as to denounce unbelief as impious, with a reference to the Witch of Endor, which was somewhat marred by being complicated in an inexplicable fashion with the story of Jonah.

"Talking of Jonah," he said solemnly, with a happy disregard of the fact that he had declined to answer several eager questions put to him on the subject, "look at the strange tales sailors tell us."

"I wouldn't advise you to believe all those," said a bluff, clean-shaven man, who had been listening without speaking much. "You see, when a sailor gets ashore he's expected to have something to tell, and his friends would be rather disappointed if he had not."

"It's a well-known fact," interrupted the first speaker firmly, "that sailors are very prone to see visions."

"They are," said the other dryly; "they generally see them in pairs, and the shock to the nervous system frequently causes headache next morning."

"You never saw anything yourself?" suggested an unbeliever.

"Man and boy," said the other, "I've been at sea thirty years, and the only unpleasant incident of that kind occurred in a quiet English countryside."

"And that?" said another man.

"I was a young man at the time," said the narrator,

517

drawing at his pipe and glancing good-humouredly at the company. "I had just come back from China, and my own people being away I went down into the country to invite myself to stay with an uncle. When I got down to the place I found it closed and the family in the South of France; but as they were due back in a couple of days I decided to put up at the 'Royal George,' a very decent inn, and await their return."

"The first day I passed well enough; but in the evening the dullness of the rambling old place, in which I was the only visitor, began to weigh upon my spirits, and the next morning, after a late breakfast, I set out with the intention of having a brisk day's walk.

"I started off in excellent spirits, for the day was bright and frosty, with a powdering of snow on the iron-bound roads and nipped hedges, and the country had to me all the charm of novelty. It was certainly flat, but there was plenty of timber, and the villages through which I passed were old and picturesque.

"I lunched luxuriously on bread and cheese and beer in the bar of a small inn, and resolved to go a little farther before turning back. When at length I found I had gone far enough, I turned up a lane at right angles to the road I was passing, and resolved to find my way back by another route. It is a long lane that has no turning, but this had several, each of which had turnings of its own, which generally led, as I found by trying two or three of them, into the open marshes. Then, tired of lanes, I resolved to rely upon the small compass which hung from my watch-chain and go across country, home.

"I had got well into the marshes when a white fog, which had been for some time hovering round the edge of the ditches, began gradually to spread. There was no escaping it, but by aid of my compass I was saved from making a circular tour and fell instead into frozen ditches or stumbled over roots in the grass. I kept my course, however, until at four o'clock, when night was

coming rapidly up to lend a hand to the fog, I was fain
to confess myself lost.

"The compass was now no good to me, and I wandered about miserably, occasionally giving a shout on
the chance of being heard by some passing shepherd or
farm hand. At length by great good luck I found my
feet on a rough road driven through the marshes, and
by walking slowly and tapping with my stick managed
to keep to it. I had followed it for some distance when
I heard footsteps approaching me.

"We stopped as we met, and the new arrival, a sturdy-
looking countryman, hearing of my plight, walked back
with me for nearly a mile, and putting me on to a road
gave me minute instructions how to reach a village some
three miles distant.

"I was so tired that three miles sounded like ten, and
besides that, a little way off from the road I saw dimly
a lighted window. I pointed it out, but my companion
shuddered and looked round him uneasily.

"'You won't get no good there,' he said hastily.

"'Why not?' I asked.

"'There's a something there, sir,' he replied, 'what
'tis I dunno, but the little 'un belonging to a gamekeeper
as used to live in these parts see it, and it was never
much good afterward. Some say as it's a poor mad
thing, others says as it's a kind of animal; but whatever
it is, it ain't good to see.'

"'Well, I'll keep on, then,' I said. 'Good night.'

"He went back whistling cheerily until his footsteps
died away in the distance, and I followed the road he
had indicated until it divided into three, any one of
which to a stranger might be said to lead straight on.
I was now cold and tired, and having half made up my
mind walked slowly back toward the house.

"At first all I could see of it was the little patch of
light at the window. I made for that until it disappeared suddenly, and I found myself walking into a
tall hedge. I felt my way round this until I came to a

519

small gate, and opening it cautiously, walked, not without some little nervousness, up a long path which led to the door. There was no light and no sound from within. Half repenting of my temerity I shortened my stick and knocked lightly upon the door.

"I waited a couple of minutes and then knocked again, and my stick was still beating the door when it opened suddenly and a tall, bony old woman, holding a candle, confronted me.

" 'What do you want?' she demanded gruffly.

" 'I've lost my way,' I said civilly; 'I want to get to Ashville.'

" 'Don't know it,' said the old woman.

"She was about to close the door when a man emerged from a room at the side of the hall and came toward us. An old man of great height and breadth of shoulder.

" 'Ashville is fifteen miles distant,' he said slowly.

" 'If you will direct me to the nearest village, I shall be grateful,' I remarked.

"He made no reply, but exchanged a quick, furtive glance with the woman. She made a gesture of dissent.

" 'The nearest place is three miles off,' he said, turning to me and apparently trying to soften a naturally harsh voice. 'If you will give me the pleasure of your company, I will make you as comfortable as I can.'

"I hesitated. They were certainly a queer-looking couple, and the gloomy hall with the shadows thrown by the candle looked hardly more inviting than the darkness outside.

" 'You are very kind,' I murmured irresolutely, 'but——'

" 'Come in,' he said quickly; 'shut the door, Anne.'

"Almost before I knew it I was standing inside and the old woman, muttering to herself, had closed the door behind me. With a queer sensation of being trapped I followed my host into the room, and taking the proffered chair warmed my frozen fingers at the fire.

" 'Dinner will soon be ready,' said the old man, regarding me closely. 'If you will excuse me——'

"I bowed and he left the room. A minute afterward I heard voices; his, and the old woman's, and, I fancied, a third. Before I had finished my inspection of the room he returned, and regarded me with the same strange look I had noticed before.

" 'There will be three of us at dinner,' he said, at length. 'We two and my son.'

"I bowed again and secretly hoped that that look didn't run in the family.

" 'I suppose you don't mind dining in the dark,' he said abruptly.

" 'Not at all,' I replied, hiding my surprise as well as I could, 'but really I'm afraid I'm intruding. If you'll allow me——'

"He waved his huge gaunt hands 'We're not going to lose you now we've got you,' he said with a dry laugh. 'It's seldom we have company, and now we've got you we'll keep you. My son's eyes are bad, and he can't stand the light. Ah, here is Anne.'

"As he spoke the old woman entered, and, eyeing me stealthily, began to lay the cloth, while my host, taking a chair the other side of the hearth, sat looking silently into the fire. The table set, the old woman brought in a pair of fowls ready carved in a dish, and placing three chairs left the room. The old man hesitated a moment, and then, rising from his chair, placed a large screen in front of the fire and slowly extinguished the candles.

" 'Blind man's holiday,' he said, with clumsy jocosity, and groping his way to the door opened it. Somebody came back into the room with him, and in a slow, uncertain fashion took a seat at the table, and the strangest voice I have ever heard broke a silence which was fast becoming oppressive.

" 'A cold night,' it said slowly.

"I replied in the affirmative, and light or no light, fell to with an appetite which had only been sharpened by

521

the snack in the middle of the day. It was somewhat difficult eating in the dark, and it was evident from the behaviour of my invisible companions that they were as unused to dining under such circumstances as I was. We ate in silence until the old woman blundered into the room with some sweets and put them with a crash upon the table.

"'Are you a stranger about here?'" inquired the curious voice again.

"I replied in the affirmative, and murmured something about my luck in stumbling upon such a good dinner.

"'Stumbling is a very good word for it,' said the voice grimly. 'You have forgotten the port, father.'

"'So I have,' said the old man, rising. 'It's a bottle of the "Celebrated" to-day; I will get it myself.'

"He felt his way to the door, and closing it behind him, left me alone with my unseen neighbour. There was something so strange about the whole business that I must confess to more than a slight feeling of uneasiness.

"My host seemed to be absent a long time. I heard the man opposite lay down his fork and spoon, and half fancied I could see a pair of wild eyes shining through the gloom like a cat's.

"With a growing sense of uneasiness I pushed my chair back. It caught the hearthrug, and in my efforts to disentangle it the screen fell over with a crash and in the flickering light of the fire I saw the face of the creature opposite. With a sharp catch of my breath I left my chair and stood with clenched fists beside it. Man or beast, which was it? The flame leaped up and then went out, and in the mere red glow of the fire it looked more devilish than before.

"For a few moments we regarded each other in silence; then the door opened and the old man returned. He stood aghast as he saw the warm firelight, and then, approaching the table, mechanically put down a couple of bottles.

" 'I beg your pardon,' said I, reassured by his presence, 'but I have accidentally overturned the screen. Allow me to replace it.'

" 'No,' said the old man gently, 'let it be. We have had enough of the dark. I'll give you a light.'

"He struck a match and slowly lit the candles. Then I saw that the man opposite had but the remnant of a face, a gaunt wolfish face in which one unquenched eye, the sole remaining feature, still glittered. I was greatly moved, some suspicion of the truth occurring to me.

" 'My son was injured some years ago in a burning house,' said the old man. 'Since then we have lived a very retired life. When you came to the door we—' his voice trembled, 'that is—my son——'

" 'I thought,' said the son simply, 'that it would be better for me not to come down to the dinner-table. But it happens to be my birthday, and my father would not hear of my dining alone, so we hit upon this foolish plan of dining in the dark. I'm sorry I startled you.'

" 'I am sorry,' said I, as I reached across the table and gripped his hand, 'that I am such a fool; but it was only in the dark that you startled me.'

"From a faint tinge in the old man's cheek and a certain pleasant softening of the poor solitary eye in front of me I secretly congratulated myself upon this last remark.

" 'We never see a friend,' said the old man apologetically, 'and the temptation to have company was too much for us. Besides, I don't know what else you could have done.'

" 'Nothing else half so good, I'm sure,' said I.

" 'Come,' said my host, with almost a sprightly air. 'Now we know each other, draw your chairs to the fire and let's keep this birthday in a proper fashion.'

"He drew a small table to the fire for the glasses and produced a box of cigars, and placing a chair for the old servant, sternly bade her to sit down and drink. If the talk was not sparkling, it did not lack for vivacity,

523

and we were soon as merry a party as I have ever seen. The night wore on so rapidly that we could hardly believe our ears when in a lull in the conversation a clock in the hall struck twelve.

" 'A last toast before we retire,' said my host, pitching the end of his cigar into the fire and turning to the small table.

"We had drunk several before this, but there was something impressive in the old man's manner as he rose and took up his glass. His tall figure seemed to get taller, and his voice rang as he gazed proudly at his disfigured son.

" 'The health of the children my boy saved!' he said, and drained his glass at a draught."

524

THE CAGE BIRD
by Francis Brett Young

FRANCIS BRETT YOUNG may still be described as one of the younger English authors of whom much is to be expected. He was born in 1884 and educated at the University of Birmingham, afterwards training as a doctor. He wrote *The Young Physician*, the best novel about the medical profession of modern times. His novel, *Love is Everything* won for him the James Tait Black Memorial Award. He served in East Africa during the European War, and now lives at Anacapri, Italy. *The Cage Bird*, which is a story about African life, is a fine example of his art as a short-story writer, so much being expressed within a small compass, while the character of the escaped convict, whose dauntless efforts to survive win our sympathy, is most convincingly portrayed.

THE CAGE BIRD

BY

Francis Brett Young

FOR story-telling there is one place that beats all
others in the world, and that is a camp-fire in
tropical Africa. It has no distractions. Even in a coy
library with curtained windows and coal-fire burning,
one's eyes will wander to the light that plays over the
backs of books or watch the creeping hands of a clock.
In Africa you get none of these things to disturb you.
The world shrinks into a small circle of firelight. Beyond
the edge of it nothing exists at all; and within it only
the story-teller and his listeners.

And that's not all: the men one meets in the scent of
wood-smoke have something to say. There are few
books in the bushveld, and those mostly bad ones; but
Africa is a country of full lives, and of these you only
hear from the mouths of the men who have lived them.
Great story-tellers! You sit and listen and the world
drifts away from you so that the sputter of a green
branch in the fire makes you jump. And then you see
yourself sitting on your haunches, the glow of the fire,
the fumes that sting your eyes; and all around you, in a
haze of Boer tobacco (that tastes like hay in Europe,
but in Africa is the best smoke in the world), you see
other listeners who have not awakened and still inhabit
the world of enchantment that you have just left. So
you reach out for another branch to throw on the
fire, or give the embers a kick. And the voice of
the chap who is telling the story goes on, and on, and
on.

The best hand at the game I ever met was Charlie
Murray, and he knew it. Get him after a dinner of

grilled eland-steak and a peg of whisky, and he'd talk you to sleep: not because his stories were sleepy, but from sheer staying power. Murray was a tremendous chap. He rode sixteen stone, with long stirrup-leathers, like the Boers, so that his feet nearly touched the ground on either side of his rat of a hunting pony. A tall, stiff figure, with shrewd blue eyes, a yellow moustache, and cheeks sun-dried like *biltong*: a dead shot, and the best of company.

When I knew him he had settled down to ranching on the edge of the Berg, which is the loveliest land in all Africa and as lovely as any in the world. He knew that it was beautiful, and warmed when one praised it; but though his life was busier than that of most men of his age, he lived in the past. And such a past! African born—his father had been a Free Stater—Murray had fought in five wars. He had seen the map of Africa shaken like a kaleidoscope, and helped to shake it. And yet he was no politician. He knew a man and esteemed him whatever his race or language: Dutch, Kafir or English were the same to him, for he spoke them all. It sounds as though I am shifting from my point; but that is not so. It is the fairness and sports-manship of the man's nature that come out so clearly in this queer story of his childhood. You can hear it and say to yourself: "That's Charlie Murray all over!" From that day to this he has scarcely changed a hair's breadth.

It happened, as I say, when he was quite a kid. They were living in Smitsdorp, a little town, important in its way, that lay a few miles north of the Caledon river that marks the Cape Colony and the Orange Free State. That is important to remember. His father was prosperous. Wool, I take it. Yes, it must have been wool; for I remember a story that Murray once told me. He was playing alone at the bottom of the garden with a little Kafir, when one of the house boys came rushing down upon them, picked them both up—one under each arm—and ran off, shaking the life out of them, to the house.

But it wasn't that. The house was full of the big, side-whiskered men of that generation, talking seriously together. All were armed, and none took any notice of Charlie.

Then came his mother, scrambling down the bamboo ladder that led to the loft, with a couple of old Dutch elephant guns: brutes that would take a couple of ounces of lead and kick you into the middle of last week. When she saw him she gave a gasp. "Thank God!" she said, but she didn't kiss him. She told him to run and fetch a pot of mutton fat, of the kind that they used to boil down from the tails of sheep, to grease the guns with. When he came back she took it from him without a word, and the room was so full that he slipped under the table with a dog called Bles and the little nigger that had been snatched up beside him.

From this refuge he caught stray words of the men's conversation. They were talking about Moshesh— Moshesh and the Basutos. And then the farm boys came running in with great bales of wool with which they began to pack the windows, so that the house grew dark. He was frightened by the dark and the trampling; he hated the greasy smell of wool, and the dust under the table made him sneeze; so he crawled out on to the *stoep* at the back of the house and asked his special chum, a Cape boy named Klaas September, what it was all about. Klaas pointed to the hills, the great lion-coloured foothills crouching in front of the Maluti Mountains. "Kafirs coming," he said. "Moshesh is a great king. They will crack your skull with their kerries like a snail-shell, and put a sharp stick into your body. Look, you can see them!"

But all that Charlie saw was a number of black dots scattered over the mountains like sheep, and a few ponies moving along the skyline; and before he knew where he was, his mother had found him again and hauled him in and put him to bed as a punishment for his wickedness and daring, in the loft where he and his elder brother slept. So he poked a hole in the thatch, and saw the men ride out from Smitsdorp. He heard shots fired and saw puffs of smoke on the mountain till he grew bored and went to sleep.

Next day, the Basutos had gone, the bales of wool were carried back to the store and the windows washed clear of the grease stains that the bales had made on them.

A long digression—but such digressions were the essence of Murray's stories.

Murray's father, then, was a wool merchant. Wool was his staple business; but in those early days a man of spirit took his turn at many things. He was also a solicitor, practising in the little Landdrost's Court at Smitsdorp. The Boers were a litigious race, and Murray's father generally had his hands full; for men who had to stand their trial knew that if they had a good case he would fight for them and that the bench respected him. Indeed, the two men with whom he had most to do in Smitsdorp were the magistrate and the governor of the jail.

The last was a deplorable affair; but in that poor country there was no money for a better. It was a great hollow square, like a cattle kraal, with high walls of undressed stone and a *chevaux de frise* of broken glass on the top. The back of the building lay up against the side of a hill, so that the innermost cells were walled with red rock through which, in the rainy season, water oozed and dripped. The safest jail in the Free State it was called. Certainly it was the most noisome, and for this reason it was the custom of the judges in Bloemfontein to send the more desperate criminals there to serve their sentences.

And here comes the most remarkable thing of all: that in a Boer country, among a race that has always recognized a colour bar, black men and white were imprisoned

together. Murray's father had always protested against
this: he had even induced the Smitsdorp burghers to
petition against it; but the answer was always the same:
the finances of the Free State wouldn't allow them to
erect separate prisons; when more money came in,
other arrangements might be made. This troubled old
Murray's mind. He knew that the jail was a disgrace
to the country. Whenever he went there he came back
sickened with its filth and its darkness, full of pity for
the chained savages inside. For they wore chains: a
heavy ring round the neck, another for each ankle, and
between them two lengths of half-inch chain that clanked
as they walked. At night they were chained together,
four to a cell.

The governor of the jail was a dark, violent Dutch-
man, a survivor of the Great Trek, who felt bitterly
towards all living creatures, and respected nobody but
Murray. He didn't live at the jail. He knew better
than that. He had his own farm a mile or more away,
and rode over in the evening to see the prisoners when
his other cattle had been kraaled. For the rest they
were left in the charge of four natives: a Griqua, named
April, and three Zulus, proud of their guns and their
uniform, lazy and tyrannous.

Except in winter, when it was swamped, the jail was
badly supplied with water, and so it came into old
Murray's mind one day that he might do himself and
the prisoners a good turn by giving them a chance of a
bathe in his dam. Rensburg, the governor, wouldn't
have understood it as an act of charity, so Murray
suggested that the prisoners might do an afternoon's
work on his land before they bathed, and Rensburg,
who was always ready to help a man who might be of
service to him in the future, particularly when he could
do so at the public expense, consented. Murray's
suggestion filled him with admiration. It was a slim
idea to get the work of twenty men for nothing under
the guise of charity. Murray knew what he was about!

And so Charlie Murray's story begins.

"By that time," he told us, "I was a boy of twelve or thirteen. They used to come over every Sunday, and I used to watch them grinding up the hill, twenty poor devils, sweating their souls out! The Zulu guard used to walk behind with a rifle, and April, the Griqua, in front with a pipe in his mouth. When they got to the top they'd halt and stand there panting like blown oxen, waiting to be told the work they had to do. Then they'd drag off with their chains into the fields. I remember how they used to make a rush for the dam—just like cattle—when the work was over, stripping off their coats and splashing the water up over their naked chests and faces. They'd some fine chests on them, too! April usually joined them, while the Zulu sat on the bank, smoking, with his rifle across his knees. While they were bathing, they became different creatures. You wouldn't believe it. They laughed and splashed one another like a lot of kids playing, and shouted out their Kafir jokes to the guard on the bank and to me. I used to answer them back in Kafir, too. It struck me as rather fine to be making jokes with murderers—particularly as I'd been forbidden to talk to them at all!

"Every Saturday, somehow or other, I managed to get down to the dam, and one day I got a surprise. I saw that one of the prisoners who had stripped along with the others was a white man. Earlier in the day, when they marched up, I hadn't noticed him. After that I couldn't help thinking of it, and when supper came along I couldn't keep it back.

" 'This afternoon one of the prisoners was a white man,' I said.

" 'How do you know that?' asked my father.

" 'I saw them bathing,' said I.

" 'Haven't you been told not to do that?' said my mother.

"But she, too, was interested. 'I thought that was all over,' she said. 'Didn't you speak about it?' She implied that if he *had* spoken about it, it was as good as done.

"'Yes,' said my father, 'I did speak about it, but it's no good! They say they have no room anywhere else.'

"'It's a scandal!' said my mother.

"'Yes, it's a scandal, but we can do nothing.'

"No more was said about it, and for some weeks I saw no more of the white prisoner. Then, one afternoon, I came down into the orchard where the convicts were earning their bathe by cultivating in between the trees. I came down there for a special reason: I wanted a nest out of the top of an almond tree. Up I went, thinking myself no end of a climber, showing off a bit, because I knew the poor devils were watching me. Then I missed my balance and came down a darned sight quicker than I'd climbed; and the next thing I knew I was sitting up, dazed, with the white prisoner on the ground beside me. 'How be 'ee, son?' he asked. 'A bit shaken up, I reckon. Was it that nest you were after?' I nodded. I didn't quite know where I was, but in another second that chap was shinning up the tree with his irons clanking on either side of him. He went up liked a darned monkey. I'd never seen a man climb so quickly. When he came down he had the eggs in his mouth and handed them over to me. 'If that's what you wanted,' he said, 'you've come to the right shop. There's not a tree in the world that I couldn't climb, even with these things on.' I asked him why. 'Because I'm a sailor,' he said, 'and a sailor has to go aloft in a gale of wind that'd blow your guts out.' I'd never seen a sailor before, and told him so. 'If you don't believe me,' he said, 'look at this!' And he stripped his arm to the shoulder and showed me the tatooing of a dragon that he'd got done in China, with flames coming out of its mouth. And on his chest he'd got a full-rigged ship with all her canvas set. 'Not a sheet out of place,' he said. And he may have been right. At any rate, you could read the ship's name. *Alabama* she was called.

"After that we stayed talking for a bit. I'd never. met a man in my life I liked better, and it was a rum experience, anyway, to be yarning with a chap that was doing time. I hoped he was a murderer; but he didn't look like it. I can see him now: a sturdy fellow with a broad chest—it had to be, to hold that ship—and bright brown eyes like a bird's. He had a beard that grew right up to them, brown and curly without a grey hair in it, and a hooked nose peeling with sunburn. The guard was smoking at the other end of the orchard, and so we sat down under the almond tree and he began telling me yarns about places he'd seen all over the world, hunting whales, diving for pearls, doing all the things that boys like to hear about but which had never come my way.

"He'd been everywhere, or said he had, and in any case, I believed him. And then suddenly he dropped back into talking about his own home in Devonshire: a place called Ditsam, if I remember rightly. My people never talked about England. My father had quarrelled with his parents and never made it up; he wanted to forget about it. But it seemed to me that boys had a much better time there than in the Free State, tickling trout in the streams and bird-nesting in the hedges. I didn't know what a hedge meant. There we sat talking, and the time slipped by. And then, all of a sudden I saw Crang rolled over from behind, and the Zulu guard kicking him as if he'd kill him. The brute had got boots on, too. Poor old Crang got mixed up in his chain, and couldn't find his feet. When he did he looked at me, and if ever I saw murder in a man's eyes I saw it that day. He never said a word. He just marched off to join the others with the Zulu blackguard kicking him behind. If he had showed fight I believe I should have joined in. I cried about it that night, though I didn't dare to tell my father. After seeing

Crang's eyes I made sure he was in for murder, and that was a point in his favour.

"So, next week, I waited for him—they were still working on the orchard, and we had another talk. By gad, it was like a new world to me. I'd never been farther from home than Bloemfontein. The week after, I pinched some of the tobacco my dad kept for the Kafirs, and gave it to Crang. It was a treat to see the chap chew! 'You've saved my life, son, and that's the truth!' he told me. It seemed to do him good to get things off his chest, to talk about the sort of life he led in the *tronk*, as the Boers call a jail. That Kafir guard was a fair devil. You can understand it. The man was a savage by nature, and no check on him, for Rensburg drew his salary for looking after the jail, and left it at that. If ever a white man suffered hell, poor Crang did. They slept four together in a hole like a pigsty. Crang lay at the end of the chain, next to a lousy Basuto horse-thief. You don't believe it? But it's true! This actually happened under the Boer Government of the Free State in the 'sixties!

"Well, my heart fairly bled for the poor devil, and when I'd plucked up my last ounce of courage, I managed to ask him what he was in for.

"'Son,' he said, 'it's manslaughter; but I swear to God I'm as innocent as a lamb!'

"To tell you the truth, I'd much rather it had been murder, and Crang guilty; but it seemed that he was merely serving a sentence of five years in chains.

"'Five years,' he said, 'and only six months gone!'

"He told me that he'd have committed suicide long ago if he'd had the chance. He would have drowned himself in father's dam. The trouble was that he could swim like a fish, and couldn't sink if he tried. 'I'd have done it at night,' he said, 'but what can you do when you're chained to a dirty Basuto? You couldn't bleed to death without waking him, and I haven't got a knife. Now, what would you do, son?'

"I took it very seriously, but I'm hanged if I could tell him. What I wanted to be getting at was the story of his crime, and I begged him to tell me.

" 'Understand first of all, that I'm innocent,' he said. And I told him I believed him.

"It was a long yarn. He had deserted his ship at Port Elizabeth, as lots of men did in those early days of the diamonds, and had been tramping to Kimberley. On the way he put up for the night at a Jew store somewhere near Bethulie, and got blind drunk. That same night some Kafirs broke into the store, killed the Jew, and left Crang asleep. Next day Crang woke to discover the murder. He was still fuddled, but clear enough to make his way to the next farm and to report the crime. The farmer was one of the Landdrost's court, and Crang, instead of being thanked, found himself arrested. Everything was against him. The Kafirs gave evidence. They had heard sounds of a struggle in the night. And here was a desperate character, an Englishman, tramping to the diamond fields with a fair sum of money in his pocket, and he too drunk to know what he had done. It was lucky that they didn't make it murder. Five years in chains, and not a friend in the country!

"Now, if there's one thing that appeals to a boy it's a sense of justice. I believed the chap. He'd cried like a child when he told me, and I'd cried with him. That night I had it out with my father; told him the whole story as Crang had given it to me. First, I got a good hiding for having talked to him; then my father said he'd see about it. And he did. I knew he would, and kept quiet, waiting to hear what he'd say. That week I only saw Crang for a second. 'I've told my dad about you,' I said. 'God bless you,' says he, 'that was the luckiest nest that ever I took.'

"Next day my father called me up to him. 'Charlie,' he said, 'I've been looking into the matter of that man Crang. I've had his papers from the court at Bloemfontein, and it's just possible he may have told you the truth.'

"It seems that he went straight up to old Rensburg and put the case to him. Then he got him to ride along with him to the *tronk*. They saw Crang together, heard his story, and talked it over. My father pointed out to Rensburg that Crang was the only white man in the place, and that it wasn't fair to chain him up to a Kafir and let him be knocked about by a black guard. Rensburg saw the force of this, particularly when my father told him that this was the way to make the Kafirs get above themselves. So they came to an agreement. My father made himself responsible for Crang. Crang swore on his honour that he wouldn't try to escape if he had his chains knocked off and was allowed to sleep in a pigsty of his own. And next time that they came to the dam I saw Crang without his chains.

"He just caught a moment to thank me. 'Charlie,' he said, 'I'll never forget you as long as I live. I tell you, it's heaven!' Well, if the *tronk* at Smitsdorp was heaven, it must have been pretty hellish before.

"And so it went on. Every Saturday we met and had a yarn: sometimes it was just a whisper. By that time I'd decided that I was going to be a sailor myself! Great times we had . . . Sometimes he'd talk about his life in the *tronk;* sometimes we didn't mention it; but all the time I knew that he was having a pretty rough passage with the guard, who could knock him about even though he wasn't chained. But Crang was a plucky fellow, and never grumbled. He'd had more than one chance of escape, and would have taken it like a bird if he hadn't given his word to my father. He told me so, quite frankly. You couldn't help admiring the chap, and so I used to do everything that I could for him; slipping a bit of meat off my plate at dinner-time, or pinching a few inches of tobacco and an old pipe of my father's. So two years passed. . . .

539

"Then we had a nasty knock. My father died. You'd never have thought it of a great strong chap like that; but the winters in the Free State are worse than anything you get up here. He got pneumonia, and wouldn't lie in. He had a case on, and his client depended on him. It was the worst thing I remember in my life; but it made a man of me. I was fifteen, and the only son. We had only the farm to live by, and I had to take on the whole weight of it. You see, I was a big chap for my age. What's more, my father had made good friends, so that if it came to sales some of them would give a lift to my stuffs, or let me in easy if I wanted to buy. It turned my head a bit, I don't mind telling you; but I worked like a horse for all that. I never saw Crang for weeks on end.

"One afternoon I came across him in the same old orchard, and the sight of him gave me a shock. The man had fallen away to nothing. His nose was like a bird's beak, and his eyes sunk in his head.

" 'Well, Charlie,' he says, 'So you've forgotten me.'

"I flushed up properly. I hadn't exactly forgotten him, but I hadn't taken any trouble to see him. He came up closer, and I saw that one eye and all that side of his temple were black with a bruise.

" 'What have you been up to?' I said.

" 'It's that blasted Zulu,' says he. 'He's got a down on me, and so have all the other niggers in the *tronk*. It's no good; it's one against twenty-three, and your poor dad's dead and gone. I'm worse off now than ever I was.'

"Then he came right up to me. 'Look here, Charlie,' he said. 'I gave your dad a promise. I've kept it. That's true, ban't it?'

" 'Certainly you've kept it,' I said.

" 'And now he's dead and gone,' he went on, 'that promise is still there. I don't want to put a slur on his memory. But this I tell you straight, I'm done. I can't go on!' I didn't need telling that, I could see that the

540

chap was done. 'It's this way,' he said. 'I reckon you've come into your father's promise. If you want to bind me to it, I'm bound. But if you release me from it, I'm off. I think I see my way to it.'

"I could say nothing. 'I'll ask my mother,' I said.

" 'Now for God's sake,' says he, 'don't go and drag a woman into it! Just tell me this: am I free of my word? Will you give it back to me?'

"Well, what could I do? 'Yes,' I said. 'As far as I'm concerned, you're free.'

"Thank God, you're a sportsman, Charlie,' he said. He gave me a good old handshake. 'And now there's one thing more. Will you help me?'

"Well, that was a question I didn't wait to answer. A lad of fifteen does not think much about laws of things of that sort. I said 'Yes' at once, and asked him what he wanted me to do.

" 'Not much,' he said. 'I want you to give me a rough chart of the country and tell me a place where I can lie quiet for the night. Then I want you to put me up some food and a suit of your dad's clothes. That's all.'

"So we had a talk about the lie of the land and the course of the Caledon river. His idea, you see, was to get out of the Free State as quickly as possible, and the river was the boundary between it and the Cape Colony. We decided that he might spend the night in a poplar thicket at the top of our valley, four or five miles above the dam. There used to be a Boer farm there, but they just went north with their wagons, like they do, and left the place to go to waste. Above the dam the hillside rises pretty steeply—it's almost a cliff—and we settled that next Saturday I should hide the clothes, with a loaf of bread and some *biltong*, at the top of it.

" 'Leave the rest to me,' said Crang; and at this the Zulu blackguard came up, and we said no more.

"That next Saturday was the most exciting day of my life up to date. It was a blazing hot morning. I

541

hid the clothes and the food at the top of the cliffs, as
we'd arranged, and then I waited in the bushes on the
other side to see what would happen. The afternoon
was a scorcher, too. The convicts came up and did
their bit of work. Then the two guards marched them
down to the dam. They began to strip for bathing.
And I lay there watching Crang. You've got to remember that he was the only man without chains.

"He didn't seem in any hurry to bathe. I saw him
at a distance, slinking round the edge of the dam like a
dog that's got scent of something, and looking out of the
corner of his eye at the Zulu who had the gun. It was
the best play that ever I saw! When the other guard
saw the prisoners in the water he couldn't resist it. He
stripped naked and went and lay in it, and the Zulu
watched him. He was stretched out on the ground with
his rifle on a rock a yard or two away. I saw old Crang
hovering over that rifle like a hawk; but the Zulu had
half an eye on it too, and there was nothing doing. It
was a queer thing—you could see that nigger thinking
of the cool water as he lay there in the heat. I kept on
saying to myself: 'Why don't you get in, you swine?'
It almost seemed as if by thinking of it you could make
him do it. Know what I mean? Poor old Crang must
have been thinking just the same as myself. . . .

"Then suddenly the Zulu got up on his haunches
and began to pull at his coat. 'It's coming,' I thought.
'By gad, it's coming!' Crang came a bit nearer, and
the guard asked him why he hadn't washed according
to orders. Crang slunk off again. I couldn't hear what
he said. The Zulu began to rub his naked chest with
his nails, like a great monkey scratching. Then he got
up and went to the edge of the water.

"It all came in a second. As soon as his back was
turned, Crang was on that rifle. The Zulu swung round.
'It's murder,' I thought, 'and if it is, I'm in it. Crang's
a white man.' But there was no need for that. Crang
swung the rifle in the air and brought it down on a rock,

splintering the butt to pieces. That was his plan. All that he feared was that rifle. Otherwise, he knew they couldn't catch him. He was off like a flash, and the Zulu after him. Up the hillside, over the rocks—I've never seen a man climb like that in my life, and the Zulu wasn't far behind him. It was a pretty even match, for poor old Crang was weak with want of food. At the top of the *kranz* the Zulu was gaining. Crang stopped and picked up a big rock. He heaved it over his head. 'You black swine,' he shouted, 'if you move another yard I'll dash your dirty brains out!' He could have done it, and the Zulu knew. He stopped, and Crang went on up the mountain like a damn rock-rabbit. And there was I, forgetting that I was supposed not to be there, standing up above the bushes shouting: 'Go it—go it!' at the top of my voice!

"I went home that evening more excited than I can tell you. I wanted to take someone into my confidence, but there was nobody but my mother, and I was scared of her. She was too good. Next morning, at daybreak, I rode up to the place I'd hidden the clothes. They were gone. 'Well, that's over,' I thought; 'I've finished with Crang for life.'

"Of course, you know the proper end of this story. Crang ought to have died a millionaire and left me his fortune. Well, he didn't, or you may bet your soul I shouldn't be here this night. For a year or two I often thought of him; and then he went right out of my mind. A good deal happened in those years.

"We sold the house and farm at Smitsdorp. After my father died there was no point in living so near the town. We moved to a new place sixteen miles away from the dorp. When I was eighteen I fell in love with my first; and that's quite enough to keep a man's mind busy.

"One evening—I can't even tell you the year—I was ploughing. None of your tractors in those days! I'd sent the niggers off to the compound, and went on ploughing myself right up to sunset. I wanted to finish a big patch for the mealies, and as I ploughed I was thinking of Bessie so that I hardly knew what I was doing. I went round and round that field so that by sunset there was only a narrow strip to finish. 'Well,' I thought, 'I may as well get it done while I'm about it.' There was a moon, you see. So I gave old Scotland a flick with the whip, and told him he'd have to finish it. You could talk to that ox like you'd talk to a dog.

"All through that last half-hour I saw that there was a fellow watching me on the edge of the ploughland. I noticed him specially because you might go for six months without seeing a stranger on our new farm. I wondered what he wanted, though I'd no intention of stopping my work to ask him. When I'd finished, I left the plough where it was and started driving the span of oxen home; and then he came to meet me, a little chap, dressed all in black, like a shopkeeper, with a bilcock hat on his head and a little black bag in his hand. He came up to me and took off his hat. I guessed he wanted to sell something, and was ready to turn him off. 'Is this Mr. Charles Murray?' he says. 'That's my name,' says I. 'Well, you've grown away all right!' he said.

"I laughed. 'And who might you be?' I asked.

" 'Don't you remember me?' says he.

" 'No, I don't,' said I.

"Then he stripped off his coat and rolled up his sleeves, holding out his arm. I thought the chap was mad.

" 'Take a look at this,' he said.

"Then I saw it was tattooed with a great dragon. 'By God!' says I, 'it's Crang!'

" 'Crang it is!' said he. 'I thought you'd remember me, son.'

"I took him by the arm. 'You'd better come along to the house and have some supper,' said I.

544

" 'No, son,' says he. 'I daren't do it. This is the Free State, and there's a warrant still out against me. But I'd like to have a yarn all the same.'

"So I left the oxen to graze, and we two sat down on the veld and talked in the moonlight. It was a queer story he told me. After he got clear of the guard on that Saturday afternoon he had gone to the poplar grove where we'd settled he should hide. In the middle of the night he'd come back for the food and the suit of clothes. And then he had a stroke of bad luck. I told you that the stuff was hidden at the top of a cliff? Well, in the dark, poor old Crang missed his footing, fell twenty feet, and smashed his arm. A fine old business for a man as weak as he was! But he stuck to it, and got his clothes, and the next night he struggled across country somehow or other to the Caledon river. And there he had another bit of bad luck. The river was in flood, and he had to swim it, broken arm and all. He must have been pretty near dead when he reached the other side.

"And here comes the funny part of the business. He had to get his arm mended somehow or other; there was no hospital nearer than Aliwal North; and, if you'll believe it, the only hospital there was the jail! Out of one jail and into another! I tell you we had a good laugh over it. But that jail was a British one, and heaven after Smitsdorp. They looked after him finely for a couple of months and turned him out cured.

"Then he went down to Port Elizabeth, and got work of some sort. He saved a bit of money—Smitsdorp had cured him of the drink for life—and set up in a coal and wood business on his own. He must have made a pretty good thing of it; money was easier to make in those days; but the man could never get the diamond fields out of his mind. So just before I saw him he'd sold up his business and treked off again, going this time by the coach that used to run from Port Elizabeth to Kimberley. That coach passed through Smitsdorp;

and when he saw the old *tronk* on the side of the hill he
had remembered me and felt it his duty to let me know
he was alive, and to thank me. That shows you he was
a good sort; for, as he said, the warrant was still out
against him. He went to the hotel in Smitsdorp, and
there he found out that we'd left the place. But that
didn't stop him. He walked a good sixteen miles over
the veld to find me, and did it, as I've told you.

"I asked him if I could help him with money, but he
opened his black bag and showed me that it was crammed
with bank-notes and gold. 'I'm a rich man,' he said,
'and in Kimberley I shall double it.' I shook my head,
but there was no stopping him. 'It's a fine moonlight
night,' he said, 'and I'd better be getting on my way.'

"So he shook hands. 'You'll see me again, son, never
fear,' he said. 'I'll write to you from Kimberley.' It
was a funny thing to see that little chap, with his black
bag, moving off into the dusk. When I was just losing
sight of him he turned and waved to me. I've never
liked any man better in my life.

"That was the last of him, and the last I heard. He
never wrote to me from Kimberley. Perhaps he lost
all his money and was ashamed. Perhaps—I don't
know—at that time the Kimberley diggings were about
the most unhealthy place on earth. They used to get a
kind of malaria or typhus—they called it 'Diggings
Fever'—and men died there like flies. I expect that was
what happened to poor old Crang. Well, he'd had a
good run for his money; he'd thanked me for the little
help I gave him, and he'd got to Kimberley. He'd
always told me that his chief ambition was to find a
rough diamond, and that's just about the best name
you could give him. I reckon we'll have another pipe,
and turn in. . . ."

COMMAND
by *Albert Richard Wetjen*

ALBERT RICHARD WETJEN was born in 1903 and, true to a race of forbears who had always suffered from "wander-lust," ran away to sea when he was fourteen. Within two years he was twice wrecked, once in the Bay of Fundy, by fire, and once near Cape Race, by fog and sea. He has been "on the beach" in Canada. After spells of rail-roading, stevedoring, farming and mining, he joined the crew of the *Berwick Castle* and was on board that ship when the captain took the Sultan of Zanzibar as a prisoner of war to St. Helena. This adventure provided Wetjen with the material for his first story. During the European War he served in the British Merchant Service and won two medals. His sea-stories are remarkable for their truth and insight into the pyschology and character of sea-faring men, and *Command* is an unforgettable study of the courage that lies beneath the apparent ease of a ship's captain.

COMMAND

BY
ALBERT RICHARD WETJEN

HE had been trained in such a school that the normal state of his features was one of impassiveness. His jaw was granite; not prominent, but terribly firm. It had had to cope with a good deal in its time. The eyes were steady and very clear in the tan of the lined face. At the temples the brown hair was a little white, though he had not yet reached his forty-fifth birthday. He walked with a firm, confident tread. He was aloof, remote and tranquil. No one, save, perhaps, another master, knew what years and immense happenings, fears and hopes had gone into making him like he was.

His name was Arthur Stewart Taplow, and he commanded the three-funnelled liner *Santhia*. She was a mighty craft, thirty thousand tons. She flew the flag of the Royal Mail. She ran to a clock-like schedule. She was the finest sort of thing that man had built for navigating the great waters.

Below her decks the engines spun ceaselessly. They did not stamp and reel and grunt after the manner of old. They were the latest turbines, as quiet almost as electric motors. The men tending them were alert and neat, not the tired grimy men the sea was used to. In her stokehold there was no rattle and clang of shovels in coal or the jarring clamour of the ash-hoist to torture the air. The *Santhia* burned oil. She was modern in every detail. Her chart room bristled with scientific devices. Wireless stations ashore kept in touch and gave her her position in case she was not sure of it. A whisper of trouble on her sea journeys and nations sprang to her assistance.

Going down the river with the *Santhia* were two other craft. One was a coast barge laden with cement. Her sails were dun-coloured and her hull was daubed with tar. The other vessel was a rusty red-sided tramp laden with coal for Mexico. On her bridge walked her captain, a fat man with a walrus moustache and dressed in greasy serges. On the poop of the sailing-barge, steering, was a man almost as fat and attired in blue dungaree pants and a flannel shirt with the sleeves rolled up. He wore a dirty peaked cap and smoked a clay pipe. The peculiar part of it all was that each man bore the same ageless, impassive look that graced the face of Captain Taplow on the *Santhia*. For you must understand that the mark of the sea is imprinted on all alike and it does not matter really, when the test comes, whether you command a smack out of Lowestoft or a white-walled liner flying the flag of the Royal Mail. And scientific devices are not of much use when the rack rips across the sky and the white-capped combers are roaring in from the horizon.

Which was why Captain Taplow, for all he walked a broad bridge and was surrounded by calm and efficient men, was just a little nervous under his outward tranquilness. He was so keyed up, so fully a creature of ships and the sea, that his ears absorbed every sound and his eyes missed nothing.

He might be saying to the pilot, "Yes, old Hamlin's a good man. Best president the Line ever had . . ." But he was thinking, "The red and white buoy over by Scorp's Landing's not in place . . . Oh, yes, it was reported removed for repairs. There's the substitute."

And even as he listened to the pilot's reply about Hamlin, he heard the hoarse shouting of a man on the fore deck of the collier, and he noticed the captain of the sailing-barge spin his wheel sharply as his great mainsail commenced to shiver. Not only did he hear and note these small matters. He was hearing and noting every other such matter that impinged upon his senses: the swirl of black water over a mud bank; the bow wave lifted by a racing launch that gave a good idea of the speed; the man standing by the collier's windlass which indicated she was very likely going to anchor; the various screechings and hootings of sirens up and down the mighty river. That was his business. Command. . . .

He sat at his table in the brilliantly-lighted saloon and smiled gravely as he listened to a New York banker dilate on the war debts. Over by the great curving main stairway a grey-haired passenger was in hot argument with the chief steward. There had been some mistake about seating him. He desired to be at the captain's table. He was a pompous and wealthy man with a vast opinion of himself, but he was also a shareholder in the company. He had brought a letter from old Hamlin, the president. The chief steward glanced across, over the heads of the diners and caught the captain's eye. The captain nodded imperceptibly and the steward grew all at once urbane and smiling. He deftly whisked an astonished young lady from her chair near the captain and flourished the shareholder into it. But by that time the captain was murmuring a very discreet joke to the stern-looking woman seated on his left.

He had barely finished and was reaching for his soup spoon when a quartermaster came down the stairway and tapped the chief steward on the shoulder. The chief crossed the saloon with a slip of paper and the captain read from between the cover of his palms: *Ice reported lat.* 47.12, *long.* 47.06. *Large berg drifting S.S.E.*

He nodded to the chief who shook his head at the waiting quartermaster. The stern-faced lady was saying, "Do you know, Captain, I feel so very nervous crossing the ocean. I suffer from the heart, leaking valve, you know . . ." The captain inclined his head, smiling, tranquil, courteous. He had heard it so many times before. A few minutes later he was deep in a calm argument about the merits and demerits of spiritualism. And no one knew that he was thinking all the time about that ice floating in latitude 47.12 and longitude 47.06.

The dining-saloon emptied slowly. The orchestra put its instruments away while it fed. Later it would appear on the promenade deck. The captain went to his bridge, his face impassive, his hands in his side pockets. He looked at the compass, at the sky, at the windward horizon, at the bridge log. He stared then straight ahead into the gathering dusk for over a quarter of an hour. A few sharp words to the mates on watch and he went slowly down the companion to the boat deck and his cabin. He sat there for a while, signing some papers, looking over reports. The surgeon came in, prim, white-bearded, professional-looking even in his evening dress. He tapped on his thumb-nail with his pince-nez and waited until the captain was ready.

"Well?"

"Just a seaman, sir. Came on board intoxicated. Rather old. I'm afraid we'll lose him."

The captain frowned. He disliked deaths at sea. It was bad on a passenger ship. Women grew nervous. Superstition, of course. But it had spoiled many people's voyages before.

"His name?"

"Just Smith, sir. William Smith. He's a bo's'n's mate, I believe."

The captain nodded. "Ah! Smith. An old ship-mate, so to speak. He was with me first on the *Brixton City*. Good man. Keep me informed."

"Very well, sir." The surgeon commenced to withdraw. The captain gestured and stopped him.

"Not a word if he . . . er . . . dies. No alarm."

"I understand, sir." The surgeon was rather stiff.

554

As if he didn't know that. He closed the cabin-door quietly behind him. The captain stared at the papers on his desk. William Smith. Plain Bill Smith, bo's'n's mate. He remembered the man. He had been an able seaman on the *Brixton City* when he, Taplow, was an apprentice. Lord, how time flew! And Smith had sailed on his ships pretty nearly ever since. Sort of understanding between them. Never had time to talk together, of course. Master and man. Bad for discipline. Why didn't the fo'c's'le hands leave liquor alone?

He rose with a sigh, put his papers away. He adjusted his uniform cap and his black wing-tie. The miniature medals tinkled on his left lapel. He caught sight of himself in a glass and stopped to grin a trifle, the impassiveness wiped away. He was a bit different from the sweating kid who'd furled royals on many an icy night and tarred down the backstays in the tropics. A bit different from the scared youngster on his first responsible watch with his certificate brand new in his sea chest. He was a captain now. But thirty-odd years had gone into putting him behind a starched shirt front and into a dinner jacket with miniature medals in a row. They thought it was easy, the youngsters.

He appeared below and moved through the lounge with unhurried strides, smiling, dropping courteous words here and there. The orchestra was playing softly behind some palms. Women were chatting in groups, a few men attending. The captain stopped by each group, listened, told a delicate set joke, rendered perhaps a little information and passed on. An hour later he reached the smoking-room.

The purser and assistant surgeon were seated at a table playing bridge. They greeted him with a jovial "Have a hand, sir?" that contained just the correct amount of respect. They each offered to rise and deliver their hands, but he waved them to be seated. The chief steward and the chief engineer were smoking cigars and drinking Scotch with a group of American salesmen.

555

The captain made for a table in the corner where he
noticed the grey-headed man who was a shareholder
in the Line. "Treat him kindly," Hamlin had written
in his grim way. It was hard sometimes, but it had to
be done. The home office couldn't be bothered with
petty grievances.

The shareholder called loudly for the best cigars the
smoke-room possessed. The captain accepted one from
the box and lighted it with care. He declined whisky
and called for ginger ale. The shareholder settled
himself and commenced to talk.

He was a good talker, a loud talker. He knew
everything and constantly asserted he was a self-made
man. He'd always worked and always would work.
Some men had easy jobs—he glared at the captain—
but not he. No, he toiled ten hours a day, sometimes
twelve when in his office. Nothing like it. A man's
business would go to bits if he wasn't paying attention.

The captain smiled and agreed. He always agreed,
with everyone. It was part of his job, as it was his job
to listen to small men and women trying to impress on
him what a great figure they cut ashore. He had gained
the art of listening to a fine degree. He could answer
logically almost any question that cropped up, look
interested and smile when required, while all the time
his mind could be miles away.

The smoke-room crowd thinned out. Some men went
to turn in. Some joined the women. More cards were
produced and bridge tables occupied. The captain
played with the shareholder, the purser and a sandy-
haired man from Chili. The second game of the rubber
was half-way through when the captain paused in the
act of playing a card and listened. The other three men
looked at him, wondering, and waited. Then the purser
relaxed. He had caught the sound. The other two
men, land-trained, heard nothing.

It was a little thing, scarcely sounding above the noise
of the smoke-room. It was merely a change in the

perpetual note of the wind singing by the open port-
holes. But it was enough to check Captain Taplow in
his game, make him murmur an apology, lay down his
cards and walk to the door. He was only gone a
minute, just stepping on to the deck and looking over
the darkling sea, but the shareholder fumed and
grumbled.

"Fine way t' go off and leave everything. How the
devil. . . ."

"He'll be right back," murmured the purser, soothingly, and added, "here he is," as the captain returned.
The game finished. The rubber was won and lost.
And no one in the smoke-room, save the ship's officers
who happened to be present, knew that the captain
had gone to look over the sea because of the faintest of
faint changes in the noise of the wind.

He had just finished dressing when the surgeon
entered his room next morning. The white-bearded
man stood on the mat inside the door and tapped his
thumb-nail with his pince-nez.

"He's dead," he said shortly.

"Smith?"

The surgeon nodded. "Overstrained heart and
arteries almost hard. Too much drink."

"No one knows?"

"Only my hospital attendants, sir."

"We'll bury him at ten o'clock."

"Very well, sir."

The captain stood shaking his head when the surgeon
had gone. Just like Bill Smith. Couldn't leave the
liquor alone. He pressed a bell and a quartermaster
knocked at the door.

"Send the mate here."

The mate came, a white-headed, reliable old man,
stopped only from high command because of a morose-
ness that made him a bad man to mix with passengers.

"Have the sailmaker sew up Smith. He's in the after
hospital, Mr. Hopkins."

"Aye, aye, sir. Shall I inform the chaplain what time the burial?"

"I'll conduct service myself. He was an old shipmate, a very old shipmate . . . when I was 'prenticed." The mate nodded, understanding. The captain paused a moment and went on. "Have four A.B.'s aft at ten, sailing-ship men if you can find them. Clear the third class promenade. An ensign over the canvas. That'll be all."

"Very good, sir." The mate withdrew, nodding. The captain reached for his uniform cap and went on the bridge. An hour later he strolled aft along the first class promenade, chatting with passengers, inquiring of ladies if they found everything all right. He straightened out two or three small matters, heard two complaints, found a child's lost ball wedged in the scupper port and reprimanded the saloon deckman for carelessly splicing grommets. Then, almost unnoticed, he dropped down the companion to the third class deck and went right aft to where the screws shook and vibrated underfoot.

A long canvas bundle with the red ensign over it rested on a grating balanced on the bulwarks. Four bare-headed A.B.'s held it level. The mate stood by. The surgeon stood by. The pale-faced ship's chaplain was in his robes and holding a prayer book.

He said, in a thin voice, as the captain approached, "You know, sir, I consider it is my duty. . . ."

The captain smiled and pulled a little black leather book from his own pocket. He answered, gently, "He wasn't much of a Christian, Mr. Winch. I don't think he'd properly appreciate it. And we were old shipmates. He's been with me a long time, since we were in windjammers."

"But . . ." protested the chaplain, quivering. He was really distressed. That a soul should go out on the water without a proper sending. But then, he wasn't a sailor.

The captain was still smiling. "He saved my life one

night, at least, I think so. It was icy on the yard and I slipped from the foot-rope. I'm sure you won't mind."

The chaplain opened his mouth, but shut it again, for, looking at the captain, he felt his will battered down to a little whimpering thing. The face he gazed at was so ageless, tranquil, confident. The face of the sea itself. He gestured wearily and stepped back. The captain cleared his throat. He looked for a gentle moment at the ensign covering the canvas and then at Mother Carey's chickens skimming the bubbling wake. A good drop for a sailor, the sea birds and the sun. He started to read the service in a subdued voice, but he was thinking of that night on the icy yard long ago. The grating tilted. There was a splash, lost in the roar of the wake. So a sailor sent a sailor to Fiddler's Green.

Three days out something happened. Many of the passengers would have talked about it for the rest of their lives had they known. But ugly things are always hidden from people who pay for cabins. The *Santhia* caught fire somewhere just for'ard of her midship fuel tank. The smoke was cleverly stifled. Men went down in the thick of it with grotesque masks over their heads. The fuel tank was pumped out, but the danger did not decrease, because there was enough oil gas left inside to rupture things severely if a spark chanced to catch.

The turbines whirled without end. The *Santhia* made her steady twenty-one knots. The band still played at meal times and in the evening. The day the fire was discovered there was even a dance on the promenade.

The captain followed his daily programme as nearly as he was able. He ate in the saloon, listened to passengers, helped entertain them. He smiled always, was always unruffled and calm. And not one of the two thousand souls he was paid to deliver safely knew that he was a man exhausted with worry or that overhead the wireless was crashing out half-hourly reports to four ships almost as big as the *Santhia* herself.

559

It was a grim, anxious time. The captain played bridge nightly in the smoking-room. He laughed heartily at the shareholder's jokes despite the fact he had heard them all before. And when the shareholder had gone comfortably to bed the captain repaired to his cabin, pulled dun-coloured overalls over his evening suit and went diving down into the bowels of his ship where men searched and fought at his order.

They were twelve hours finding the seat of the fire and just fifteen minutes extinguishing the whole thing! Had they been a little later the empty fuel tank would have blown up. As it was, matters were smoothed and there was no trouble. Nothing was changed save that a few more lines were etched in Captain Taplow's face.

When it was all over he went to try and get some sleep, but his foot was only over his cabin storm step when a wireless message was handed to him. The ice was lower. Lat. 43.12, Long. 48.20. A berg six hundred feet long and two hundred feet high had been sighted right across the main sailing route. The captain closed his cabin-door, went up on the navigation bridge, called for a cup of strong black coffee and settled himself to watch and pilot his course with care.

That night he sent his regrets to the shareholder. He was unable to play bridge with him. He was going to be busy. And the shareholder, who had no understanding, anyway, only grumbled. "What for? Pretty easy he's got it. Enough officers to run a dozen ships."

It was true. There were enough officers to cover with their sharp eyes every point of the compass. Right at that moment, while Captain Taplow was on the bridge, there were two mates with him. From each bridge wing watched an apprentice. Two quartermasters eyed the sea from where they stood near the chart-house. There was even a man on the fo'c's'le head. And yet Captain Taplow, who needed sleep, must walk his bridge as nervous as the newest master out of London. And this because it was no light thing to hold in trust thirty thousand tons and over two thousand souls. Whatever might befall, the responsibility was his. The officers might be efficient. They were. They might be calm and confident and good men. But if they made a mistake it was the captain who was broken. He was responsible. Officers were given him for him to command and order, not to take responsibility from him. And officers had been known to make mistakes before. So how could a master mariner sleep when there was ice abroad and to a certainty fogs as well? That was what it meant, command. . . .

The shareholder who grumbled so much, who considered that Captain Taplow might have come down to have his game of bridge, never knew that at one o'clock that morning the *Santhia* shot suddenly into a night mist and was slowed to half-speed. Nor did he know that half an hour later she barely skimmed a berg as large as a mountain, so that the hair of every watcher stood on end and the heart of at least one man contracted until it pained in his breast.

The dawn broke grey and chilly, strangely chilly after the summer weather that had gone. The ice blink was on the northern horizon, but straight ahead the sea appeared clear. It was a grey sea, a steely sort of swelling with little jumbles of white foam capping it. The sky was blue between patches of grey cloud. The horizon was a little dim.

As the light strengthened and day settled into being, a haggard, unshaven Captain Taplow took a good look around and sighed with relief that he had come safely through the night. There was danger still, great danger, ahead. But it could be seen approaching and even a new officer could steer a ship out of the way.

He stopped in his walk beside the senior third mate, who was on watch.

"I'm going below, Mr. Stevens. Got to get some sleep. We dock to-morrow and it'll be hard work going up to the harbour . . . Give me a call if it gets thick."

"Aye, aye, sir. Call you if it thickens."

"Don't forget! We don't want another *Titanic*!" He frowned irritably as he turned away. There was no need for him to use such a tone of voice to a junior. Of course, he was tired, that accounted for it. He went down the companion to his room and sank into a chair. He rang and a steward brought him some coffee and an omelette. He managed to consume that and then pulled off the high rubber sea-boots he had been wearing. When he had them off he padded across the room in his socks to look at the barometer and frowned worriedly.

Two decks below, the shareholder was turning over under the warm sheets and gazing up at the deck head. He was very comfortable and rested. He smiled, thinking of the breakfast he was going to eat. He was disturbed when he caught the faint sound of the third mate's voice shouting to a quartermaster. He didn't know what it was and he didn't care, but he wished whoever it was would be quieter.

As a matter of fact, the third mate was anxious, which was why his voice was raised. As a consequence, a somewhat surly quartermaster tapped at the door of the captain's cabin and poked his head inside. The captain was just peeling off his jacket..

He looked up and said, "Well?"

The quartermaster blinked. "Third mate says it's getting thick, sir."

The captain sighed. He slipped on his jacket and reached for his sea-boots. "I'll be right up," he said. He sighed again as he stamped out on to the boat deck and started for the navigation bridge, the first thin wisps of the fog wrapping about him.

The third mate peered at him as he came up the

companion and started, "Sorry, sir. Didn't like to disturb you. . . ."

"That's all right," murmured the captain wearily. "Half-speed. Siren, there!" And so he took over again, to bring his thirty thousand tons and his two thousand souls to safety. That was what it meant, command. . . .

THE ARGONAUTS OF THE AIR
by H. G. Wells

DESPITE his voluminous activities as journalist, publicist and creator of "outline" histories, H. G. Wells still bestrides the modern world of fiction like a colossus. His novels of social life, imaginative scientific romances and tales of strange experiences fill many volumes. To quote his own words he has "probably experimented in more directions than any living author." Born at Bromley, in 1866, the son of a one-time professional cricketer who achieved records as a bowler, Wells lived in humble surroundings until, by dint of self-education and perseverance, he emancipated himself from an early, uncongenial apprenticeship to a draper and became, at sixteen, an assistant master at Midhurst Grammar School. Afterwards, he obtained a scholarship at South Kensington School of Science and for a time was a science teacher. It was not until a temporary breakdown in health enforced rest that Wells discovered his talent for fiction. It is not too much to say that he re-invented the short story, showing how it could be brought much closer to life as well as illuminated by imaginative conjecture. *The Argonauts of the Air* vividly describes an episode, partly derived from the author's personal experience of aviation; it will always live as a masterly account of the pluck and enterprise of pioneers in air-flight.

THE ARGONAUTS OF THE AIR

BY

H. G. WELLS

ONE saw Monson's Flying Machine from the windows of the trains passing either along the South-Western main line or along the line between Wimbledon and Worcester Park—to be exact, one saw the huge scaffoldings which limited the flight of the apparatus. They rose over the tree-tops, a massive alley of interlacing iron and timber, and an enormous web of ropes and tackle, extending the best part of two miles. From the Leatherhead branch this alley was foreshortened and in part hidden by a hill with villas; but from the main line one had it in profile, a complex tangle of girders and curving bars, very impressive to the excursionists from Portsmouth and Southampton and the West. Monson had taken up the work where Maxim had left it, had gone on at first with an utter contempt for the journalistic wit and ignorance that had hampered and irritated his predecessor, and had spent (it was said) rather more than half his immense fortune upon his experiments. The results, to an impatient generation, seemed inconsiderable. When some five years had passed after the growth of the colossal iron groves at Worcester Park, and Monson still failed to put in a fluttering appearance over Trafalgar Square, even the Isle of Wight trippers felt their liberty to smile. And such intelligent people as did not consider Monson a fool stricken with the mania for invention, denounced him as being (for no particular reason) a self-advertising quack.

Yet now and again a morning trainload of season ticket holders would see a white monster rush headlong through the airy tracery of guides and bars, and hear the further stays, nettings, and buffers snap, creak, and groan with the impact of the blow. Then there would be an efflorescence of black-set, white-rimmed faces along the sides of the train, and the morning papers would be neglected for a vigorous discussion of the possibility of flying (in which nothing new was ever said by any chance), until the train reached Waterloo, and its cargo of season ticket holders dispersed themselves over London. Or the fathers and mothers in some multitudinous train of weary excursionists, returning exhausted from a day of rest by the sea, would find the dark fabric, standing out against the evening sky, useful in diverting some bilious child from its introspection, and be suddenly startled by the swift transit of a huge black flapping shape that strained upward against the guides. It was a great and forcible thing beyond dispute, and excellent for conversation; yet, all the same, it was but flying in leading-strings, and most of those who witnessed it scarcely counted its flight as flying. More of a switchback it seemed to the run of the folk.

Monson, I say, did not trouble himself very keenly about the opinions of the Press at first. But possibly he, even, had formed but a poor idea of the time it would take before the tactics of flying were mastered, the swift assured adjustment of the big soaring shape to every gust and chance movement of the air; nor had he clearly reckoned the money this prolonged struggle against gravitation would cost him. And he was not so pachydermatous as he seemed. Secretly he had his periodical bundles of cuttings sent him by Romeike, he had his periodical reminders from his banker; and if he did not mind the initial ridicule and scepticism, he felt the growing neglect as the months went by and the money dribbled away. Time was when Monson had sent the enterprising journalist, keen after readable matter, empty from his gates. But when the enterprising journalist ceased from troubling, Monson was anything but satisfied in his heart of hearts. Still day by day the work went on, and the multitudinous subtle difficulties of the steering diminished in number. Day by day, too, the money trickled away, until his balance was no longer a matter of hundreds of thousands, but of tens. And at last came an anniversary.

Monson, sitting in the little drawing-shed, suddenly noticed the date on Woodhouse's calendar.

"It was five years ago to-day that we began," he said to Woodhouse suddenly.

"Was it?" said Woodhouse.

"It's the alterations play the devil with us," said Monson, biting a paper-fastener.

The drawings for the new vans to the hinder screw lay on the table before him as he spoke. He pitched the mutilated brass paper-fastener into the waste-paper basket and drummed with his fingers. "These alterations! Will the mathematicians ever be clever enough to save us all this patching and experimenting? Five years—learning by rule of thumb, when one might think that it was possible to calculate the whole thing out beforehand. The cost of it! I might have hired three senior wranglers for life. But they'd only have developed some beautifully useless theorems in pneumatics. What a time it has been, Woodhouse!"

"These mouldings will take three weeks," said Woodhouse. "At special prices."

"Three weeks!" said Monson, and sat drumming.

"Three weeks certain," said Woodhouse, an excellent engineer, but no good as a comforter. He drew the sheets towards him and began shading a bar.

Monson stopped drumming, and began to bite his finger-nails, staring the while at Woodhouse's head.

"How long have they been calling this Monson's Folly?" he said suddenly.

"*Oh!* Year or so," said Woodhouse carelessly, without looking up.

Monson sucked the air in between his teeth, and went to the window. The stout iron columns carrying the elevated rails upon which the start of the machine was made rose up close by, and the machine was hidden by the upper edge of the window. Through the grove of iron pillars, red painted and ornate with rows of bolts, one had a glimpse of the pretty scenery towards Esher. A train went gliding noiselessly across the middle distance, its rattle drowned by the hammering of the workmen overhead. Monson could imagine the grinning faces at the windows of the carriages. He swore savagely under his breath, and dabbed viciously at a blowfly that suddenly became noisy on the window-pane.

"What's up?" said Woodhouse, staring in surprise at his employer.

"I'm about sick of this."

Woodhouse scratched his cheek. "Oh!" he said, after an assimilating pause. He pushed the drawing away from him.

"Here these fools . . . I'm trying to conquer a new element—trying to do a thing that will revolutionize life. And instead of taking an intelligent interest, they grin, and make their stupid jokes, and call me and my appliances names."

"Asses!" said Woodhouse, letting his eye fall again on the drawing.

The epithet, curiously enough, made Monson wince.

"I'm about sick of it, Woodhouse, anyhow," he said, after a pause.

Woodhouse shrugged his shoulders.

"There's nothing for it but patience, I suppose," said Monson, sticking his hands in his pockets. "I've started. I've made my bed, and I've got to lie on it. I can't go back. I'll see it through, and spend every penny I have and every penny I can borrow. But I tell you, Woodhouse, I'm infernally sick of it, all the same. If I'd paid a tenth part of the money towards some political greaser's expenses—I'd have been a baronet before this."

Monson paused. Woodhouse stared in front of him with a blank expression he always employed to indicate sympathy, and tapped his pencil-case on the table. Monson stared at him for a minute.

"Oh, *damn!*" said Monson suddenly, and abruptly rushed out of the room.

Woodhouse continued his sympathetic rigour for perhaps half a minute. Then he sighed and resumed the shading of the drawings. Something had evidently upset Monson. Nice chap, and generous, but difficult to get on with. It was the way with every amateur who had anything to do with engineering—wanted everything finished at once. But Monson had usually the patience of the expert. Odd he was so irritable. Nice and round that aluminium rod did look now! Woodhouse threw back his head, and put it, first this side, and then that, to appreciate his bit of shading better.

"Mr. Woodhouse," said Hooper, the foreman of the labourers, putting his head in at the door.

"Hallo!" said Woodhouse, without turning round.

"Nothing happened, sir?" said Hooper.

"Happened?" said Woodhouse.

"The governor has just been up the rails swearing like a tornader."

"*Oh!*" said Woodhouse.

"It ain't like him, sir."

"No?"

"And I was thinking perhaps——"

"Don't think," said Woodhouse, still admiring the drawings.

Hooper knew Woodhouse, and he shut the door suddenly with a vicious slam. Woodhouse stared stonily before him for some further minutes, and then made an ineffectual effort to pick his teeth with his pencil. Abruptly he desisted, pitched that old, tried, and stumpy servitor across the room, got up, stretched himself, and followed Hooper.

He looked ruffled—it was visible to every workman he met. When a millionaire who has been spending thousands on experiments that employ quite a little army of people suddenly indicates that he is sick of the undertaking, there is almost invariably a certain amount of mental friction in the ranks of the little army he employs. And even before he indicates his intentions there are speculations and murmurs, a watching of faces and a study of straws. Hundreds of people knew before the day was out that Monson was ruffled, Woodhouse ruffled, Hooper ruffled. A workman's wife, for instance (whom Monson had never seen), decided to keep her money in the savings-bank instead of buying a velveteen dress. So far-reaching are even the casual curses of a millionaire.

Monson found a certain satisfaction in going on the works and behaving disagreeably to as many people as possible. After a time even that palled upon him, and he rode off the grounds, to everyone's relief there, and through the lanes south-eastward, to the infinite tribulation of his house steward at Cheam.

And the immediate cause of it all, the little grain of annoyance that had suddenly precipitated all this discontent with his life-work was—these trivial things that direct all our great decisions—half a dozen ill-considered remarks made by a pretty girl, prettily dressed, with a beautiful voice and something more than prettiness in her soft, grey eyes. And of these half-dozen remarks, two words especially—"Monson's Folly." She had felt she was behaving charmingly to Monson; she reflected the next day how exceptionally effective she had been, and no one would have been more amazed than she, had she learned the effect she had left on Monson's mind. I hope, considering everything, that she never knew.

"How are you getting on with your flying machine?"

she asked. ("I wonder if I shall ever meet anyone with the sense not to ask that," thought Monson.) "It will be very dangerous at first, will it not?" ("Thinks I'm afraid.") "Jorgon is going to play presently; have you heard him before?" ("My mania being attended to, we turn to rational conversation.") Gush about Jorgon; gradual decline of conversation, ending with—"You must let me know when your flying machine is finished, Mr. Monson, and then I will consider the advisability of taking a ticket." ("One would think I was still playing inventions in the nursery.") But the bitterest thing she said was not meant for Monson's ears. To Phlox, the novelist, she was always conscientiously brilliant. "I have been talking to Mr. Monson, and he can think of nothing, positively nothing, but that flying machine of his. Do you know, all his workmen call that place of his 'Monson's Folly'? He is quite impossible. It is really very, very sad. I always regard him myself in the light of sunken treasure—the Lost Millionaire, you know."

She was pretty and well-educated—indeed, she had written an epigrammatic novelette; but the bitterness was that she was typical. She summarized what the world thought of the man who was working sanely, steadily, and surely, towards a more tremendous revolution in the appliances of civilization, a more far-reaching alteration in the ways of humanity than has ever been effected since history began. They did not even take him seriously. In a little while he would be proverbial. "I *must* fly now," he said on his way home, smarting with a sense of absolute social failure. "I must fly soon. If it doesn't come off, soon, by God! I shall run amuck."

He said that before he had gone through his pass-book and his litter of papers. Inadequate as the cause seems, it was that girl's voice and the expression of her eyes that precipitated his discontent. But certainly the discovery that he had no longer even one hundred

575   oo

thousand pounds' worth of realizable property behind him was the poison that made the wound deadly.

It was the next day after this that he exploded upon Woodhouse and his workmen, and thereafter his bearing was consistently grim for three weeks, and anxiety dwelt in Cheam, and Ewell, Malden, Morden, and Worcester Park, places that had thriven mightily on his experiments.

Four weeks after that first swearing of his, he stood with Woodhouse by the reconstructed machine as it lay across the elevated railway, by means of which it gained its initial impetus. The new propeller glittered a brighter white than the rest of the machine, and a gilder, obedient to a whim of Monson's, was picking out the aluminium bars with gold. And looking down the long avenue between the ropes (gilded now with the sunset) one saw red signals, and two miles away an ant-hill of workmen altering the last falls of the run into a rising slope.

" I'll *come*," said Woodhouse. " I'll come right enough. But I tell you it's infernally foolhardy. If only you would give another year——"

" I tell you I won't. I tell you the thing works. I've given years enough——"

" It's not that," said Woodhouse. " We're all right with the machine. But it's the steering——"

" Haven't I been rushing, night and morning, backwards and forwards, through this squirrel's cage? If the thing steers true here, it will steer true all across England. It's just funk, I tell you, Woodhouse. We could have gone a year ago. And besides——"

" Well?" said Woodhouse.

" The money!" snapped Monson over his shoulder.

" Hang it! I never thought of the money," said Woodhouse, and then, speaking now in a very different tone to that with which he had said the words before, he repeated, " I'll come. Trust me."

Monson turned suddenly, and saw all that Woodhouse

had not the dexterity to say, shining on his sunset-lit face. He looked for a moment, then impulsively extended his hand. "Thanks," he said.

"All right," said Woodhouse, gripping the hand, and with a queer softening of his features. "Trust me."

Then both men turned to the big apparatus that lay with its flat wings extended upon the carrier, and stared at it meditatively. Monson, guided perhaps by a photographic study of the flight of birds, and by Lilienthal's methods, had gradually drifted from Maxim's shapes towards the bird form again. The thing, however, was driven by a huge screw behind in the place of the tail; and so hovering, which needs an almost vertical adjustment of a flat tail, was rendered impossible. The body of the machine was small, almost cylindrical, and pointed. Forward and aft on the pointed ends were two small petroleum engines for the screw, and the navigators sat deep in a canoe-like recess, the foremost one steering, and being protected by a low screen, with two plate-glass windows, from the blinding rush of air. On either side a monstrous flat framework with a curved front border could be adjusted so as either to lie horizontally, or to be tilted upward or down. These wings worked rigidly together, or, by releasing a pin, one could be tilted through a small angle independently of its fellow. The front edge of either wing could also be shifted back so as to diminish the wing area about one-sixth. The machine was not only not designed to hover, but it was incapable of fluttering. Monson's idea was to get into the air with the initial rush of the apparatus, and then to skim, much as a playing-card may be skimmed, keeping up the rush by means of the screw at the stern. Rooks and gulls fly enormous distances in that way with scarcely a perceptible movement of the wings. The bird really drives along on an aerial switchback. It glides slanting downward for a space, until it has gained considerable momentum, and then altering

577

the inclination of its wings, glides up again almost to its original altitude. Even a Londoner who has watched the birds in the aviary in Regent's Park knows that.

But the bird is practising this art from the moment it leaves its nest. It has not only the perfect apparatus, but the perfect instinct to use it. A man off his feet has the poorest skill in balancing. Even the simple trick of the bicycle costs him some hours of labour. The instantaneous adjustment of the wings, the quick response to a passing breeze, the swift recovery of equilibrium, the giddy, eddying movements that require such absolute precision—all that he must learn, learn with infinite labour and infinite danger, if ever he is to conquer flying. The flying machine that will start off some fine day, driven by neat "little levers," with a nice open deck like a liner, and all loaded up with bombshells and guns, is the easy dreaming of a literary man. In lives and in treasure the cost of the conquest of the empire of the air may even exceed all that has been spent in man's great conquest of the sea. Certainly it will be costlier than the greatest war that has ever devastated the world.

No one knew these things better than these two practical men. And they knew they were in the front rank of the coming army. Yet there is hope even in a forlorn hope. Men are killed outright in the reserves sometimes, while others who have been left for dead in the thickest corner crawl out and survive.

"If we miss these meadows—" said Woodhouse presently, in his slow way.

"My dear chap," said Monson, whose spirits had been rising fitfully during the last few days, "we mustn't miss these meadows. There's a quarter of a square mile for us to hit, fences removed, ditches levelled. We shall come down all right—rest assured. And if we don't—"

"Ah!" said Woodhouse. "If we don't!"

Before the day of the start, the newspaper people got

wind of the alterations at the northward end of the framework, and Monson was cheered by a decided change in the comments Romeike forwarded him.

"He will be off some day," said the papers. "He will be off some day," said the South-Western season ticket holders one to another; the seaside excursionists, the Saturday-to-Monday trippers from Sussex and Hampshire and Dorset and Devon, the eminent literary people from Hazlemere, all remarked eagerly one to another, "He will be off some day," as the familiar scaffolding came in sight. And actually, one bright morning, in full view of the ten-past-ten train from Basingstoke, Monson's flying machine started on its journey.

They saw the carrier running swiftly along its rail, and the white and gold screw spinning in the air. They heard the rapid rumble of wheels, and a thud as the carrier reached the buffers at the end of its run. Then a whirr as the flying machine was shot forward into the networks. All that the majority of them had seen and heard before. The thing went with a drooping flight through the framework and rose again, and then every beholder shouted, or screamed, or yelled, or shrieked after his kind. For instead of the customary concussion and stoppage, the flying machine flew out of its five years' cage like a bolt from a crossbow, and drove slantingly upward into the air, curved round a little, so as to cross the line, and soared in the direction of Wimbledon Common.

It seemed to hang momentarily in the air and grow smaller, then it ducked and vanished over the clustering blue tree-tops to the east of Coombe Hill, and no one stopped staring and gasping until long after it had disappeared.

That was what the people in the train from Basingstoke saw. If you had drawn a line down the middle of that train, from engine to guard's van, you would not have

579

found a living soul on the opposite side to the flying machine. It was a mad rush from window to window as the thing crossed the line. And the engine-driver and stoker never took their eyes off the low hills about Wimbledon, and never noticed that they had run clean through Coombe and Malden and Raynes Park, until, with returning animation, they found themselves pelting, at the most indecent pace, into Wimbledon station.

From the moment when Monson had started the carrier with a "Now!" neither he nor Woodhouse said a word. Both men sat with clenched teeth. Monson had crossed the line with a curve that was too sharp, and Woodhouse had opened and shut his white lips; but neither spoke. Woodhouse simply gripped his seat, and breathed sharply through his teeth, watching the blue country to the west rushing past, and down, and away from him. Monson knelt at his post forward and his hands trembled on the spoked wheel that moved the wings. He could see nothing before him but a mass of white clouds in the sky.

The machine went slanting upward, travelling with an enormous speed still, but losing momentum every moment. The land ran away underneath with diminishing speed.

"*Now!*" said Woodhouse at last, and with a violent effort Monson wrenched over the wheel and altered the angle of the wings. The machine seemed to hang for half a minute motionless in mid-air, and then he saw the hazy blue house-covered hills of Kilburn and Hampstead jump up and rise steadily, until the little sunlit dome of the Albert Hall appeared through his windows. For a moment he scarcely understood the meaning of this upward rush of the horizon, but as the nearer and nearer houses came into view, he realized what he had done. He had turned the wings over too far, and they were swooping steeply downward towards the Thames.

The thought, the question, the realization were all the business of a second of time. "Too much;" gasped Woodhouse. Monson brought the wheel half-way back with a jerk, and forthwith the Kilburn and Hampstead ridge dropped again to the lower edge of his windows. They had been a thousand feet above Coombe and Malden station; fifty seconds after they whizzed, at a frightful pace, not eighty feet above the East Putney station, on the Metropolitan District Line, to the screaming astonishment of a platform full of people. Monson flung up the vans against the air, and over Fulham they rushed up their atmospheric switchback again, steeply —too steeply. The 'buses went floundering across the Fulham Road, the people yelled.

Then down again, too steeply still, and the distant trees and houses about Primrose Hill leapt up across Monson's window, and then suddenly he saw straight before him the greenery of Kensington Gardens and the towers of the Imperial Institute. They were driving straight down upon South Kensington. The pinnacles of the Natural History Museum rushed up into view. There came one fatal second of swift thought, a moment of hesitation. Should he try to clear the towers, or swerve eastward?

He made a hesitating attempt to release the right wing, left the catch half released, and gave a frantic clutch at the wheel.

The nose of the machine seemed to leap up before him. The wheel pressed his hand with irresistible force, and jerked itself out of his control.

Woodhouse, sitting crouched together, gave a hoarse cry, and sprang up towards Monson. "Too far!" he cried, and then he was clinging to the gunwale for dear life, and Monson had been jerked clean overhead, and was falling backwards upon him.

So swiftly had the thing happened that barely a quarter of the people going to and fro in Hyde Park, and Brompton Road, and the Exhibition Road, saw anything of the aerial catastrophe. A distant winged shape had appeared above the clustering houses to the south, had fallen and risen, growing larger as it did so; had swooped swiftly down towards the Imperial Institute, a broad spread of flying wings, had swept round in a quarter circle, dashed eastward, and then suddenly sprang vertically into the air. A black object shot out of it, and came spinning downward. A man! Two men clutching each other! They came whirling down, separated as they struck the roof of the Students' Club, and bounded off into the green bushes on it southward side.

For perhaps half a minute the pointed stem of the big machine still pierced vertically upward, the screw spinning desperately. For one brief instant, that yet seemed an age to all who watched, it had hung motionless in mid-air. Then a spout of yellow flame licked up its length from the stern engine, and swift, swifter, swifter, and flaring like a rocket, it rushed down upon the solid mass of masonry which was formerly the Royal College of Science. The big screw of white and gold touched the parapet, and crumpled up like wet linen. Then the blazing spindle-shaped body smashed and splintered, smashing and splintering in its fall, upon the north-westward angle of the building.

But the crash, the flame of blazing paraffin that shot heavenward from the shattered engines of the machine, the crushed horrors that were found in the garden beyond the Students' Club, the masses of yellow parapet and red brick that fell headlong into the roadway, the running to and fro of people like ants in a broken ant-hill, the galloping of fire-engines, the gathering of crowds —all these things do not belong to this story, which was written only to tell how the first of all successful flying machines was launched and flew. Though he failed, and failed disastrously, the record of Monson's work remains—a sufficient monument—to guide the next of that band of gallant experimentalists who will sooner or later master this great problem of flying. And between Worcester Park and Malden there still stands that portentous avenue of ironwork, rusting now and dangerous here and there, to witness to the first desperate struggle for man's right of way through the air.

THE STAKE AND THE PLUMB LINE
by Sir Gilbert Parker

GILBERT PARKER was a Canadian by birth, an Imperialist by conviction. He was born in 1862 and came to England to complete his education at Trinity College, Cambridge. He travelled extensively in the intervals of writing and preparing for a political career, visiting the South Sea Islands, the East and his own homeland. He was member of parliament for Gravesend for many years. In 1904 he initiated and organized the first Imperial Universities Conference, and he acted as chairman of the Imperial South Africa Association. Most of his novels and short stories describe adventurous life in North-West Canada, but he also wrote some diverting stories about British officers in India under the title of Donovan Pasha. The Seats of the Mighty is one of the most successful of his stories written on a theme much favoured by him—the salvation of a weak man's character through the influence of a woman. Gilbert Parker died in 1932.

GILBERT PARKER was a Canadian by birth, an Imperialist by conviction. He was born in 1862 and came to England to complete his education at Trinity College, Cambridge. He travelled extensively in the intervals of writing and preparing for a political career, visiting the South Sea Islands, the East and his own homeland. He was member of parliament for Gravesend for many years. In 1903 he initiated and organized the first Imperial Universities Conference, and he acted as chairman of the Imperial South Africa Association. Most of his novels and short stories describe adventurous life in North-West Canada, but he also wrote some diverting stories about British officers in India under the title of *Donovan Pasha*. *The Stake and the Plumb Line* is one of the most successful of his stories written on a theme much favoured by him—the salvation of a weak man's character through the influence of a woman. Gilbert Parker died in 1933.

THE STAKE AND THE PLUMB LINE

BY

SIR GILBERT PARKER

SHE went against all good judgment in marrying him.
She cut herself off from her own people, from the
life in which she had been an alluring and beautiful
figure, popular beyond any other girl of her brief epoch
of girlhood, witty and full of a humour not to be suppressed. Washington had never had two such seasons
as those in which she moved, for the diplomatic circle
who had had "the run of the world" knew her value,
and were not content without her. She might have
made a brilliant match with one ambassador thirty
years older than herself—she was but twenty-two—and
there were at least six attachés and secretaries of legation
who entered upon a tournament for her heart and hand.
All her fine faculties of tact and fairness, of harmless
strategy and unexpected humour, were needed to keep
her cavaliers constant and hopeful to the last; but she
never faltered, and she did not fail. The faces of old
men brightened when they saw her; and one or two
ancient figures, who for years had been seldom seen at
social functions, now came when they knew she was to
be present. There were, of course, a few women who
said she would coquette with any male from nine to
ninety, but no man ever said so; and there was none
—from first to last—but smiled with pleasure at even
the mention of her name, so had her vivacity, intelligence, and fine sympathy conquered them. She was
a social artist by instinct. In their hearts, they all
recognized how fair and impartial she was; and she drew
out of every man the best that was in him. The few
women who did not like her said that she chattered; but

the truth was, she made other people talk by swift suggestion or delicate interrogation.

After the blow fell, Freddy Hartzman put the matter succinctly, and told the truth faithfully, when he said: "The first time I met her, I told her all I'd ever done that could be told, and all I wanted to do, including a resolve to carry her off to some desert place and set up a kingdom of two. I don't know how she did it. I was like a tap, and poured myself out; and when it was all over I thought she was the best talker I'd ever heard. But yet she'd done nothing except look at me and listen, and put in a question here and there that was like a baby asking to see your watch. Oh, she was a lily-flower, was Sally Seabrook, and I've never been sorry I told her all my little story. It did me good. Poor darling! It makes me sick sometimes when I think of it. Yet she'll win out all right—a hundred to one she'll win out. She was a star."

Freddy Hartzman was in an embassy of repute; he knew the chancellories and salons of many nations, and was looked upon as one of the ablest and shrewdest men in the diplomatic service. He had written one of the best books on international law in existence; he talked English like a native; he had published a volume of delightful verse, and had omitted to publish several others, including a tiny volume which Sally Seabrook's charms had inspired him to write. His view of her was shared by most men who knew the world, and especially by the elderly men who had a real knowledge of human nature, among whom was a certain important member of the United States Executive, called John Appleton. When the end of all things at Washington came for Sally, these two men, by tacit consent, united to bear her up that her feet should not stumble upon the stony path of the hard journey she had undertaken.

Appleton was not a man of much speech, but his words had weight, for he was not only a minister, but he came of an old family which had ruled the social destinies of a state and had alternately controlled and disturbed its politics. On the day of the sensation, in the fiery cloud of which Sally disappeared, Appleton delivered himself of his mind in the matter, at a reception given by the President: "She will come back, and we will all take her back—be glad to have her back. She has the grip of a lever which can lift the eternal hills with the right pressure. Leave her alone—leave her alone. This is a democratic country; and she'll prove democracy a success before she's done."

The world knew that John Appleton had offered her marriage, and he had never hidden the fact. What they did not know was that of all the world—save her own father and mother, and Freddy Hartzman—she had told him what she meant to do before she did it. He had spoken plainly, bluntly, to her, with a voice that was blurred and a little broken, urging her against the course towards which she was set. It had not availed; and, realizing that he had come upon a powerful will underneath the sunny and so human surface, he had ceased to protest, to bear down upon her mind with his own iron force, through which there ran as fine an affection as was ever given to any woman, albeit he was fifty-five and she but twenty-two. When he realized that all the reasoning was wasted, that all worldly argument was vain, he made one last attempt—a forlorn hope.

"There is no position you cannot occupy," he said. "You have the perfect gift in private life, and you have a public gift. You have a genius for ruling. Say, my dear, don't wreck it all. I know you are not for me, but there arc better men in the country, and out of it, than I am. Hartzman will be a great man one day—he wants you. Young Tilden wants you; he has millions, and he will never disgrace them or you, the power which they can command, and the power which you have. And there are others. Your people have told you they will turn you off: the world will say things—will rend you. There is nothing so popular for the moment as the fall of a favourite. But that's nothing —it's nothing at all, compared with the danger to yourself. I didn't sleep last night as I thought of it. Yet I'm glad you wrote me. It gave me time to think, and I can give you the truth as I see it. Haven't you thought that he will drag you down—down—down, wear out your soul, break and sicken your life, destroy your beauty? You are beautiful, my dear, beyond what the world sees, even. Give it up; say, give it up, and don't break our hearts. There are too many people loving you for you to sacrifice them—and yourself, too. You've had such a good time."

"It's been like a dream," she interrupted, in a far-away voice; "like a dream, these two years."

"And it's been such a good dream," he urged, "and you will only go to a bad one—from which you will never wake. The thing has fastened on him; he will never give it up. And penniless, too—his father has cast him off. My girl, it's impossible! Listen to me. There's no one on earth that would do more for you than I would—no one!"

"Dear, dear friend!" she cried with a sudden impulse, and caught his hand in hers and kissed it before he could draw it back. "You are so true, and you think you are right. But—but"—her eyes took on a deep, steady, far-away look—"but I will save him, and we shall not be penniless in the end. Meanwhile, I have seven hundred dollars a year of my own; no one can touch that. Nothing can change me now; and I have promised."

When he saw her fixed determination, he made no further protest, but asked that he might help her, be with her the next day when she was to take a step which all the experience of the world would say must lead to sorrow and a miserable end.

The step she took was to marry Jim Templeton, the

drunken, cast-off son of a millionaire senator from Kentucky, who controlled railways and owned a bank, and had so resented his son's inebriate habits that for four years he had never permitted Jim's name to be mentioned in his presence. Jim had had twenty thousand dollars left him by his mother, and a small income of three hundred dollars from an investment which had been made for him when a little boy. And this had carried him on; for, drunken as he was, he had sense enough to eke out the money, limiting himself to three thousand dollars a year. He had four thousand dollars and his tiny income of three hundred left when he went to Sally Seabrook—after having been sober for a month—and begged her to marry him.

Before dissipation had made him look ten years older than he was, there had been no handsomer man in all America. Even yet, he had a remarkable face, long, delicate, with dark-brown eyes, as fair a forehead as man could wish, and black, waving hair, streaked with grey —grey, though he was but twenty-nine years of age. When Sally was fifteen and he twenty-two, he had fallen in love with her and she with him; and nothing had broken the early romance. He had captured her young imagination, and had fastened his image on her heart. Her people, seeing the drift of things, had sent her to school on the Hudson, and the two did not meet for two years. Then came a stolen interview, and the fastening of the rivets of attraction, for Jim had gifts of a wonderful kind. He knew his Horace and Anacreon, and Heine and Lamartine and Dante in the originals, and a hundred others; he was a speaker of power and grace, and he had a clear, strong head for business. He was also a lawyer, and was junior attorney to the great business. It was because he had the real business gift, not because he had a brilliant and scholarly mind, that his father took him into his great concerns, and was the more unforgiving when he gave way to temptation. Otherwise, he would have pensioned Jim off and dismissed him from his mind as a useless, insignificant person, for Horace, Anacreon, philosophy and history were to him the recreations of the feeble-minded. He had set his heart on Jim, and what Jim could do and would do by and by in the vast financial concerns he controlled; but Jim had disappointed him beyond calculation.

In the early days of their association Jim had left his post and taken to drink at critical moments in their operations. At first high words had been spoken; then there came the strife of two dissimilar natures, and both were headstrong, and each proud and unrelenting in his own way. Then, at last, had come the separation, irrevocable and painful; and Jim had flung out into the world, a drunkard who, sober for a fortnight, or a month, would go off on the spree in which he quoted Sappho and Horace in taverns, and sang bacchanalian songs with a voice meant for the stage—a throw-back to an ancestor who had sung upon the English stage a hundred years before. Even in his cups Jim Templeton was a man marked out from his fellows—distinguished and very handsome even after his darling vice had submerged him. Society, however, had ceased to recognize him for a long time, and he did not seek it. For two or three years he practised law now and then. He took cases—preferably criminal cases, for which very often he got no pay; but that, too, at last ceased. Now, in his quiet sober intervals he read omnivorously and worked out problems in physics, for which he had a taste, until the old appetite surged over him again. Then his spirits rose, and he was the old brilliant talker, the joyous galliard, until, in due time, he became lethargically drunk.

In one of his sober intervals he had met Sally Seabrook in the street. It was the first time in four years, for he had avoided her; and though she had written to him once or twice, he had never answered her—shame was in his heart. Yet all the time the old song was in

Sally's ears. Jim Templeton had touched her in some distant and intimate corner of her nature where none other had reached; and in all her gay life, when men had told their tale of admiration in their own way, her mind had gone back to Jim, and what he had said under the magnolia trees; and his voice had drowned all others. She was not blind to what he had become, but a deep belief possessed her that she of all the world could save him. She knew how futile it would look to the world, how wild a dream it looked even to her own heart, how perilous it was, but, play upon the surface of things as she had done so much and so often in her brief career, she was seized of convictions having origin, as it might seem, in something beyond herself.

So when she and Jim met in the street, the old true thing rushed upon them both, and for a moment they stood still and looked at each other. As they might look who say farewell for ever, so did they dwell upon each other's faces. That was the beginning of the new epoch. A few days more, and Jim came to her and said that she alone could save him; and she meant him to say it, had led him to the saying, for the same conviction was burned deep in her own soul. She knew the awful risk she was taking, that the step must mean social ostracism, and that her own people would be no kinder to her than society; but she gasped a prayer, smiled at Jim as though all were well, laid her plans, made him promise her one thing on his knees, and took the plunge.

Her people did as she expected. She was threatened with banishment from hearth and home, with disinheritance, but she pursued her course; and the only person who stood with her and Jim at the altar—she would be married in church, so sacred the task to which she had set herself—was John Appleton, who would not be denied, and who had such a half-hour with Jim before the ceremony as neither of them forgot in the years that the locust ate thereafter. As he knelt beside her awaiting the benediction, a sudden sense of the enormity of this act came upon him; and for her sake he would have drawn back then, had it not been too late. He realized that it was a crime to put this young, beautiful life in peril; that his own life was a poor, contemptible thing, and that he had been possessed of the egotism of the selfish and the young.

But the thing was done, and a new life was begun. Before they were launched upon it, however—before society had fully grasped the sensation, or they had left upon their journey to the far north of Canada, where Sally intended they should work out their problem and make their home, far and free from all old associations —a curious thing happened. Jim's father sent an urgent message to Sally to come and see him. When she came, he told her she was mad, and asked her why she had thrown her life away.

"Why have you done it?" he said. "You—you knew all about him; you might have married the best man in the country. You could rule a kingdom; you have beauty and power, and make people do what you want. And you've got a sot!"

"He is your son," she answered quietly.

She looked so beautiful and so fine as she stood there, fearless and challenging before him, that he was moved. But he would not show it.

"He was my son—when he was a man," he retorted grimly.

"He is the son of the woman you once loved," she answered.

The old man turned his head away.

"What would she have said to what you did to Jim?"

He drew himself round sharply. Her dagger had gone home, but he would not let her know if he could help it.

"Leave her out of the question; she was a saint," he said roughly.

"She cannot be left out—nor can you. He got his

596

temperament naturally; he inherited his weakness. From your grandfather, from her father. Do you think you are in no way responsible?"

He was silent for a moment, but then said stubbornly: "Why—why have you done it? What's between him and me can't be helped. We are father and son; but you—you had no call, no responsibility."

"I love Jim—I always loved him, ever since I can remember—as you did. I see my way ahead. I will not desert him. No one cares what happens to him—no one but me. Your love wouldn't stand the test—mine will."

"Your folks have disinherited you. You have almost nothing—and I will not change my mind. What do you see ahead of you?"

"Jim—only Jim—and God."

Her eyes were shining, her hands were clasped together at her side in the tenseness of her feeling, her indomitable spirit spoke in her face.

Suddenly the old man brought his fist down on the table with a bang.

"It's a crime! Oh, it's a crime, to risk your life so! You ought to have been locked up. I'd have done it."

"Listen to me," she said quietly. "I know the risk. But do you think that I could have lived my life out feeling that I might have saved Jim, and didn't try? You talk of beauty and power and ruling; you say what others have said to me. Which is the greater thing: to get what pleases one, or to work for something which is more to one than all else in the world? To save one life, one intellect, one great man—oh, he has the making of a great man in him—to save a soul, would not life be well lost, would not love be well spent, in doing it?"

"Love's labour lost!" said the old man slowly, cynically, but not without emotion.

"I have ambition," she continued. "No girl was ever more ambitious, but my ambition is to make the

597

most and best of myself. Place? Jim and I will hold
it yet. Power? It shall be as it must be; but Jim and
I will work for it to fulfil ourselves. For me—ah, if I
can save him—and I mean to do so!—do you think that
I would not then have my heaven on earth? You want
money, money, money, power, and to rule; and these
are to you the best things in the world. I make my
choice differently, though I would have these other
things if I could, and I hope I shall. But Jim first—your
son, Jim, my husband, Jim."

The old man got to his feet slowly; she had him at
bay.

"But you are great," he said, "great! It is an awful
stake—awful! But if you win, you'll have what money
can't buy. And listen to me. We'll make the stake
bigger. It will give it point, too, in another way. If
you keep Jim sober for four years from the day of your
marriage, on the last day of that four years I'll put in
your hands for you and him, or for your child—if you
have one—five millions of dollars. I am a man of my
word. While Jim drinks, I won't take him back; he's
disinherited. I'll give him nothing now or hereafter.
Save him for four years—if he can do that, he will do
all—and there's five million as sure as the sun's in
heaven. Amen and amen!"

He opened the door. There was a strange, soft light
in her eyes as she came to go.

"Aren't you going to kiss me?" she said, looking at
him whimsically.

He was disconcerted. She did not wait, but reached
up and kissed him on the cheek.

"Good-bye," she said with a smile. "We'll win the
stake. Good-bye."

An instant, and she was gone. He shut the door,
then turned and looked in a mirror on the wall. Ab-
stractedly he touched the cheek she had kissed. Suddenly a change passed over his face. He dropped in a
chair, and his fist struck the table as he said:

"By God, she may do it—she may do it! But it's life and death—it's life and death!"

Society had its sensation, and then the veil dropped. For a long time none looked behind it, except Jim's father. He had too much at stake not to have his telescope upon them. A detective followed them to keep Jim's record. But this they did not know.

From the day they left Washington, Jim put his life and his fate in his wife's hands. He meant to follow her judgment, and, self-willed and strong in intellect as he was, he said that she should have a fair chance of fulfilling her purpose. There had been many pour-parlers as to what Jim should do. There was farming. She set that aside because it meant capital, and it also meant monotony and loneliness; and capital was limited, and monotony and loneliness were bad for Jim, deadening an active brain which must not be deprived of stimulants—stimulants of a different sort, however, from those which had heretofore mastered it. There was the law. But Jim would have to become a citizen of Canada, change his flag, and where they meant to go—to the outskirts—would offer few opportunities for the law, and with not enough to do there would be danger. Railway construction? That seemed good in many ways, but Jim had not the professional knowledge necessary—his experience with his father had been financial, not practical workmanship. Above all else he must have responsibility, discipline, and strict order in his life.

"Something that will be good for my natural vanity, and knock the nonsense out of me," Jim agreed as they drew farther and farther away from Washington and the past, and nearer and nearer to the Far North and their future.

Since their marriage there had come into Sally's face that illumination which only belongs to souls possessed of an idea greater than themselves—saints, patriots;

faces which have been washed in the salt tears dropped for others' sorrows, and lighted by the fire of self-sacrifice.

What did Jim's life mean?—it was only one in the millions coming and going, and every man must work out his own salvation. Why should she cramp her soul to this one issue when the same soul could spend itself upon the greater motives and in the larger circle? A wide world of influence had opened up before her, power, position, adulation could have been all hers, as John Appleton and Jim's father had said. She might have moved in well-trodden ways, through gardens of pleasure, lived a life where all would have been made easy, where she would be shielded at every turn, and her beauty would be flattered by luxury into a constant glow. She was not so primitive, so unintellectual, not to have thought of all this, else her decision would have had less importance; she would have been no more than an infatuated, emotional woman with a touch of second-class drama in her nature. She had thought of it all, and she had made her choice.

She had a heart and mind for great issues. She believed that Jim had a big brain, and would and could accomplish great things. She knew that he had in him the strain of hereditary instinct. His mother's father had ended a brief life in a drunken duel on the Mississippi, and Jim's boyhood had never had discipline or direction, or any strenuous order. He might never acquire order, and the power that order and habit and the daily iteration of necessary thoughts and acts bring; but the prospect did not appal her. She had taken the risk with her eyes wide open; had set her own life and happiness in the hazard. But Jim must be saved—must be what his talents, his genius, entitled him to be. And the long game must have the long thought.

As they drew into the great Saskatchewan Valley, she gave him his course. As a private he must join the mounted police, the red-coated riders of the plains, and work his way up through every stage of responsibility, beginning at the very foot of the ladder.

She believed that he would agree with her proposal; but her hands clasped his a little more firmly and solicitously—there was a faint, womanly fear at her heart—as she asked him if he would do it.

His face fell for a moment when she made the suggestion, but it cleared presently, and he said, with a dry laugh:

"Well, I guess they must make me a sergeant pretty quick. I'm a colonel in the Kentucky Carbineers!"

She laughed too; then for a moment afterwards, woman-like, wondered if she were right, and was a little frightened. But that was only because she was not self-opinionated, and was more anxious than any woman in all the north land.

It happened as Jim said; he was made a sergeant at once—Sally managed that; for, when it came to the point, and she saw the conditions in which the private lived, and realized that Jim must be one of them, and clean out the stables, and groom his horse and the officers' horses, and fetch and carry, her heart failed her, and she thought that she was making her remedy needlessly heroical. So she went to see the commissioner, who was on a tour of scrutiny on their arrival at the post, and, as better men than he had done in more knowing circles, he fell under her spell. If she had asked for a lieutenancy he would probably have corrupted some member of parliament into securing it for Jim.

But Jim was made a sergeant, and the commissioner and the captain of the troop kept their eyes on him. So did other members of the troop, who did not quite know their man, and attempted, figuratively, to pinch him here and there. They found that his actions were greater than his words, and both were in perfect harmony in the end, though his words often seemed pointless to their minds until they understood that they had conveyed truths through a medium more like a heliograph than a telephone. By and by they began to understand his heliographing; and when they did that they began to swear by him—not at him.

In time it was found that the troop never had a better disciplinarian than Jim. He knew when to shut his eyes, and when to keep them open. To non-essentials he kept his eyes shut; to essentials he kept them very wide open. There were some men of good birth from England and elsewhere amongst them, and these mostly understood him first. But they all understood Sally from the beginning, and after a little they were glad enough to be able to come, on occasion, to the five-roomed little house near the barracks and hear her talk, then answer her questions, and, as men had done at Washington, open out their hearts to her.

They noticed, however, that while she made them barley-water, and all kinds of soft drinks from citric acid, sarsaparilla, and the like, and had one special drink of her own invention which she called cream-nectar, no spirits were to be had. They also noticed that Jim never drank a drop of liquor; and by and by, one way or another, they got a glimmer of the real truth before it became known who he really was, or anything of his history. Interest in the two and in Jim's reformation spread through the country, while Jim gained reputation as the smartest man in the force, officers or privates.

They were on the outskirts of civilization; as Jim used to say, "One step ahead of the procession." Jim's duty was to guard the columns of settlements and progress, and to see that every man got his own rights and not more than his rights; that justice should be the plumb line of march and settlement. His principle was embodied in certain words which he quoted once to Sally from the prophet Amos: *"And the Lord said unto me, Amos what seest thou? And I said, a plumb line."*

On the day that Jim became a lieutenant, his family increased by one. It was a girl, and they called her Nancy, after Jim's mother. It was the anniversary of their marriage, and, so far, Jim had won, with what fightings and strugglings and wrestlings of the spirit only Sally and himself knew. She knew as well as he, and always saw the storm coming before it broke—a restlessness, then a moodiness, then a hungry, eager, helpless look, and afterwards an agony of longing, a feverish desire to break away and get the thrilling thing that stilled this demon within him.

There had been moments when his doom seemed certain. He knew and she knew that if he once got drunk again he would fall never to rise again—humiliation would break his spirit. On one occasion, after a hard, long, hungry ride he was half-mad with desire, but even as he seized the flask that was offered to him by his only enemy—the captain of B Troop at the next station east of them—there came a sudden call to duty, two hundred Indians having gone upon the warpath. It saved him, it broke the spell. He had to mount and away, with the antidote and stimulant of responsibilty driving him on.

Another occasion was equally perilous to his safety. They had been idle for days in a hot week in summer, waiting for orders to return from the rail-head, where they had gone to quell a riot, and where drink and hilarity were common. Suddenly, more suddenly than it had ever come, the demon of his thirst had Jim by the throat. Sergeant Sewell, of the grey stubble head, who loved him more than his sour heart had loved anybody in all his life, was holding himself ready for the physical assault he must make upon his superior officer if, and when, he raised a glass to his lips, when salvation came once again. An accident had occurred far down the railway line, and the operator of the telegraph-office had that very day been stricken down with pleurisy and pneumonia. In despair, the manager had sent to Jim, eagerly hoping that he might help them, for the Riders of the Plains were a sort of Court of Appeal for every trouble in the Far North.

Instantly Jim was in the saddle with his troop. Out of curiosity he had learned telegraphy when a boy, as he had learned many things. Arrived at the scene of the accident, he sent swift messages and received them —by sound, not on paper, as did the official operator— to the amazement and pride of the troop. Then, between caring for the injured in the accident, against the coming of the relief train, and nursing the sick operator through the dark moments of his dangerous illness, he passed a crisis of his own disease triumphantly; but not the last crisis.

So the first and so the second and third years passed in safety.

"Please, I want to go too, Jim."

Jim swung round and caught the child up in his arms.

"Say, how dare you call your father *Jim*? Tell me that."

"It's what mummy calls you—it's pretty."

"I don't call her mummy because you do, and you mustn't call me *Jim* because she does. Do you hear?"

The whimsical face lowered a little, then the rare and beautiful dark blue eyes raised slowly, shaded by the long lashes, and the voice said demurely:

"Yes—Jim."

"Nancy, Nancy," said a voice from the corner in reproof, mingled with suppressed laughter. "Nancy, you mustn't be saucy. You must say 'father' to——"

"Yes, Mummy, dear. I'll say 'father' to—your Jim."

"You imp—you imp of delight!" said Jim, as he strained the dainty little lass to his breast, while she appeared interested in a wave of his black hair which she curled around her finger.

Sally came forward with the little parcel of sandwiches she had been preparing, and put them in a saddle-bag lying on a chair at the door, in readiness for the journey Jim was about to make. Her eyes were glistening, and her face had a heightened colour. The three years which had passed since she married had touched her not at all to her disadvantage, rather to her profit. She looked not an hour older. Motherhood had only added to her charm, giving it a delightful gravity. The prairie life had given a shining quality to her handsomeness, an air of depth and firmness, an exquisite health and clearness to the colour in her cheeks. Her step was light as Nancy's, elastic and buoyant—a gliding motion which gave a sinuous grace to the movements of her body. There had also come into her eyes a vigilance such as deaf people possess, a sensitive observation imparting a deeper intelligence to the face.

Here was the only change by which you could guess the story of her life. Her eyes were like the eyes of an anxious mother who can never sleep till every child is abed; whose sense is quick to hear the faintest footstep without or within; and who, as years go on, and her children grow older and older, must still lie awake hearkening for the late footstep on the stair. In Sally's eyes was the story of the past three years; of love and temptation and struggle, of watchfulness and yearning and anxiety; of determination and inviolable hope. Her eyes had a deeper look than that in Jim's. Now, as she gazed at him, the maternal spirit rose up from the great well of protectiveness in her, and engulfed both husband and child. There was always something of the maternal in her eyes when she looked at Jim. He did not see it. He only saw the wonderful blue, and the humour—the humour which had helped him over such difficult places these past three years.

The baby Nancy had done much to brace her faith in the future, and comfort her anxious present. The child had intelligence of a rare order. She would lie by the half-hour on the floor, turning over the leaves of a book without pictures, and before she could speak would read from the pages in a language all her own. She made a fairy world for herself, peopled by characters to whom she gave names, to whom she assigned curious attributes and qualities. They were as real to her as though flesh and blood, and she was never lonely and never cried; and she had buried herself in her father's heart. She had drawn to her the roughest men in the troop, and for old Sewell, the grim sergeant, she had a specially warm place.

"You can love me if you like," she had said to him at the very start, with the egotism of childhood, but made haste to add: "Because I love you, Gri-Gri." She called him Gri-Gri from the first, but they only knew long after that "Gri-Gri" meant "grey-grey," to signify that she called him after his grizzled hairs.

What she had been in the life-history of Sally and Jim they both knew. Jim regarded her with an almost superstitious feeling. Sally was his strength, his support, his inspiration, his bulwark of defence; Nancy was the charm he wore about his neck—his mascot, he called her. Once, when she was ill, he had suffered as he had never done before in his life. He could not sleep, nor eat, and went about his duties like one in a dream. When his struggles against his enemy were fiercest he kept saying over her name to himself, as though she could help him. Yet always it was Sally's hand he held in his darkest hours, in his brutal moments; for in this fight between appetite and will there are moments when only the animal seems to exist, and the soul disappears in the glare and gloom of the primal emotions, a throwback to savagery. Nancy he called his "lucky sixpence," but he called Sally his "guinea-girl."

From first to last his whimsicality never deserted him. In his worst hours, some innate optimism and humour held him steady in his fight. It was not depression that possessed him at the worst, but the violence of an appetite most like a raging pain which men may endure with a smile upon their lips. He carried in his face the story of a conflict, the aftermath of bitter experience, and through all there pulsed the glow of experience. He had grown handsomer, and the graceful decision of his figure, the deliberate certainty of every action, heightened the force of a singular personality. As in the eyes of Sally, in his eyes was a long reflective look which told of things overcome, and yet of dangers present. His lips smiled often, yet the eyes said: "I have lived, I have seen, I have suffered, and I must suffer more. I have loved, I have been loved under the shadow of the sword. Happiness I have had, and golden hours, but not peace—never peace. My soul has need of peace."

In the greater, deeper experience of their lives, the more material side of existence had grown less and less to them. Their home was a model of simple comfort and some luxury, though Jim had insisted that Sally's income should not be spent except upon the child, and should be saved for the child, their home being kept on his pay and on the tiny income left by his mother. With the help of an Indian girl, and a half-breed for outdoor work and fires and gardening, Sally had cared for the house herself. Ingenious and tasteful, with a gift for cooking, and an educated hand, she had made their little home as pretty as their few possessions would permit. Refinement covered all, and three or four-score books were like so many friends to comfort her when Jim was away, like kind and genial neighbours next door when he was at home. From Browning she had written down in her long, sliding handwriting, and hung up beneath Jim's looking-glass, the heartening words:

"One who never turned his back, but marched breast
    forward,
  Never doubted clouds would break,
Never dreamed, though right were worsted, wrong
  would triumph,
  Held we fall to rise, are baffled to fight better,
  Sleep to wake."

They had lived above the sordid, and there was something in the nature of his life to help them to it. He belonged to a small handful of men who had control over an empire, with an individual responsibility and influence not contained in the scope of their commissions. It was a matter of moral force and character, and of uniform, symbolical only of the great power behind, of the long arm of the State, of the insistence of the law, which did not rely upon force alone, but on the certainty of its administration. In such conditions, the smallest brain was bound to expand, to take on qualities of judgment and temperateness which would never be developed in ordinary circumstances.

It had not come to him all at once. His intellect at first stood in his way. His love of paradox, his deep observation, his insight, all made him inherently satirical, though not cruelly so; but satire had become pure whimsicality at last; and he came to see that, on the whole, the world was imperfect, but also, on the whole, was moving towards perfection rather than imperfection.

In all that he had changed a great deal. His heart was still the heart of a boy, but his intellect had sobered, softened, ripened, even in this secluded and seemingly unimportant life; as Sally had said and hoped it would. Sally's conviction had been right. But the triumph was not yet achieved. She knew it. On occasion, the tones of his voice told her, the look that came into his eyes proclaimed it to her, his feverishness and restlessness, his burning eyes made it certain. How many a night had she thrown her arm over his shoulder, and sought his hand and held it, while in the dark silence, and wide-eyed, dry-lipped, and with a throat like fire, he had held himself back from falling! There was liquor in the house —the fight would not have been a fight without it. She had determined that he should see his enemy, and meet him in the plains and face him down, and he was never many feet away from his possible disaster. Yet for three years all had gone well. There was another year. Would he last out the course?

At first the thought of the stake for which she was playing, in terms of currency, with the head of Jim's father on every note, was much with her. The amazing nature of the offer of five millions of dollars stimulated her imagination, roused her; gold coins are counters in the game of success, signs and tokens. Money alone could not have lured her; but rather what it represented —power, width of action, freedom to help when the heart prompted, machinery for carrying out large plans, ability to surround with advantage those whom we love. So, at first, while yet the memories of Washington were much with her, the appeal of the millions was strong.

But, all through, the other thing really mastered her —the fixed idea that Jim must be saved. As it deepened, the other life that she had lived became like the sports in which we shared when children, full of vivacious memory, shining with impulse and the stir of life, but not to be repeated—days and deeds outgrown.

When Nancy came, the lesser idea—the stake, took on a new importance; for now it seemed to her that there was a duty which she owed the child to secure for it its rightful heritage. Then Jim, too, appeared in a new light, as one who could never fulfil himself unless working through the natural channels of his birth, inheritance and upbringing. Jim, drunken and unreliable, with broken will and fighting to find himself, the waste places were for him until he was the master of his will and emotions. Once, however, secure in ability to control himself, with cleansed brain and purpose defined, the widest field would still be too narrow for his talents, and the five, yes, the fifty millions of his father must be his!

She had never repented having married Jim; but twice in those three years she had broken down and wept as though her heart would break. There were times when Jim's nerves were shaken in his struggle against the unseen foe, and he had spoken to her querulously, almost sharply. Yet in her tears there was no reproach for him, rather for herself—the fear that she might lose her influence over him, that she could not keep him close to her heart, that he might drift away from her in the commonplaces and monotony of work and domestic life. Everything so depended on her being to him not only the one woman for whom he cared, but the woman without whom he could care for no other.

"O my God, give me his love," she had prayed. "Let me keep it yet a little while. For his sake, not for my own, let me have the power to hold his love. Make my mind always quiet, and let me blow neither hot nor cold. Help me to keep my temper sweet and cheerful, so that he will find the room empty where I am not, and his footsteps quicken when he comes to the door."

Twice had she poured out her heart so, in the agony of fear that she should lose favour in Jim's sight. She did not know how alluring she was in spite of the constant proofs offered her. She had had her will with all who came her way, from governor to Indian brave. Once, in a journey they had made far north, soon after they came, she had stayed at a Hudson Bay Company's post for some days; while there came news of restlessness among the Indians, because of lack of food, and Jim had gone farther north to steady the tribes, leaving her with the factor and his wife and a half-breed servant.

While she and the factor's wife were alone in the yard of the post one day, an Indian chief, in war-paint and feathers, entered suddenly, brandishing a long knife. He had been drinking, and there was danger in his black eyes. With a sudden inspiration, she came forward quickly, nodded and smiled to him, and then pointed to a grindstone standing in the corner of the yard. As she did so, she saw Indians crowding into the gate, armed with knives, guns, bows and arrows. She beckoned to Arrowhead, and he followed her to the grindstone. She poured some water on to the wheel and began to turn it, nodding at the now impassive Indian to begin. Presently he nodded also, and put his knife on the stone. She kept turning steadily, singing to herself the while, as with anxiety she saw the Indians drawing closer and closer in from the gate. Faster and faster she turned, and at last the Indian lifted his knife from the stone. She reached out her hand with simulated interest, felt the edge with her thumb, the Indian looking darkly at her the while. Presently, after feeling the edge himself, he bent over the stone again, and she went on turning the wheel, still singing softly. At last he stopped again and felt the edge. With a smile, which showed her fine white teeth, she said: "Is that for me?" making a significant sign across her throat at the same time.

The old Indian looked at her grimly, then slowly shook his head in negation.

"I go hunt Yellow-Hawk to-night, I go fight. I like marry you when I come back. *How!*" he said, and turned away towards the gate.

Some of his braves held back, the blackness of death in their looks. He saw.

"My knife is sharp," he said. "The woman is brave. She shall live and eat; go and fight Yellow-Hawk, or starve and die."

Divining their misery, their hunger, and the savage thought that had come to them, she had whispered to the factor's wife to bring food, and the woman now came running out with two baskets full, and returned for more. Sally ran forward among the Indians, and put the food into their hands. With grunts of satisfaction they seized what she gave, and thrust it in their mouths, squatting on the ground. Arrowhead looked on, stern and immobile, but when at last she and the factor's wife sat down before the braves with confidence and an air of friendliness, he sat down also; yet, famished as he was, he would not touch the food.

At last, Sally, realizing his proud defiance of hunger,

offered him a little lump of pemmican and a biscuit,
and with a grunt he took it from her hands and ate it.
Then, at his command, a fire was lit, the pipe of peace
was brought out, and Sally and the factor's wife touched
their lips to it, and passed it on.

So was a new treaty of peace and loyalty made with
Arrowhead and his tribe by a woman without fear,
whose life had seemed not worth a minute's purchase;
and, as the sun went down, Arrowhead and his men
went forth to make war upon Yellow-Hawk, beside the
Nettigon river. In this wise had her influence spread
in the land.

Standing now with the child in his arms and his wife
looking at him with a moisture of the eyes, Jim laughed
outright. There came upon him a sudden sense of
power, of aggressive force—the will to do! Sally understood, and came and laughingly grasped his arm.

"Oh, Jim," she said playfully, "you are getting
muscles like steel! You hadn't these when you were
colonel of the Kentucky Carbineers!"

"I guess I need them now," he said, smiling, and,
with the child still in his arms, drew her to a window
looking northward.

As far as the eye could see, nothing but snow, like a
blanket, spread over the land. Here and there in the
wide expanse a tree silhouetted against the sky, a tracery
of eccentric beauty, and off, in the far distance, a solitary
horseman riding towards the post—riding hard.

"It was root, hog, or die, with me, Sally," he continued, "and I rooted—I wonder—that fellow on the
horse—I have a feeling about him. See, he's been
riding hard and long—you can tell by the heavy way
the horse drops his legs. He sags a bit himself. But
isn't it beautiful and all that out there—the real quint-
essence of life?"

The air was full of delicate particles of frost on which
the sun sparkled; and though there was neither bird nor
insect nor animal, nor stir of leaf, nor swaying of branch

or waving grass, life palpitated in the air, energy sang its song in the footstep that crunched the frosty ground, that broke the crusted snow, in the delicate wind that stirred the flag by the barracks away to the left, hope smiled in the wide prospect over which the thrilling, bracing air trembled. Sally had indeed chosen aright.

"You had a big thought when you brought me here, guinea-girl," he added presently. "We are going to win out here"—he set the child down—"you and I and this lucky dollar." He took up his short fur coat. "Yes, we'll win, honey!"

Then he added, with a brooding look on his face:

> "The end comes as came the beginning,
>   And shadows fall into the past;
> And the goal, is it not worth the winning,
>   If it brings us but home at the last?
> While far through the pain of waste places,
>   We tread, 'tis a blossoming rod,
> That drives us to grace from disgraces,
>   From the fens to the gardens of God!"

He paused reflectively.

"It's strange that this life up here makes you feel that you must live a bigger life still, that this is only the wide porch to the great labour-house. It makes you want to do things. Well, we've got to win the stake first," he added, with a laugh.

"The stake is a big one, Jim—bigger than you think."

"You and her and me—me that was in the gutter."

"What is the gutter, Dadsie?" asked Nancy.

"The gutter—the gutter is where the dish-water goes, midget," he answered, with a dry laugh.

"Oh, I don't think you'd like to be in the gutter," Nancy said solemnly.

"You have to get used to it first, miss," answered Jim.

Suddenly Sally laid both hands on Jim's shoulders and looked him in the eyes.

"You must win the stake, Jim. Think—*now?*"

She laid a hand on the head of the child. He did not know that he was playing for a certain five millions, perhaps fifty millions, of dollars. She had never told him of his father's offer. He was fighting only for salvation —for those he loved; for freedom. As they stood there, the conviction had come upon her that they had come to the last battlefield, that this journey which Jim now must take would decide all, would give them perfect peace or lifelong pain.

To her adjuration Jim replied by burying his face in her golden hair, and he whispered:

"Say, I've done near four years, my girl. I think I'm all right now—I think. This last six months, it's been easy—pretty fairly easy."

"Four months more, only four months more! God be good to us!" she said, with a little gasp.

If he held out for four months more, the first great stage in their life journey would be passed, the stake won.

"I saw a woman get an awful fall once," Jim said suddenly. "Her bones were broken in twelve places, and there wasn't a spot on her body without injury. They set and fixed up every broken bone except one. It was split down. They didn't dare perform the operation; she couldn't stand it. There was a limit to pain, and she had reached the boundary. Two years went by, and she got better every way, but inside her leg those broken pieces of bones were rubbing against each other. She tried to avoid the inevitable operation, but Nature said, 'You must do it, or die in the end.' She yielded. Then came the long preparations for the operation. Her heart shrank, her mind got tortured. She'd suffered too much. She pulled herself together, and said: 'I must conquer this shrinking body of mine by my will. How shall I do it?' Something within her said: 'Think and do for others. Forget yourself.' And so, as they got her ready for her torture, she visited hospitals, agonized cripple as she was, and smiled, and talked to the sick and broken, telling them of her own miseries endured and dangers faced, of the boundary of human suffering almost passed; and so she got her courage for her own trial. And she came out all right in the end. Well, that's the way I've felt sometimes. But I'm ready for my operation now whenever it comes, and it's coming, I know. Let it come when it must."

There came a knock at the door, and presently entered Sewell.

"The commissioner wishes you to come over, sir," he said.

"I was just coming, Sewell."

"Everything's ready, sir; but there's to be a change of orders—something happened somewhere—some bad job up in the Cree country, I think."

A few minutes later Jim was in the commissioner's office. The murder of the Hudson Bay Company's man had been committed in the Cree country. The stranger whom Jim and Sally had seen riding across the plains had brought the news for thirty miles, word of the murder having been carried from point to point.

The commissioner was uncertain what to do, as the Crees were restless through want of food and the absence of game, and a force sent to capture Arrowhead, the chief who had committed the murder, might precipitate trouble. Jim solved the problem by offering to go alone and bring the chief in to the post. It was two hundred miles to the Cree encampment, and the journey had its double dangers.

Another officer was sent on the expedition for which Jim was preparing, and he made ready to go upon his lonely duty. His wife only knew three days after he had gone what the nature of his mission was.

Jim made his journey in good weather with his faithful dogs alone, and came into the camp of the Crees armed only with a revolver. If he had gone with ten men

615

there would have been an instant mêlée, in which he would have lost his life. This is what the chief had expected, had prepared for; but Jim was more formidable alone, with power in the distance behind him which could and would come, with force, and destroy the tribe if resistance was offered, than with fifty men. His tongue had a gift of terse and picturesque speech, powerful with a people who had the gift of imagination. With five hundred men ready to turn him loose in the plains without dogs or food, he carried himself with a watchful coolness and complacent determination which went home to their minds with great force.

For hours the struggle for the murderer went on, a struggle of will, of mind over inferior mind and matter.

Arrowhead was a chief whose will had never been crossed by his own people, and to master that will by a superior will, to hold back the destructive force which, to the ignorant minds of the braves, was only a natural force of defence, meant a task needing more than authority behind it. For the very fear of that authority put in motion was an incentive to present resistance—— to stave off the day of trouble. The faces that surrounded Jim were thin with hunger, and the murder that had been committed by the chief had, as its origin, the foolish replies of the Hudson Bay Company's man to their demand for supplies. Arrowhead had killed him with his own hand.

But Jim Templeton was of a different calibre. Although he had not been told it, he realized that, indirectly, hunger was the cause of the crime, and might easily become the cause of another; for their tempers were sharper even than their appetites. Upon this he played; upon this he made an exhortation to the chief. He assumed that Arrowhead had become violent because of his people's straits, that Arrowhead's heart yearned for his people, and would make sacrifice for them. Now, if Arrowhead came quietly, he would see that supplies of food were sent at once, and that arrangements would be made to meet the misery of their situation. Therefore, if Arrowhead came freely he would have so much in his favour before his judges; if he did not come, then he must be brought by force if need be; and if they raised a hand to prevent it, then destruction would fall upon all—all save the women and children. The law must be obeyed.

As he ended his words a young brave sprang forward with his hatchet raised. Jim's revolver slipped down into his palm from his sleeve, and a bullet caught the brave in the lifted arm. The hatchet dropped to the ground.

Then Jim's eyes blazed, and he turned a look of anger on the chief, his face pale and hard.

"The stream rises above the banks; come with me, chief, or all shall drown. I am master, and I speak. Ye are hungry because ye are idle. Ye call the world yours, yet ye will not stoop to gather from the earth the fruits of the earth. Ye sit idle in the summer, and women and children die round you when winter comes. Because the game is gone, ye say. Must the world stand still because a handful of Crees need a hunting-ground? Must the maker of cities and the wonders of the earth who fill the land with plenty—must they stand far off, because the Crees and their chief would wander over a million acres, for each man a million, when by a hundred, ay, by ten, each white man would live in plenty—and make the land rejoice? See! Here is the truth. When the Great Spirit draws the game away, so that the hunting is poor, ye sit down and fill your hearts with murder, and in the blackness of your thoughts kill my brother. Idle and shiftless and evil ye are, while the earth cries out to give you of its plenty, a great harvest from the little seed, if ye will but dig and plant, and plough and sow, and reap and lend your backs to toil. Now, hear and heed. The end is come. For this once ye shall be fed—by the blood of my heart ye shall be fed! And another year ye shall labour, and get the fruits of your labour, and not stand waiting, as it were, till a fish passes the spear, or a stag shall water at your door, that ye may slay and eat. The end is come, ye idle men. O chief, hearken! One of your braves would have slain me, even as you slew my brother —he one, and you a thousand. Speak to your people as I have spoken; and then come and answer for the deed done by your hand. And this I say that right shall be done between man and man! Speak!"

Jim had made his great effort—and not without avail. Arrowhead rose slowly, the cloud gone out of his face, and spoke to his people, bidding them wait in peace till food came, and appointing his son chief in his stead until his return.

"The white man speaks truth, and I will go," he said. "I will return," he continued, "if it be written so upon the leaves of the tree of Life; and if it be not so written, I will fade like a mist, and the tepees will know me not again. The days of my youth are spent, and my step no longer springs from the ground. I shuffle among the grass and the fallen leaves, and my eyes scarce know the stag from the doe. The white man is master —if he wills it, we shall die; if he wills it, we shall live. And this was ever so. It is in the tale of our people. One tribe ruled and the others were their slaves. If it is written on the leaves of the tree of Life that the white man rule us for ever, then it shall be so. I have spoken. Now, behold I go."

Jim had conquered; and together they sped away with the dogs through the sweet-smelling spruce woods where every branch carried a cloth of white, and the only sound heard was the swish of a blanket of snow as it fell to the ground from the wide webs of green, or a twig snapped under the load it bore. Peace brooded in the silent and comforting forest, and Jim and Arrowhead, the Indian ever ahead, swung along, mile after mile, on their snowshoes, emerging at last upon the wide, white prairie.

A hundred miles of sun and fair weather, sleeping at night in the open in a trench dug in the snow, no fear in the thoughts of Jim, nor evil in the heart of the heathen man. There had been moments of watchfulness, of uncertainty, on Jim's part, the first few hours of the first night after they left the Cree reservation; but the conviction speedily came to Jim that all was well; for the chief slept soundly from the moment he lay down on his blankets between the dogs. Then Jim went to sleep as in his own bed, and waking, found Arrowhead lighting a fire from a little load of sticks from the sledges. And between murderer and captor there sprang up the companionship of the open road which brings all men to a certain land of faith and understanding, unless they are perverted and vile. There was no vileness in Arrowhead. There were no handcuffs on his hands, no signs of captivity; the two ate out of the same dish, drank from the same basin, broke from the same bread.

One hundred miles of sun and fair weather, and then fifty miles of bitter, aching cold, with nights of peril from the increasing chill, so that Jim dared not sleep lest he would never wake again, but die benumbed and exhausted! Yet Arrowhead slept through all. Day after day so, and then ten miles of storm such as only come to the vast barren of the north lands; and woe to the traveller upon whom the icy wind and the blinding snow descended! Woe came upon Jim Templeton and Arrowhead the heathen!

In the awful struggle between man and Nature that followed, the captive became the leader. The craft of the plains, the inherent instinct, the feeling which was more than eyesight, became the only hope. One whole day to cover ten miles—an endless path of agony, in which Jim went down again and again, but came up, blinded by snow and drift, and cut as with lashes by the angry wind. At the end of the ten miles was a Hudson Bay Company's post and safety; and through ten hours had the two struggled towards it, going off at tangents, circling on their own tracks; but the Indian, by an instinct as sure as the needle to the pole, getting the direction to the post again in the moments of direct peril and uncertainty. To Jim the world became a sea of maddening forces which buffeted him; a whirlpool of fire in which his brain was tortured, his mind was shrivelled up; a vast army rending itself, each man against the other. It was a purgatory of music, broken by discords, and then at last—how sweet it all was, after the eternity of misery!—"Church bells and voices low," and Sally singing to him. Nancy's voice calling. Then nothing but sleep—sleep, a sinking down millions of miles in an ether of drowsiness which thrilled him—and then—no more.

None who has suffered up to the limit of what the human body and soul may bear can remember the history of those distracted moments when the struggle became one between the forces in man and the forces in Nature; agonized body and smothered mind, with yet the divine intelligence of the created being, directing, even though subconsciously, the fight.

How Arrowhead found the post in the mad storm he could never have told. Yet he found it, with Jim unconscious on the sledge and with limbs frozen, all the dogs gone but two—the leathers over the Indian's shoulders as he fell against the gate of the post with a shrill cry that roused the factor and his people within, together with Sewell, who had been sent out from headquarters to await Jim's arrival there. It was Sewell's hand which first felt Jim's heart and pulse, and found that there was still life left, even before it could be done by the doctor from headquarters, who had come to visit a sick man at the post.

For hours they worked with snow upon the frozen limbs to bring back life and consciousness. Consciousness came at last with half delirium, half understanding; as, emerging from the passing sleep of anæsthetics, the eye sees things and dimly registers them before the brain has set them in any relation to life or comprehension.

But Jim was aroused at last, and the doctor presently held to his lips a glass of brandy. Then from infinite distance Jim's understanding returned; the mind emerged, but not wholly, from the chaos in which it was travelling. His eyes stood out in eagerness.

"Brandy, brandy!" he said hungrily.

With an oath, Sewell snatched the glass from the doctor's hand, put it on the table, then stooped to Jim's ear and said hoarsely, "Remember your wife and child! For God's sake, sir, don't drink!"

Jim's head fell back, the fierce light went out of his eyes, the face became greyer and sharper. "Sally— Nancy—Nancy!" he whispered, and his fingers clutched vaguely at the quilt.

"He must have brandy, or he will die—the system is pumped out. He must be revived." The doctor reached again for the glass of spirits.

Jim understood now. He was on the borderland between life and death; his feet were at the brink.

"No—not—brandy, no! I will die first!" he moaned. "Sally—Sally, kiss me," he said faintly, from the middle of the world in which he was.

"Quick, the broth!" said Sewell to the factor who had been preparing it. "Quick, while there's a chance." He stooped and called into Jim's ear: "For the love of God, wake up, sir! They're coming—they're both coming! Nancy's coming. They'll soon be here."

What matter that he lied! A life was at stake.

Jim's eyes opened again. The doctor was standing with the brandy in his hand. Half madly he reached out. "I must live until they come," he cried; "the brandy—ah, give it! Give it—ah, God save me from it!" he added, gasping, his lips trembling, his hands shaking.

Sewell held the broth to his lips. He drank a little,

yet his face became greyer and greyer, a bluish tinge spread about his mouth.

"Have you nothing else, sir?" asked Sewell in despair.

The doctor put down the brandy, went quickly to his medicine-case, poured into a glass a few drops from a phial, came over again, and poured a little between the lips, then a little more, as Jim's eyes opened again; and at last every drop in the glass trickled down the sinewy throat.

Presently, as they watched him, the doctor said:

"It will not do—he must have brandy; it has life—food—in it."

Jim understood the words. He knew that if he drank the brandy the chances against his future were terrible. He had made his vow and he must keep it. He must win the stake—for Sally, for Nancy, for himself. He must win it or die. Yet the thirst was on him; his enemy had him by the throat again, was dragging him down. Though his body was so cold, his throat was on fire. But in the extremity of his strength his mind fought on—fought on, growing weaker every moment. He was having his last fight. They watched him with an aching anxiety, anger in the doctor's face—he had no patience with these forces arrayed against him.

At last the doctor whispered to Sewell:

"It's no use; he must have the brandy, or he can't live an hour!"

Sewell weakened; the tears fell down his rough, hard cheeks.

"It'll ruin him—it'll ruin him—it's ruin or death!"

"Trust a little more in God, and in the man's strength. Let us give him the chance. Force it down his throat —he's not responsible," said the doctor, to whom saving life was more than all else.

Suddenly there appeared at the bedside Arrowhead, gaunt and weak, his face swollen, the skin of it broken by the whips of storm.

"He is my brother," he said, and stooping, laid both hands, which he had held before the fire for a long time, on Jim's heart. "Take his feet, his hands, his legs, and his head, in your hands," he said to them all. "Life is in us; we will give him life." He knelt down and kept both hands on Jim's heart, while the others, even the doctor, awed by his act, did as they were bid. "Shut your eyes. Let your life go into him. Think of him and him alone. Now!" said Arrowhead, in a strange voice.

He murmured, and continued murmuring, his body drawing closer and closer to Jim's body, while in the deep silence, broken only by the chanting of his low, monotonous voice, the others pressed Jim's hands and head, and feet and legs—six men under the command of a heathen murderer.

The minutes passed. The colour came back to Jim's face, the skin of his hands filled up, they ceased twitching, his pulse got stronger, his eyes opened with a new light in them.

"I'm living, anyhow," he said at last, with a faint smile. "I'm hungry—broth, please!"

The fight was won, and the pagan murderer drew over the fire, and crouched down beside it, his back to the bed, impassive and still. They brought him a bowl of broth and bread. He drank it slowly, and placed the empty bowl between his knees. He sat there through the night, and though they tried to make him lie down, he sat where he was until the morning.

As the light came in at the windows, Sewell touched him on the shoulder, and said, "He is sleeping now."

"I hear my brother breathe," answered Arrowhead. "He will live." All night he had listened, and had heard Jim's breath, as only a man who has lived in waste places can hear. "He will live. What I take with one hand, I give with the other."

He had taken the life of the factor; he had given Jim his life. And when he was tried three months later for murder, someone else said this for him, and the hearts of all, judge and jury, were so moved they knew not what to do.

But Arrowhead was never sentenced, for at the end of the first day's trial he lay down to sleep, and never waked again. He was found still and cold, and there was clasped in his hand a little doll which Nancy had given him on one of her many visits to the prison during her father's long illness. They found a piece of paper in his belt with these words in the Cree language: "With my hands on his heart at the post I gave him the life that was in me, saving but a little until now. Arrowhead, the chief, goes to find life again where is the well at the root of the tree. *How!*"

On the evening of the day that Arrowhead made his journey to "the well at the root of the tree," a stranger knocked at the door of Captain Templeton's cottage; then, without awaiting admittance, entered.

Jim was sitting with Nancy on his knee, her head against his shoulder, Sally at his side, her face alight with some inner joy. Before the knock came to the door, Jim had just said:

"Why do your eyes shine so, Sally? What's in your mind?"

She had been about to answer, to say to him what had been swelling her heart with pride, yet she had not meant to tell him what he had forgotten—not till midnight. But the figure that entered the room, a big man, with deep-set eyes, a man of power who had carried everything before him in the battle of life, he answered for her.

"You have won the stake, Jim," he said in a hoarse voice. "You and she have won the stake, and I've brought it—brought it."

Before they could speak, he placed in Sally's hands bonds for five million dollars.

"Jim—Jim, son!" he burst out, turning to him.

624

Then suddenly he sank into a chair, and putting his head in his hands, sobbed aloud.

"My God! But I'm proud of you! Speak to me, Jim! You've broken me up."

He was ashamed of his tears, but he could not wipe them away.

"Father, dear old man!" said Jim, and put his hands on the broad shoulders.

Sally knelt down beside him, and took both the great hands from the tear-stained face, and laid them against her cheek. But presently Sally put Nancy on his knees,

"I don't like you to cry," the child said softly. "But to-day I cried too, 'cause my Indian man is dead."

The old man could not speak, but he put his cheek down to hers. After a minute, "Oh, but she's worth ten times that," he said, as Sally came close to him with the bundle he had thrust into her hands.

"What is it?" said Jim.

"It's five million dollars—for Nancy," she said.

"Five million—what?"

"The stake, Jim. If you did not drink for four years —never touched a drop—we were to have five million dollars for the child, or for us."

"You never told him, then—you never told him that?" asked the old man.

"I wanted him to win without that," she said. "'If he won, he would be the stronger; if he lost, it would not be so hard for him to bear.'"

The old man drew her down and kissed her cheek. He chuckled, though the tears were still in his eyes.

"You are a wonder—the tenth wonder of the world!" he blurted.

Jim stood staring at the bundle in Nancy's hands. "Five millions—five million dollars for her!" he kept saying to himself.

"I said she's worth ten times that, Jim," The old man caught his hand and pressed it. "But it was a d——d near thing, I tell you," he added. "They tried

625

to break me and my railways, and my bank. I had to fight the combination, and there was one day when I hadn't that five millions there, nor five dollars! Jim, they tried to break the old man!"

"And if they'd broken me, they'd have made me out a scoundrel to her—to this wife of yours, who risked everything for both of us, for both of us, Jim—for she's given up the world to save you, and she was playing like a soul in Hell for Heaven. If they'd broken me, I'd never have lifted my head again. When things were at their worst I played to save that five millions —her stake and mine!—I played for that! I fought for it as a man fights his way out of a burning house. And I won—by the Eternal, I won! And it was by fighting for that five millions I saved fifty—fifty, son! They didn't break the old man, Jim. They didn't break him —not much!"

"There are giants in the world still," said Jim, his own eyes full as he squeezed his father's hand.

He knew now his father and himself, and he knew the meaning of all the bitter and misspent life of the old days. He and his father were on a level of understanding now.

"Are you a giant?" asked Nancy, peering up into her grandfather's eyes.

The old man laughed, then sighed.

"Perhaps I was once, more or less, my dear," saying to her what he meant for the other two. "Perhaps I was, but I've finished. I've had my last fight."

He looked at his son.

"I pass the game on to you, Jim. You can do it. I knew you could do it, as the reports came in this year. I've had a detective up here for four years—and I knew all. I had to do it. It was the devil in me. You've got to carry on the game, Jim; I'm done. I'll stay home and potter about. I want to go back to Kentucky, and build up the old place, and take care of it a bit —your mother always loved it. I'd like to have it as

626

it was when she was there long ago. But I'll be ready
to help you when I'm wanted, understand?"

"You want me to run things—your colossal schemes.
You think——"

"I don't think. I'm old enough to *know!*"

He knew. Fifteen years have gone since then; and
Jim Templeton, masterful, daring, and human, has
preserved his inheritance, has kept the pledge that
saved him. Sally—as she was, so she is, and her old
lovers are her lovers still. Jim has no jealousy, for the
world knows their story, and she may live in the White
House yet.

THE RUNAWAY GUN
by Victor Hugo

A N interval of thirty-one years elapsed between the writing of Victor Hugo's first important work of fiction, *The Hunchback of Notre Dame*, which he wrote in order to revive an interest in the ancient landmarks of France, and *Les Miserables*, his greatest novel. This long interval, however, was fully occupied in the writing of poems and dramas. Hugo was born in 1802. His early years were full of success and honour; the French Academy elected him a member when he was only thirty-nine, and a few years later he was created a peer of France. In 1851 Hugo, with a price on his head as the result of his implication in the famous *coup d'état*, fled to the Channel Isles, where he remained in exile for the rest of his life. Love of liberty is the inspiring force of Hugo's great mind and animates all his work. He died in 1885.

THE RUNAWAY GUN

BY

VICTOR HUGO

THE corvette, *Claymore*, had been detached from a small fleet of British ships, which was cruising off the eastern point of Jersey. Although the *Claymore* was, to outward appearance, a merchant vessel, in reality she was a fighting ship. She lumbered along with the pacific air of a trader, but it would have been unwise to trust her, for she had been constructed to serve a double purpose: deception and fighting. She must mislead the enemy, if possible, but, when necessary, she must join action. For the special service for which she had this night been detailed, her covered deck, which ran from end to end of the ship, had been cleared, and the place of her usual freight had been taken by thirty bronze-wheeled carronades of large calibre. To guard against the hazards of rough weather, or, more probably, with a view to a smart and ship-shape appearance, these thirty carronades were close set, and strongly shackled with triple chains. A corvette, as a rule, has all her guns mounted on her flush-deck, but the *Claymore* had no armament visible. For purposes of surprise and ambush, she carried all her guns between decks. The crew, for this special occasion, consisted entirely of Frenchmen, for the *Claymore*, though a British ship, was co-operating with French Royalists in common cause against the dominant Republican power in France. Not a man on the ship but was a good soldier, a good sailor, and a good Royalist. Her captain was the Count du Boisberthelot; her second-in-command, Lieutenant La Vieuville, of the Gardes-Françaises.

But the circumstance that particularly indicated that

the ship was bound on some unusual adventure was the presence on board of a stranger, an elderly man of severe countenance, and of tall, erect, and powerful figure. At the moment of his stepping on to the corvette, his sea-cloak had been thrown partly open, and it was seen that he was wearing the complete dress of a Breton peasant. And it was as "the peasant" that he was designated by the crew, although when he came on board he had been escorted by the Governor of Jersey, who had addressed him as "General," and by Prince de la Tour d'Auvergne, who had called him "Cousin." This peasant friend of princes and governors spoke not at all, except occasionally to address a curt remark in a low tone to the captain, who listened with deference, and appeared to consider his passenger as in a position of higher authority than himself.

After conducting the "peasant" to his cabin, which was, in fact, the captain's own quarters, Count du Boisberthelot and the Chevalier La Vieuville regained the deck, where they paced up and down in the darkness. As they walked, they lamented the miserable state of France, and the deplorable absence of leadership in the Royalist party. They speculated more especially, but in lowered tones, as to the identity of their mysterious passenger, and the possibility of his being the chief whom their cause so sorely needed.

As La Vieuville was speaking, his remarks were cut short by a sudden cry of distress, while simultaneously strange sounds arose, which resembled nothing that is heard in everyday life. These extraordinary noises and the despairing cry proceeded from the interior of the ship. The captain and the lieutenant rushed from the bridge and made an attempt to descend to the covered deck, but the entrance was choked by the gun-crews, who were swarming up in panic from below.

A terrible thing had happened. One of the carronades of the battery, a "twenty-four," had broken loose. Of all the perils of maritime life, this is, perhaps, the most daunting. No more terrifying disaster can threaten a battleship under full sail in the open sea. A gun which has broken loose straightway becomes a supernatural brute, baffling description. A mere machine is transformed into a living monster. The unwieldy mass of metal glides along on its wheels with movements like those of a billiard ball, staggering when the ship rolls, plunging when she pitches, advancing, retreating, pausing as if to reflect, setting off again, traversing the ship from end to end with the speed of an arrow, gyrating, dodging, eluding, rearing, charging, demolishing, slaughtering, exterminating. It is like a ram butting at a wall for its amusement. But mark this. The ram is of iron; the wall is of wood.

It is as though inert matter has suddenly achieved independence. The bondsman of eternity seems bent on taking its revenge. The malevolence latent in objects, which we describe as inanimate, bursts forth with sudden fury. The thing appears to have lost patience and to be wreaking a weird, incomprehensible vengeance. There is nothing so inexorable as the wrath of the inanimate. This raging mass of metal bounds like a panther and strikes like the lightning. It has the ponderousness of an elephant, the nimbleness of a mouse, the relentlessness of an axe, the unexpectedness of waves, the insensibility of the tomb. It weighs many tons, and it bounces like a child's ball. In the midst of a turn it will suddenly shoot off at a right angle. What can one do? How can one cope with this peril? A tempest subsides; a cyclone passes over; a gale blows itself out. A broken mast can be replaced, a leak can be stopped, and a fire can be extinguished. But how will you control this monster made of gun-metal? You can reason with a mastiff, take a bull by surprise, charm a boa constrictor, frighten a tiger, conciliate a lion. But there is no expedient available against an escaped carronade. You cannot kill it; it is dead already. Yet at the same time it is alive. It is instinct with sinister life, which it derives from the infinite. Beneath it is the deck, on which it is poised. The gun is moved by the ship, the ship by the sea, the sea by the wind. The destroyer is a plaything in the clutches of the vessel, the winds, and the waves, and from these it borrows its awful vitality.

What can be done against such a combination of forces? How frustrate this formidable apparatus of wreckage? How forestall those rushes to and fro, those recoils, those hesitations, those concussions? Each blow that it strikes the bulwarks may founder the ship. How anticipate its terrible meanderings? You are matched against a projectile, which appears to reason, to have ideas, and which is forever swerving in a new direction. How can you stop something you dare not go near? The terrible carronade is beside itself with rage. It rushes hither and thither, hitting out left and right, retreating, shooting past, baffling stratagems, demolishing all obstacles, crushing men as though they were flies.

The whole horror of the situation arises from the fact that the deck is never steady. How contend with an inclined plane which has caprices of its own? It is as if a thunderbolt were imprisoned in the belly of the ship—a thunderbolt which seeks to escape, a thunderbolt which is rolling about on the top of an earthquake.

In a moment the whole ship's company was aroused. The man responsible for the disaster was the gun-captain, who had neglected to tighten the bolt of the shackling chain and to secure the four wheels of the carronade. The result of this omission was to give free play to the underbody and the chase, thus throwing the two planes out of position and finally tearing the recoil tackle from the ringbolts. The drag-rope, too, had parted, and the carronade was no longer attached to its base. Fixed recoil-ropes had not as yet been introduced.

The ship had lurched to a heavy sea, and the carronade, being insecurely fastened, had been violently hurled backwards. It had broken its chain, and

636

embarked upon its disastrous career in the covered deck. A drop of water sliding down a window-pane will give some idea of its curious, gliding motion.

At the moment when the chain parted, the gun crews were in the battery, occupied, singly or in groups, with sundry duties preparatory to clearing the decks for action. Flung forward by the pitching of the ship, the carronade cut a lane through the closely-packed throng, and with one bound crushed four of the men to death. A fifth unfortunate victim was cut down as the carronade was dragged back, and again swept forward, by the roll of the vessel. Then it charged a piece of ordnance on the port side, and dismounted it.

Such was the explanation of the agonized cry which had been heard on the open deck. All the survivors made a rush for the ladder, and the battery was deserted in the twinkling of an eye.

The formidable carronade was master of itself; it was master of the ship. It could work its will on her. The whole ship's company, men who were wont to go laughing into battle, were trembling. No words can describe the horror that prevailed.

Brave men though they were, Captain du Boisberthelot and Lieutenant La Vieuville paused at the head of the ladder. As they stood there, silent, pale, irresolute, gazing into the battery, a man pushed past them down the steps. It was their passenger, the mysterious peasant, whom they had been discussing a moment ago. At the foot of the ladder he halted.

Backwards and forwards the carronade took its course in the covered deck. It was like the living chariot in the Apocalypse. Oscillating at the forward end of the battery, the ship's lantern shed upon the scene bewildering alternations of light and shade. The outlines of the gun were blurred by the violence of its movements. It loomed now black in the light, now vaguely white with reflected gleams in the darkness. It proceeded with its

637

work of destroying the ship. It had already shattered four other pieces of ordnance and had made two great breaches in the side of the vessel. Happily these were above the water-line, but in the event of a squall, the sea would pour in through them. The gun hurled itself frantically against the ribs of the ship. Curved pieces of wood possess a special solidity, but though the riders resisted its onslaughts, they could be heard cracking under the blows of that tremendous mallet, which, incredibly ubiquitous, delivered its attacks in every direction at once. It rattled from side to side as wildly and as quickly as a pellet of lead shaken in a bottle.

The captain was quick to recover his self-possession. By his orders, everything that might serve to check and hamper the gun in its mad career was flung through the hatchway into the battery: mattresses, hammocks, spare sets of sails, coils of rope, kit-bags. But what was the use of these trifles when no one had the courage to go below and place them where they were wanted? In a few minutes they were reduced to shreds.

There was just sufficient sea to make the catastrophe as complete as possible. A gale would have been preferable, for it might have overturned the carronade. Once on its back, with its four wheels in the air, it would have been easily mastered. In the meantime, the damage was becoming more and more serious. The masts, which are socketed in the woodwork of the keel, and run up through the decks like great, round columns, were scored and splintered. The foremast had cracked under the frantic onslaughts of the gun, and even the mainmast had suffered. The battery was breaking up. Ten guns out of the thirty were rendered unfit for service. Further breaches appeared in the bulwarks, and the corvette was beginning to take in water.

The stranger remained standing at the foot of the ladder like a statue in stone, grimly observing the havoc that had been wrought. He did not stir from the spot.

It seemed impossible to take a single step inside the battery. Each movement on the part of the runaway gun threatened to sink the corvette. A few moments more, and nothing could save her. It was a case of instantly averting the peril or losing the ship. Some action must be taken. But what was the right thing to do? The raging lunatic had to be caught; the lightning seized; the thunderbolt brought down.

"Do you believe in God, Chevalier?" du Boisberthelot asked La Vieuville.

"Yes and no," replied La Vieuville. "On certain occasions."

"Such as a storm?"

"Yes; and in moments like the present."

"Certainly only God Himself can get us out of this."

All were silent, while the carronade continued its hideous clamour. The concussions of the gun were answered from without by the thud of the waves breaking against the ship. It was as though two hammers were delivering blows alternately.

Suddenly, within that unapproachable arena a man appeared. He was carrying an iron bar. He was the gun-captain, to whose culpable negligence the disaster was due. The mischief was his doing, and he was anxious to make amends. In one hand he grasped a tiller-rope with a slip-knot at one end; in the other, a handspike. He had jumped into the battery through the hatchway.

A grim scene was now enacted, a titanic spectacle: the duel of gun and gunner, the struggle of matter against mind, the battle of the thing against its creator. The man had taken up his position in a corner of the battery. Grasping his bar and his rope in both hands, he stood with his back against one of the ship's timbers, with his legs, which were like two steel columns, well braced. Pale and calm, a tragic figure, he seemed rooted to the deck while he bided his time. He was waiting for the carronade to pass close to where he stood.

639

The gunner knew his gun, and he felt the gun must know him, too. How often he had thrust his hand into its maw! It was his own familiar monster. He began speaking to it, as if it were his dog and he were fond of it. "Come here!" he called, as if trying to attract it. But if it obeyed him it must hurl itself upon him, and he would be lost. He could never escape being crushed. All the onlookers gazed at him in terror, with bated breath—with the sole exception, perhaps, of the mysterious stranger, who remained, a sinister witness, alone in the battery with the combatants. Like the gunner, he ran the risk of being crushed to death, but he did not stir. Beneath them the forces of ocean blindly directed the battle. Just as the gunner had committed himself to that desperate hand-to-hand conflict, the carronade, by some chance movement of the waves, hung motionless for a moment, as if taken aback. "Come now!" said the man.

The gun seemed to be listening to him. Suddenly it charged him, but he jumped aside. A battle began, such a battle as had never been waged before. It was fragile man pitted against invulnerable matter. The brute of metal was attacking the man of flesh and blood, who was his keeper. On the one side, force; on the other, a human soul. The whole scene was enacted in semi-darkness. It was like some dim, fantastic vision.

The carronade seemed likewise to possess a soul—a soul that was fraught with rage and hatred. Blind though it was, it appeared to have eyes. The monster seemed to be stalking the man. Cunning lurked within that mass of metal. The carronade, too, knew how to choose its moment. It was like some preposterous insect of iron, a gigantic grasshopper, endowed with demonic purpose. First it would batter against the low-pitched roof of the covered deck. Then it would drop down on its four wheels, like a tiger on its paws, and resume the pursuit of its human foe. Supple, agile and alert, the gunner turned and twisted like a snake, in his efforts to avoid these lightning attacks. But the bows which he eluded fell upon the ship and hurried on the work of destruction. A length of broken chain was left hanging to the carronade. It had become twisted in the elevating screw. One end was fast to the gun-carriage. The other hung loose, and swung violently round and round with the gun, enhancing the deadly effect of its plungings and rearings. The screw held it tight like a clenched fist. Whenever the gun delivered its ram-like blows, the chain whirled madly round, lashing out like a thong, an iron whip in a brazen clutch. This was an additional complication.

The man, however, did not relax his efforts. At times he even attempted a counter-attack. Grasping his rope, he crept along the side towards the gun. But the carronade appeared to divine his purpose. It fled before him, as though suspecting a trap. Its menacing human foe followed in pursuit.

The situation could not last for long. The carronade seemed suddenly to say to itself:

"Come, I must put an end to this." It paused. All felt that the climax was approaching. To the onlookers, who had come to regard it as a living thing, the gun seemed to be savagely brooding. The next moment it had hurled itself at the gunner. He sprang to one side, and as it shot past him, he exclaimed with a laugh:

"Try again!"

The gun vented its wrath by crushing a carronade on the port side. Then, as if caught in an invisible catapult, it was slung to starboard at the gunner, who again escaped. Three carronades collapsed under the weight of its attack. Then, as though suddenly indifferent, the gun turned its back on its enemy and rolled the whole length of the deck from stern to bow, damaging the stem and making a breach in the boarding. The man had taken refuge at the foot of the ladder, a few paces from the stranger, who was witnessing the scene. The gunner stood holding his handspike like a couched spear. The carronade appeared to catch sight of it, and without troubling to turn round, it recoiled upon its enemy with the suddenness of a falling axe. The man crouched against the side; it seemed as if nothing could save him. A cry of horror burst from the whole ship's company.

But the stranger, who had hitherto remained motionless, now sprang forward with a swiftness which exceeded even the carronade's fierce rushes. He snatched up a bundle of kit-bags, and at the risk of being crushed, he contrived to thrust it between the wheels of the gun. He carried out this daring and decisive feat with a precision and promptness which could not have been equalled by a man trained in all the exercises in Durosel's "Gun-drill at sea." The bundle of bags acted as a wedge, just as a mere pebble may serve to obstruct a rock, or the branch of a tree avert an avalanche. The gun tottered, and the gunner took advantage of this perilous juncture to thrust his iron bar between the spokes of the back wheel. The carronade stopped dead, and began to stagger. Using the bar as a lever, the gunner caused it to rock from side to side, until at last it turned completely over with a crash like that of a bell falling from a steeple. The gunner, with the sweat pouring from his body, threw himself headlong upon it, and passed the slip-knot round the neck of the fallen monster.

All was over. The man had triumphed. The ant had routed the mastodon. The pygmy had captured the thunder. The soldiers and sailors clapped their hands. In a moment the whole crew had rushed to the spot with chains and ropes, and the gun was made fast.

The gunner saluted the stranger.

"Sir," he said, "I owe my life to you."

The old man, however, had resumed his usual imperturbability, and made no reply.

The man, indeed, was victorious, but the carronade,

too, might be said to have conquered. The danger of immediate shipwreck was averted, but the safety of the corvette was by no means assured. The ship appeared to have sustained irreparable damage. There were five breaches in her boarding, and of these a very large one was situated in the bow. Twenty out of the thirty carronades were lying crippled. The gun, which was now recaptured and chained up, was itself unfit for service. The elevating screw was jammed, and levelling was, therefore, impossible. The battery was reduced to nine pieces of ordnance. Water was pouring into the hold. The first essential was to repair the damaged parts and to set the pumps working. Now that the battery could be examined, it presented an appalling spectacle. It was like the havoc in the cage of a mad elephant. However important it might be for the corvette to escape notice, the question of her immediate safety was still more urgent. It was necessary to light up the deck, and ship's lanterns were hung here and there along the sides.

During the whole course of that tragic interlude, the ship's company had been so deeply absorbed in watching the desperate conflict that no heed had been paid to what was happening without. The fog had thickened, and the weather had changed. Left to the mercy of the wind, the corvette had been driven out of her course; she was now so far south that she could be sighted from both Jersey and Guernsey. The sea was rapidly rising, and great waves touched with their sinister kisses the corvette's gaping wounds. There was menace in the rocking of the sea. The breeze had freshened to a northerly wind. There were all the signs of an approaching squall, or even a gale. It was impossible to see further than four waves ahead.

While the crew were hastily and summarily repairing the damage between decks and stopping the leaks, and while the guns that had escaped disaster were being prepared for action, the stranger had returned to the

643

open deck, where he stood leaning his back against the
mainmast. He paid no attention to certain proceedings
which were taking place around him. La Vieuville
had assembled the marines on either side of the mainmast, and at a whistle from the boatswain, the sailors,
who were working the ship, manned the yards.

Count du Boisberthelot approached his passenger. He
was followed by a man, who was haggard, panting and
dishevelled, but who wore, none the less, a look of com-
placency. It was the gunner, who had so opportunely
proved himself a tamer of wild beasts, and had brought
the carronade into subjection.

The count saluted the stranger in the peasant's dress.
"Here is the man, General."

The gunner stood with downcast eyes in the correct
attitude of attention.

"General," resumed Count du Boisberthelot, "in
view of what this man has done, do you not consider
that there is something his chiefs should do for him?"

"Undoubtedly."

"Will you give your orders?"

"That is for you to do. You are the captain."

"But you are the general," replied du Boisberthelot.

The stranger looked at the gunner.

"Come here," he said, and the man stepped forward.

The stranger turned to Count du Boisberthelot,
removed from the captain's coat the Cross of St. Louis
which he was wearing, and fastened it to the gunner's
tunic. The sailors broke into a cheer, and the marines
presented arms. Then, pointing to the gunner, who was
dazed with joy, he said:

"Now take this man away and shoot him."

The enthusiasm gave way to consternation. The old
man's voice rang out through a death-like silence:

"The ship has been imperilled by an act of carelessness, which may yet prove fatal. To be at sea is to be
in the presence of the enemy. A ship crossing the ocean
is an army fighting a battle. The tempest may not

644

manifest itself, but it is always lying in wait. The whole sea is an ambush. Death is the penalty for every error committed in the presence of the enemy. No blunder can be remedied. Courage must be rewarded, and negligence must be punished."

Word followed word, slowly, solemnly, with a kind of inexorable rhythm, like the strokes of an axe upon an oak.

Looking at the soldiers, the old man added:

"Do your duty."

The man upon whose breast glittered the Cross of St. Louis bowed his head. At a sign from Count du Boisberthelot, two sailors went below and returned with a hammock shroud. They were accompanied by the chaplain, who had been at prayers in the wardroom ever since the ship left harbour. A sergeant detailed twelve men from the company and arranged them in double file. Without a word the gunner placed himself between the two files. Crucifix in hand, the chaplain stepped forward and stood beside him.

At the word of command from the sergeant, the squad marched slowly away in the direction of the bow. The two sailors followed with the hammock. A sullen silence sank down upon the ship. The mutterings of a distant storm were heard.

A moment later there was a flash through the gloom. A volley rang out. Then all was still, and presently a sound was heard as of a body falling into the sea.

645